LORD OF THE EMPTY ISLES

LORD OF THE EMPTY ISLES

Jules Arbeaux

HODDERSCAPE

First published in Great Britain in 2024 by Hodderscape
An imprint of Hodder & Stoughton
An Hachette UK company

1

Copyright © Jules Arbeaux 2024

The right of Jules Arbeaux to be identified as the Author of the Work has been asserted by them in accordance with the Copyright, Designs and Patents Act 1988.

All rights reserved. No part of this publication may be reproduced, stored in a retrieval system, or transmitted, in any form or by any means without the prior written permission of the publisher, nor be otherwise circulated in any form of binding or cover other than that in which it is published and without a similar condition being imposed on the subsequent purchaser.

All characters in this publication are fictitious and any resemblance to real persons, living or dead, is purely coincidental.

A CIP catalogue record for this title is available from the British Library

Hardback ISBN 978 1 399 72497 5
Trade Paperback ISBN 978 1 399 72498 2
ebook ISBN 978 1 399 72496 8

Typeset in Sabon MT by Manipal Technologies Limited

Printed and bound in Great Britain by Clays Ltd, Elcograf S.p.A.

Hodder & Stoughton policy is to use papers that are natural, renewable and recyclable products and made from wood grown in sustainable forests. The logging and manufacturing processes are expected to conform to the environmental regulations of the country of origin.

Hodder & Stoughton Ltd
Carmelite House
50 Victoria Embankment
London EC4Y 0DZ

www.hodderscape.co.uk

*To every person for whom healing is a declaration of war
on the forces that tried to unravel you*

Chapter One

*Red for the fated ones,
lovebonds bright gold.
Green for the boundless, o'er seas they will hold.
Blue for the piecebound—two fragments made whole.
Gray for the hollow ones.
Black for the cold.*

— Unknown
Verdinian nursery rhyme

Remy Canta hurries down narrow back streets toward home, bloody knife cupped between his hands like a prayer.

This is how he'll make things right.

Brandishing the blade, he pushes through the doorway's gauzy curtain to the sparse but elegantly furnished room he and Tirani use to conduct their business.

"Tirani, I found it!"

But Tirani isn't alone. Remy has a moment to take in the blushing couple sitting across from her—hands clasped, bodies pressed so close they might just fuse—before they scramble away and shriek at his entrance. He grimaces. She wasn't supposed to have any more customers today.

He sidesteps out of the doorway, lowers the knife, and adopts a more businesslike expression.

"Thanks for your patronage! May your bonds be forever strong and unbroken." He slides the blade behind his back. "This isn't what it looks like."

It's almost exactly what it looks like.

The setting sun makes something molten of Tirani's hazel-brown eyes as she glares at him, her dense curls an inferno in the red light. They'll have words later, clearly.

She arranges her face into a brilliant smile and returns her attention to the couple. One finger traces a line in the empty air between them—an affectation. She's lucky. She can only see tethers, not touch them.

Her vision gives her insight, though, the kind that sappy young lovers pay through the nose for. They eat it up when she clasps their hands and theatrically describes the gilded glimmer and unbreakable thickness of loyal, patient lovebonds or the color-shifting blue of the piecebonds that link people with complementary skillsets. Tirani probably knows more flattering descriptors for hues of gold and red and blue and green than the most celebrated poets.

"Rest assured," she says. "Your souls are aligned and the tether that binds them is thick as any rope. Please, finish your tea and be well."

The young couple gulps the delicate floral tea and scrambles out holding hands, their footsteps an urgent drumbeat on the cobblestones outside.

Once the noise of their retreat fades, Remy summons an apologetic smile for Tirani. "Sorry, I can—"

Something flies through the doorway and nails him in the back. He stumbles forward, coughing, and twists his non-knife-bearing hand to pat at the point of impact between his shoulder blades. Hissing and pulling the curtains open, he finds a dirty shoe on the ground and an angry, hunched woman on the path outside. Age has collapsed her into a compact ball of aggression, not unlike the ugly pseudo-moon she was named after. *Fluora*.

"Remy Canta, don't think I didn't hear that couple tittering! A knife? You'll give us all a bad name."

"You do that well enough by yourself," Remy mutters.

Like Tirani, Fluora is a weaver, but she's been plying her trade longer than Tirani and Remy have been alive. Where the outside of the home they share bears a simple, elegant piece of rope art in the shape of a star above the door, Fluora's place of work is bedecked with tacky ribbons in gold, red, blue, and green that billow from the windows with every breeze.

"I heard that," Fluora rasps. "Now you give me that shoe back, rotten boy."

Remy snatches the mud-crusted sandal up. "You're the one who threw it."

He fights the urge to return it in the way it arrived, but this is the woman who took Tirani in when she had no one else. He can't brain her with a shoe. Sighing, Remy lobs the sandal out onto the cobblestones, and with a conversation-ending *hmph*, Fluora wiggles her cracked foot back inside and begins her slow trek toward her garish shop.

"She's right, for once." Tirani paces over, leaning out the doorway to make sure Fluora gets home. Her eyebrow goes up, and with it goes the little mole beside it, like the world's most judgmental exclamation point. "You're lucky they paid before the consultation."

Remy slips past her. On the wall behind the consultation table, a much larger version of the rope art star decorates the wall, with silken ropes in the four healthy tether colors tied to a central square. A pentagon of five nails representing the five connection points surrounds the square. Every tether at the center square loops around each connection point, creating a colorful star. Remy plucks at a nail to hear it twang. "Were they really aligned?"

Tirani laughs. "Yeah, mutually-anchored. They'll be fine."

Lucky bastards. Anchored tethers connect at the hands. Of the locations tethers can rest—head, heart, gut, hands, and feet—anchored ones are the least likely to rot or travel. Once a bond has settled there, it's likely to remain. Remy likes to think he and Cameron might have become anchored one day, if they'd had more time.

The embedded screen beside the door flashes red to scold him for failing to play this morning's broadcast. He used to watch those things religiously, hoping maybe the next one (or the next) would be the one where the Chancellor announced the capture of his brother's killer. But for all his paternal warmth and competence in other areas, the Chancellor's awful at catching criminals.

But they have a plan, Andrew, the Chancellor's Vice-Enforcer, keeps telling him. A *plan*, like that justifies five years of a killer's continued freedom. Every time, it's a different excuse.

Delaciel was smart about it—his connection to Cameron's death is tenuous. It's been hard to make a case.

He has citizen support and acts outside the area we can realistically observe.

He uses banned tech. We were so damn close, but he slipped away.

Stuff like that, every time. *But we're turning the tide!* Andrew keeps saying. *The Chancellor has a plan. Just wait.*

Remy's sick of waiting.

Tirani tucks a sweat-curled lock of hair behind his ear. "You're a mess. I ate the last of your soup today, so I made stir-fry, but . . ."

Remy nudges the floor cushions back to order with his foot. "But?"

Tirani pauses long enough that he stops what he's doing. Finally, she says, "Lara came."

A grin stretches Remy's lips, his taut muscles relaxing. "Don't scare me like that! I thought it was something bad."

He pulls a bag from his pocket and drops the knife inside. He and Lara know the same pain. Her husband and Cam both passed in the same month five years ago. It's been their journey, these intervening years. "Is she still here? Lara!"

"I had her wait in the kitchen."

"Perfect." Remy sinks onto the embroidered cushions—tether colors in interweaving ropes—and fumbles into the table's supply drawer for the tincture that'll ease Lara's pain. Her tether, like Remy's, never faded like it should've. She must be here for her next batch.

His fingers find only empty space. The realization comes too slow: Lara is early. Very early. Her previous bottle should have lasted weeks longer. They shouldn't see her until fall.

"... Something happened?" Remy ventures. His hand clenches in sympathy over his sternum.

"Something happened."

Remy bites his lip. It'll take Tirani at least a week to prepare another batch—a week of pain for Lara. He heads to the washroom, where his own tincture sits in a little glass bottle on the windowsill, and calls, "I'll give her mine!"

He already has it in hand when Tirani calls back, "What? No, Remy, wait! It's not—"

Clutching the bottle (translucent sky-blue with an iridescent glaze, like the plumage of the allura birds Cameron once lifted Remy on his shoulders to see) he hurries back out. "Not what?"

Two pairs of wide eyes pin him when he slides into his seat again.

Lara freezes in the middle of settling onto the cushions opposite Tirani.

"Perfect timing." Remy holds the bottle out to her. "It's not full, but it's a really strong batch. It'll last you a while."

Lara just stares, stricken, at the dark fluid sloshing inside its glass cage.

"Remy." Tirani's hand falls on his shoulder, heavy like an urn.

Her touch would usually be comforting, but the tiny shake of her head and the way Lara's hands lie palm-up on the table like dead spiders make a shiver scale his spine.

"She wants your help today, not mine."

His help.

The skills Remy sells aren't nearly so sweet as Tirani's. He squeezes his eyes shut. Pulls the bottle back and drops it in the supply drawer with shaking hands. Something whistles in his ears, in his skull. "No."

"His family visited." The words tumble from Lara's mouth like a plea. "His father looks just like him, but he's nothing like him. His laugh is nothing like him. He doesn't throw my boy up in the air like him. Please, Remy. It hurts."

Of course it does. That's the cost of loving.

"You'd cut him out of your life just because it hurts?"

She flinches like Remy slapped her.

"Remy!" Tirani growls. "You know it's not like that."

He most certainly doesn't.

Tirani turns back to Lara. "Even a fully rotbound tether will attenuate on its own in a few months when the bearer is willing to move forward." She slants a glance at Remy. "There's nothing wrong with choosing to heal."

Lara wilts in her seat. "But it'd be more likely to come back."

"Healing isn't always linear. In any case, it'd be easier to manage even if it did." Tirani retrieves Remy's discarded tincture, the potent mixture of medicinal herbs that dulls the pain from rotbonds and aids in healing. Remy doesn't take it nearly as often as Tirani thinks he should. "With these drops, you could keep it from ever fully rethreading."

Lara looks to Remy instead. "Please. Just sever it."

Remy can't spin beautiful stories about tethers like Tirani. He can't see them at all, but he can cut them.

"Find someone else."

The widow seizes his wrist before he can stand. "There is no one else!"

Weavers like Tirani are uncommon enough, with just a handful in the city. Witherers are rarer still. "Why?"

"It's been five years. It's time. My baby can read now. He's a whole person. I need to be whole for him, too."

Traitor. As if severing herself from her love could ever make her whole. Remy would never cut Cameron away. Pain is a small price to pay for keeping this last piece of him close.

Lara withdraws a pouch from the pocket of her dress. Delicate blue-and-white flowers decorate the exterior. She opens it, and the fading light glints off coins stamped with the Chancellor's striking profile. It's nearly twice what Tirani usually makes in a month; benefits of being the only practicing witherer on the island.

"You want this," he says.

The all-important question. If she doesn't, even a severing might not keep her bond from rethreading forever.

"I need it." Tired. Peaceful.

Remy wrenches the supply drawer open again to prepare for the ritual that will allow him to handle her tether, fingers freezing over the tins and bottles.

He wants to tell her she'll regret it, wants to beg her to stop, or maybe ask what she had to do to steel herself for this—to forgive herself for it. It is not his business to ask these questions, but it is a business, so he presses his lips into a shape he hopes is kind and pulls out a jar of raw honey, a pouch of ash from the corpse of the person he once loved more than life.

His eyes burn. His breath comes short. Swallowing the rock of sickness pushing itself up his throat, Remy smears honey over his fingers. He sprinkles his brother's ashes onto his hands, then uses the pad of his thumb to spread the awful mixture across his bottom lip.

It's a job. It's a job. It's a job.

He's severed tethers after nasty divorces, or when a bond was one-sided or unhealthy or unbalanced and began to rot. He's even severed a few tethers broken by loss. This is different. He and Lara have survived this pain together. He thought they'd survive it forever.

Needle-like tingling sweeps from his fingertips to his wrists. Remy can't see the spun gold of Lara's lovebond, but it's visceral; it'll be near her gut. He closes his eyes, rubs his hands to smear the mixture that allows him to touch tethers evenly across his palms, and reaches out.

There. Fever-hot like something sick unto death. Slick with rot.

It's not just half rotbound. It's decayed almost all the way to its anchor, nearly as bad as Remy's. Even after all these years, though, her orphan tether is more rope than thread. It must have been beautiful while it lived.

He follows it until his fingers skim the cornflower blue linen of her dress, then farther, until he's pressing against her stomach, where the spiritual knot that once tied her to the man she still loves pulses with a dying heart's beat.

He cinches his fingers at the base.

One brutal instant of intent and the whispered tune that makes it real. The honey heats against his hands. Sweet smoke blurs the air, and that thrumming knot, the last living evidence of Lara's love, dissolves like so much ash. Severing, with her will to lose the bond and his to break it, only takes a moment.

She sighs, like a baby sighs before falling asleep. Like a body before it never breathes again. But then Lara inhales. She presses her hands to her stomach and sobs.

"It's done," Remy whispers, voice raw.

She nods—fast, up and down—and keeps crying. If she's gonna cry like that, she shouldn't have made him do it.

"Can't be *un*done, so don't ask."

"I know." She stands. "My baby'll be coming home soon. I have to . . ." She wipes her eyes, and she's weak, but Remy can't hate her for it, and that's worse. She's out the door before she can finish her sentence.

The coins glitter on the table.

"Remy," Tirani whispers, reaching for him.

Remy pushes up and away, stomach twisting. In the washroom, he hangs his head over the basin until the nausea recedes, then sets his cheek on the cold porcelain. His dirty hands find the frayed tether that once bound him to his brother, still as thick as it was in life. As soon as he washes off Cameron's ashes, he won't be able to touch it, so he holds it now and breathes.

Grasping. That's what they call tethers connected at the heart, intimate and instinctive, loyal to the last. If he could see it, the bond would be rotbound-black through and through. It's warm, though, with a beat almost like life. Heart- and gut-connected tethers like his and Lara's—the hungriest and most emotional bonds two people can share—are also the most likely to rot. Anchored bonds, knotted at the hands, are the least, followed by the joyfully intellectual ruminant tethers that connect at the head or spine and reckless tethers knotted at the feet. How strange, that hands are the most willing to let go.

Remy twists away to avoid touching the living tether beside Cameron's—thick and healthy, untouched by rot. Tirani talks about that bond like it's his future, like there's someone out there waiting to fill the space Cam's death left.

Whoever's at the other end of it, Remy hates them. He hopes they never meet.

The anniversary of his brother's death is next week. It's funny— Cam used to say Remy's hands were for helping, for healing. If they ever were, they aren't now. He'll buy his healing in blood, like any good witherer should.

Severing, for all its quiet horrors, is benign. Legal. *Healing*. It only lasts if it's mutually desired.

A withering is unspeakable—lethal and illegal. It's what took his brother from him. A witherer just like Remy did the deed. Helpless while his brother died shade by shade for weeks, Remy offered a soothing tea, another pillow, a hand to hold. He should have sharpened himself like a blade instead.

Witherings don't need consent. They need blood.

Almost five years to the day, and he has the blood he needs on that knife. Tonight, he'll perform the ritual to kill the man his brother was building a case against when he was murdered.

Idrian Delaciel, Lord of the Empty Isles, a criminal who's crowned himself king of the cursed pseudo-moons that light the sky at night— and the man who ordered the withering that took Cam's life.

If he'd known it back then, Remy would have extracted the name of whichever witherer Delaciel paid to do the deed and killed them both. His brother would have lived.

A withering, after all, cannot survive the death of the witherer.

There are two ways to end one, and they both involve murder. The first, of course, is for the victim of a withering to personally kill the caster, but Cam was too kind to become a killer. He would never have hurt anyone to save himself, which is why Remy hung all his hopes on the second method: a close blood relative of an affected victim can act as proxy and kill the witherer in the victim's place. Remy would have been glad to do it, even at fourteen. When Cam first fell ill, he begged his brother to give up the name of his killer—or a lead, or anything—so he could kill the witherer to save Cam's life. But Cam kept his silence. Only on the night before the end, far too late for Remy to do anything, did he confess his killer's name and press the pendant he always wore into Remy's hands like an apology.

Tirani waits in the doorway with his tincture in her palm, fluid already pulled into the dropper. "You want . . . "

He should. His chest throbs with every breath. "Not today."

The sun-powered hivelights overhead—hexagonal glass-and-solarfibre bubbles built into the ceiling to light the house from sunset until curfew—flicker on as the sun sinks.

"We can talk," Tirani whispers.

She'd listen. She'd run her fingers through his hair like he did for her when she confided that she'd forgotten her sister's face-splitting troublemaker's grin, her dad's booming laugh. She was barely three when her family abandoned her. She loses pieces of them one by one. The first thing she lost was her surname.

What a pair they make. She hurts because she can no longer remember; Remy hurts because he can't forget.

"I wish you could see it like I do. What you did for Lara, it's like cleaning an infected wound."

"You said you made dinner?" He angles to move past her.

Her shoulders sag. "Yeah. Lima and honey-glazed rib meat with smoked rama seeds over rice."

That sounds unexpectedly edible. " . . . You add anything else?"

"My turn, my rules." Her laugh is quiet but genuine. "I diced a rainfruit in for sweetness. And field onion—just for you—to balance it. Be grateful. And put down that *damned* knife."

Ah. It's still in his hand. Remy lifts it, purpose flooding his limbs. "Tirani, I found it!"

"Eat first." She paces to the kitchen and he follows, filling a chipped bowl halfway with rice and picking around the spongy, whitish chunks of rainfruit to top it off.

"The knife," he garbles around a bit of rice. "It's Idrian's blood. I can end it, Tirani."

"Are you sure?"

It'll be fine even if he isn't. If the name Remy speaks and the blood he offers don't match, the withering will fail.

"Pretty damn. The guy I bought it off had a recording." It was the highlight of Remy's day to see shaky footage of some guy stabbing Idrian Delaciel on one of the fringe islands. "Only way I could be more sure is if I stabbed him myself."

"You know what I mean. Are you sure this is what you *want*?"

He gathers a perfect bite but doesn't eat it. "I'm sure. I just need him gone."

"And anyone he's fatebound to? You'd kill them, too."

Remy scoffs. Vital red, fatebonds are the strongest and rarest of all tether types, indicative of a perfect and complementary alignment of goals. Other tethers speak to relationships—enduring ones, passionate ones, selfless and dedicated ones—but fatebonds indicate not only a profound connection but one meant to transform the world around it. They're the only bonds thick enough to carry a curse like an artery. Remy wasn't even fatebound to his *brother*. "You think a bastard like that is fatebound to anyone? Please. You're plucking at threads."

"What if he has family, then? They'll have to watch him die, just like—"

Remy drops his spoon and pushes back from the table. "Don't."

"—like you watched Cameron. Do you want to make another you?"

"I'm trying to prevent another me!"

"Remy, it's been *five years*. I hoped maybe you'd . . ." Her fingers curl, bloodless, around her spoon. "Didn't you use to like him when you were little? You can't really want to kill him."

Can't he? So many things have changed from back then. The glow from the hive overhead ripples in Remy's funneled vision. He snaps at the knife on the table. Misses. Grabs it on his second try. Stands, bowl spinning.

Tirani follows him into the consultation room. "You won't be able to undo this if you get your head on straight later!"

"*Good.*" He stomps upstairs, grabs his heavy backpack from his bed, and stalks down again. "You don't have to agree with me, just don't get in my—"

"Remy?" A warm, deep voice stops him dead at the foot of the stairs, and Remy staggers back at the sight of a lean silhouette on the other side of the curtain. "Is that you?"

Shit.

Andrew Delacour, Vice-Enforcer to the Chancellor, a man with hound-like senses for illegal behavior. He always shows up when Remy's planning something reckless. Tirani has to be involved, somehow.

An *officer of the law* is the last thing Remy needs. He has to get out of here.

"Tirani?" Andrew calls again. "We're coming in, all right?"

We. He's not alone. That's worse.

Remy casts around the wide-open room—nowhere to hide.

The washroom. It has a window he can escape through.

Remy skids inside just as he hears Andrew bustling into the consultation room. He tugs the washroom's window as wide as it'll go and slips his pack from his shoulders. The window isn't wide enough to let him through with it on his back, but he can grab it once he's out.

He leans out the window, startling a fluffy gray stray cat from an acrobatic round of butt-cleaning. Grisly glares up with her one eye but doesn't move from the cozy bathing nest that's conveniently situated where he needs to land.

"Grisly!" Remy begs. "You need to move."

She slow-blinks and begins to purr, rolling to show him her belly. Remy groans. He grabs his pack and swings it above her head, hoping the motion might startle her, but she only watches it curiously as his elbow aches from the strange angle and the weight of the pack.

"Go on!" he pleads to no avail.

"Yeah, he's here," Tirani's saying from the consultation room. Loud. Too loud. A warning. "Maybe in the washroom, but I doubt he's in the mood for company. I can check on him and see—"

Remy pulls the bag back inside. He'll have to throw it, but that might break the raw crystal bowl he needs for the withering. He wrenches the bag open and grabs the bowl.

Footsteps pad down the hall. Remy's blended irritation and relief melt to terror when the approaching person speaks.

"Oh no, dear, don't trouble yourself. I need to wash my hands, anyway."

That familiar baritone. Those steady footsteps. Remy knows with sudden, numb horror exactly who Andrew's guest is: the Chancellor himself. Of course it would be him.

Gentle and cheery, the Chancellor always insists Remy call him Aram when he visits. He granted the Canta Manor to Remy after Cam's death in hopes of giving him somewhere he'd feel safe. He treats Remy like a son, but he still rules over the hundreds of islands that make up the Protectorate. If he sees what Remy has in the bag, he'll have no choice but to sentence him to death—or worse, to the Isles.

There's no time to think, no time for a careful descent. Remy flings his bag outside (thankfully, Grisly flees) and shoves the crystal bowl against his chest. He tips out the window backward, vision sparking with bright stars and air punched from his lungs with the impact. He grabs his pack, shoves the bowl inside, and yanks it onto his shoulders before he can catch his breath.

A knock sounds on the wall of the washroom as he finds his feet.

"Remy?" the Chancellor's voice sifts through the still-open window. "I was in the area helping with festival prep and wanted to see how you were doing. I know this time of year is hard for you..."

It takes everything inside Remy not to give into muscle memory and sink into the respectful bow Cam taught him when he was six: one closed fist behind his back for preservation, an open hand over his heart for progress. The Chancellor used to laugh when little Remy jumped into the formal pose every time they met. Even at nineteen, it's a hard habit to break.

He snaps himself free and flees around the corner just as the Chancellor's figure blots a dark line into the light pooling from the washroom's window.

None of the Chancellor's bittersweet stories, none of Andrew's tired pleas to *just wait*, none of Tirani's promises that he doesn't want to do this can stall him tonight.

Outside the home Remy shares with Tirani, the seaside city has grown cool with night, the octagonal hivelights' warm glow illuminating every tightly packed, brightly painted building, spilling light onto narrow, cobbled streets. The houses grow farther apart as Remy ascends the winding uphill paths and staircases toward the city's peak. Here in the Chancellor's cliffside capital, rich and poor alike have solar-powered hives to light their homes along with the same restrictions on energy use. The currency of wealth is space to roam and permission to fill it. Remy was lucky to be born to high officials: his parents were allowed a second child. When his mom died giving birth to him and his father followed five years later, he still had Cam.

The Empty Isles—the man-made moons Idrian Delaciel has claimed as his base of operations—loom over the Glass Sea as Remy hurries onward.

Alta, Fluora, and Toxys: for hundreds of years, they held Verdine's survivors while they watched their wounded planet heal from the damage its own people wrought. When the moons were abandoned to allow the survivors to return to Verdine, they became known as the Empty Isles: a reminder of the people's folly and a symbol of their promise to nurture their recovered world.

But in the century since Verdine's survivors descended, the Isles have turned from cradle to curse: the fading pseudo-moons are now a prison for those too dangerous to live on the surface, while criminals like Idrian gouge precious resources from the planet to keep the moons' inhabitants luxuriously fed.

Silvery and cracked with blue light, for years they've been a reminder of what Delaciel stole from Remy, but he looks up at them tonight without flinching.

White ribbons tied into bows on the guardrails brush Remy's fingers as he walks, a promise of the coming festivities: next week's centennial Resurrection Festival—a celebration of the planet's healing and a reminder of how close it came to destruction—will be the biggest Verdine has ever seen.

When selecting one of the archetypal masks for the festival each year, Remy usually chooses the mask of the Mourner, black and white with mirror shards and a tragically down-turned mouth. The Mourner: the one who saw the end coming but could do nothing but watch.

This year, once Idrian's dead, he'll don the mask of the Reveler—smiling and bright and many-colored, fringed with hammered coins.

This year, Remy will have everything in the world to celebrate.

Chapter Two

Visceral, or gut-connected, tethers signify a primal connection—powerful, passionate bonds as likely to illuminate as they are to immolate. Bearers of visceral bonds long to consume. Like grasping bonds, they resist the slow fade of attenuation and are more likely than any other tether type to rot and require therapeutic intervention.

— From *On the Manipulation of Tethers*

Alta stares down from the city's peak like a judge.

As beautiful as they are during the day, the ring of statues that preside over Verdine's thriving capital take on a certain eeriness at night. Of the ten, Alta—the then-Chancellor who spearheaded the construction of the Isles—is the tallest by far. Her arms raised to support a bronze recreation of the pseudo-moon named after her, she represents the one in every ten people who survived the rising waters and smoke-choked air.

The statue beside her kneels, covering its agonized face, while the next, sitting slumped, could almost be sleeping. The final statue is little more than a pile of bones. They represent the lost.

Alta is a shadowed giant, all-knowing and unknowable, bearing the weight of a world. *Preservation.* That was her credo when the world fell apart. She'd probably tell Remy that every life is precious, even Idrian Delaciel's.

Alta can go fuck herself.

Remy ducks into the coverage of the trees that shade the path to his childhood home and away from her accusing eyes.

He stops dead before hitting the front porch's first stair.

There's nothing scary about the dirt-clogged windows with faint suggestions of dead houseplants on the sills or the manor's cheery eggshell-blue facade. Cam's well-loved but ugly floral umbrella probably still waits in the entryway. The bronze hook inside the door must still hold the keys he so often forgot. Yet, Remy's pulse thuds dizzily in his throat, stomach greasy with nausea, and he turns away.

He can't go in through the front door. He'll never walk into this house like he's coming home again.

He enters through the back.

Everything inside is blanketed in years of dust, caught in cutting beams of moonlight. Remy chooses the most indirect route to his room: through the back hallway and down the staff corridor into the kitchen. Past the staff baths. He can almost pretend he's in someone else's home.

He's fine until he gets to the sitting room. Against his will, his eyes settle on the yellow-and-gold cushions in the window-seat where his brother, when asked how work was going, concocted elaborate adventures with shootouts and daring duels instead of boring Remy with descriptions of the endless paperwork he did for cases he argued before the Chancellor. In this room, Cameron Canta was immortal. He was a hero, a fortress, a father.

He was thinner than Remy when he died.

Remy navigates the space blind—here, the gouge in the wall from enthusiastic play-fighting. There, crackling between floorboards, sand from their attempts to germinate neverdesert beans for a class project. He runs his hand over the wallpaper he drew stick figures on when he was six. Cam tried so hard to scold him (it was just after their father passed, when he was still trying to fill the Canta patriarch's shoes), but he ended up shaking his head and painting two stick figures of his own in broad, black strokes. Loudly, he pronounced, "What's paper for, if not to draw on?"

They never stopped drawing on it after that.

Here and there, stick figures and math problems and unrealistic airships scuttle between and behind the subdued geometric print on the wallpaper. Cam drew flowers, vibrant bouquets of them. A glittering trio of crystals and a string of bloom-studded ivy (Cam's) traversed by a badly drawn cat (Remy's) guide him down the hall. His breaths crowd the narrowing space.

Somewhere, there must still be drawings of a charismatic figure with windblown hair and blue-toned glasses, with a long, dark coat and knee-high boots, saving the world or the ocean or the endangered allura birds or whatever else Remy thought Idrian Delaciel could save that day.

Before he murdered Cam, Idrian Delaciel was Remy's hero, but Delaciel saves no one—and if Remy has his way, no one will save Delaciel.

Remy steps into his old room, giddy with the promise of it: he can finally atone. Swiping everything from his desk, Remy opens the curtains and throws the window wide. A cool breeze puffs dust into the air.

He opens his pack and gets to work. He's done plenty of research on witherings these past five years. He has everything he could need.

The bowl, raw crystal for ease of energy transfer.

Blood of the withered (flecked from the knife) and blood of the witherer (drawn with its blade).

Ghost-lace (picked before it flowered, dried and crushed into a fine powder) sprinkled over the blood.

Ghost-lace (fresh, picked with flowers newly blossomed and ground into a paste) to pack the wound on his middle finger—his fate-finger, a direct line to his heart.

Cameron's ashes, as much as he can hold between the pinched fingers of one hand.

Hands of a clockwork timepiece worn for at least two generations.

This last step creates a mark on the skin of the cursed. Remy needs Delaciel to bear it, to know the desperation that comes with the countdown it'll paint on his skin.

Remy cups both hands over the bowl, eyes closed.

Your hands aren't meant to destroy, his brother told him when he found out Remy inherited their mother's unspeakable gift. But Cam isn't here to tell Remy how goodness begets goodness. He's not here to water the irises he planted that still bloom each year behind the house. And Remy has work to do.

In spirit, he follows the blood to the man it still sings for. Delaciel is somewhere far away, but Remy, reaching out, finds him in an instant.

He lifts the knife once more to draw blood from the fate-finger of his right hand. He smears a drop over his lips before readying the song that will allow him to lay a withering.

Like everything else about Remy's work, the song is a sacrifice. Like the ash—which can only come from the body of someone he loved—the song has to be one he treasures.

Remy's is a lullaby Cam used to sing. It was the only thing that could soothe him to sleep after their parents died. The song can be cycled through endlessly for severings, but witherings use it up. The words Remy sings today are ones he can never use again. He burns through the first stanza and the first lines of the second before the withering begins to work.

Intent—poisonous and angry, cultivated for years—ignites in his veins, and Remy pushes it into Idrian's blood.

This will be the end of it. Once it's done, maybe Remy will finally sleep without dreams and wake without pain.

This must be what Tirani was talking about: the cleansing of an infected wound. For the first time in years, there's only silence in his head and the beat of his heart in his chest.

Five years, one knife, and a fleck of dried blood. He couldn't save Cam, but he can ensure Idrian Delaciel can never take another life. A laugh cracks out of Remy, breathless and helpless and free. He's on fire with the joy of it all the way to his fingertips.

He's on fire.

The books say the heat should dissipate, but the energy he pushed into the blood ignites again, not cleansing but cataclysmic. His breath seizes and Remy staggers against his desk.

Something's wrong.

This is how a withering should feel for the *target*, not the caster.

He grasps for the bowl, for his chest where Cam's dead bond aches and aches—for anything worth holding onto—but can't find purchase.

His vision shutters black, and he falls.

~

It must be hours later when Remy wakes, arm throbbing and the pre-dawn light through the open window like an awl lodged in his eyeballs.

He doesn't dare pull back his sleeve to look at his left hand, not when he's mere feet from Cam's old bedroom and the drawings on the wallpaper stare down at him with the solemnity of executioners. Not when he did this to atone.

"Fuck," Remy whispers, his aching left hand twisting in his tunic.

His knowledge of withering is elementary at best, gleaned from an ancient textbook and an ancestral diary his mother kept in the Canta library, but he knows this: when it comes to witherings, there's only success once the process has been set in motion. The withering worked. He *felt* it. Idrian Delaciel will die.

But if Remy got backlash, too—

He can have his answer in an instant. All he needs to do is unclench his hand and look at his fingers. The fear and horror that chased him into the dark flood back, crushingly hot and close. Remy has to look. He owes Cam an answer, owes himself the truth.

He uncurls his hand from his tunic, eyes closed.

He'll open them and check. He *will*. In three, two . . .

A rhythmic crashing interrupts Remy's countdown, and his hand flies to the floor when he identifies the source of the sound.

Running footsteps.

A man's voice booms through the halls. "Remy?"

Andrew. Remy's stomach churns with a combination of adrenaline and relief. He forces himself onto his elbows just as Andrew arrives, wild-haired and gasping.

He clenches his hands into fists against the hardwood. Later. He'll look later.

"There you are! Tirani said you never came home last night. I'll have you know we ate nearly all the cookies I brought. I thought you might—"

By his unbreathing stillness, Remy knows the exact moment Andrew sees the bowl stained with dried blood.

"Damn it, Remy. I distinctly recall asking you to *wait*." Andrew sags to support his hands on his knees. "This complicates things."

He has no idea how much.

Remy has never dared to pit Andrew's care for him against his dedication to his work before. Cautiously, pulling his feet underneath him in case he has to run, Remy says, "You gonna arrest me?"

"Don't tempt me." Andrew's hands hook under Remy's arms, lifting him and patting at his shoulder to make him walk. "Let's get you out of here."

Remy keeps his eyes closed to slits until Andrew guides him down to the floor of the covered porch.

"I did save one for you," Andrew admits, pulling a tissue-wrapped and slightly squished sandwich cookie from his pocket and passing it over. The butter rum filling has turned the tissue translucent. Remy huffs a laugh as he unwraps it and stuffs the whole thing into his mouth. Work must be getting to Andrew if he's stress-baking.

The pendant Andrew wears spills from his shirt as he settles in beside Remy, its shape somewhere between a clenched fist and an anatomical heart, made from hammered metal and stripes of a brutally bright, fatebond-red glass. The necklace Cam gave Remy is just the same.

Remy wasn't the only one who lost Cam. He's not even the only one to lose a family member to Delaciel. Andrew was sworn to silence, but after Cam's death, he shared the ugly truth with Remy, sitting on this same porch: years before Cam, Idrian sharpened his skills with another murder. He tracked down Andrew's father, the previous Minister of the Environment, during a visit to a fringe island for a conference.

The official story about Alister Delacour's death, crafted to preserve public faith in the Protectorate, is that the man passed peacefully among family, in his own home.

The truth is anything but peaceful. Andrew's father was tortured and then executed.

Andrew talks like he's so happy to wait for justice, but he gets how Remy feels, even if he won't admit it.

Remy says, "It worked, you know. I cursed that bastard to death."

Andrew just keeps staring, expression hollow.

"Good," he finally whispers, low enough that Remy couldn't swear he heard it if called upon to do so. He cups his pendant in his palm. "I shouldn't— I know I shouldn't want that, but . . ." His hand closes, tight enough to shatter glass. "You know he didn't go by any last name before what he did to my dad? *Delaciel*. It's like he chose it to mock us."

"Not for much longer," Remy says.

"He ruined everything. They made Mom retire, said she was *a potential target*. She loved her work." This, Remy knows. She chose Cam to take on the mantle of Intermediary when she left. Andrew sighs. "As a defender of the law, I should be slapping you in cuffs."

He should. The remnants of the withering in that bowl are more than enough evidence to convict.

"But as my father's son . . ." Andrew's expression hardens. He tucks his pendant away and stands. "You probably need to head out, right? It's not like you to leave dirty dishes lying around. I'll wash them for you, just this once."

Fear is a sharp thing in his gut as Remy scrambles onto his knees. "You can't—"

If Andrew cleans up his mess, he's party to Remy's crime.

"Cam asked me to take care of you, and I have. I *will*. I don't make those sorts of promises lightly." Andrew paces back toward the entrance and pauses in the doorway. "It'd be best if you were gone before I got back."

Remy tests his legs, manages a few solid steps. "Thank you."

"Don't thank me, just . . ." Andrew turns to grasp Remy's wrist, and Remy freezes with the awful terror that he *knows*.

But Andrew grabbed the wrong arm, and he only tugs a pen from the pocket of his vest and opens the clenched fingers of Remy's right hand. On his palm, Andrew writes five numbers. 8-8-4-1-2.

"That's my personal code. Enter it into any Protectorate-installed keypad and it'll send a signal for help. We're as good as family, Remy. If you need me, I'll find you."

Andrew disappears inside to erase the evidence of Remy's crime. Only when his footsteps fade does Remy lift the loose sleeve of his tunic—ash-gray printed with bone-white floral accents—and turn his left hand.

Cam's rotten bond squeezes his heart, warning and punishment at once.

Look. He has to look.

A quick glance is all he can manage. It's more than enough.

Hands of a clockwork timepiece worn for at least two generations. Well, it fucking worked.

There, unmistakable, from the tip of his fate-finger to the inside of his wrist, the advancing line of his own withering is colored the red of dried blood. He'll die when it reaches his heart.

Idrian Delaciel will bear one just like it.

Delaciel—and anyone fatebound to him.

How funny. How rare, how *impossible* to be bound to the man who ruined his life. Fatebound, like their paths in life are tether-sworn to run parallel. Like they've walked the same roads, want the same things.

What sort of twisted, sick fuck is Remy, and what sort of cruel thing is so-called fate, to bind him to the man who made him into this? Tirani has always said tethers are echoes of truth, not architects of it, but there can be no truth in this. He wouldn't betray Cam by being bound to the man who killed him.

His own withering burns up his arm, evidence that he already has.

Chapter Three

Listen, children, running wild
heed your father's warning cries.
Shadow-hunter, slick, beguiling
stalks the moons and paints the night.
Water-gouger, island-breaker
cuts and ruins all that's green.
Thief and killer, man most vile—
reckless, ruthless, rude, obscene.

— Tune sung by the Enforcers in the children's capture game, "Lord of the Empty Isles"

Remy slips back into his room before sunrise.

He drops onto the end of his bed, clothes strewn over his blanket and pack open but empty. No matter how hard he scratches the dark line of the withering on his hand, it won't disappear. His pulse roars in his ears, adrenaline demanding he fight this or flee from it. Instead he sits, frozen. The only way to unravel a withering is to kill the witherer. Kill himself to free himself. What a joke.

A helpless noise scrapes out of his throat, and he buries his face in his hands.

Fatebound. To *Idrian Delaciel*.

There's no precedent, no literature to guide him. There are plenty of books about the therapeutic benefits of severing, and more than a few about the capture and sentencing of famous witherers who've turned to murder, but, unsurprisingly, Remy hasn't found any how-to guides or problem-solving methods for lethal curses.

He does know this: the mark on his arm is a death sentence, and it's advancing far faster than it should. Something's amplifying the curse's effects. Maybe the ritual interpreted Remy's blood as both blood of the witherer and blood of the withered, making him doubly-cursed—both direct target and indirect recipient of the curse through the fatebond. Cam survived for weeks. At the rate Remy's is going, he has days.

Maybe he's not *really* bound to Delaciel.

Maybe it's some old, dead tether the ritual mistook for a fatebond, left over from when he was young and Idrian's actions sounded daring rather than deadly. Maybe hate is a fate in itself. Maybe he can tear it out.

Hope sings through him.

Maybe he can. General wisdom says a witherer can't sever his own tethers, just as weavers like Tirani can't see their own bonds, but general wisdom doesn't account for mistakes like this one. When his only other option is waiting to die, it's worth a try.

Remy spreads honey and ash over his hands. For the first time, he purposefully reaches for the grasping tether to the right of his brother's, over his heart. He loses his breath at the texture of it.

If anything binds him to Idrian Delaciel, it should be rotted and thread-thin, coarse with malice. It should make his fingers bleed just to touch it.

This is not a thin, splintered thing. The sturdy rope is finely-woven and warm, as thick as Lara's but infinitely healthier. It's all wrong.

It has to be. There are no paths he and Idrian Delaciel could walk together, no ideals they could share.

Remy grips the tether and hums the song for a severing.

Agony and heat flood through the bond and knock him to his knees, blotting his vision white. He jerks away as ashy smoke fogs the air. His palms sting, muscles contracting with an electric surge of pain.

Why won't it *break?*

When he reaches for the tether once more, the honey on his hands sizzles on contact. He ignores the pain. *Again.*

Again with the electric jolt of agony. The thick tether remains unharmed, molten-hot and unwilling to be torn. He pulls his stinging hands away, teeth clenched and body curled in on itself.

Remy's fingers skim Cam's bond as he withdraws, and he jerks away from its roughening, frayed ends, slippery with rot-sickness. Cam's tether shouldn't have to share space with *this*.

"What are you doing?" The voice comes from his doorway.

Tirani, eyes dark with exhaustion.

"Nothing!" Remy tears his tunic over his head and wraps it around his hands to scrub the evidence of an attempted severing away.

"I was worried. Where were you last night?"

Remy winces. She knows, surely, even if she doesn't want to believe it.

He stands, dropping the dirty shirt and opening his pack. He snaps up a shirt and slings it over his arm.

"Can I get some privacy?"

"No," she says cheerfully. "Isn't that mine?"

He considers the tunic, embroidered with wide leaves and florals in blue, turquoise, orange, and coral pink. He'd rather die than trap himself in the fitted shirts with high, ribbed collars that are so popular with other young men right now. Old ladies like Fluora love to chide him: *You'll never find a partner like this!*

It rarely occurs to them to ask if he's looking for one. Remy's always known it's all right to like whoever he likes. Cam fell in love with a new person each month. The boy in the garden with the sharp jawline and soft words. The blacksmith's daughter with her reckless grin and laughter like poetry. The tall artist by the shore with their black hair twisted in a silky bun and fingers stained with clay. For Cam, the answer to the question of attraction was *all of the above*. For Remy, it's always been *none*, and his life has been no less rich for it. He's never longed to be desired—not how people like Fluora expect him to—so it seems useless to choke himself with clothes other people might like to see him in. Wearing what he loves and having someone who understands him at his side is enough.

Years of friendship have given him and Tirani that sort of understanding in most things, including their tastes in clothing. They've been stealing each other's clothes so long he hardly remembers what belongs to whom. He lets her borrow his leggings, the ones that lace up the calves, and they share the chunky brown heels that match everything in their shared wardrobe. Remy runs his fingers over the rounded leaves that start at the bottom left of the tunic in question and lifts it over his head.

"Could be." It's one of his favorites. He'll fight her for it.

"Whatever." Tirani slips into the room and examines the array of supplies on his bed. "Chancellor offered me a job again after you ran out on us."

Remy winces. "You said no?"

"I could hardly say yes!"

Not least because, as a government-employed weaver, she'd be promise-bound to report any crime her abilities made her aware of. Her skills could greatly benefit the Enforcement branch. A killer can smile and lie, but lies are easy to see through when Tirani can discern tether health with a glance. Weavers can identify witherers, too. Their tethers naturally look hyper-saturated to a weaver, the colors brighter than any others. The tethers of a witherer who has used their abilities to kill are brighter still, nearly painful in their intensity. Tirani's eyes can't tell her of Remy's intentions—she's bound to him, so his tethers appear colorless to her—but Remy's talked about his murder plans often enough that she wouldn't need her eyes to condemn him.

She sighs. "What are you doing?"

He should say *nothing* again, but he's no good at lying to her, or to anyone. "I don't know."

A warm hand lands on his shoulder, and he stops himself from reaching to hold it. "Tell me about it?"

He wants to, but telling her means saying he went through with the withering (which she'll hate), and confessing that he's affected (which he hates), so he shakes his head. "I don't think I can stay here."

"Vacation, then. We'll go together."

"No." He lifts her hand from his shoulder, turning his wrist to reveal its mark.

She curses, grabbing his hand to pull it closer. "Remy, *why?* Did they . . .?"

The truth is bitter on his lips. Tirani used to make up stories about the mystery tether next to Cam's and the kind of person it might link him to. None of her stories came close to this. He's ready for mockery when he finishes explaining, but she only brushes hair from his eyes and presses her forehead to his. She traces the rusty line from his fingertip to his wrist.

"It's moving fast."

Too fast. But at least Tirani's safe. Whatever form their friendship takes, it's not a fatebond. Her hands bear no marks.

"It can't be real. I wouldn't betray Cam like this. There's no way . . ." He grits his teeth. There's just no way.

"Tethers aren't something you *do*. Whatever it is, it's speaking to something true." Before he can argue, she says, "It could mean so many different things."

"I'll tear it out. I'll find a way."

Tirani lifts his chin to make him look at her, a wild smile lifting her lips. "That's not a bad idea. Let's find him."

"What?"

"Idrian. We track him down. Everyone talks about killing the witherer to reverse it, but I'll bet there are tons of other ways—maybe even things *you* could do. Maybe they're just not common knowledge because witherers have never *wanted* to undo their own work."

It's certainly possible. To pay for the ritual with the ashes of their beloved dead, a witherer has to be pretty damn sure of their intent. "If he was nearby, it'd give me more time to find a way to free myself," he says. "Some way to cut it."

Finding Delaciel would do more than allow Remy to try to untangle himself from the curse. It might just save him. Fatebonds don't only carry curses. They carry life.

Fatebound souls heal each other with nearness—not enough to counteract a withering, but enough to slow it. If Remy finds Delaciel and stays close, the double-time advance of his curse will slow down to match the pace of Idrian's. He'll have weeks to find a solution rather than days.

Remy's ears buzz. His joints throb, body urging him northeast. Wherever this pain is leading him, that's where he'll find Delaciel.

He grabs a small bag with the tools of his trade and drops it in his pack, then starts on the clothing. "All right. I'll find him."

This cursemark will be his camouflage. Other than the ash and honey at the bottom of his bag, there's nothing that could expose Remy as a witherer. But this curse, the same one Delaciel bears—that'll paint him as an ally. Delaciel will believe him to be nothing more than a fatebound partner in crime. A fellow victim. By the time he realizes Remy is the person he should be hunting, it'll be too late.

"*We'll* find him. Do you even know where to look?"

Remy points in the direction the pain is pulling him, along the coastline.

Tirani laughs. "See, this is why you need a weaver. Precision tracking." She aims his finger out over the ocean. "*That's* where your tether leads."

She snatches a leaf-green tunic with gold embroidery from his hands and slings it over her shoulder. "Come on. First ship departs at sunrise."

~

Remy dies inch by inch in darkness, where the air tastes of salt and sweat.

The hold of the ship they managed to buy passage on will be empty until it picks up a lima shipment from one of the fringe islands, so the crewmen were happy to take cash on the down-low.

By the following morning, the cursemark is halfway up his forearm. By evening, it sits in the crook of his elbow.

Just after moonrise on the second day, he spikes a fever that burns him from the inside out. In near-perfect darkness, Tirani hums songs. When he recognizes them, he hums along.

The curse races the boat. Tirani watches the water, navigating by a tether he can't see.

By the morning of the third day, when they arrive on the trade island of Auni, the mark has advanced to the ball of his shoulder.

Remy pulls aside the neck of his shirt to examine the withering. It's in its final stages, the crisp line unraveling into rust-red threads. It hasn't started retreating yet; they'll need to get closer to Delaciel.

"When we meet him, Remy..."

"I *know*, I won't stab him." Tempting though the idea is. "You can stop reminding me."

"I will as soon as you stop looking like you're lying."

Tirani's right. He has to control himself. Delaciel is the nexus of the curse; the moment he dies, no matter how he dies, anyone else affected by the curse dies, too. Killing him would be suicide.

They disembark before sunrise to the overpowering stench of the docks—fish guts and waste and saltwater.

"Where to now, oh great weaver?" Remy manages three shaky steps before falling to his knees, world rolling in time with the splash of the waves.

Beside him, Tirani makes a choked noise.

"I'm fine," he says. "Just lemme catch my breath. Can't be much farther."

"No," she whispers. "Look."

When he turns to her, his blood runs cold. Because she's doing that thing she does, dark eyes tracking something he can't see. Tracking a tether. But she's not looking farther inland, where they'll find the man they're searching for.

Expression lax with horror, she's staring back the way they came.

"They... just left. They had to've—Remy, shit."

With the speed the curse is traveling, he'll be unable to move in mere hours, and then dead by mid-afternoon.

Tirani grabs his shoulder, kneeling at eye-level. "We must've just missed him. I'll find a ship heading back out. You stay here, all right?"

"Right here?"

A burly fisherman stomps past, giving them a suspicious stare.

Tirani hooks a hand under his arm. "We'll stand. On three."

She half-drags him up to the island proper, dropping him on a bench across from a line of pastel-painted, ocean-facing shops before returning to the docks alone. Brightly dyed cotton banners flutter from the storefronts. The first sliver of sun peeks above the clear waters, lighting the fog and strings of birds that ring the nearby islands and glinting blue on the energy-storing, Protectorate-mandated solarfibre weaving in the shops' honeycomb windows.

Heat creeps through Remy's veins, ever closer to his heart.

We'll find him, Tirani promised.

But if they can't, she'll have to watch him die. He can't sever his own tether to spare Tirani pain, but he can at least spare her that. Better that she doesn't know the waxy chill and rigidity of dead skin.

He first met her a few months after he lost Cam, back when he'd fall asleep in alleyways with stray cats on his lap or against trees in strangers' orchards to avoid returning home. Both orphans, they formed a family of their own.

If he makes it far enough away, perhaps Tirani won't have to see his body at all. Down on the docks, she scrambles from one worker to the next, gesturing as fiercely as she does anything.

Remy forces himself to his feet. He doesn't have Tirani's precision, but he has a decent enough sense for Delaciel's location that he can search on his own. If he fails, he'll die alone. No mess.

The pull in Remy's chest guides him first to the west, in the direction of Tirani's seaward-pointing finger as she argues with a gruff gentleman, toward a section of dock caught in the impenetrable blue shadow of a neighboring island. The houses get smaller as he goes, huddled closer in the cold shade. It figures Delaciel would be on *this* side of the island.

Remy's chest aches, vision fizzing with static as the pull in his chest guides him inexplicably around a corner, then up the rickety stairs to a pedestrian path and through a narrow alleyway, past a hunched and grizzled man burning the pages of an old book over a trash can fire. Maybe Delaciel forgot something and is heading back?

He follows the tug into an alley where the reek of rotting things chokes him, then to a dead end.

Ah.

Tirani was right. His sense of direction is terrible. Weakness rolls through Remy in a cold wave, and he slumps against the alley's slippery wall.

"Nice *shoes*," a mocking voice says behind him.

Remy turns, and his wavering vision shows him a man—a few inches taller than Remy, with shoulders twice as broad and a cruel twist to his lips. Remy glances from his own chunky heels to the man's pale, brown-stained feet.

"Better than yours."

"Oh, you've got a mouth on you! Kids like you don't usually visit this side of Auni."

Remy scowls. "I'd prefer to die in peace, if you don't mind."

"Hmm?"

"Is this *your* stinky alleyway? I can go—"

The man spreads his arms to block Remy's exit, and the pale light glints on something sharp clenched in one fist. Remy stumbles back, away from the point of the man's blade.

"Mm," the man says, thoughtful. "There's a toll. For passage, you know. Got any coin?"

"Not a one, I'm afraid." He'd left his pack on the bench where Tirani dropped him.

"Then give me the shirt. I know someone who'd buy it."

Remy will not be dying *shirtless*, thank you. "I don't think so."

"You can give it, or I can cut it off you."

"You know what? I think I'll just—" Remy's heart skips a beat, and the next one comes with rending pain that dims his vision and tips him against the wall. When it clears, the first things he sees are the livid red threads of his own branching withering on his chest.

This man is taller, wider, stronger, and the withering doesn't have far to go. Remy won't make it out of this alleyway, one way or another. That's not so bad. The moment his heart stops, the curse will be irreversible. Idrian Delaciel can't kill the witherer to save himself if Remy's already dead.

But he's not going to make surrendering his shirt to this asshole his last living act.

Remy eyes the space under the man's raised knife-wielding arm. He could duck through it and run.

"Do what you will." He smirks as he catches his breath. Strange that it should be so easy to breathe, this close to the end. He points a finger at his own aching chest, taking a slow step forward. "This thing here? It just means you'll be doing me a favor."

"What thing where?" the man growls. "Don't you try to trick me. You give me what I want, I'll leave you be."

"Fine." He makes as if to remove his shirt. Another step closer. When he's near enough, Remy goes for the space beneath the man's arm, but he catches on, bringing the knife-hand down in a brutal swing.

Remy sidesteps, nearly stumbling into one of the man's big, bare feet. He glances down.

Perfect.

This asshole can say what he likes about Remy's heels. He lifts his foot and brings the chunky, tapered heel down hard on his attacker's instep, splitting skin and cracking bone with a satisfying crunch. Let him try to pursue Remy now.

But as Remy tries to push past, he overbalances, landing on the grimy cobblestones on his back. The man looms over him, expression warped with pain and knife raised.

Remy spares a moment for regret. This will not be much better than dying shirtless.

"I'll teach you—"

A hand closes around his attacker's wrist before Remy learns what he's about to be taught.

"Excuse us," a stranger's voice says, honey-smooth and quiet. "But this one's ours."

Remy's attacker turns, eyes widening. The knife clatters from his hand, pinging off the cobblestones. "*You.*"

"Me," the stranger says cheerily. He lets go, and the man flees.

The intruder pulls Remy to his feet and out of the alleyway, and Remy inhales the sweeter scent of morning dew and sea salt, bent double as he hauls in a deep breath.

His eyes catch on his own heaving chest, but he doesn't find the dark, spreading threads of an end-stage withering. There's only clear, if irritated, skin. A quick examination reveals the withering halfway down his upper arm, still retreating. The dizziness and pain, the blackness that haunted the edges of his vision, they're all gone.

And if *that's* happening—

Slowly, Remy looks up at his savior.

Ribbed boots lace up the man's calves, brushed by a leather coat, deeper blue than the velvety dark of night and studded with silver buttons like stars. The thin brown strap of a holster crosses over the man's left shoulder and disappears beneath the coat. Silver-blond waves of hair escape from a messy low ponytail. Ocean-blue sunglasses shield pale eyes even in the early-morning shade. Pinpricks of fresh blood blossom on his white linen shirt just above his hip— the stab wound that gave Remy blood for the curse.

Idrian Delaciel—self-proclaimed Lord of the Empty Isles—grins, exposing a brutal, brilliant smile with all the swagger Remy worshipped as a boy, and claps a hand on Remy's shoulder. When he speaks, his voice is softer than Remy ever imagined.

"*There* you are."

Chapter Four

Reckless, or foot-connected, tethers signify a connection characterized by a desire to support. Their health and thickness may be affected by physical or emotional distance. Bearers of reckless tethers long to serve—and in serving, to thrive. In an unusual reversal, these tethers readily attenuate or travel to a new location when they are no longer of use. If they rot, it is because they linger too long.

— From *On the Manipulation of Tethers*

For a moment, all Remy can feel is awe.

It fades fast.

"We've been up and down the whole damned island looking for you. Your dying was quite the distraction." Eyes inscrutable behind the blue glasses, Delaciel spreads his curse-marked hand toward Remy's matching mark. "This isn't how I'd have preferred to meet the next member of my crew."

In the abstract, it was easy to imagine pretending to be Delaciel's ally. Reality isn't so kind. Nausea slithers in Remy's belly, a shudder crawling through him from the proprietary hand Delaciel hasn't taken off his shoulder.

Tirani was right to warn him. All he wants is to watch this man suffer every bit as much as Cam did. The fact that killing him would be as good as suicide doesn't make it any less tempting.

Remy twists away from Delaciel's touch. "I'm not your *crew*."

"If only that were true." The edges of Delaciel's smile could draw blood.

"Idrian!" A tall woman with voluminous black curls, a cutting frown, and both hands cocked on her hips steps out from behind him. "Be nice to the new kid."

"Look at him, Roca! Look at his clothes."

Remy glances down at his embroidered tunic, fitted maroon leggings, and heeled boots. He wonders whether Idrian Delaciel needs all the bones in his feet intact. Surely not. "And what, exactly, is wrong with my clothes?"

A man steps out of the little group behind Delaciel, willow-thin with ash-brown hair spilling over amber eyes. He wears a fitted, floral teal vest over a coral pink dress shirt rolled up around his elbows and sports a smile that promises slow death. "Yes, Idrian, do tell. Is there something wrong with those clothes?"

"No!" Delaciel scowls over at Remy. "*Yes.*"

The man with the excellent vest taps his foot, gunshot-staccato. "How so?"

"Really, Thomlin? Is no one else seeing this? The material, the make? He's fucking rich. Bet my blood he's from the viper's nest itself."

"Ex*cuse* you. One snazzy outfit does not a rich man make." The man named Thomlin gestures at himself, fingernails painted the same vibrant teal as his vest. "Case in point. Regardless, you've bet plenty enough of your blood. Keep the rest of it inside you."

"I didn't bet it, that squirrelly bastard stabbed me. And that's beside the point. Seriously, I'm fatebound to *this*?"

Remy squints at the blood dots on the shirt that conveniently mark the location of Delaciel's wound. Clearly, the guy who stabbed him to get the blood for Remy's withering didn't do a thorough enough job. Remy could punch him there. Stab him again, twist it deep—

"The sentiment's mutual," he grits out instead.

"Glad we've established that," Delaciel drawls. "Time to go. We're on the clock."

That's when it hits him. His shoulders are free of the pack with all his supplies, but that's not all he left behind. "We can't! My friend's here. She can't be far. She was just—"

"Tough. I've found myself short of friends on Auni thanks to your Chancellor, and stopping for you made us late. We don't have time to wait."

"Hey, guys?" the tall woman—Roca—says.

"That's too bad." Remy crosses his arms. "I won't be leaving without her."

"Excellent!" Delaciel throws an arm around Roca's shoulders. "Y'hear him, Roca? He *wants* to die here."

Thomlin interjects, "*I* don't want him to die here, not if we have to feel it happening like that again. It was remarkably unpleasant." He gives Remy a weak shrug. "More for you than for us, I'm sure."

"All of you!" Roca steps out of the loop of Delaciel's grabby arms to turn Remy around by his shoulder. "New kid, calm down." She points downhill. "Is that your friend?"

Remy follows her finger to the distant figure approaching at a furious pace, tasseled shawl flying. He pulls free of Roca and waves. "Tirani! Over here!"

"Don't *yell*," Delaciel hisses. "What sort of outlaw are you?"

Remy wants to retort that he's not an outlaw, but given that he recently laid a very illegal withering to kill this man, he doubts he'd sound convincing.

When Tirani arrives, the first thing she does after catching her breath is shove Remy's abandoned pack into his arms with enough force to push a shocked *oof* from him.

"Tirani, I'm—"

"You idiot! You left." She throws her arms around him. "You left me. I thought—you *know* what I—" The rest of her sentence dies in a choked sigh against his nape.

A chill spreads in Remy's belly. He *is* an idiot. Her family disappeared the same way, with a promise never kept. He thought to spare her the sight of his corpse, but he hurt her instead. Remy puts his arms around her, tentative, and she squeezes tighter, breath hitching. They're not allowed to leave each other. It's their rule, even when they argue. They sit with it, maybe in different rooms, but they never leave. "Sorry," he whispers. "That was an asshole move."

"It certainly was!" She pulls back and rubs her eyes. "You're lucky I'm a better tracker than you. I saw your tether shifting and followed it. Are they—is he . . . ?"

"Oh," Roca says from behind Tirani, rapt and wondering, one hand extended like Tirani might be an illusion and she has to make sure she's tangible. "You're a *weaver*," at the same time Delaciel growls, "A *fucking weaver?*"

Delaciel has a head and shoulders on Remy in height, but he squares himself in front of the man. "Careful what you say about my friend."

Delaciel's eyes narrow on Tirani. "Weavers are liars."

"No they're—" Remy clamps his mouth shut. Old Fluora's tether readings are as gaudily ornamented as her shop—it's why she's so successful. Everyone loves pretty half-truths. "Tirani isn't a liar."

"You sure about that?"

"*You two* . . ." Roca throws an arm between them, and that's when Remy sees it. It's fainter on the darker skin of her finger, but it's still there. The burgeoning cursemark sits halfway down her fate-finger.

Thomlin bears the same.

"Both of you . . . ?" Remy whispers.

"All of us," Thomlin says. "Unlucky, right? As far as 'ways of discovering you're fatebound to someone' go, this might be my least favorite."

All of them.

"You didn't know," Tirani breathes.

"Not for sure, until this thing showed up." Thomlin taps the withering. "We didn't exactly have time to do a cute group trip to a weaver, given the fugitive thing."

"Over my dead body," Delaciel says primly.

"Lucky for you, it just might be," Thomlin grouses. "Anyway, to be honest, I'm not one bit surprised. Idrian doesn't do things by half measures. Being fatebound to every last one of us seems like something he'd do."

Remy crushes down a surge of sickness and shifts away from Thomlin.

He didn't plan for this. Delaciel's entire crew is fatebound to him? What's the likelihood of anyone—especially a bastard like Idrian Delaciel—being fatebound to so many people? It shouldn't be possible.

Tirani's face reflects Remy's horror, magnified. She meets his eyes with a sort of desperation that, put to words, would probably translate to *do something*, but there's nothing he can do.

Tirani drags him back into the stinky alley while the others watch, bemused, and leans close to hiss, "*Remy.*"

"Stop looking at me like I killed someone," he whispers back.

"You're about to kill several someones. I told you. I *warned you*—"

Remy flinches, darting a glance to the crowd outside the alley. "Should we really be having this conversation now?"

Delaciel's quiet voice spears the silence that follows: "Something wrong? Weaver girl seems upset."

Tirani moves to the mouth of the alley and speaks at full volume, laying on the innocent act. "You're all—this is a lot to take in. It's just . . . more than we were expecting."

Remy scowls at the double meaning.

Tirani gives Remy a quelling stare, but her attention doesn't linger long. She walks closer to Delaciel, tilting her head as she stares at him. "I don't need you to believe my work is legitimate. To be honest, if you were a customer, I'm not sure I'd know where to start reading your tethers. I've never met a person with so many of them. I can barely see you between them."

"Spare me." Delaciel flicks his hand in front of his chest, as if to show that nothing's there, and Tirani smiles thinly.

"You do have a few grasping tethers," she admits. "But most of them are reckless. Thousands, like a road stretching out behind you."

Remy swallows a laugh. Reckless, really? Idrian Delaciel hardly seems like the giving type. Nurses and teachers and the right sort of leaders might have a profusion of foot-connected tethers, but this guy, selfless and self-sacrificing? Remy leans toward Tirani. "You're kidding. Are they all rotbound?"

"No." Tirani's silent for a long moment. "Just one," she says, quiet.

Delaciel turns away. "We're leaving."

Roca grabs him by the shoulder before he can go. "Don't be rude. Invite the kid to come."

"Kids!" Thomlin chimes in. "Two for the price of one."

"I'm not a kid," Remy says. He's nineteen. Old enough to be a murderer and die for it.

The expression that curls Delaciel's lips up is not a smile. "That's what all children say. Come along or stay behind. Doesn't matter to me."

Roca sighs. "Were you listening to anything I said? We leave him and we have to feel him die again. You can't tell me you'll be able to work like that."

"I've worked through worse."

"*Idrian.*"

"The one with the mark, then. We leave the girl. We don't need more dead weight."

Roca stands straighter. "We do *not* leave the girl."

There must be something in the way she says it, because Delaciel turns fully to look at her.

Roca meets him without flinching. "She can help us. Hate them if you want, but having a weaver could help us find the person who did this to us."

Roca has no idea how right she is, though in this case it has nothing to do with being a weaver and everything to do with being his friend. If Tirani were so inclined, she could point them toward the witherer right now.

Finally, Delaciel growls, "Fine."

"What part of *be nice*—" But he's already several steps away. Roca's sharp eyes return to Remy. "He's grumpy when he doesn't sleep. Mind you, this whole thing is awfully strange. I know proximity's supposed to make a withering go slower, but this is the first time I've ever heard of distance making it *worse.*"

Adrenaline sparks through Remy. Distance wouldn't make it worse in any case other than his, but there's no way Roca could guess what happened. Remy's case has to be one in a million, maybe even the only one of its kind. They have no reason to assume he's anything other than a peculiarly-affected victim. His withering has receded to match everyone else's, sitting barely halfway down his fate-finger. As long as they don't discover he's the culprit, he has more than enough time to figure out a way to save himself and run. He forces himself to walk calmly when Roca sets off after Delaciel.

He shrugs. "Don't ask me. I'm just in this to survive."

"That'll be easy." Thomlin laughs. "Idrian, who'd you piss off lately?"

Roca gives it a few moments while Delaciel stalks ahead of them before she drops what must be some agreed-upon punchline. "Only the whole planet."

Thomlin again: "Idrian and his big damn heroism are gonna get us all killed."

"How's that different from any other day?" Roca turns her eyes on Delaciel's back with the same, silent judgment Tirani uses like a well-honed blade on Remy. "I *told* you we should have tried harder to track the knife after that coward ran off with it. We wouldn't be in this position if we'd found it."

Delaciel doesn't hesitate. "You were right. I knew it then. But we didn't—" His face darkens. "We didn't have *time*."

The cheery mood in the group evaporates. Their pace picks up.

Down the winding path they go, past shuttered shops and rows of vendors laying out their wares. Before they get to the docks, Roca stops dead, staring at a cart displaying skewers with greasy chunks of meat, thick slices of wild onion, and buttery-smooth mushroom. The grease has flooded off the dish meant to catch it and made mud of the dust on the ground.

"Oh," Roca whispers, spellbound. "Those look terrible. Idrian—"

He sighs, and something sails through the air. It lands in Roca's hand with the clink of metal against metal.

"Just you. Get enough to share. And *hurry*."

They take a sharp right and pace along the narrowing paths. They leave the docks behind, and the salt-stink of the sea. Houses and vendors thin out, then disappear. They follow a barely-trodden path, then something that can't rightly be called a path at all, up through the tall grasses and then a grove of thick, ancient trees. Remy's gasping by the time they leave the shadow of the wood and step into a clearing still decorated with the morning's low fog.

There, a behemoth waits.

In the low light, the ship's smooth metal shines bluish, beautiful and horrible like the things that live in the deepest parts of the sea. Remy traces the lines of the thing, catches the numbers half-scratched-off along the side, and scowls. He doesn't know a ton about hybrid interstellar vessels, but he's Cameron Canta's brother. He knows the law.

"That thing's ancient. Wasteful and harmful and fuel-inefficient. No *way* it's still legal to operate under the updated Sustainability Standards," he says. And because he used to idolize Idrian and knows to look for it, he can still make out the indistinct numbers and—in a different color, underneath them—the opalescent, fading shine of the infamous ship's name. *Astrid*.

The door hisses open when Delaciel draws near, but he pats the side of the vessel and doesn't enter. "That's what you're worried about? She's plenty flight-worthy."

"Yeah," Remy mutters. "If you want to poison the planet again."

"Because those new solar ships are so much better."

"They are."

"They're not *reliable*. Liable to sputter out as they are to start, and they're slower than Roca in the morning." Delaciel's pleasant expression takes on a delighted edge. "But by all means, tell me where to get the funds I'd need to procure a more *efficient* mode of transportation and the permits to operate it. Except I'd need to jump through a hundred hoops to do that, and with all the shit your Chancellor's pinned on us, I wouldn't make it to the first, never mind through it."

"*Pinned* on you? It's nothing you don't deserve. I saw what you did to Veida," Remy spits. Delaciel flinches, turning away, and Remy pushes a step closer. The pictures played out over the Chancellor's broadcasts for months after Cam's death, each bit of footage worse than the last. Veida was a thriving fishing island. When Delaciel drained the aquifer that watered it, the bright green island wilted. Veida was built around its aquifer. When it ran dry, more than half the village's homes and the belongings the displaced villagers had to leave behind were lost to sinkholes. To this day, no one's been able to live there again.

Delaciel's voice is rough when he finally speaks. "We make do with what we have, or we die. You stick around long enough, you'll figure that out, Greenie."

The others all enter, and Tirani crowds in close to Remy and pushes him through the door and down the hall, hissing, "You keep antagonizing him, he'll kick you out and you'll die. Is that what you want?"

Delaciel doesn't immediately follow them inside, and Remy's about to ask why when the trees in the woods rustle to reveal Roca, who carries a platter stacked alarmingly high with greasy skewers. She walks inside, a woman on a mission. Delaciel follows behind her, the entrance hissing seamlessly shut behind him. The ship's interior is silver and cream, with accents in lavender. It's old, all of it, but well-maintained.

Heavy platter precarious on the spread fingers of a single hand, Roca leads them into a cozy common room, where she sets the platter in the middle of a long table. Chairs with coats and blankets and books and even an offensively adorable and massive stuffed bear crowd around it. Benches line the wall. A fuzzy blue blanket adorns what looks like a game table in the back of the room, with a rolled-up jacket and an open travel book with pictures of distant islands with flower-specked hillsides in one corner.

Roca grabs a small but lethal-looking hammer from the corner of the table and bashes it into a little bell on the wall. The sound it produces is loud enough to shatter eardrums.

"First bell for your last meal!" she bellows. "Come one, come all, for your shitty street food! There's enough grease on these to kill everyone on Alta." She looks to Remy and Tirani. "Sit in any empty chair."

Tirani and Remy remain standing. There's not a single chair without something on it.

Roca throws the coin pouch back at Delaciel, who catches it without looking and stuffs it into his pocket. He takes the chair at the head of the table, so the giant stuffed bear sits to his left.

"Last meal?" Tirani whispers.

Roca snatches a skewer from the platter and tugs a chunk of rare meat from its end with her teeth. She drops into a chair draped in a red-and-orange shawl. "It's tradition. We do it before every fuel run. I'm not saying it *is* our last meal, but I'm not saying it isn't. And what makes a gal feel more alive than bad street food?" She moans appreciatively as she stuffs an onion and slice of mushroom into her mouth. "If we're gonna die, we might as well die with full bellies."

Delaciel looks up, and he's still wearing those damn sunglasses. "Eat," he says. "Roca and I will break off in a smaller vessel for fuel and supplies. You'll come with us."

"*What?*" Remy blurts. "No."

"It wasn't a request. If you being here can slow down this curse or your friend can help us find whoever did this, that's great, but if you think I'd leave you here, where you could hurt my people or sabotage my ship, you're an idiot. Thom and Emil are too nice to kill you if you get rowdy. You're both coming with me."

"You don't trust us," Tirani says.

"I don't *know you*. I don't care if I'm bound to him or whatever. There are plenty of bonds more inviolable than these that people break every day." He spits out the words like they're rotten. "Trust is a thing you earn by doing. You're strangers to me. I've got no qualms about putting you down if I think you're a danger to us." Delaciel reaches across the table and pulls a thick book toward him.

Remy's breath freezes in his chest at the embossed cover, the title stamped in forest green along the side. *A Rumination on Rights and Responsibilities.* Cam used to carry that book with him everywhere, using everything from Remy's drawings to blades of grass to mark favorite pages. His notes were so thick in the margins he must have written half again the book's length.

Delaciel flips it open, and Remy's chest aches. There are no wobbly underlines in this copy. No found bookmarks or notes. Delaciel lifts one page between his fingers and nods before tightening his hold and tearing it from the book.

Remy doesn't mean to make the noise that escapes him, but Delaciel looks up. Wordless, he takes in Remy's expression, his hand half lifted. He raises an eyebrow and holds Remy's gaze while he tears another page out, then flattens it on the table and begins to fold it.

"How dare you—"

"It's my book," Delaciel says. "I'll do what I want with it."

It's not his book. It's a treatise on the line between liberty and personal responsibility in regard to the safety of their recovered world. It's tantamount to treason to mistreat it. Delaciel rips a couple strips from the page to make it square and then swipes the strips onto the floor.

In the mess on the table, Remy spots other pages, folded—inconceivably—into roses. One paper rose adorns the giant plush bear's head like a hat.

Thomlin comes in and drops into the messiest chair at the table. The space in front of him is strewn with notes, a large coat, a plush blanket, miscellaneous wires, and a stack of books. He

Jules Arbeaux

reaches over the mess to grab a few skewers. "Hold on, everyone," he says.

Before Remy can ask why, the *Astrid* rocks into motion, and Remy scrambles to keep his feet as it lifts off.

Thomlin throws out an arm to keep his belongings from sliding away. "Maybe we could steal better stabilizers," he says, and is soundly ignored. "Nobody? New kid, surely you agree."

To Remy's right, Delaciel mutilates a universally beloved book of philosophy. Across the table, Thomlin has wrapped a wire around one of his fingers like a snake.

Thomlin glances between Remy and his own finger, then quietly removes the wire spiral. "Ah! Apologies. We never officially introduced ourselves, did we? How rude."

He gently shoves aside the pile of books and wires that nearly obscures him. "Thom Nash, would-have-been mechanical engineer, now fixer-upper for an infamous outlaw. And of course, you've met our beloved asshole, Idrian, who neither needs nor deserves an introduction. First time we spoke, I punched him in the mouth, so let me just say he's an acquired taste. I'm sure he'll warm up to you."

"You're *sure*, are you," Delaciel deadpans. He covers a massive yawn, then props his chin up in the cup of his hands.

"Shut it. Now, the woman who could choke you and probably make you thank her for it—" at this, Roca raises a cheery hand, mouth full of skewered meat "—is Roca Aravel. And the quiet guy behind you—"

Remy spins and chokes on a startled curse. There is, in fact, a man behind him. He's short and compact, with cropped black curls, three watches on his wrist, and at least three days of stubble. "When did *you* get here?"

"I've been here since we found you," the man says, voice as unassuming as his manner.

Remy tries to think back, but he can't recall meeting a fourth crew member. "No," he says.

"Yes," Thom responds, laughter in his voice. "It's hilarious, right? That's Emil Carteau. Stealthiest fella any of us have ever met. You'd think he'd be a perfect criminal, right?" He doesn't wait for Remy's reply. "He's the worst! We sicced him on swiping some jerk's souped-up nano-surgery setup because I wanted to re-gift it, and he botched it so bad he nearly got us all killed. Good thing he's a fantastic navigator, pilot, and keeper-together of our shit."

Emil passes around the table, kissing Roca's head on the way. Roca lifts the two skewers she's been keeping tucked between the first and third fingers of her free hand. "Saved some for you. You set the course?"

He nods. "Yeah, better get back. We'll be there in an hour."

Emil walks out with a skewer in each hand.

"Be where in an hour?" Remy asks.

"The OSS," Roca says, like that's a remotely acceptable answer.

The motion of the *Astrid* isn't to blame, this time, when he nearly loses his footing. "You're stealing from the OSS?" He's never personally seen the Orbital Supply Station, but stealing from it seems unwise.

Clearly, no one shares his concern.

"Sit, sit!" Roca gestures around the table. "Anywhere you can find room."

Roca beckons Tirani into the seat beside her, which means the only chair that seems easy to clear is occupied by the massive plushie.

"Idrian, move the damn bear," Roca says.

When he just continues leaning forward on the table, chin in hands, Roca growls and leans over to tear the stuffed animal from its seat. It sails through the air and lands on top of the blanket half-folded across the game table.

"Sit," Roca says again. "Eat."

Remy's stomach turns at the prospect of sitting near the man who killed Cameron. He takes the journey step by step, and when he drops into the chair, he refuses to look over. Roca, lips lifted in a half-smile, pulls two of the three remaining skewers from the platter and gives them to him.

He tries to ignore Delaciel next to him. Delaciel with his still-bleeding wound. His presence burns at Remy's side. He barely tastes the first bite of meat, chewing mechanically.

A snuffling noise to Remy's right startles him, and he glances over before he can stop himself, shock loosening his hands where they clench around the skewers.

Delaciel didn't respond to Roca's request because he's sound asleep sitting up, eyes closed behind the ocean-blue lenses of his sunglasses.

"Ah." Roca stands to brush a half-folded paper flower from the table. "He does that. Good news is, he'll probably be less of a mess with an hour of sleep in him. He'll slip and knock his head on the table in a few minutes. Always does."

She retrieves the discarded bear from the game table and drops it in front of Delaciel.

"As funny as it'd be to see him break his nose, we have work to do, and our window of opportunity's really small thanks to our detour to find you. You finished?"

Remy contemplates his half-eaten skewer. He's not hungry. "Yeah."

"More for me. This way, both of you. I'll show you where you'll be sleeping."

The unmarked room she leads Tirani and Remy to is dusty and empty of anything but a corner desk and a wall nook with bunk beds set into it. Only one contains a mattress. Roca offers a sheepish grin, one of Remy's skewers already emptied. She shoves the other into Tirani's hands. "We'll call this a work in progress, shall we? Let's get you some furniture. Follow me."

Remy winces. He'd rather not spend time with these people. "Uh, Tirani, you wanna . . . ?"

Tirani, already exploring the dusty room, waves him away. "You go ahead. Leave your bag and I'll unpack for you."

Her voice is cheerful, but she stares at the ground, hands loose at her sides.

"Are you sure? I could stay."

"No. I just need to put everything in order." Tirani upends her backpack on the floor. "Go on, I'm fine."

She clearly isn't. Remy bites his tongue. He's stuck with Roca, then.

He trails after her down the hall.

She defended Tirani earlier and seems particularly knowledgeable about tethers. "So are you a weaver or something? A witherer?"

As soon as the words are past his lips, he wishes he could swallow them down his throat again. But Delaciel must have a pet witherer, and she's the most likely candidate. He can blame his curiosity on his friendship with Tirani, if she asks.

She belts out a laugh. "Me? Hardly. Just an interested party. We do have a witherer, though. The best." It's a promise and a threat in one. "We got lucky with your girl—we haven't had a weaver until today."

"She's not my girl," Remy mutters. "And her name is Tirani."

Roca stares like she intends to crack him open with it. "That's a very unique name."

"Yeah, well. So's yours." All the questions Remy can't ask echo in his skull. *Who? Where? Is your witherer here? Somewhere else? Give me a name. Give me his* blood. And, blade-sharp and climbing his throat, *Why? Why kill a man as kind as Cameron Canta?* Instead, he says, "So we're all gonna die soon, I guess."

"I wouldn't bet against us just yet. We've got a pretty damn good track record of wriggling out of tight spots, and now that you're here, the withering will advance even more slowly."

She's definitely the one he needs to watch out for.

"Does your *witherer* know how to fix this?"

Roca's steps don't falter, but she tosses him a narrow-eyed look over her shoulder. "Don't know. We've had more important things to deal with."

"More important than dying?"

"More important than the five of us dying. Ah! Here we are." She stops at a clearly marked room. Delaciel's name adorns a plaque on the door, carved in lazy, slanting letters.

The door slides open when Roca speed-taps a code into the pad by the door, and Remy gapes. While the room at least contains a bed and has a pile of stuff on the desk in the corner, it isn't much better than the room they left Tirani behind in. Bare, except for the frankly alarming profusion of stemmed paper flowers.

"What the—"

Without a moment's pause, Roca strides inside, nods firmly, and hefts Idrian Delaciel's entire mattress over one shoulder. She drags it to the door, tipping her head to urge him to follow. "Grab the pillow!"

Remy obeys, clutching it against his chest. "Did you just *steal his bed*?"

Roca laughs. "Better question: when will he notice?"

The frame, without its mattress, is an empty shell, an eyesore. It's not the sort of thing a person can miss.

"Anyway," Roca says, "You don't need to worry about a thing. With our witherer and your weaver, we'll figure a way out of this mess as soon as we've sorted the fuel thing."

The OSS. Right. Remy shudders. "That sounds like a bad idea."

"We subsist on bad ideas." She stares down the hall, free hand clenching at her side. "It always seems hopeless, and we always manage." She runs a thumbnail down the line of the curse on her fate-finger. "No reason this has to be any different."

Remy follows behind her as she starts back toward his room. "You're pretty confident."

Roca throws a sharp smile over one shoulder. "I have to be. Anyone less confident would've given up on this shit show years ago. But see, we're in luck for once. We don't have to comb through the millions of people who'd love to kill Idrian. We only have to comb through the *witherers*. I'll find the bastard who's trying to kill us—" Roca swipes her hand across her throat, and Remy feels the pressure on his, cold like a blade "—then I'll return the favor."

They know they can kill him to save themselves, then. That's . . . not ideal. Remy swallows. "You—uh, you have any leads?"

"I *will*."

Her unwavering faith wrings a shiver from him. Witherings aren't considered nigh-untraceable for nothing. If he were on the surface—even if they had Tirani or another weaver to identify active witherers by the vibrancy of their tethers—they'd have to comb through thousands of settlements on hundreds of islands. Hundreds of witherers, and not a single shred of evidence to guide them. He's made it easier by coming to them, but as long as Remy's careful, he's just another victim.

Still, it doesn't change the fact that he's on their turf, in their hands. Remy skims his fingers over his palm, where Andrew wrote those numbers. All he needs to turn the tables is a Protectorate-installed keypad.

The numbers have smeared into illegibility, but he remembers them. He can ping Andrew with his location, get them all arrested. If they're in custody, he can still take advantage of their nearness to find a way to save himself without having to interact with them. Andrew would be thrilled, surely, to have his father's murderer in prison.

Roca's tone shifts to cheerful as the door to his dusty room opens again, an instant switch that jolts Remy from his thoughts. She drops Delaciel's mattress on the floor and kicks it into the corner. It grazes Remy's pack, and he can't help imagining it tipping over, spilling his clothes onto the floor and exposing the little tin at the bottom with its incriminating ashes and honey. But it only wobbles in place.

Roca directs a quick wave at Tirani, who faces the wall, folding her clothes and lining them up in a drawer. "Settling in, Tirani?"

Tirani nods without looking their way.

Roca pulls the pillow from Remy's arms and flings it onto the mattress. "See? Looking more like a home already."

"If you say so."

"Come on." She starts walking again. "We have more work to do."

But Remy can't look away from the room's thick, dusty window. There's no sunlight beyond the glass—nothing of Verdine's clear blue skies. All Remy sees through the window is airless impenetrable blackness. He's closer to the stars than he's ever been, but they look far more distant than they did when he sprawled on his back as a boy and tried to count them. He feels abruptly untethered; he's never been farther from home than this.

He shakes the mixed feeling of awe and horror away and says, "Why help us?"

Roca lifts both hands. "Why not? The more people we have, the slower the curse goes. Anyway, it's how these things go, you'll see. We drag people into our mess, show them subpar but earnest hospitality, and they never leave."

Remy scoffs. "Sorry to disappoint, but this—" he waves at the flickering lights in the time-worn hallways "—isn't my thing. I won't be sticking around."

"Thomlin said that, too." Her face splits into a gleeful grin, and between her wine-red lips, her incisors are threateningly sharp. "Speaking of!" She speeds up, and, when she arrives at a room at the end of the hall, knocks loud enough to wake the dead. "Thom, you incurable hoarder! I'm here to rob you!"

The door whines open to reveal Thomlin's scowling face, a pair of safety goggles lopsided on his nose. "Please remember I'm the reason we have hot water for washing and I can be the reason we don't."

Roca pushes past him into the room, which is, frankly, a disaster. Various machines and wires and tools lie on surfaces not meant to hold them. Something sparks at the corner desk he must have just stood up from, spitting gold light and emitting a concerning growl. Boxes and baskets, carefully lined up underneath the workbench at the far left of the room as if to assert some semblance of order, disgorge their mechanical contents onto the floor.

Still, there's a very clear walking area. Remy has seen Andrew's office in the Chancellor's estate enough to understand there's order at work here, too.

"Remy and his friend need a room, but all we have so far are mattresses and one pillow."

At this, Thomlin makes an impolite noise and tips his head to the ceiling. "Idrian's?"

Roca just grins.

"We doing a betting pool? 'Cause I say it's a full cycle before he realizes it's gone."

"Put your money where your mouth is, Nash. How much?"

"The usual." He paces over to his bed and grabs another pillow, a couple threadbare towels, and, finally, a folded quilt.

"Gotta stay warm in here. Heating doesn't work for shit. You'll need this."

The quilt becomes uglier the closer it gets to Remy, made up of swatches of the most abhorrent colors he's ever seen. Bile-yellow and green-brown. Primary red and blue polka-dots on a lime-colored background.

"It's really okay." Remy holds his hands out in the universal—but soundly ignored—gesture for *stop*. "You can keep it."

"Oh no," Thomlin says dryly, pushing the thing toward him. "I insist."

"It's tradition." Roca shoves the quilt into his arms. "New blood gets the blanket."

"Enjoy the nightmares. Thing's cursed."

Roca cackles. "Only if you're weak enough to fall under its thrall. Be ready to pay up."

She takes the blanket from Remy and unfolds it to tip the towels and pillow inside before cinching the ends with a fist and swinging it all over her shoulder.

"I won't tell you how to store your stuff, but careful what you keep outside the drawers. Anything on the floors could get tossed if we have to do emergency maneuvers."

On the tip of Remy's tongue is, *Maybe don't be murderers and you won't have to do emergency maneuvers*, but he bites it back and offers a bland nod.

"We drop this stuff and go." Roca hurries down the dim hallways. "We've got ten minutes. We get your friend, we wake Idrian, and we're out. It's time to steal from the fucking Chancellor."

Chapter Five

Alta, Fluora, Toxys—these moons
may have been mothers and wombs to you.
Look up, at night, from your growing place. See
their glow, bone-white,
gravid and mourning.

— Unpublished poem from Toxys, author unknown

After pulling Delaciel's face from the stuffed bear and poking him awake, Roca leads them to what must be the ship's cargo bay, a wide, rounded space as dark as an ocean cave, and gestures at a tiny vessel in the center with a flourish. "Your ride awaits, Greenie."

Remy stares. Tirani makes an awkward hiccupping noise and retreats a step.

"There's plenty of room inside, don't worry! It's the trip back that's gonna be interesting."

That's not what Remy's worried about. He means to be delicate about it after the warning Tirani gave him about blending in, but all that comes out is a flat, "It has teeth."

Hooks. But they look like teeth—razor sharp in rows upon rows, protruding from the mouth of the tapered cylindrical vessel. The narrow window on the vessel's front resembles nothing more than a set of grinning eyes. It looks *hungry*.

Roca guffaws, hand to chest, and Delaciel's lips tick up.

"It's called a Lamprey," Delaciel says, so quiet Remy has to strain to hear him. "It's a parasitic stealth vessel—small enough that it won't tip off any of the station's sensors when we approach. The 'teeth' secure us to the station so we can siphon fuel. Ideally, we'd have a larger vessel that could hold more supplies, but we're not that lucky. So, we hit hard and we prioritize. Climb up." He taps Remy on the shoulder and then urges him forward with a hand on his back.

Remy jerks away from the contact and climbs up.

Roca must catch his expression as she steps in after him, because she chuckles. "Damn, I forgot. Y'all down on Verdine and your space bubbles. You can tell him to stop, and he'll try, but personal space is a complicated concept for him. For most of us."

Personal space. If only Remy's problem with Idrian Delaciel were so simple. When Delaciel's hands fall on him, all Remy wants is to hurt him, every thoughtless touch a reminder of what he stole from Remy.

Angry words swell inside him, but he catches them in his throat and hurries into the toothy vessel, away from Roca's smirk and Delaciel's nearness. He forces his eyes to his surroundings, absorbing them to distract himself from the way his insides knot, and the bones of his hands groan from clenching them so tightly.

The Lamprey is, indeed, surprisingly spacious inside. Two short benches line either wall, each one big enough for two people. Two spinning seats sit at the front, facing an array of screens and instruments. The *Astrid* is so ancient as to be illegal, but this is newer, more efficient, and clearly built for storage. The floor of the round vessel is an echoing metal mesh, with a trapdoor built in so the space beneath can be filled. Drawers and doors line everything that isn't the benches or the tiny cockpit. It's nice. Delaciel probably stole it.

Roca turns to give Tirani a hand up, and then Delaciel, who's *still* wearing his sunglasses.

Delaciel slips seamlessly into the pilot's seat and buckles a harness around himself. "Strap in. I've been told I'm a bad driver."

Tirani chooses the bench across from Remy rather than squeezing in beside him. She makes sense of the series of belts and hooks just before the vessel lifts off. Remy isn't so lucky. He slams against a secured but un-tightened harness with a guttural *oof,* teeth clacking in his skull.

"Told you to buckle in, Greenie," Roca says.

"Don't call me that," he grits out.

Roca doesn't turn around. "What else would I call you? You've spent your whole life well-fed and pretty down there."

"As opposed to . . . ?"

"Working for anything," Delaciel says.

"Greenie 'cause you get—I dunno, trees and shit," Roca adds. "But also 'cause you're soft. Green."

"Immature," Delaciel adds, cold.

Remy pushes against the choking strap across his chest toward Delaciel, but before he can speak, Tirani does.

Her voice is so much like Delaciel's—the sort of quiet that can't be ignored. "That isn't fair."

"Isn't it?" Delaciel says. "I'm not saying your life's been perfect. You were half dead when we found you; clearly you've had a bad day or two. But you've had food. Lived in a place with *light,* where living things grew from the ground. I bet you didn't have to watch—"

Roca's hand clenches on the corded muscle of Delaciel's lean arm, and his grip relaxes. He subsides. "Sorry," he says, but it's not directed at Remy or Tirani.

Remy's jaw aches, teeth locked together.

"He's right," Roca says. "By an order of magnitude, your experiences will be better than what even the most fortunate person on the Isles experiences."

Remy growls, "They're criminals. They deserve it."

This time, it's Delaciel who grabs Roca's arm, her hand closed so tight around the armrest Remy can see the sharp stars of her knuckles. She sits in her chair, impossibly still and straight, and pulls a headset from the wall. She snaps it loudly over her ears.

Tirani stares down at her lap, both hands clasped around her harness as if to keep them still. She didn't have it easy, either. Though she was raised on an agricultural island where the overpopulation prevention laws were more lax, an injury forced her dad to find work in the capital. She tells Remy, sometimes, what she remembers of the journey—skimming her fingers in an ocean so blue and clear she could see all the way to the bottom while her father hooked his hands under her arms to keep her from falling in. The way she tells it to Remy, her parents promised an aunt would take her in for a while, to keep her safe.

Whatever was supposed to happen, it fell through before they arrived. All she remembers of their arrival is being left for the night with old Fluora, her parents' kisses and tight, lingering hugs and their promises of *we'll figure this out* and *we'll see you in the morning*. Her parents never came back. For years, Tirani asked every day when she'd see them again, but when Fluora couldn't give an answer, Tirani made up her own: the city permitted her parents to have one child, so they chose the one they liked best. Who do these people think they are, to say pain isn't pain if you have *trees*?

If they were closer, Remy would hold Tirani's hand. Or she'd hold his. Like Roca with Idrian. They soothe each other. It doesn't feel good to realize that snakes, too, find warmth together.

The tense silence never does lift, but it softens. Remy shifts his attention to the small viewing window.

It fills with white and sleek silver when the Orbital Supply Station finally comes into view. Light glances off the solarfibre weaving of the station's exterior with a cold blue glow. The OSS, according to Cam, is a dead-end assignment for public servants whose careers have been less than distinguished. Its skeleton crew is responsible for delivering food, fuel, and comfort items to the criminals on the Isles. It is, Cam once told him, barely different from the Isles themselves, except that the officers who handle the OSS have twice-yearly leave to spend time on the surface.

Remy can't make much sense of the station's shape—dense at the center, with protruding spokes and docks on a rotating wheel that makes the whole thing look like a top spinning out into the stars.

The groan of metal lets Remy know the Lamprey has attached itself to the exterior, and Delaciel takes hold of a joystick and fixes his attention on a small screen. The vessel makes an odd noise, like something's unfurling beneath Remy's feet, but before he can make sense of it, Delaciel says. "All right, we're siphoning. Time to go."

He unhooks his seatbelt and stands, and Roca follows. Remy, again, is the last to untangle the harness from around him. By the time he's free, Delaciel has settled in front of a second screen with dim video footage, where he types in a series of instructions. A claustrophobic tunnel-like extension, sealed at the other end, unfolds from the vessel. Before Remy can ask where it's heading, Delaciel guides it to a small door—"Emergency Fuel Access Hatch," it reads—and nods as the tunnel suctions all the way around the door.

After a light on his screen turns green, he shoos them inside with a light touch at their shoulders.

Remy tenses. "*Don't.*"

He seals his lips and turns away too fast to see how Delaciel responds. A shudder rolls through him as he swallows hard. He's not sure how much longer he can keep this up.

Maybe he won't have to. There could be a way to expose them here. The OSS is the Chancellor's domain. Remy just needs an opportunity.

"All right, wow," Delaciel says, in the tone of someone who probably has both hands raised. "Fine, just keep it moving. We've got someone on the inside who blocks off the hallway for 'cleaning' when we need to use it. Picking you up slowed us down, but we're still barely within our projected time-frame."

Roca taps in a code on the exterior keypad like she's done it a thousand times, and there's a loud clank somewhere inside the door. She spins the hatch to open it and urges Tirani in ahead of her. "Me and Tirani'll keep watch."

The interior is painfully white and empty, the only sound the sigh of air through the vents.

Delaciel nods. "Be careful." He jerks his chin at Remy. "You. With me."

"Isn't this dangerous?" Remy whispers.

"Nah, this is one of the least dangerous things we do. Security's lax as fuck here."

Delaciel starts down the hall, and Remy follows.

The halls they hurry down are cold silver, the lighting depressingly dim, blinking on only as they draw near. Delaciel walks fast, without pausing; the flickering lights guide them forward.

Dust and silence meet them in the halls—dirty windows on closed doors that may never have been opened, in a pristine hallway that looks like it's never seen a dirty boot. Delaciel stops at a door a bit less derelict than the rest and taps another code in.

The console blinks red, and Delaciel curses. "You make me nervous, Greenie."

He hums and re-enters the passcode. This time, the panel flicks green.

Remy huffs. "I don't know why you do this. The Isles are meant to be a punishment. Getting all this extra stuff for them ruins the point."

The cold glance Delaciel aims at Remy could draw blood. "Y'know, you're allowed to shut up about things you don't understand."

Before Remy can retort, the door slides open and they step into the room beyond it.

It's ridiculous to call it a room.

It's a *world*. It's so high the few dim lights on the distant ceiling are a net of stars, and the skyscraper-sized piles of boxes cast the ground in impenetrable shadow. A keypad identical to the one outside waits at the same location inside the door, and a group of little flat storage robots huddle near it. Delaciel nudges them awake, and they follow him like ducklings into the dark.

They stop in front of a mile-high tower of boxes, well off the only travel-worn path. On a multi-tiered metal shelf, a massive crate has been freed of its wrapping, its contents decimated. Clearly, Delaciel's been here before.

"Here." He hefts one, two, three small boxes on top of each other. Then more, and more. He passes them to Remy until there's a modest tower stacked on the nearest flatbed. They're not terribly heavy, and they rustle like they're filled with something small and hollow. They head to the next stack, where another crate of boxes is partially opened. There's a little bit of ghostly light here, enough to see that their expiration date was last year.

"These are expired," Remy says.

Delaciel shrugs. "They're *vintage*."

He passes Remy a box so heavy his spine nearly breaks with it. Then another. Sixteen of these. Remy's sweating by the time they're finished.

They fill several bots with boxes from other stacks, packing as many as they can fit on the flat surface, and then more, until it's three layers deep and the nearest bot is gasping *over capacity, over capacity*. Delaciel removes a box and tucks it under his arm.

"You grab one too." Delaciel gestures to the oblong boxes. "More if you can."

Remy manages to grab two while Delaciel kneels, programming something into the bots' screens. They obediently turn and whir (and *clank-clank-squeak*) into the distance, back toward the Lamprey.

One of the bots loses a pile of boxes as it creaks up an incline in the hall, and Delaciel winces and hurries over to replace them.

The last bot to approach the door is the slowest one—clearly the oldest. It jolts to a stop before leaving the room, garbling out, *Obstructed rear wheel. Obstructed rear wheel.* In the hall, Delaciel lifts some of the fallen boxes onto the dolly and calls, "Just give it a good kick, come *on*."

The bot's stuck close to where it slept when they entered, beeping and humming and intermittently attempting to move. As Remy approaches, a bright glow draws his eyes to his right—to the interior keypad, with a winged logo engraved in the bottom corner. A delicate chain winds up around the base of the wings from top and bottom, meeting in a lock shaped like an anatomical heart. The Chancellor's crest, symbolic of both freedom and preservation.

A Protectorate-installed keypad.

Of course. This is his opportunity. Remy clenches the fist Andrew wrote on. *It'll send a signal for help*, he said.

It could be so easy, tipping the balance of power in his favor—making the man who killed Cam face justice.

Remy sucks in a breath. Outside, Delaciel's gathering the last few fallen boxes. "A *real* kick, Greenie. Hard enough to break your toes."

Remy turns, muscles taut with fear. "It loosened a stack of boxes. Give me a moment, I'll get it moving."

This could be his only chance.

"Make it quick."

So he does.

Before he can second-guess himself, he taps in the code Andrew gave him—8-8-4-1-2—then presses and holds the send key. Fingers stinging with adrenaline and heart roaring in his ears, he kicks the bot as hard as he can and coughs to obscure the keypad's cheery beep.

The wheel doesn't budge, but it makes a sad whine. Three more kicks yield nothing but a hot, sore foot.

Delaciel paces in, swings a booted foot at the wheel just once, and makes it move. "Weakling. Should've known by now that if I want something done, I have to do it my damn self."

The bot whines and wobbles its way out the door, and Delaciel trails after it. He has no idea what Remy just did, what it will mean for him. Remy strides along beside him, resisting the urge to look over, certain that if Idrian catches his eye, he'll know.

They're almost halfway back when a scream shatters the tense silence. It's faint from so far away, but it surges through Remy like electricity.

That's *Tirani*.

Delaciel outpaces Remy as he careens through the halls, footsteps clanging.

When they stop, the first thing Remy sees is blood, bright in the cold silver of the hallways. It's on the wall, in splatters and smears. On the floor in drips. On Tirani's arms and sleeve.

On a uniformed body on the ground, spreading.

On Roca, too.

"Remy," Tirani whimpers, showing him her hands. "We . . ."

Roca kneels beside Tirani, both of them on the floor now, and wipes a spray of blood from her cheek. The shit-eating grin on Roca's face is both softened and made infinitely more horrifying by all the blood on her as she declares, "There, there. You're not even the one who's hurt."

Tirani turns toward Roca like a flower to the sun, expression blank with shock.

Delaciel bursts into action, helping Roca to rise. The left side of her face, through the hand she uses to cover it, is a mess of red, her dark curls dripping.

"I got him," Roca whispers when she's upright again. "Bastard came . . . outta nowhere. Heading straight for us. Jacques is a filthy liar. Incompetent . . ."

Delaciel's expression shifts deadly dark, but it's gone as fast as it appeared. He slides in close to Roca, long fingers framing her face and tipping it into the light, gently drawing her cupped hand away from the wound.

"Shit," he whispers. "No, no, no." The shredded skin on her cheek and brow hangs and gushes blood over her face. It's impossible to tell whether her eye got caught up in it. Delaciel's hands shake so hard her face bounces in his grip, his lips bloodless and eyes wide behind his sunglasses, greasy cold sweat bright on his skin. "Hey, it'll be okay. You'll be all right."

Her bloody left hand cups his cheek, leaving a bright smear. "Idiot, I know that," she rasps. "*You* know that. Calm down. We've got work to do."

At this, Delaciel's hands steady. He leans in, forehead meeting hers. "Let's get you back to the Lamprey. I'll carry you."

"Please, you'd break in half if you tried to carry me. You know head wounds are dramatic little rotters. I'll be fine. Just do what you need to do."

"Okay. I'll find . . . I'll find Jacques." To Tirani, without looking away from Roca, he says, "You keep an eye on her. Med pack's under the seat. If someone sends up an alarm, you head out. You *leave* us. Supplies'll be inside soon."

A quick glance reveals the empty bots creaking through the hall behind them, having relieved themselves of their burdens.

Tirani, still shock-hollow, doesn't do anything until Roca taps at her back. She answers only with a nod.

"You," Delaciel's pale eyes, through the glasses, pin Remy. "With me."

"Won't they find us?"

Delaciel pushes him along. "We're fine. Even if we're not, we're *all* dead if we don't do this; won't matter whether we get away or not." They head down the same hallway they traveled before, but deeper, until they arrive at a closed door with a foggy window. The room is some kind of monitoring area, with a spinning chair set in front of a wall of translucent, flexible screens. Some show video feeds. Others show scrolling lines of text. A glass with plaster-like liquid congealing in rings at various levels sits to the side of the keyboard, half-finished.

There's a man in the spinning chair. Remy ducks as soon as he sees him, heart racing.

Delaciel knocks hard on the window and startles the man, who scurries to his feet and opens the door with an awkward smile. He's just a gangly kid, brown hair fluffed over eyes that widen as he takes Delaciel in.

Delaciel is a sight to see, hands wet with blood, cheek and forehead stamped with it like some grotesque bloom. Twin smears lie on the legs of his pants where he wiped his palms.

"Jacques." Delaciel steps inside, face unnervingly blank.

"Whoa, are you okay? You're— shit, that's a lot of blood," the young man—Jacques—says.

Delaciel doesn't speak, and a chill slithers down Remy's spine. Ash-blond hair haloed in the cold light of the supply station, he's something set apart, pale and vengeful. He traces the grooves in the handle of the gun holstered at his side. "Jacques, you lied to me."

"What? No. Everything I told you was true. I got it straight from Lia. She wouldn't lie to me. We're lovebound!" He backs up to his console, kissing his fingers and reaching to skim a cluster of photographs on the wall beside it. A grinning group of five, Jacques in the center surrounded by older men and women who are probably his parents and grandparents. A young woman, partly out of focus except for her wide grin, a space between her two front teeth and a constellation of freckles over her cheeks. Jacques' fingers settle on the photo. "I trust Lia."

"You guaranteed the corridor was marked off-limits, patrols rerouted."

"It is! I sent the order in myself. Lia put up the cones and everything."

"There was an armed officer."

"There . . ." Jacques considers the blood again. "Roca?"

"They'll notice he's gone. Even if we throw the body outside, they'll look for him. They'll look *close,* and they'll notice our thefts. You know what else they'll find?"

Jacques' eyes flick to his consoles, then back to Delaciel.

"*You,* Jacques."

Jacques steps back. "This won't happen again." The tips of his fingers touch his sternum. "On my bond, it won't! Sever my tether and spit on my palm." In the cold metal chill of the Orbital Supply Station, the childish promise is absurd on his lips. Jacques spits on his palm and holds it out for a shake.

Delaciel doesn't take it.

The world outside the door is dim and calm. No alarms, now, in the halls or on Jacques' consoles.

"No," Delaciel says. Remy's never heard a word so quiet, so flat. "No, it won't happen again."

Jacques nods. "I won't let you down. You know how much I value your work."

Something that could be pain or grief or rage draws Delaciel's eyebrows together, and he closes his eyes. "Has anyone called in a body?"

"Uh, let me see." Jacques, hands skittering, drops into his chair and spins to face the monitors. "Ah! This one's kinda interesting. There was an acti—"

Delaciel withdraws the gun from the holster under his arm and fires before Jacques finishes his sentence.

One bullet to the back of the head, ear-piercing in the small room. Blood sprays the bright consoles, and something pinkish. Flecks of sharp white.

Jacques slumps forward and floods the keyboard red, and all Remy can see is his slim hand twitching to stillness across from that freckled photo, the mist of blood on his half-empty glass. All he can think about is Jacques' Lia, who will cry for this boy now that he's gone.

Jacques swore on his tether, hand to heart: he must have been grasping lovebound, his tether knotted at the chest, just like Remy's. Pain throbs beneath Remy's sternum, fingers twisting in his shirt as his vision blurs.

A hand falls on his shoulder, fingernails digging in. "*Move,*" a voice says over the ringing in his ears.

Remy moves.

Out of the room. Into the hallway. He can't feel his feet, his hands, his face.

Delaciel walks silent like a ghost, soft-soled shoes absorbing the sound of his steps. He's covered in blood but none of it is his, and the gun is still in his hand, and he's not shaking at all.

Delaciel walks like he didn't just kill a man. Remy tries to walk like he didn't watch someone die.

They're at the open door before he even realizes it, and they duck into the suctioned hallway that leads back to the Lamprey.

Tirani whimpers, "Remy," as he draws close. The floor is flooded with boxes, barely any room to move. "Remy, she—she's . . ."

Remy thinks he says, "No," as he drops down onto the bench, but he's not sure. He's not even sure what he's saying no to. This time, ridiculously, he gets his seatbelt secured on the first try.

Roca sits slumped over her chair, dripping blood through a makeshift bandage. She looks up at Delaciel with her one visible eye, but she says nothing.

She must already have withdrawn the fuel-siphoning hose, because Delaciel taps a button to retract the hallway that allowed them to board the OSS before pressing something on the keypad beside it. Then he stands there, sagging like a puppet stringless. Remy wants to shake him. He doesn't get to act that way, not when he's the one with a murder weapon still clutched in his left hand.

"Idrian." Roca's voice.

Delaciel doesn't make a sound. Doesn't do anything but look at her.

"Come on. Time to go."

He moves toward her. Into the seat, like an automaton.

Roca reaches for his hand. He flinches but doesn't withdraw, and she loosens the grip he has on his handgun until it sits in her palm. She gently presses it back into the holster at his side.

"Hey." A hand under his chin, making him meet her eyes. "For Alta."

Lord of the Empty Isles

His eyes close, like he's *comforted*. He shakes his head and turns to the control panel. "For Astrid," he echoes, almost too quiet to hear. The only Astrid Remy has heard of is Idrian's famous ship. It didn't occur to him to wonder about the vessel's namesake.

They withdraw before he can consider it further, the Lamprey's teeth releasing the vessel.

It's silent all the way back except for Tirani's quiet sobs.

Remy envies her. His eyes remain stubbornly dry, his vision filled with bone-flecks and brain matter on bright screens. Then, with awful clarity, Jacques' final words: *There was an activation.*

Delaciel was in such a hurry to plug the hole in their security that he wasn't listening, but Remy was. Roca bleeds and an eager love-bound boy is dead, and *there was an activation*. Remy's activation.

8-8-4-1-2. A call for Andrew.

Remy presses his head back against the unyielding metal behind him. Surely it didn't have to be his. It could have been any activation. Could even have been coincidence. Remy never wanted something like this. He just wants Delaciel stopped. In his lap, his hands are numb and still while Tirani muffles sobs into a trembling, bloodied fist.

Remy may be a monster, but with the gunshot still echoing in his ears, he grabs a sharper truth and holds it close.

Even if he is a monster, Delaciel is a far worse breed of beast.

~

Arrival is chaos. As soon as they've landed in the glaring brightness of the cargo bay, Delaciel's people flood in to surround the Lamprey.

Someone's carrying the huge bear. It wears an absurdly festive feathered hat. Before they exit the Lamprey, what waits for them is an air of celebration.

Delaciel steps out first, with Roca leaning heavily against him. Her skin has gone sandstone-pale with blood loss. Delaciel's long coat hangs from her shoulders and brushes her ankles: she's been complaining of the cold and increasingly confused on the way back.

The smiles on the welcome party's faces fade.

Emil bursts into motion at the sight of her and takes her from Delaciel. "What *happened*?"

"We burned the OSS. Can't use it again."

"What? Shit, that means— how? *Why*?"

"Later. Get her to med bay. I'll be there soon. Just have to . . . " He shakes his head, voice growing fainter with each word.

Thomlin, pink shirt still rolled up and teal vest impeccable, jumps down, having clearly just examined the supplies. Only the wild mess of his hair, like he's been tearing his hands through it, speaks to his state. "You got a lot." He runs his hand through his hair again, shaking his head. "But it won't last long. We're screwed."

Remy should be able to feel good about this.

One move, and he's brought the man responsible for Cameron's death closer to justice than anyone's managed in years. It's an ugly thing, though, seeing it in person. Roca's blood, and Thomlin's smiling face wiped free of joy, and Emil holding Roca and examining her with gentleness before guiding her out the door.

Tirani, shock-slow and wide-eyed, flecked with Roca's blood, trails after the couple without a word.

He should be happy, shouldn't he?

He makes a fist of the hand Andrew wrote those numbers on. They're *criminals*. These people have disrespected and compromised the rule of the Chancellor. Stolen and destroyed. Consorted with the scum on the Isles and, through theft, allowed them to flourish. They've murdered or been party to murder. Those are facts.

They are, but with Roca's blood flecking the floor and the gaudy bear splayed on the ground, Remy still feels sick and untethered.

His eyes catch on Delaciel, and the choking weight on his chest eases, replaced with the reliable throb of pain from his rotbound bond. Delaciel paces from the room, hand trailing the wall as if to support himself. Remy stalks after him.

 He shot that boy in cold blood.

Cameron was close to capturing him five years ago. So close. He'd not been allowed to share the details of the case, but he'd said he could feel it—he could blow the whole thing wide open soon. He rarely traveled for his cases, but he traveled that time. All the time.

Then he started coming home exhausted, when he came home at all. Sleeping later. Three weeks in, he couldn't stand for more than a few minutes without getting dizzy. He got awful nosebleeds. In that final week, he couldn't leave his bed.

The farther they walk, the dimmer the lights get, until Delaciel, divested of his coat, stops, silhouetted in the hallway ahead of him.

"Get lost, Greenie."

Without the coat, there's nothing to him. He's all height, no substance. No hero. Not even a villain.

It's sick. It's sad. It's *funny* that someone so insubstantial could evade justice for so long. Andrew said the Chancellor had some grand strategy, but what benefit could they possibly see in delaying? Today, Delaciel killed another innocent.

Remy seizes Delaciel's wrist. "Is this what you do? If anyone could get you caught, you kill them?"

Delaciel doesn't turn. Doesn't even pull his hand free. "Yes."

"Just like that?"

"Just like that."

"That boy had someone he loved. He was trying to help when you *shot him in the fucking head*."

Delaciel moves too fast for Remy to react, spinning him by Remy's grip on his wrist. The breath bursts from Remy's lungs, spine aching as he collides with cold metal. Delaciel's free hand, fingers splayed, slams against the wall beside his head. "I had no choice. They would've traced everything back to Jacques. The things he could've told them . . ."

"Just because he could doesn't mean—"

"He *would have*. You've got no idea the methods they'd use to get it out of him. I did him a favor. You get in my way, Greenie, I'll do you the same favor."

In the dimness, with nothing to reflect off his glasses, Delaciel's ice-pale gaze is sharp and unwavering.

Something like fear curls in Remy's gut. He glares at the arm blocking his retreat down the hall, and his eyes find an irregularity—a raised, round white scar on Delaciel's wrist, like he put out a cigarette on it. Or maybe someone else did. Maybe countless people have tried to take his life. Cruel satisfaction twists through Remy. No matter how many have tried, Remy will be the last.

"You're a coward," he spits. "You're not allowed to decide what he would have done."

The hand withdraws, and Delaciel frees his other wrist from Remy's grip. "I made a judgment call. You've got no idea what's on the line."

"I know that you—!" Remy bites his tongue so Cameron's name won't spill out, pressing until the bitter-sharp sting of pain fills his mouth.

He can't say it. Not now. Not *yet*. His next words drag themselves up his throat like glass shards. They're not the right ones, but they're as close as he's allowed to get. "I know you're a murderer."

"We covered that one already."

Like it's a joke. Like the bodies he's left behind him have not been mourned.

"Anyway, call me what you like, but if you're right, what does that make you?"

"What?"

Delaciel's sickle-smile is sharp enough to cut. "We're *bound*. I might be a killer, but you're the one fatebound to me. What do you think that says about you?"

Chapter Six

*Verdant green **boundless** tethers are unusual in that, while other bonds attenuate over great distances, boundless tethers thrive. Those connected boundlessly may influence one another from afar or carry on related work and remain dedicated to one another despite the physical distance that separates them.*

— From *On the Manipulation of Tethers*

Remy doesn't know how long he paces the dim halls, trying to catch his breath and calm his seething thoughts. When no amount of exertion will banish the sick, nameless urgency clawing its way up his throat, he goes to the infirmary seeking Tirani's calming presence. He finds the whole damn crew there.

Thomlin sits, leg jumping nervously and apron tied over his clothes, at a supply-strewn table by the foot of the room's single cot, jotting notes into some sort of form. Emil sprawls, dead asleep, in a rigid foldout chair so close to the cot it might as well merge with it, hand twining between the rails to knot his fingers with Roca's.

Wide awake, Roca rests propped up on the cot, wound swathed with clean bandages and black hair poking from between them.

Delaciel didn't take the foldout chair on Roca's other side, like a reasonable human being. Instead, he sleeps on the cot, shoved

Lord of the Empty Isles

up against the rails, hand thrown over Roca's belly and head tucked under her arm.

They don't look like murderers. If Remy hadn't seen the gun leveled at Jacques' head, he wouldn't believe Delaciel pulled the trigger. It's not *right*.

Roca follows his entrance and greets him with a quiet, "What did I tell you?" She tips her head to where Delaciel clings to her like a limpet. "No sense of personal space."

Tirani hunches in an extra chair beside Roca's bed, sipping at a green, sludgy drink like she's halfway abandoned her body. She looks up when Remy enters, eyes red and cheeks tacky.

"You okay?" Remy draws in close, hand reaching to rub down her back.

She shivers but lifts the cup, face wan and smile weaker. "Want some? It's terrible."

"It's *nutritionally complete*," Thomlin sniffs from his table. "And also terrible. You get used to it. Would you actually like some, Remy? We can suffer together."

Remy leans in to steal a drink from Tirani.

It's very green. Licking the sludge from his teeth with a grimace, he bumps Tirani's shoulder with his body and stays that way until the scent of blood and disinfectant in the air banishes the chalky salt-and-sweetness of the drink. "I'll pass, thanks."

Tirani's warmth at his side and the pressure as she leans against him is a balm. His breath comes even. She sighs and wraps an arm around his waist, and he tips his head against hers.

Roca smiles at them, her visible eye crinkling. "That's pretty damn adorable, you two. I'm glad."

Tirani looks at the floor instead of answering.

Remy gestures to where Idrian Delaciel snores into Roca's armpit. "Wish I could say the same, but that's kind of gross, actually. I don't even want to know."

"Not much to know. Idrian, Emil, and I sleep together, as you can see."

Remy pauses, not sure how he's supposed to translate that.

"If it helps, this isn't even the weirdest place he's fallen asleep this week. He took a nap on the game table the other day, and there was that one time he fell asleep in the hollow of a big-ass tree when we were being pursued—alarms blaring, guys with guns, and this asshole was out like a light." She looks like she's about to smile but grimaces instead.

"What's the news? Your eye . . ."

She shrugs. "The damage was mostly to my cheek and eyebrow. My vision should survive. A shame. I'd look badass with an eye patch, and y'all know it."

Thomlin huffs a laugh and massages his temples. "Not if Yves has any say in it. They'll put my bad patch-up job to shame."

Roca twists her head to show off the tight, precise bandages with tufts of hair bursting between them. "I think your work is charming."

"Mummy chic." Thomlin jots a few notes. "You shouldn't die of infection, at least."

A pause. Too long.

Then: "Oh," Thomlin says, faintly.

It's the tone of his voice that makes Remy turn.

There's a trail of red droplets, growing larger by the second, on his paperwork. Blood on his hand, spread wide like he's examining it. Blood on his lips and chin. His teeth.

"Fuck." Thomlin shoves a hand up under his nose. He rifles through the contents of the medical kit disgorged all over his desk and finds a wad of gauze he uses to mop up the paperwork and his face.

"Thom?"

He turns away. "Just a nosebleed. Used to get these all the time in university." He squeezes his nostrils shut. "Yves is getting my notes just like this. I'm *not* rewriting them."

Remy says, "Maybe tipping your head back . . . ?"

Thomlin laughs, an odd sound with his nose blocked. "Thanks, but I won't be swallowing any blood today. Done enough of that for a lifetime. Ugh." He leans over and spits blood into the trashcan. "It's the worst when it gets in your mouth."

Roca sits up, but Thomlin shakes an irritated hand at her and she subsides. "Thom, are you . . . ?"

He points an open palm at her, still and calm (and smeared with his own blood), and maybe that's why it takes them all longer than it should to see what he's showing them with his middle finger pushed farther forward than the rest: under the blood, a little more than halfway down his fate-finger, the rusty red line of Remy's withering.

Remy shivers.

Thomlin's right. This is how it starts. A withering, in the early stages, chips at the weak places.

Remy loses minutes staring blankly across the room, but when he looks back over, Thomlin's still squeezing his nose shut with red hands, looking irritated. "I don't even have my spray," he grumbles. "Haven't needed it in *forever*. Seriously, can you all look somewhere else? Why am I the first to be hit?"

Roca laughs. "To be fair, I don't think I'd notice minor aches and pains on top of the whole eye thing. And Idrian's like a cat—the bastard would rather find a nice cozy hole to die in than let on that anything's wrong."

Thomlin leans back in his seat and lets it rotate toward them. He surveys the group of them, Roca and Delaciel still in their bloody clothes and Emil drooling in his chair.

"We're all a mess," he says to Remy and Tirani. "It won't get any better from here."

"Yves'll *freak* when they see you," Roca says.

"Yves will be busy enough without having to worry about all of us. Especially now. We're *late*." Thomlin lets go of his nose, testing for a moment, then growls and squeezes it closed again with a curse.

"Who's Yves?" Tirani asks, but her eyes are on all that blood.

"Yves Radenne," Thom says. "They're an overworked kinda-doctor on Alta. Jack of all trades." He shows off a delicate floral partnership tattoo, inked in boundless green on the back of his right hand. His tether must be anchored, then—secure despite the distance that often characterizes boundless tethers. "And my spouse."

Tirani makes a pained noise, and Remy turns to her. "Tirani . . . ?"

She doesn't answer.

Awkwardly, Remy waves at the tattoo. "That's awfully permanent."

Thom shrugs. "So's love. Mind you, I *tried* partnership jewelry. Had this gorgeous ring, prettiest layer of green gem all the way through the middle, but it got greased up and I lost it in an engine. Tried a bracelet, but I broke the damn clasp. Would've been easier to be bound anywhere else, but I use my hands too much."

He's not wrong. Ruminant-bound partners usually have symbolic piercings in their ears or noses with gems the color of their bond. Grasping couples often choose pendants that hang over their hearts, and visceral-bound pairs gravitate toward navel jewelry. Spouses with reckless bonds often select toe rings or anklets to symbolize their connection. Some choose nothing. Remy has little doubt that Roca and Emil are bound, but they wear no jewelry he can identify. It's not a surprise. Roca seems to have a lot of faith in tethers. Some couples don't need physical reminders of their bonds.

Even with her left eye obscured, Roca leans toward Emil with an easy, instinctive faith. She nudges him until he startles awake, his eyes instantly finding hers. "Mm, Roca, y'okay? Something wrong?"

"Shh, everything's fine. How far out are we from Alta?"

Emil rubs his eyes and squints at the wide screen of one of the watch-like devices around his wrist. "'Bout thirty minutes. Why?"

"No worries, go back to sleep."

Emil doesn't need to be told twice.

Alta. Biggest of the three Isles, cast in the shadow of the true moon. Once the most luxurious of the Isles, where the most affluent congregated while the planet healed, it's now where the worst criminals get sentenced. They'll eat people like Remy and Tirani alive there.

"Is that really a good idea?" Remy blurts.

"Is what a good idea?"

"Going to Alta. Isn't there more important stuff to do?"

Roca waves a hand with blood still dried under the nails. "Nah. Dropping off supplies won't take long. We'll have more time to figure this mess out after. I'll get Idrian to write down all the really high-profile stupid shit he's done, the sort folks might want to kill him for. We'll start with stuff that happened around this time of year. Then we'll get Tirani here to investigate them—one of them's gotta be a witherer."

Remy pulls the cup of green nutrient sludge from Tirani's suddenly slack fist so he'll have something to do with his mouth other than gape.

Roca really will be the death of him. Tirani can't use her weaver sight to identify Remy as a witherer, and wouldn't even if she could, but she won't need to, not if they figure out he's Cameron's brother. Not since, like a fool, he cast this withering just before the anniversary of Cam's passing. He chokes down a too-large gulp of the chalky drink, scowling at the way it coats his teeth, and manages to rasp, "That sounds . . . efficient."

"Yes," Roca says. "I think it will be."

Thomlin scrubs at his face with his clean hand. "It'd be nice if we could get it all sorted before Alta. I'm not looking forward to telling Yves about the withering. I wish . . ."

Remy tightens his arm around Tirani, but she shrugs it off.

"Sorry," she murmurs, chair clattering as she stands, "I need a minute."

Before Remy can ask what's wrong, she's slipped from the room, leaving the door to hiss closed behind her.

∼

Remy feels like he wanders for hours, seeking her. To and back from the little room they share. To the table they ate at. To rooms he doesn't even know the name of.

It's like she disappeared.

Something twisted-up and unnameable steals his breath as he slips into every open room, calling her name.

He's an idiot. Something's clearly been bothering her. She was inconsolable on the way back, and that's weird for her, and he should have *noticed*. She's not a crier, usually. Not like that. She makes work of anger, and silence of sadness.

He's been so tangled up in his own worries that he left her alone with all of this. He speeds up his search, calling for her loudly enough to drown the urgent patter of his heart.

He doesn't know how much time has passed when he finally finds her in an empty room at the end of a darkened corridor. An apology freezes on his lips.

Lord of the Empty Isles

The room is wide-open and lightless except for the window. The whole far wall is a window, feet thick with a thin rail running along it at waist height. Outside, the faint light of the planet below and the distant stars flooding by cast a cold glow into the room. It hits Remy again—the awful newness and strangeness of all of this.

Tirani's first words to him are, "They don't seem bad, Thomlin and Emil. Roca."

Remy looks away, but he can't deny it.

"She saved my life, you know."

It takes him only a second to figure out what she's saying, to feel the first slow curl of guilt. "Tirani . . ."

"That guard—I saw him first, and I froze. Roca jumped in to protect me. It's my fault she's hurt."

"I'm glad you're safe."

"I'm the only one who is. Thomlin has a *partner*! Emil and Roca are involved, I think. Remy, you have to see it. Even Idrian—"

An image flashes into his head: bone-fragments on a bright screen. A keyboard flooded red. "You weren't there today."

Tirani finally turns to him. "What?"

"You didn't see it. There was this guy—probably *our* age, and he had someone he loved, too. Delaciel greeted him by name and *shot him in the head* while he was trying to help. Maybe you're right. Maybe Thomlin isn't so bad, or even Roca, but that guard she killed, you think he didn't have a family?"

Tirani flinches, then wipes her cheeks and watches the stars for so long Remy thinks maybe that's the end of it, but then she says, "I can't see the color of her tethers."

The quiet words land like a punch. She can't see the color of Remy's tethers, either. Tirani's bound to Roca. Whatever bond they share could linger and rot when Roca dies. Of all the people to be affected by what he's done, he'd do anything to keep it from hurting Tirani. "Shit. Tirani, I wouldn't make you choose . . ."

Tirani wraps her arms around herself, more embrace than blockade. "You already have. They want to use me to *hunt* you, Remy."

"I doubt they'll need to go that far. And we have—if they're planning to figure it out after this, we have time."

"To do *what?* I've never heard about a case like yours. Or theirs. There are so many of them. Can you really let them all die?"

"Should I tell them what I did and let them kill me?"

"No!" Warm hands seize his shoulders. "Remy, I don't want them *or* you to die. I want everyone to live."

"Witherings don't work like that."

"But I want you to *live*," she says again, nonsensically.

"Then let me do this, and I'll find a way. I'll make them put us on research duty or something. They've gotta have books, and maybe those books will have a way I can wriggle free of this thing."

"That's not what I mean." Tirani's hands cup his cheeks and turn his face toward her. "This whole time, you've been tearing yourself to pieces for the dead. Sometimes I think you're hurting yourself just to keep the wound fresh, but it's been five years, Remy. Your brother is *dead*."

Pain drives itself through Remy's ribs. "You think I'd be here if he weren't?"

"That's my point. You say you're trying to prevent more people like you, but you've made so many more."

"And they haven't? That boy's name was Jacques! I don't even know the name of the guard, and—"

"Those people weren't my friends! You are. And now there's—there's Roca, too, and I don't know how we're bound but I wish

I had time to find out, and instead you're both going to die. Sometimes you're right beside me and it still feels like you're gone. I'm *here,* and Cameron is dead, and I'm not your brother but I'm alive and I'm with you and it hurts all the time. I don't want you to leave."

Like my family goes unspoken, but it sits like an elegy in the air between them.

"Please, Remy. Just let it go."

Remy clenches his fist atop the rotbound throb in his chest, and it's awful. It's cleansing. It's not nearly enough, but it's something.

He can't hold Cam's tether, but he grips the wire-and-glass pendant Cam used to wear, life-warm through his shirt, and the weight of the metal and the reliable throb of pain from his rotten bond allow a thread of air into his closing throat. "You don't get to say that. You of all people—"

"If I don't, who does?" Tirani sounds so defeated. She presses her face against his neck to hide it, but he still feels the heat of her unsteady breaths against his skin, and he *aches* because he knows why she's saying this but she still doesn't get it, why he needs this to happen. "I feel like I'm doing this all by myself. I'm tired, Remy. I just want you to be okay."

Like it's that easy. Like *being okay* is something a person can want and just have. Remy isn't even allowed to want it, not yet. He owes this pain to his brother. "I'll be okay when this is over."

When it's over, they can go back home to the cliffside city strung with white ribbons for the Resurrection Festival. They can pull out their old masks and take a picnic to the apple orchard in front of the Chancellor's estate. It'll be Remy's turn to make dinner. He could put rainfruit in, just for her.

"It doesn't work that way." She pulls back and traces the mark of the withering on his hand. "Where we're heading, it's where most of Idrian's tethers lead. It doesn't matter what kind of people he's connected to, they're people who care what happens to him. Remy, I can't even count them. How many people need to hurt for this to end? I'm not sure if the you that comes back from it is someone I want to know."

Betrayal, like a spear through his chest. "If you don't want to, you don't have to."

He knows as the words leave his lips that they're cruel. Even if he didn't, the gutted expression on Tirani's face would tip him off.

She blurts, "Why don't you see it? You say he's bad, but aren't you just like him?"

Remy shakes his head, vision swimming, pain in his chest so thick it's like his lungs are filled with sand.

He opens his mouth but the words won't come out. "I'm not—" He backs up. "How could—" Finally, he manages, "I'm *nothing* like him. Why would you say that?"

He isn't. He's different. Remy isn't like Idrian at all.

The stars in his blurring vision become islands, dim and cold. He can barely force his next words from his throat. "You know what . . ." He pulls away, and Tirani nearly staggers with it. "You don't want to see what this makes me, then go."

She doesn't move, frozen.

"Or I will."

"I don't want to—I don't want you to leave." It's barely audible, the raw plea of a child left behind. "I just want—"

She wants him to let go. To change. She wants someone less broken—like Lara, whose cut tether turned to dust in Remy's hands.

He shouldn't leave. It's their rule.

Remy clenches his teeth against it and turns around. He starts walking.

"Remy, don't." The clank of her feet on the floor says she's ready to follow. Remy walks faster.

He freezes, because Emil, that stealthy bastard, is standing in the doorway, hair sleep-ruffled but eyes alert.

"Ah, sorry, I should've . . . called out or something. We're two minutes from touchdown. You need to get outfitted, both of you. Tirani, Roca thinks she has a suit in your size, and Remy—"

Remy pushes past Emil and out the door.

Emil follows behind him.

"That was a private conversation," Remy says, heart hammering. He means, *how much did you hear?*

"Door was open," Emil says. "And you weren't exactly whispering. Look, I didn't hear a lot, but I heard Jacques' name—and hey, I don't like it either, but you have to understand—"

Remy walks faster. All these people asking for understanding, and no one gets it. "Not now."

"Sure." Emil skips ahead and gestures for Remy to follow.

There must be a neat solution to this, something that'll make everything better. He's just not seeing it. Remy hurries down the narrow corridor, thoughts racing faster than his feet as he moves in and out of puddles of light, but he doesn't get closer to any sort of answer.

Chapter Seven

One in the cradle
Just one in the crib
One at the table, all smiles with a bib.
One in the arms for the lullaby-night
One, only one
or this green world you'll blight.

— Verdinian children's playground rhyme

Remy stands at the closed cargo bay door, separated from the barren, lawless chaos of the Empty Isles by less than a foot of metal. It's almost worse, not having windows. *Knowing* but not seeing. There's perfect, eerie silence from the other side. No prisoners beating at the hull or using unspeakable machinery to claw it open because they're *late*. That's good, right?

"You sure you don't wanna talk about it?" Emil lifts the lid of a deep metal trunk built into the side wall.

Remy presses his lips together and says nothing.

"Fine, fine." Emil, rifling through the trunk, tasked with the job of "getting him ready"—whatever that means—releases a triumphant cry and rises at last with a ribbed gray garment slung over one arm. He throws it at Remy. "I knew we still had one! Might not be stylish but wear it. You're skinny enough, I think you could break Haeland's record."

"Record?" Remy slips his feet into the wetsuit-like garment and tugs it up awkwardly until he can slide his hands into the long sleeves.

"Yeah. One minute." Emil points down, wiggling his bare toes before he slips into his own suit. "Frostbite—lost his little toe 'cause the fucker was wearing *sandals*." He gives Remy a once-over. "Don't be like Haeland. Haeland is no longer with us."

He spins Remy by the left shoulder of the strange suit and depresses something against his right shoulder that makes a heavy click and then a low, pleasant trill. Emil comes back around front. "Still working! Good, good." He pulls flexible tubing from a slit on the front. It ends in a clip. Emil smiles. "You'll want this."

He tugs his own out and clips it into his nostrils. The piping that connects it to his suit dangles gaily from the end as he smiles. He looks ridiculous.

"Yeah, no thanks," Remy says. "I'm good."

"Now, normally I'd say *suit yourself*." Seeming to realize his pun, Emil devolves into deafening guffaws. He guides Remy to slip his suited feet into impossibly heavy boots ("You'll be grateful," he offers, and nothing more). "But in this case, it's non-optional. You'll look like a fool with the rest of us. Atmosphere on the surface of the Isles isn't something any living thing should sample."

Emil pulls the tubing out and winds it behind Remy's ear and around to his nose before clipping it on. It pushes dry air into his nose, and he coughs. "Wh-what?"

"You'll be glad I did this!" Emil presses a button on the back of the suit and something oil-slick bright rushes up and covers his field of vision with a mechanical whir. After a while, it lets out a puff of air and turns glass-clear. "Give it a sec to adjust the pressure."

Remy reaches up with clumsily gloved hands to touch what feels like a solid dome around his head, transparent at every angle.

"All set!" Emil announces.

Hardly. "What about a gun?"

"To do what? Shoot the stars?"

"What part of *lawless prison planet* don't you understand?"

"Yeah. Dangerous criminals everywhere." The expression on Emil's face takes on a funny twist. "I imagine you'll get a very *frosty* reception. *Ice-cold* bastards, all of them. They won't be doing anything to hurt you, though."

Remy snorts. "Why, because I'm *in* with their lord?"

Another laugh, except it's nothing like the ones before. Hollow and sharp, it fades as fast as it started. "Nah, man." A smile ticks his lips up, dim but warm. "'Cause you're too tall."

∼

Delaciel exits first, suit-clad, his wild blond hair pulled back with a blue ribbon. Roca, Emil, Thomlin, Tirani, and Remy follow. Thomlin, who packed his nostrils with reddening gauze in the half-hour since Remy last saw him, has already stained the inside of the dome around his head with a couple drops of blood. Tirani walks close to Roca and doesn't look at Remy; in his peripheral vision, she stands unnaturally straight, eyes red-rimmed.

Aren't you just like Idrian?

The accusation echoes in his skull. He's *not*, but Tirani wasn't entirely wrong. He didn't mean for it to happen, but he'd be a fool not to acknowledge the effects are the same. Tirani, too, will know every merciless moment of watching a withering chip away at the life of someone she's bound to, and Remy's the one who set it in motion.

Maybe—maybe he can find a way to save Roca, too.

The surface of Alta is as ugly as it looked from Verdine: barren and cold, pocked with outhouse-sized protrusions that cast impenetrably dark shadows. Worm-like metal pipes snake along the ground to trip up his clumsy feet. Some sort of vent belches an unidentifiable vapor as he passes, and someone snickers when he jumps and yelps. Even with the protection of the suit, Remy's fingers go numb with a cruel chill and alternating stabs of pain, like ice crystals are forming in his blood. The air he sucks in tastes like a sharp knife feels. Remy coughs and rubs his gloved hands together as he passes into the seamless shadow cast by one of the sharp-edged protrusions.

Emil was right about the gravity. Even with the heavy boots, Remy's feet are light on the ground, like Alta could be convinced to give him up to the air if he makes one wrong move.

"It's a bit nippy!" Emil yells.

Delaciel is still half asleep, still wearing the shades Remy has never once seen him take off. The light from the distant sun glitters blue on their treated surface. Remy can't see his eyes.

"Little bit," Delaciel says. "It's been worse. Remember that time we were stranded—"

Roca hisses.

Delaciel turns to face her immediately, a question on his lips.

Roca speaks, low and urgent. "To the left, Remy, it's—"

Something crunches under his foot. Remy looks down and immediately wishes he hadn't.

It's a hand. A human hand, warped and frozen solid, barely an inch off the ground. Remy's footfall snapped off three icy fingers—a jagged cross-section of flesh and bone.

Remy gags.

Roca grabs his shoulder and guides him left.

The hand is connected to an arm, a torso, everything frost-rimmed and frozen, face set in an expression of horror. It's not the only body. Others have fallen, too—on their backs, on their bellies like they were crawling away from or toward something, their open hands barely at ankle-height.

Emil chuckles. "What did I tell you? You're too tall. Criminals can't reach high enough to hurt you."

The rest of the trip is a blur. In one of the windowed, doorless protrusions from the underground, he sees a plant, frail and grayish-teal, leaning in lacy spirals toward the distant sun.

He doesn't remember going underground, but he must have. He goes from razor-cold to an anvil-like wet heat. His suit is immediately stifling, skin on fire with the change in temperature. The door closes behind them, burying them in near-perfect darkness, and only then does a second door open.

Seamless darkness all around. Hot, humid air. Narrow like a grave. The dome around Remy's head vanishes with a series of whirs, folding in on itself and retreating into the suit, which at least helps with the crush of claustrophobia.

No light, except for a sea of yellow and orange eyes staring up, unblinking, from the floor. Remy's heart rockets to life in his chest.

"Shit," Emil says. "This many? We're not *that* late."

Remy can't *see*. Nothing but those yellow eyes. He hears only the rasp of labored breath—a distant moan. "What . . ." he manages to whisper. The others walk ahead of him, boots clattering on the floor, but he's paralyzed, limbs locked, breaths coming fast.

A hand on his shoulder, then Roca's voice. "Come on."

Remy shakes his head. "Dark," he breathes between gasps.

Roca huffs out a laugh. "Not that dark. Give it a minute." She calls out to the others. "Our little sunshine boy isn't a fan of Alta's lighting."

The footsteps ahead of them stop, and Roca's hand doesn't leave his shoulder, heavy and steady. He breathes, shakes. Gathers himself.

Lord of the Empty Isles

He moves to pull the tube from his nostrils, but Roca stops him. "I wouldn't do that if I were you. I don't think you'd like the air here any better than you like the lighting."

He keeps it in, sucking cool air through the tube until his vision clears.

It's not completely dark in here. Strip lights at waist-height glow a sickly ash-blue, dimmer even than the yellow and orange lights.

Lights, not eyes. Lights glowing up from droplet-shaped implants in the wrists of bodies in every size. Children and adults, sprawled across the floor and against each other. Children. Why are there *children* here? This isn't right. In all the storybooks, the Isles are painted in watercolor blues and purples, with faceless people tending to growing things or staring longingly through viewing windows at the healing Verdine. In the storybooks, the halls of Alta are wide and well-lit, and the walls spill over with greenery. Water trickles from pretty fountains, cycled and recycled. Alta, of all places, is not supposed to be like this.

"A-are they dead?"

"Not yet." Roca grimaces. "Some of them come to the door when it gets bad—like if they can just get *out*, they'll be okay."

The image of the corpse's frozen, shattered hand flashes through Remy's mind, bringing a surge of nausea. The outside won't offer any kindnesses for these people but a quick death.

A man up ahead rolls onto his back, mouth opening but no sound coming out. The corpse-toned light glints off tear tracks on his cheeks. His yellow light shifts orange.

An orange light shifts red on a little girl half Remy's size, and a piercing whine rises from the implant at her wrist. Remy nearly trips over her in his shock.

"She's—" he says. In the dim light, her chest rises and falls too fast, her lips bluish. She has a button nose and a scattering of freckles that seem morbidly dark on her face in this light. The fingers of one bony hand twitch faintly.

"This is the way of the Isles," Roca whispers, like this is a tomb or a holy place. "They make whatever air they can, but there's not enough for the huge underground population. Those who can't adapt die. Yellow is dangerous oxygen saturation levels. Orange is critical." She gestures to the girl. "Red is terminal."

"She needs *help!*" He's whispering, too, his voice a thready whine, and he hates himself for it.

The girl is so thin she looks alien.

Something ugly unfurls in Remy's stomach and yawns: this is what his brother looked like in his final days. But this is what everyone looks like on the Empty Isles.

The red light flashes, urgent, and its shrill whine pierces Remy's ears.

"It's a high-stakes game," Roca says. Delaciel and Emil wait ahead, shoulders tight and heads turned away. "There are too many people here, and more arrive each month. They'll dispatch a medical team to respond to the alarm with portable oxygen. If she's lucky, she'll be alive when they get here."

Delaciel murmurs, "If everyone else here is lucky, she won't."

Remy should do something, but he's frozen stiff, eyes locked on the girl's blue lips.

The only reason he stops looking is because something blocks his view, a sharp exhale of breath rising over the whine of the alarm. "Screw this," says a voice.

Delaciel. He rises with the girl in his arms and strides down the hall, and even Emil and Roca can't keep up. Emil guides Remy by the shoulder, and he hates that he's grateful, but he is. He still stumbles on unseen obstacles, vision obscured in the semi-darkness.

Delaciel's sunglasses still sit over his eyes, but he walks with such speed and confidence it's like he's in full daylight. He pulls the tubing from his face and gives it to the girl, rubbing her cheeks and chest, urging her to breathe. "Come on," he says. "Come on. You can do this."

He lifts her head with a hand in her straw-blond curls and calls her Astrid, and Roca looks away. The girl's red light shifts mercifully to orange. The whine of the alarm cuts out. Orange to yellow, to yellow-green, to green as they hurry through the halls.

Delaciel effortlessly breathes the lethally-thin air of the underground and strides through the corridors like he owns them, and Remy remembers his hand slamming into the wall in the ship's hallway, remembers the scar at his wrist, round and puckered. Like a cigarette burn, he thought at the time.

Remy's blood goes cold and his cheeks go hot as he re-contextualizes everything he thought he knew about Idrian Delaciel.

No. Not like a burn. Like he dug one of these implants from his own flesh.

Chapter Eight

*Charcoal-colored **rotbonds** are not a type of tether but a result of damage to a once-healthy connection. They are evidence of love living on, even when it should not. By contrast, ash-gray **hollowbonds** signify an unrequited interest—a failed attempt at bringing a love to life. Though they may be thick at their source, they quickly attenuate to thread-like thinness. If there is any contact at the other end, it is fine and difficult to discern.*

— From On the Manipulation of Tethers

They careen through winding hallways in dreamlike lighting, Idrian with a dying girl in his arms.

The Isles aren't anything like Remy thought. None of this is like he's been told. Remy tries to tell himself it doesn't change anything, but he can't make himself believe it. It changes everything. Reeling, he sucks air from the tube on his suit and strains to make out the shape of the world ahead. His eyes have almost adapted to the eerie dimness when light bursting from a doorway blinds him. He throws a hand over his eyes.

Delaciel barges inside without introduction. "Yves! Oxygen."

The room's only standing occupant, white-coated and lean with round glasses and red-blond hair buzzed on one side and chin-length on the other, doesn't even look up at the ruckus. Bent over a prone body on one of many cots, the doctor who must be Yves retorts, "Wait your turn."

Delaciel ignores the order and finds an empty cot. A mask and canister hang from a hook beside it, and he drops the girl onto the bed, pulling the mask down and twisting a valve on the canister. He pulls the tube from the girl's face and presses the mask on instead. "Breathe."

The girl grins through the mask, breathing just fine. It's sickening, though, how huge the thing is on her.

At last, the white-coated doctor turns, exposed right ear glinting in the cold light, more piercings than skin. "I see you've taken matters into your own hands, Idrian."

"You were too slow, Dr. Radenne," he says, sugar-sweet and unsmiling.

Yves must notice the blood that's leaked through the bandages and spotted the shirt on his lower left side. "And you've clearly been taking top-notch care of yourself." They tut and tug gloves on. "What is it this time?"

Delaciel leans away. "I'm fine. Check on her."

With a sigh, Yves strides over to kneel at the girl's bedside, turning her wrist to look at the implant then doing a cursory examination. "Her oxygen saturation is suboptimal but survivable. She doesn't need supplementary air. Save it."

Delaciel moves between Yves and the girl. "She needs it."

"The next person will need it more."

Delaciel doesn't budge. Instead, he ignores Yves entirely, slipping a small pack from his back and unzipping it to pull something out. One of those stupid paper flowers, complete with a stem. You'd think he'd given the girl the world by how her eyes go wide and her mouth drops open, upsetting the mask. Idrian situates it back over her nose and mouth.

"For *me*?" the girl says.

"If you want it," Idrian says, lips curling up.

"I want it!" She shakes it, bats him in the face with it, then draws it close to shove her fingers inside the paper petals. "What is it?"

"A flower. They're all over the place, down on Verdine."

"What do you use them for?"

Yves snickers.

"Not much, I suppose. They're beautiful," Idrian says. "And they smell nice."

The girl pulls her mask off and stuffs her face in the flower.

"Not that one." He lifts the mask over her mouth again. "I'll bring a real one next time. But you'll have to be careful. They have teeth. They'll bite you if you don't watch out."

The girl throws the paper flower onto the bedsheets. "They have *teeth*?"

"*Idrian.*" Yves brushes pale hair from their eyes. To the girl, they say, "Flowers do not have teeth. Stop corrupting the children, Delaciel, and sit your ass down. It's your turn."

When he only raises an eyebrow, arms crossed, Yves turns to Remy with narrowed eyes. "I see you brought friends."

"The little grumpy one's fatebound to Idrian! His name's Remy," Emil chirps from just behind him, and Remy jumps.

"Why am I not surprised?" Yves drawls. "And . . ." They lean closer to Tirani. "You look familiar. Do I know you?"

Tirani leans back. "I don't think so? I'm—"

Roca claps a hand down on Remy's shoulder as she pushes forward and waves to get Yves' attention. "Introductions later. If you don't mind, these bandages are starting to *itch*. And, uh, if you want your floor clean, Thom's gonna need some more gauze soon."

"Thom?" Remy flinches at the way Yves' expression warps when they see the red fingers he cups under his nose. Yves hurries to him, hissing, "What *happened*? The only thing I ask of you is to take care of yourself, and you can't even—"

Thom grabs Yves' hand before it can touch his face. "Whoa, hey. Um. I'd hug you, but . . ." He waggles his bloody fingers. "Just a nosebleed. Almost finished now, I think. Roca needs your expertise more than I do."

"All of you! Out of my sight for a few weeks and look what you've done to yourselves. I don't have enough beds for this, don't have enough *meds* for this. Thom, hemostatic spray's where it always is. Sit down after you use it. Roca, take a seat by the light. And *Idrian*—"

"The stabbing was days ago. I'm fine. Look after the others first."

"Oh," Yves says, dry. "The *stabbing*. Truly, go fuck yourself. What have you even been doing?"

Thom leaves to treat his nosebleed, and Emil follows Roca to a spinning chair by a flimsy, bare-bulbed lamp that sheds bluish-white light onto a disorganized desk and an endless list that tumbles down from high on the wall to spill onto the desk's surface. That leaves Remy alone in the doorway, Tirani an awkward several steps behind him in the dim hall. Remy can't make himself look her in the eye. It's probably a good thing. He's not sure what he'd say.

He turns back to where Yves pats at Roca's bandages. "Do I even want to know?"

From the door, Tirani whispers, "It was my fault. She protected me."

Yves' eyebrows climb up into their hairline. "*Roca* did? What, you actually have a heart in there? Don't think I won't check." They lift the stethoscope slung around their neck like a threat and direct an expansive shrug at Tirani. "She never tells me anything."

When Roca doesn't answer, Yves moves on, examining the bandages. "Pretty well-wrapped. Did you disinfect?"

Thomlin is in the middle of inhaling hemostatic spray, but he gives a thumbs-up while hissing and wincing and clawing at the air. "Damn, that stuff stings!" He pulls a piece of paper from the breast pocket of his vest. "Sutured, too, as well as I could. Ignore the blood, but that's a list of what I did."

Yves snatches the paper and unfolds it. "Looks good." Yves tilts Roca's head. "There are a lot of things a better-supplied doctor could do for you, but as I'm neither well-supplied nor fully-qualified, just let me know if you start dying, and I'll prevent it if I can."

"It's not a big deal," Roca says. "Considering."

Yves massages their temples. "If the bleeding has stopped, Thom, can you help me convince your asshole-in-chief that stabbings are not something one should ignore?"

"Gimme a sec. I'm gross."

Yves waves him over to a tiny sink.

While Thomlin wipes his hands, Idrian drops onto the end of the girl's cot. The girl leans closer, pulling off her mask, but Idrian gently replaces it before turning to Yves with an implacable stare. "I'm fine. Like I said, it was days ago."

"How nice for you. Lift your shirt."

"Don't you have patients?"

"For fuck's sake! If you won't accept friendly concern, accept my greedy self-preservation. If you're out of commission, we all die."

Die? Remy's body flushes hot with shock, questions crowding up his throat, but Idrian doesn't react to what must surely be hyperbole.

All he says is, "It's pretty much healed already."

A tiny hand seizes Idrian's coat and tugs. As if magnetized to the motion, Idrian spins to face the little girl.

"You're hurt, mister?"

The look in Idrian's eyes, even from Remy's vantage point, is the wide-open blankness of the hunted.

"You're bleeding!" the girl cries, mask tumbling from her face and huge green eyes filling with tears.

"No. I mean yes. It's mostly old—" Idrian looks to Yves and then to Roca, and even to Remy, but he's already moving to lift his shirt as the girl's lip begins to wobble. "It's fine. I'm *fine*. You shouldn't waste resources on me."

"Since you're so eager to waste them on others, I don't see why not." Yves grins at the girl. "I might have to hire you on. Thom, the cart?"

Thom, with efficiently cleaned hands, pushes a rolling cart over, and Yves sets to peeling off the wound's covering. "You've pulled a couple stitches, no surprise. Doesn't look like there's any infection, which is a miracle considering the state of this dressing. Disinfectant?"

Thom holds it out just as Yves pats Idrian's side none-too-gently and offers up a dry pronouncement of, "You'll survive."

That's when Yves freezes—rigor-still, halfway through grabbing the disinfectant from Thom's hand. The sound that claws from their throat is quiet. Gutted.

Thom looks slowly down, hand extended, before hastily closing his fist. "Damn, I forgot."

Idrian winces. "We meant to tell you."

Remy steps closer to see what they're looking at, and his breath leaves his chest.

Yves traces the rust-red line of Remy's withering down Thomlin's fate-finger. "*No.*"

Thomlin rubs the back of his head with his free hand. "Sorry. I was gonna let you know right away, but Idrian—then the girl—"

Remy knows the expressions that cross Yves' face so well they evoke physical pain.

The blank laxity of horror.

A twist of grief, quickly suppressed.

Fear that tightens their grip on Thom's hand, like he'll drift away if they let go.

Rage. A calm, knife-like animosity more terrifying than its destructive counterpart.

"I'll kill them. I'll find the bastard who did this to you and I will *kill* them."

It hits in a terrible sort of way, that Tirani was right. It doesn't feel good to have to watch this happen to others. To have *made* it happen. It might have been easier if Yves was only angry. Vengefulness is a language Remy speaks. But they close their fists in Thomlin's nice button-up (Thomlin doesn't say a single word, only pulls them closer) and tuck their face into his shoulder before murmuring again, helplessly, "I'll kill them."

Thom laughs. "I know you will."

Remy turns away, eyes roving the room for something, anything apart from this. Normally, he'd look for Tirani, but he can't do that today. He finds the confused girl on the bed and hurries over. "Hey, you feeling any better . . ." He wracks his brain for the name Idrian called her. "Astrid?"

On the end of the bed, in Remy's peripheral vision, Idrian goes so still he could be dead.

The girl drops her mask again, grinning. "I'm not Astrid, silly! I'm Beni."

Remy turns. "But he called you—"

"Don't you say her name," Delaciel snarls, pushing to his feet. He levels a cutting look at Remy from above. "Not some coddled rich kid like you."

There can't be a name for the knotted-up mess of feelings inside Remy. All the words he's not allowed to speak clog in his throat. Before he can say anything, Delaciel turns away.

"Gotta start the fuel and water transfer."

Delaciel paces from the infirmary before anyone can answer.

Thomlin grimaces. Roca gets up. "We should help."

"Those boxes are heavy," Emil mumbles. "If I don't supervise, that idiot'll try to move 'em all himself."

Tirani waits, quiet, outside the door when everyone else has passed, arms crossed over her chest like she's trying to keep something in. She tries a smile, but even as her lips tip up, she takes two steps back into the hall, half-turning. "I'll go check if I can help with anything. See you later, Remy?"

"See you later," he echoes, numb.

Yves moves to the bed and turns the oxygen off. "I was hoping to shoo him out of the room so he'd stop wasting air on this kid, but wow. You're a real piece of work."

The girl obediently gives the mask back when Yves holds a hand out for it.

"He *called* her that, though."

Yves sucks in air through their teeth. "Count it a lesson learned. I wouldn't say it again unless you're after a reaction like that one."

It's not a good feeling, knowing that Idrian, too, has names that wound him. "Who was she, Astrid?"

Yves slants him a cold look. "It's not my story to tell. You wanna know, ask Idrian."

"You just told me not to."

Yves shrugs, eyebrows raised like they want him to make an issue of it—like they'd jump at any excuse to draw blood after what they learned from Thom. Remy knows the feeling.

Into the crackling silence, Beni chirps, "Can I go? I promised I'd play airball with Patrice."

Yves sighs. "It's not like there's much more I can do for you." They turn to Beni, expression mock-serious. "You can go, but I need your help with something first."

Beni's expression goes terribly solemn to match, eyes bright. "What is it?"

"I'm about to go do my rounds, but this one—" they jerk their chin toward Remy "—doesn't know the area. I need an assistant."

Beni's face splits into a smile. "I'll be your assistant!"

Yves' expression warms. "Let it never be said I refused helping hands when they were offered. Both of you. Come on, then."

Remy takes a couple of stuttering steps forward. "I didn't offer?"

"You're here, aren't you? Hurry up."

Yves packs oxygen canisters and other supplies onto a small cart while Beni bounds around the room. She insists on pushing the cart, even though it's nearly as tall as she is.

"Block A, first!" Yves calls, taking up a leisurely pace behind Beni.

Beni turns sharply down a hallway and looses a loud whoop.

Remy can't help a traitorous curl of warmth at the sight of her tromping through the dim and echoing halls, mumbling a song as enthusiastic as it is nonsensical. The implant on her wrist glows yellow-green, so much better than the shrieking red when they found her.

Idrian had one of those implants.

Remy turns to Yves. "Delaciel, he . . ." He gestures at his wrist. "He lived here."

It feels strange to say it, incompatible with everything Remy thought was true.

"Grew up here," Yves corrects him.

Remy's steps echo on the grated floor, the light here too dim even for shadows. Beni's song guides him forward. The expression on Delaciel's face before he left lingers behind Remy's eyelids. The twist of bitter pain. The way his face turned away, as if from a blow.

All he can think is that Tirani told him, back when they first met the crew, that Delaciel had just one rotbound bond. Remy banishes the thought with a greasy twist of sickness.

He and Idrian are not alike.

Too soon, they arrive at a branching corridor with doors at regular intervals. Many of the doors are open. Music and laughter and hacking coughs blend into a strange tune. Children litter the hallways, holding toys or holding hands or crouched over with fingers spread out like claws.

Prison planets, everyone says. For the unrepentant.

"How are there so many children here?"

Yves chuckles, mirthless. "Haven't you heard? We're animals with no mind for the planet or the people we harm. Children under ten make up about 18% of the inhabitants on the Isles. If you expand that age to fifteen, it's a solid 20%. Some were sent here—"

"That's not—" They couldn't. Surely the Chancellor wouldn't send children here.

Yves' glare could melt metal, their eyes a silver-blue paler than ghost-lace in moonlight.

"I suggest you think twice before calling me a liar."

Remy presses his lips together.

"But yes, quite a few were sent with their families. We have 'environmental criminals' here, of course, and all flavors of violent and destructive crime, but you wouldn't be able to pick the worst criminals out just by looking. Every new arrival, violent or innocent, learns they'll either play nice or suffer the consequences of exile."

Yves gracefully uncurls their long fingers and gestures *up*, to where the surface of Alta is stocked with the frozen bodies of those who did not play nice. *Exile* is such a nice word for "send you out onto Alta's lethally-cold and airless surface to die." At Remy's expression, they say, "You've seen it, then. Of course Idrian didn't dock! He made Thom walk the long way 'round the first time, too. Thought he was too soft, I suppose. What an absolute *bastard*." But they're grinning.

They could've *docked*?

"Anyway, the majority of crimes boil down to contradicting the Protectorate's pet narrative. Parents who purposely or accidentally had more children than the Chancellor permitted for population control. Dissidents whose arguments got too loud. People who violated the many conservation and sustainability standards often enough to get labeled as *unrepentant*. Some kids came with their parents, but the rest were born here."

"Who would bring a *child* into a place like this?"

Yves laughs. "Bestial, are we, just like they say? We skim the broadcasts off the satellites, so I've heard the shit the Chancellor's feeding you. But why don't *you* try to deny anyone here one of very few acts that provides a pleasure they don't have to earn in blood."

Remy grimaces. "Fine, but shouldn't they—"

Yves' fingers grab Remy's chin. "*Look around,* Greenie. We don't have enough air. You think anyone's nice enough to provide the contraception they pump into your water down there? Prenatal vitamins? Postnatal *care*? We don't even have the supplies to safely abort—not that I've been trained for it. Infant mortality is over 20% in the weeks after birth. I won't even tell you how many people don't even survive pregnancy. That's the only reason our population hasn't exploded. It's no accident. If we're monsters for bringing children into this, it's because your Chancellor has made monsters of us."

Remy shakes his head. "He wouldn't . . ."

"Wouldn't he? Deliveries are spaced so we run lethally low on food and oxygen just before the next shipment. Our next *official* delivery won't arrive for four more days. We've had people dying since last week. On the bad months, new shipments of the Chancellor's castaways arrive before supplies, and we have more mouths to feed than we have food. Never mind the effects of the environment. Higher rates of depression and anxiety. Loss in bone density and muscle mass thanks to comparatively weaker gravity. Vascular issues. The children born and raised here, if they survive, could not thrive in your world. It might literally break them to *walk* on the planet you take for granted. I'm the most qualified doctor these people have, but I'm not a real doctor and *I cannot save them.*"

Yves is shaking, fists clenched at their sides.

The boxes Idrian took—they were expired. (Vintage, he called them.)

Why didn't Remy stop to wonder why? If the deliveries were arriving as scheduled, no boxes should remain behind to expire. Remy feels *wrong*, heavier than the flimsy gravity that barely holds his feet to the ground. Spoiled, with the tube on his suit feeding air into his lungs. "I didn't know."

"Is that your excuse?" Yves scoffs. "Come on. We're here."

Beni (who has at some point slipped away and run halfway down the hall) spreads her arms wide and yells, "I'm Dr. Radenne's *assistant* today!"

Yves doesn't spare Remy a glance before striding down the hall. Block A's occupants exit their rooms with haunted resignation, but they come alive at the sight of Yves.

"Supplies?" someone whispers with brittle reverence.

"Delivering them now," Yves says.

The news sweeps through the block. Fuel. Water, food. Air.

Spouses hold each other tighter. A small boy pats an older woman's hand while she rocks and cries into his hair.

The Chancellor was warm and paternal when he pinned an award on Cameron's vest to thank him for his contribution to the great city. He gave Remy a personal tour of his estate that ended with fresh apple turnovers in the kitchen. Andrew only ever speaks of him with respect. But *this*—it must be a lie, but Remy can't find a single thread to unravel it from.

A few people glance his way, but Yves introduces him as a new member of Idrian's crew, and the uncertainty morphs to acceptance. An old woman—eighty, at least—comes forward to clap a papery hand on Remy's shoulder and offer thanks he doesn't deserve.

The old woman then shuffles over to Yves and murmurs, "My Martha would have loved to hear the news, but she couldn't make it. I'd have told you earlier, but . . ." The woman's rheumy eyes crinkle. "She looks almost like she's sleeping. I didn't want to disturb her."

Yves pulls the woman in and presses their forehead to hers. "I'll be by for her later, Mrs. Olsen."

It settles like a stone in Remy's gut: they're talking about a dead woman.

They leave Block A and the people in it. No one there accepted oxygen from the tank on Beni's cart, even though a dizzy-looking trio with yellow indicators held onto each other in their room's doorway while speaking to Yves.

Once they're around the corner, Yves turns to face the wall and brushes their hair behind one ear with a shaking hand. Beni walks up, quiet, and closes a small hand around their fingers.

"Dr. Radenne?"

"Hmm?"

She tugs a sparkly green and lima-pink clip from her hair and presses it into Yves' hand. "You can use it, if you want, to keep your hair out of your face."

Yves manages a small smile. "Thank you." They clip back some of the hair that keeps falling down, but the clip is almost comically small, at odds with their cold silver piercings and the sharp glint of light off their glasses.

Beni pats the doctor's hand. "You'll be okay!"

Yves fans that hand over their face, hiding their eyes. "Don't tell me that. With this, with *Thom*—please don't lie to me."

"Okay." Beni stands straighter. "What should I say?"

Yves huffs a laugh into their hand. "Tell me there's work to do. Tell me to get a fucking move on."

Beni gasps, mouth opening wide. "That's a grown-up word!" She grins and skips away, yelling back at Yves, "Get a fucking move on!"

She slaps her own cheeks and giggles after she says it, kicking her feet in the air with naked delight.

Block B is very much like Block A. Different faces; similar joy when Yves shares the news. There aren't as many children there, but there's a boy who's half Remy's size with an ego twice as big as he is and a blinking orange light on his wrist. He says, "I'm *fine*, Dr. Radenne," even as they press a mask to his face until the light on his wrist shifts to yellow-green. Eyes halfway hidden beneath the mask, he grins and holds out a grimy, multi-colored rope and asks Remy, "Wanna play tether says?"

In theory, tether says is supposed to make the abstract concept of tethers accessible to young children. One child ties a rope to a blindfolded partner, and the pair must work together to navigate obstacles. At the finish line, the leader and follower swap places and do the same thing in reverse. Last pair standing wins. It sounds very nice in theory, but in practice, it's an excuse to tie a rope to a friend's foot or neck (no one ever chooses the less-perilous tether locations) and drag them through the mud.

Remy squints at the boy, whose grin expands alarmingly.

"I'll lead," the boy says. "It'll be fun."

"You'll do nothing of the sort," Yves tuts. "You need to rest."

"But that's *boring*."

Yves confides as they leave Block B that the boy will not last the year. His name, Yves tells him, is Zanan.

Dr. Radenne knows everyone by name. Perhaps that's what the long list spilling over the desk in the infirmary is for.

"Block D!" Beni yells. She pushes her cart in drunken lines, then pushes it hunched over like she's a hundred, then pushes it with her shoulders while walking backward. Yves doesn't rebuke her, only occasionally reminding her not to let anything fall.

"Next is Block D!" Beni says again.

Remy's pretty sure the alphabet doesn't work like that. "What happened to C?"

Yves' smooth stride falters. "We don't visit C."

They pass a closed door with a series of cruel red lights lit beside it. BLOCK C is printed in crisp white letters over the closed door, but a massive X slashes out the name.

Before Remy can ask why, they arrive at Block D.

Beni runs inside, dodging visible piping taped together inside the doorway. The walls groan as Remy enters, a light overhead flickering as if irritated by his arrival.

Beni pushes her cart down the hall, greeting each person by name. This must be her block. She skips into an open room at the end of the hall and is shooed out by a remarkably grumpy old man. The man, supporting himself in the doorway, has a face etched into a deep and permanent scowl and the sort of jawline that says he might not have teeth. His gray eyebrows sit like birds' nests, the odd strand curling up over his forehead or down into his eyes.

"I don't need anything!" he growls at the girl skipping around his legs. "G'won, get outta here!"

His other hand rises, and it's odd not for what's on it but for what it lacks. Where yellow and yellow-green lights pierce the gray dimness from every other wrist, the man's wrist is smooth—not even scarred.

"Ox-sat monitors are optional," Yves breathes from beside him, following his eyes. "They demand a certain sacrifice of privacy, since they track the wearer's location to allow us to seek them out to administer rescue oxygen. Some folks have had enough control and oversight on Verdine. About 8% of our population isn't monitored. It's why, at any given time, there are more corpses lying around than I know about."

"I'm Dr. Radenne's *assistant*," Beni chirps, hands clasped behind her back.

"Terrible assistant. Too noisy!" the man shoots back. Finally, he shoves a liver-spotted hand into his pocket and withdraws a wrapped candy with a guttural curse. It's dirty, but Beni grabs it and dances in a circle.

"To get you out of my hair," the man sighs.

That's what he says, but his expression softens as Beni whoops and sweeps down the hall. One or two people have already inferred the purpose of Yves' presence and Beni's supply cart, and the news of the supply delivery blows through Block D like a spring breeze.

On the way out, Beni staggers, looking pale.

Yves tuts and directs her to sit on the flat cart, beside the supplies. "There's far too little air for that level of excitement," they chide. "Be excited tomorrow, little one."

But riding on the cart is far from a punishment, and Beni still chirps her news at everyone they pass.

Their journey through the rest of the blocks goes much like that. Blocks I, S, V, and X are the same as Block C, their names crossed out and unspoken, the silence surrounding them too fragile to prod at with questions.

Beni is asleep on the cart when they finish, curled up around the tanks and first aid kit.

They take a detour on the way back, and Remy can't figure out why until, up ahead, a painfully-bright light paints the floor. Yves pushes their cart into the light.

"Look, Greenie, that's you."

Remy steps underneath and looks up—but it's not a light. It's a window.

After so long in the dimness of Alta's underground, the sight through the window is an assault. The planet of Remy's birth sears his eyes against the lightless backdrop of space. Alta's viewing window stretches overhead, the vision through its thick pane frost-cracked at the edges. Remy shivers.

"I'd kill you for it, you know," Yves whispers, not even loud enough to make Beni stir.

Remy turns away from the planet's brutal glow. It lingers even when he blinks, a blinding disk floating across his eyes like a marble, a moon. A cup he can drink from. Its afterimage obscures Yves. "That seems a bit antithetical, for a doctor."

"Not a doctor." A laugh rasps from Yves' throat. "I was only halfway through my program when I started getting wind of what was happening here. You'd think my studies would've been more useful here, but I was going into surgery. Last thing these people need is for me to cut them open—not that I have any of the advanced tools I was trained with. But I'm what they have." Yves gestures at Verdine. "Look at all that fucking water. You had as much as you wanted, growing up, didn't you?"

Words perch on the tip of his tongue—rationalizations and excuses and apologies, each one heavier and more childish than the last. But of course he did. Even in his shared house with Tirani and that cracked set of bowls, they never lacked for anything. Not in the Chancellor's great city by the sea.

The hallway ahead of and behind him sinks into dimness. This window must be the brightest place on Alta. Suddenly, Remy understands why Idrian never takes his sunglasses off. This place must accustom every eye to the dark.

"Don't take this personally, but I hate you." Yves doesn't look away from the planet, their shadow on the grated floor sharply cut. "Do you know how we make oxygen here?" They don't wait for an answer. "Electrolysis, mostly. We supplement with massive algae vats that produce extra oxygen and recycle CO_2. Both of those things require water. Back when they housed Verdine's survivors, the Isles used to have large-scale equipment to recombine the hydrogen byproduct with environmental CO_2 to make water for the moon's occupants, but Alta housed the wealthiest way back when, and they hadn't learned their lesson from almost killing Verdine. They used this place hard. A lot of our equipment stopped working ages ago, and fuck if anyone living knows how to keep it fixed for long. So when deliveries don't come on time . . ."

Remy flinches.

"We can survive days without water. Minutes without air. We ration both, and those who can't bear it die while we wait for your Chancellor's backhanded goodwill." Yves' expression twists. "I was very much like you when I lived in the capital. I'd stake my life on that being where you're from."

If that's all Yves ever gleans about where he came from, he'll be lucky. Remy grasps for the anger that guided him for the past five years, but it's in tatters. Desperately, he says, "Delaciel shot someone on the OSS. A boy . . ."

"Is that so terrible?" Yves finally looks away from Verdine, pale eyes blinking fast. "Your Chancellor has killed five, just today. Idrian should be finished loading the supplies. We'll go to meet him, and I suggest you keep that name to yourself."

Astrid.

Yves continues walking, their long strides leaving Remy behind.

Mere hours ago, Remy watched Idrian execute a boy who trusted him. He killed Cam, and Andrew's father, and probably more people whose names Remy doesn't know. But in this dark, hopeless place, he's a symbol, and Remy no longer knows what face he can show the man who preserves with one hand and destroys with the other.

Chapter Nine

*And with these laws we do so swear
we will create and keep
a bright green world, a thriving place,
where all may breathe in peace.*

— Fragment from the Verdinian anthem

The first time Remy's suit chirps at him, he ignores it. Yves gives him a long look, and Remy offers to push the cart just to get away from their unblinking stare.

Beni and the supplies aren't exactly heavy, but he gets winded *fast*. His head pounds, a throb for every frenzied beat of his heart. Unmarked doors blur past but if there are numbers or letters to identify them, Remy can't see them.

Yves, strolling along behind him, blandly offers to take the cart back.

"I'm fine." Remy's wheeze nearly drowns out the suit's second beep.

"Gonna do anything about that?" Yves asks.

On the cart, Beni mumbles and curls around a first aid box like it's a pillow.

They walk.

It's getting darker. Remy blinks hard, sucking on the tube and then opening his mouth to pull in whatever air Alta has to offer, but it's like he's breathing through a wet rag. Dark shapes skitter across his vision. When his suit finally lets out a long, uninterrupted whine, it blends so well with the droning in his skull that he almost doesn't hear it.

Remy trips over one of his heavy-booted feet and nearly breaks his nose on the cart's glinting metal handle. "Something—something's wrong."

"You don't say. Those beeps were to warn you the suit's supplementary oxygen supply was running low."

Remy's arms weigh two tons each, vision washed black except for the straw-thin funnel where Yves' indifferent face stares at him.

"Welcome to Alta. Not very welcoming here, is it?"

There's no air. "Please, I can't . . ."

"You can." Yves sucks in a slow breath, arms crossed over a chest that rises and falls without difficulty. "It's easy, Greenie. Just breathe."

He *tries*. So many breaths, so long and deep his ribs ache with them, but he's starving for air, unmercifully conscious.

Yves sighs and unwinds Remy's hands from the cart. For an awful moment, Remy thinks they'll push it onward and leave him here, but instead they do something he can't see, and after what feels like hours, press something against his face.

This time, Remy's hungry gasps feed his body.

"Weak." Yves snaps an elastic band behind his head and shoves something heavy into his arms: one of the large rescue canisters they've been using to administer air in the blocks. "When we get back, I'm switching you to a cannula and something more portable, and I'll be decreasing the amount of oxygen it feeds you at regular intervals. I won't have you wasting our air. Don't fall behind."

They resume pushing the cart, and Remy follows, ashamed and grateful.

Lord of the Empty Isles

Instead of returning to the infirmary, they stop in front of an unlabeled door. When Yves waves the implant on their wrist in front of it, it opens with an obliging whir (and only the faintest groan).

When Remy was seven or eight and began to hear stories from Cameron about Idrian's reckless thefts, the outlaw's actions struck him as delightfully free. When he got tired of his teachers lacing him into the choking ribbed collars on the shirts of the boys' uniform, he liked to imagine what he'd do if he could be like Idrian, fearless and untethered. He'd come to school in a ribboned blouse like the one his teacher wore. He'd *dare her* to comment.

At nine, Remy came home crying, scratching at the neck of the shirt, and told Cam his teacher said that *boys wear the boys' uniform*. Cam had unlaced the shirt and taken their father's cooking scissors and cut the thing to shreds while Remy gaped. Boys, Cam informed him, wear whatever the fuck they want to. And that was that. Remy still played Lord of the Empty Isles. While everyone else wanted to play Enforcers, Remy pulled a blue blanket around his shoulders and volunteered to sneak around as Idrian. The Lord of the Empty Isles, too, did whatever the fuck he wanted. In more than one memorable instance, he roped Cam, Andrew, and even the Chancellor into the game. Back then, the three of them hunted him through the house to tag him and capture him for the Protectorate's judgment. He lurked in corners, giggling and hunting them back: his touch would turn them to allies. Everything felt simple back then, no problem too big to solve.

Years later, when Cam breathed Idrian's name on his last night alive, Remy's childhood imaginings took on a darker color. Idrian became, to him, suddenly and irrevocably real—the sort of person who could kill.

The two images blur and blend into the person in front of him. Inside the room, oblivious to Remy's struggle, Idrian Delaciel sits in front of a large screen, empty cart beside him and shelves lining the walls stocked with hundreds and hundreds of oxygen canisters.

Even if he were allowed to speak them, Remy doesn't know if there are words for the things he wants to say. Tirani's always been better at naming things.

"Just finished bringing in the last of the supplies!" Idrian glances over to greet them and his eyes land on Beni, drooling onto the medical kit. A complicated expression flits over his face. "Is she . . . ?"

"Sleeping. Little idiot tired herself out running through every single block," Yves says. "She'll be fine. *This* one, however, started dying on the way back. Alta's air is clearly not up to his standards."

Idrian laughs and turns back to his screen. "It's an acquired taste."

Yves stalks the walls and pulls out a smaller canister than the unwieldy one in Remy's arms and a long tube. With a bit of fiddling, they swap the smaller one for the larger, clipping the new canister to Remy's suit and hooking the cannula into his nostrils.

"What is this place?" Remy approaches the screen. On it, a map spreads out, showing a long circle with regular branches, like a child's drawing of the sun. Thousands of moving dots populate the branches in green and yellow and orange. One turns red and the screen emits a shrill noise, but soon an icon that looks like a moving person replaces the red dot.

"Are they . . . ?"

"This is Rescue Room #1," Idrian says. "There are three more on Alta, each with a screen like this and rescue oxygen. They've saved a lot of lives, for all the good it does."

"Tooting your own horn, are you?" Yves says. "Idrian makes the rooms possible."

Another red blip. Another running man icon.

"That's to show someone's handling it." Idrian taps the screen. "This room serves Blocks A through E."

Remy clenches his fists at his sides for a lack of anything better to do with his hands. The space beside him has never felt so cold and empty. "Is Tirani here?"

Idrian slants him a pitying expression. "Nah. I get to stay because Roca reminded me you might die if I didn't. The others took the—took my ship out to deliver supplies to Toxys and Fluora. Your friend went along."

Remy makes himself nod. He doesn't blame her.

Idrian tangles his fingers in his hair. "Roca'll take care of her. Seems to have a soft spot for the girl. Don't know what happened between you two, but give her time. Sometimes that's all it takes."

Not this time. The more he learns, the more complicated everything gets. Instead of answering, he glances around the room. Lots and lots of tanks, but nothing else. "Why aren't there cots? To carry the worst ones to the infirmary?"

Yves says, "We have to be careful how we spend our resources. If the person can't stand to seek further treatment after on-site oxygen therapy, the air we'd spend keeping them alive is usually a waste."

Idrian scowls. "If I could bring more supplies..." He goes still. "Shit. Yves, I forgot. We burned the OSS. I don't know if I'll be able to get in again for what we need."

Shame surges through Remy. *He* burned the OSS, and everyone on the Isles will suffer for it.

Yves drags a hand over their eyes. "What has this day come to, when that's not even the worst thing I've heard?"

Idrian traces the arc of the hallways on the screen with one finger. "Roca tried to find the bastard who stabbed me, but whoever it was, he'd planned it in advance. By the time she caught up, he'd hidden the knife or traded it off with someone else. *Maybe* we could've hunted 'em down if we made a scene and searched every person on Yenefria, but we were already running late. I made the decision to finish siphoning from the lake and leave. Someone else'll take up our work after we're gone."

Remy's lungs are airless pockets in his chest. Bleeding from the wound that fed Remy's withering, Idrian chose to save people even if it meant his death. Today, he fired a gun that ended an innocent life. Vigilante or villain—the two images won't resolve into one.

Yves grips the back of Idrian's seat. "Don't talk like that. I'll—"

"I know. You'll save us. I know you'll try."

"Don't you give me *platitudes*, Idrian Delaciel."

Idrian turns away from the screen, profile silhouetted as he pins Yves with a dry stare. "Then stop acting like you need 'em."

Another whine from the screen picks up. A red dot not far from them, at the end of one of the spokes. Remy steps closer when someone doesn't immediately claim it. Must be one of theirs. "Hey . . ."

"I'm not acting like I need them, Idrian."

The whine hasn't stopped. It's joined by another in the same location, then one more.

"Could've fooled me," Idrian says.

"*Hey*. The dots?"

"I do not *need* them. I need them to be true, you great idiot! I'm tired of watching people die. I'll kill my way through every single witherer on that rotten, beautiful planet if I have to. I will *not*—"

Another high whine. Another red blip.

Yves blinks first, turning to the screen. "That's unusual."

Then there are countless more.

One spoke on the map's great wheel flushes red in a sweeping wave, the combined noise physically painful. Alerts pop up at the fringes of the screen, but Remy doesn't have time to read them, because the floor beneath his feet trembles, nearly knocking him to his knees.

Idrian has no such issue. He's already upright, pulling armfuls of canisters from the shelves and dropping them into the cart he must have carried them in on. Yves joins him.

That's probably why, when Beni jolts awake at the nerve-rattling whine, Remy's the only one who sees her rub her bleary eyes and squint at the screen. The only one to see her lips shape the words, "Block D."

Block D with its grumpy old man, with its groaning floors and the taped-together mass of piping inside, with its flickering bulbs. Dread crawls up Remy's throat and his mind serves up images of other blocks with glowering red lights and doors painted closed.

Beni's on her feet in an instant. Before Remy can stop her, she's ducked past him and run from the room.

"Beni!"

His cry turns Idrian's head.

"She's gone," Remy says, foolishly. "It's—it's Block D. It's her block."

He has to find her. Remy runs out, but he speeds past the infirmary before he realizes he's gone the wrong way. By the time he turns around, Yves and Idrian are already pushing carts into the hall. Remy doesn't meet Beni until he's at the entrance to Block D.

The taped-together piping from earlier is on the floor, along with a shattered light and what looks like a huge mass of ductwork and a portion of the ceiling. The ductwork must deliver the block's air, little as it is, into each room. Without it... Remy's vision flashes back to the screen, to all those red dots, all those vents no longer carrying thin air. The whole obstruction is a hissing, spitting mess, crushed into the doorway at an angle so there's barely any room between the awful mass and the floor.

Barely any room. Not *no* room. Plenty enough for a girl as small as Beni.

"Wait! Please, at least take my—" Remy tugs at the canister on his suit, but it's locked on, and she's not listening.

Beni drops to her belly and wriggles through the opening, screaming names Remy doesn't recognize.

He tries to shove himself through the debris after her, but his shoulders run up against the fallen metal, hands slipping in glass as he reaches for her and touches warm skin. "Beni?"

Another voice meets him, faint and interspersed with awful gasps. Something small and soft pushes up against his hand. "My son . . ." the voice says.

The woman doesn't have the strength to push the boy any farther, and the only thing Remy's fingers reach is downy hair on what can only be an infant's head. He tries to grab at it, but the fine hair tears out in his hand. The boy makes a warble of distress in response.

Dust from debris stings his eyes, his breath deafening in the claustrophobic narrowness. He pushes his shoulder in, and *in,* until his muscles scream and his fingers finally close around soft cloth. Remy pulls his whole body back through the door with the infant, who is still and very, very quiet in his arms. He rocks the baby, pats its cheeks and rubs at its cold feet.

Idrian and Yves arrive, and Remy doesn't know what he's supposed to do. Helplessness crawls up his limbs with prickly insect feet, and he lifts the child, hoping someone will take it from him.

All at once, the baby breathes, spending his first breath on an ear-shattering wail. Remy hopes his mother is still alive on the other side, that she hears it.

The other side. "Beni!" Remy blurts, turning to Yves and Idrian. "She went in. I can't get through."

Yves shakes their head. "I've called for hydraulics, but it'll take time."

"We don't have time." Idrian shoves himself up against the chunk of collapsed ceiling. It doesn't budge.

Without words, he sets to tearing away any bits of debris that can be moved. The door keeps making aborted whirs. It wants to close and lock those people in without air. Remy passes the baby into someone's waiting arms and joins the effort, the skin of his hands tearing on sharp metal. Others join in. Still more run off to assist with carrying tools and supplies.

The more they pull, the more mess falls from the ceiling to join the pile. While they work, Yves outfits the tiniest members of the crowd with masks and a rescue tank or two. "Go in," they say. "Give it to anyone conscious enough to receive it and come back for more."

Children younger than Beni slip through the gap one after another as piles of debris fill the hall behind them. A child drags a smaller boy back with her on her first trip. Still. Lips blue.

Someone calls, "Two minutes on the hydraulics!"

"Two *minutes*," Idrian growls. "Remy, get the cart. If I fail, wedge it in to keep the opening accessible."

Remy obeys. Idrian aims for the corner that looks lightest, where a huge stretch of ductwork lies diagonally in the doorway. He lies on his back and pushes until the metal whines and groans against the wall. Other people, seeing what he's aiming for, lend their strength, but the doorway is narrow and it's already an awkward fit with so many.

Idrian pushes from below until the gap Beni escaped into widens enough that he's holding his arms all the way up with his elbows locked. He wedges himself into the space and keeps pushing.

Remy saw him, earlier, without the coat. There's not much to him, but he's made a tool of his body without a second thought to help these people.

Remy's never felt more foolish, standing awkwardly with the cart. He drags it close to the debris and frees a hand to help clear away the rubble. A woman and two men on the ground help Idrian lift. When his arms shake, seeming moments away from giving out, the woman kneels and wedges her shoulder in.

The people working at the debris pull a massive chunk away, and the rest of it rises in a jolt. Finally, Idrian is halfway upright, supporting the weight of the rubble on his shoulder, and Remy's bones ache where he's clutching uselessly at the handle of the cart.

Acid helplessness slops in his belly. Idrian, who bolted into action without pause, has probably never tasted this feeling. Remy watched death happen before, unable to stop it. He won't watch it again.

He's already got a cannula that'll feed him air. He's better-equipped to do this than anyone else here. He shoves canister after canister under his arm and pushes through the crowd to where Idrian is shaking and sweat-slick, holding the rubble up.

"I can make it through," Remy says. "I can help."

Something sparks in Idrian's eyes, which linger on Remy for longer than since he arrived. After a while, he nods. "Be careful in there," is all he says, and Remy kneels.

Something wet drips onto his forehead as he wriggles through the gap. He wipes it onto his shoulder and sees red.

It's not sweat. The dark sleeve of Idrian's coat hides it, but his left arm is soaked, his hand and the exposed bit of his wrist a macabre map of intersecting red lines.

"Go on," Idrian says. "I'm good here."

Remy goes. He starts by grabbing the mother's body, her hand still outstretched, and pushing her toward the door. Her son's still screaming on the other side.

First her, then everyone else who's near. If they're not moving, he pushes them through. If they're disoriented but conscious, he gives them oxygen.

Again and again, arms aching, into one room after another, each one packed with people—five or eight of them to a room smaller than Remy's back home. Back for tanks and then back inside. He's sweating, hands torn open from glass and debris.

Idrian holds the rubble up and bleeds.

To some of the moving ones, Remy gives oxygen so they can recover enough to assist.

A young man lays just outside his door. An older couple rests in bed, unnaturally still. The rough grate of the floor must be torture on their skin as he drags them out.

"Triage!" Yves yells through the obstruction. "Oxygen to the ones who're moving *first*. Worry about the rest later."

But how can he ignore the girl, maybe four, wrapped around a dirty doll on the floor, just because she isn't moving? He calls for Beni so much his throat goes raw. At some point, the hydraulic device Yves was talking about takes Idrian's place. Idrian grabs an ax and beats at the chunk of ceiling that's sagged into the path of the duct and blocked the airflow. When it falls to the ground with a section of mangled ductwork, thin air rushes down, but it's not enough. The system in the ceiling that should carry air to each room is no longer connected, so the directionless air floods out only near the entrance. Still, it's *something*.

Remy keeps going until his shoulders and back burn and his legs nearly buckle from the weight of the bodies he pulls out. There's a crowd of people in here now, Idrian among them even though he looks half an inch from collapsing himself.

That's when he finds her.

The first thing Remy sees is a solid red light.

Beni lies in a boneless sprawl on the opposite side of an unmade bed in the second-to-last room, cradled in shadow.

Her hand is locked around the wrist of the man on the bed, who's collapsed on his side as if reaching for Beni. Remy knows without having to look closer at the unmarred wrist that it's the grumpy old man with the candy.

Remy can't bear to pull Beni away from him, so he staggers back to the doorway. "Two more," he cries. His voice is wrecked, barely breaking free of his throat. "A cart!" He shoves his palms against his eyes and the darkness bursts with color. "In here! I need some help."

He sucks in a breath but it rushes from his chest as he kneels beside Beni with hands shaking almost too badly to get one of the canisters going and put the mask on her face. She's quiet in a way she wasn't even back in the hall when they found her. It's a silence nearly obscene in contrast to how she clanked through the halls pushing her cart, yelling about being *Dr. Radenne's assistant today*.

He barely knows her. This shouldn't hurt.

She's not moving, so she shouldn't get air. The mask still dwarfs her face when he straps it on. When the Chancellor ordered them manufactured, he probably wasn't thinking of how small some of the people he'd kill in this cold place would be.

Remy pushes at Beni's chest with desperate pumps. There's oxygen for her. She just has to breathe it in. But her implant is red, and it's red, and it's red. It's fading.

The whine stops first, then the light blinks out.

If he were the least bit courageous, he'd feel for a pulse.

Beni is so much smaller than Cameron was, but the weight of a body is just the same. Some people talk like the wasted ones are light, but Remy has never held anything heavier than a corpse. Living limbs are so easy to lift, even when they're trying not to be. A body with no one inside it is unspeakable, as painful as a tether with no one on the other end. Remy wonders if she died afraid, if there's anyone living who will ache for her.

A woman comes with a cart and tries to pull Beni from him, but he can't let go. She deserves this, to be held. Not hours before, Idrian scooped her into his arms and gave her breath and saved her life, but all Remy can do is hold her in the aftermath.

The woman drags the old man onto the cart instead, and Beni's hand drops from the man's wrist and slams on the bedframe. The first thing his mind offers up is, *that'll bruise.*

He gasps in a noise that could be a hiccup or a laugh, because Beni's lips are still blue and her chest isn't moving. She will not feel a bruise.

Remy makes himself stand with her body in his arms.

There are probably still people yelling, rushing ahead of him to drag out the few who remain inside, but all sound fades to white noise as he walks.

Beni's neck tips back over his arm at an awkward angle, and he readjusts her so he's supporting it, and it's stupid. He knows it's stupid, but it's something he can still do.

~

He doesn't remember getting outside to join the others, but there are hands on his shoulders he pushes away. He kneels on the ground and lets Beni down.

Behind him, there's a clatter and a tinkle and a thud, and Block D's door snaps closed with a flash of red.

He blinks down at Beni, and someone is screaming. Hands grab at him, jolting him from the haze he's sunken into.

A little boy claws at Beni, saying her name between sobs, and *give me back my sister.*

Hands close again on Remy's shoulders, Idrian's voice like a verdict from above, barely audible: "She's not yours. Let her go, Remy."

Remy's hands release her.

Beni's brother is about as big as she is, with a face just like hers and a mess of golden curls. He doesn't touch her much at first. Just says her name. *Beni, Beni. Beni?* like it might wake her.

Maybe the boy doesn't understand, because she's still warm, her eyes closed as if in rest. Her brother tugs on her hand, then slaps at it, then pulls her from Remy's grasp and holds her.

"She's dead," Remy whispers. It comes out like a secret, or a confession, or maybe even a question, but the boy who no longer has a sister doesn't answer.

A person who loses a spouse can be a widow or widower. A child without parents is an orphan. But what is a child who loses a sibling? A boy who loses his world? Remy left blood everywhere he touched her. Smears on her shoulders and her pale, pale chin and her mask. Under her eye. Handprints like wings on her chest where he failed to convince her to breathe. He hasn't turned off the air, still pumping into the mask like she has any use for it.

He turns his hands palm up in his lap and stares at the gouges oozing blood.

He forgot about the broken glass. A sickle-shaped shard curves from the soft part of his palm beneath his thumb. The rusty line of his withering mocks him, sitting just shy of his wrist. Remy didn't even notice it advancing so far. It *hurts*.

Why did he ever think more death could pay for a life?

Cameron said his hands were for healing.

Remy curls over them and laughs until he can't breathe between hitching, nearly voiceless sobs, and he's not even sure what he's grieving.

Chapter Ten

*Those connected by vital red, transformative **fatebonds**, the rarest of all tethers, walk the same paths and share the same pains. Of all bonds, fatebonds are thickest. When in proximity to each other, fatebound pairs may bolster the health or speed the healing of their fellows. Fatebonds share in health as they share in misfortune: these bonds are also the only type thick enough to communicate a curse.*

—From *On the Manipulation of Tethers*

Time and sound come to Remy across oceans. Voices blend into a background hum, continents removed, then farther still. Cries. Somewhere are the raw, animal noises of the grieving—shattered-glass sounds torn from throats too choked to give them up—but Remy is a star, far enough away that their pain can't cut him.

Two voices, nearer. Remy shakes his head to dislodge them, but they won't go away.

"Shit, he's a mess. You're not supposed to pick 'em this green, Idrian."

A laugh close by. Too close. It should surprise him. He should shift away. He hates that voice, doesn't he?

He can't make himself move.

His world rocks, a soothing motion. He's a boat on another world's ocean, salty ocean breeze for all who breathe, a place where he doesn't walk into a room with clumsily made porridge to find his entire life has gone cold while he slept.

No. He's a boat on another world's ocean.

"Cam." The word tumbles, ragged, from his own throat. It *hurts*. He has a throat.

"Hey, Greenie. Remy? Look, Roca told me you aren't so much into the touching but I'm gonna help you up. You can't stay here."

"Neither of you can. You're bleeding all over the place, and I—" A frustrated growl. "I don't have time to treat you. I have to—I think the cafeteria might fit all of them. Clean up and come join me. I'll need all the help I can get."

Hands hook under Remy's arms but their owner makes a noise of pain and retreats. "A little assistance? Can't lift him."

"Idiot." The other voice says, oddly gentle. "You're a mess. Bleeding's gonna be the least of it." Arms, again, lifting him, and the same voice: "I've got work to do. Up with you."

Up he goes.

His eyes find a tiny, mop-headed boy crouched over a—

Someone turns him away, but the vision lingers like it was tattooed on his eyes. A warm, wet hand settles on his shoulder, guiding him.

The world moves. His feet move him, and the halls are cold, and he's cold, a chill that starts in his extremities and creeps toward his core. Womblike dimness. Silence and one step after another.

"Good," the voice says.

Then the hand on his shoulder is gone, and he's sitting down. Something soft, and the voice is there but it's the buzz of an annoying bug.

A crash, a curse.

And *plink, plink.* It's a terrible sound, blunt and irregular. It's not a noise he can get lost in.

Plink.

"I-Idrian?" It feels wrong to use his first name aloud, the word sweet and ashy in his mouth, like a severing. He can't even pinpoint where he started thinking of Idrian that way.

"There you are. Welcome back. C'mon, your hands are a mess and I can't fix 'em."

"Stop it," Remy says. Something warm. A hand? Remy leans away from it. "Don't."

Plink. Plink-plink.

"Look, I'm shit at words, but if that's what you want, it's what you get. You heard this song before? Get fucking ready for it. It's terrible, but my singing voice is worse."

His voice is, indeed, worse. Remy groans and turns away.

"We make a rotten pair, don't we, Greenie?"

That *word*.

"Greenie? Don't like that, do you. C'mon, Greenie, the world's spinning and I can't keep this up. Immature. Rich kid. C'mon, special boy, snap to. Y'ever wonder why all the universities are in or around the capital?"

The voice pierces Remy's cozy haze, stirring irritation like embers in his chest. "M'not . . ." he manages to say, and he blinks. He's in the infirmary.

The *plinks* are Idrian's blood leaking from a treatment table to the floor.

Remy sinks into his body and hates it. He's on a plush bench next to the wall with his knees pulled up to his chest. His hands sting; his shoulders are bruised. Every muscle burns and he *remembers*.

"You never did, did you?" Idrian laughs, raw and dry.

Never did what? Remy scowls at Idrian, who's trying to tighten a wrapping around his upper arm with his teeth. Down on Verdine, a nurse with a steritape gun could paint disinfecting lines of bioglue over every wound in a minute and send Idrian on his way. This is ridiculous. "Shut up."

"Nah, if me being a jerk is what keeps you from doing the space-out thing, I do a real good bastard impression. Okay, so, wait for it."

Plink.

"All the universities are in the capital, see, 'cause it's where all the monsters are."

"It's . . . it's about population density," Remy rasps. He crosses his arms over his knees and buries his face in them. His lungs don't feel like they're his. "It's not a conspiracy. The universities are there because the people are there."

Idrian huffs and speaks with the bandage still in his teeth. "'Zat what they say? Sometimes I'm jealous and sometimes I'm just sad for you." A violent jerk and a hiss as he attempts to knot the bandage over the biggest wound. "Use your head. It's about *oversight*. They've gotta control the flow of knowledge. Why d'you think Yves got booted before raising any alarms once they started getting suspicious? It's easier for your Chancellor to make sure his propaganda machines are running smoothly if all the universities are under his control. Knowledge is a weapon. When people aren't fighting to live, they've got time to think. It's tricky business, making sure they think along the right track. You're all nice dulled-down little blades. 'Specially those bastards at Astoria."

The smile Idrian casts at Remy is half mocking, half pitying. Like he's sure he has the size of Remy just by knowing where he was born. Remy imagines, for a second, the look Idrian might wear if he learned that Remy cast his withering.

This *dulled-down little blade* is poised to take his life.

"That's a real look you're giving me. You knew folks at Astoria, huh?"

The drips speed up, an off-beat *p-plink, plink p-plink* that pounds on Remy's eardrums. Idrian's bandage is soaked through, fingers slick with blood. Under the icy-cool light of the infirmary, his face shines with cold sweat, eyelashes flickering.

P-plink.

"You've gotta wrap it *tight*," Remy growls.

Idrian doesn't turn his head. Just his eyes, sleepy and half-lidded—unimpressed. "Can't get a grip with these hands."

Remy grits his teeth, rifling through the box beside him.

"Spray's on the floor," Idrian says, " . . . dropped it earlier trying to pick it up."

Remy almost falls over when he gets to his feet, but he finds the hemostatic spray Yves recommended for Thomlin's nosebleed. Yves was so gentle about it with Thom.

Remy paces up to Idrian, plucks the bandage from around his wound, and sprays the weeping flesh in three long bursts.

"Shit, that smarts!" Idrian wrenches his arm away. But the spray does its work. *Finally.* No more drips. "You could've warned me."

"My brother graduated Astoria," is Remy's answer. He retreats to his bench, dropping the spray back in its box. "Look, I don't expect some fancy nano-surgery setup, but you don't even have steritape here?"

Idrian sighs. "We have what I can get my hands on and stealing medtech's next to impossible nowadays. Hemostatic spray's as good as it gets. Speaking of, get your hands while you're at it. Those look nasty."

Remy sprays his torn-up hands, and the pain of it is a half-step removed from him, a curious thing he can take the shape of. Blood gathers itself and the wounds stop oozing. Remy stares at the mess and thinks of healing. His eyes settle on an ugly crevasse of torn flesh that bisects the line of his withering, and then on his hands, then the wound, then the blood still inside it.

"Your brother, huh?" Ear-splittingly loud, tearing Remy from his peace. "Astoria grad? I'll bet he's a real upstanding guy. Model citizen with a head full of top-quality nonsense—"

"Shut up!" Remy's on his feet before he knows it, aching hand fisted in Idrian's coat. "You don't get to talk about him like that."

His hands are wet with Idrian's blood and his own, teeth clenched so hard his jaw ticks in his skull. But he doesn't wind up and punch Idrian in his smug mouth. He doesn't say anything, because the moment he does, Idrian will know the witherer he means to hunt is right beside him. So Remy dams up the words and aches with them. He just says again, quietly, "Shut up."

It's not enough.

Idrian's smirk vanishes. "Damn, is he . . . ?"

Idrian stops before he can say *dead*, but the word hangs heavy in the air between them.

Remy squeezes his eyes shut. "He was . . ."

Cameron was stupid. He was bright. He sang the gentlest lullabies and made the worst food.

"He was good."

Idrian rubs the tip of his shoe through the blood he dripped on the floor, and it finally hits Remy that he's not wearing his sunglasses. Those pale aqua-green eyes, the precise shade of the Glass Sea at its clearest, are uncovered for the first time since Remy met him, staring into Remy's with an intensity that makes him desperate to turn away.

"My mom went to Astoria," Idrian confesses. "Didn't save her when she was sent here."

The cultivated flatness to his voice is something Remy knows well.

"I'm sorry," Remy says. "About your mom."

They're hollow, grating words, but he's never heard any that aren't in the face of loss.

Idrian's eyes fly to his, surprised. "It's f—" He shrugs. "S'been a long time, anyway."

"Does it matter how long?"

"Nah. What happened to him, your brother?"

You happened, Remy can't say. He twists his fingers in his shirt at his side to keep them from going to Cam's pendant. "He got sick, and he never got better. I couldn't save him."

"Capital's army of doctors couldn't do anything?"

"It wasn't something doctors could fix." A better answer swells in Remy, and he catches it behind his teeth: *I would've killed anyone to keep him alive. I could have, if he'd only let me.*

"Yeah." Idrian's eyes slip closed, freeing Remy from that incisive stare. "Fuck doctors. There're tons of things they can't fix. Astrid . . . my sister, she was three. She was half as big as me but I'd—" He shakes his head. "I'd drag her here and pester the old bastard until he helped her. It didn't . . ." He looks at his red-stained hands. "It only made her suffer longer."

Astrid. The fading, iridescent shine of his crumbling ship's name. The name he breathed in the hallway, unthinking, when they arrived. Perhaps Idrian's sister looked like Beni. Sympathy and jealousy twist in Remy's gut: Idrian barely had a chance to know his sister, but at least he can talk about her openly. Remy has to swallow Cam's name like a secret if he wants to keep his head on his shoulders.

"Shouldn't even have made it to three," Idrian says, and his eyes are on Remy but they're miles and years away. "But she saw beauty fucking everywhere, you know? In status lights and stars and the shapes of the grates on the floor. Eyelashes and *condensation*. She sang. Barely ever said anything to anyone but me, but she'd sing. One of my only memories before I came here is of this—this massive garden at home. I tried to count the flowers but I could only count to three because that's how old I was, and there were thousands. Then we were here, and Astrid was *born* in this shithole, and there weren't any flowers at all. She found things to love about the filth in this place, but I never got to show her one beautiful thing."

Remy thinks of Idrian's room, filled with paper blossoms. The ever-present pang in his chest calms to a thrum, noticeable only in its absence.

Idrian *understands*. Remy knows the sharp edges in those words better than he knows his own heart. There's a twisted-up peace in the fact that the people who broke Remy have never been whole, themselves.

"Never told anyone else that." Idrian's eyes slowly focus on Remy again. "Must be the blood loss. Roca knows, of course. She and her parents came here when I was twelve. I never needed to tell her. She'd lost someone, too."

"It was like that for me and Tirani," Remy whispers.

She'll get a kick out of being right again. He and Idrian really aren't so different. The Isles carved Idrian apart. He did the same to Remy. Now, Remy's curse will take everything from him. It'll kill Remy, too, if he doesn't find a way out. Nausea coils inside him, and Remy lurches to his feet and wanders the room.

Now-empty cots. Drips and puddles of blood. The bed where Idrian pressed the mask to Beni's face.

Idrian speaks up. "Get your hands, if you can. Wrap 'em, I mean. Gauze in the cupboard. Disinfectant's . . ."

On the cart, where Yves numbly dropped it after finding Thom's cursemark.

It's like a chain, each link inseparable. Who will Yves harm to make up for the loss of Thom? How many other people will Idrian's death, and Roca's, and Emil's tear apart? Who will those people hurt?

Remy follows Idrian's gesture to a closed cupboard with glass doors hiding rolls of gauze and bottles of pills.

He makes quick work of wrapping his hands, then sighs. He has the disinfectant in hand, anyway. He walks over to Idrian. "You'll get blood everywhere," he mutters.

"Nothing new."

Remy spritzes the wound on Idrian's arm with disinfectant before he thinks better of it and wrenches a shred of gauze off the roll, then follows it with a strip of self-adhering wound-tape. He winds them around Idrian's upper left arm without looking at anything but the ragged mouth of Idrian's wound. When he's tightened the tape around it—and it's terrible, they'll probably both die of infection before the withering can take them—he turns away.

"Thanks," Idrian says.

"Yves'll be pissed if you bleed all over the place."

Idrian just grins.

Remy drops the disinfectant and seeks out the farthest seat from Idrian. He finds himself at Yves' desk, flanked by the file cabinet on one side and an empty space for Yves' rolling cart on the other. It's all surprisingly organized, aside from the list that floods down the wall onto the desk. Remy lifts it, peering at its contents. There's nothing but names—hundreds of them, maybe thousands, in careful handwriting, some encased in parentheses and some not. Beneath the list is a lamp, its cord wrapped around a small pole and plugged into the wall, balanced on top of a stack of books on either side with space between.

Remy loses his breath at what he finds beneath the light.

Maybe there were no flowers here when Idrian was little, but there are flowers here now.

There's a pot wedged between the books, under the grow light. Because it *is* a grow light. The pot is a nondescript gray thing, but from it spills a beautiful, delicate crawling plant with frosty-green, spade-shaped leaves and small starbursts of veiny, translucent flowers. Two or three desiccated bunches of the leaves hang on the wall behind the lamp and the endless list.

Remy's mouth goes dry.

Ghost-lace. That's *ghost-lace.*

He tugs the desk's drawer open with gauze-clumsy fingers and—there.

In the back: a closed, airtight container. Remy opens it and finds ashes. Finds, beside it, four or five old wristwatches. Several handwritten notes. A few locks of hair. Tiny jars: one has a baby's tooth in it.

"Yves," Remy breathes. "*Yves* is your witherer?"

Of course they are.

Five years he's been dreaming of finding this room and making the person who cursed his brother bleed. Five years too late, and now that he's here, he finds himself frozen.

Idrian frowns. "They didn't do this to us, if that's what you're thinking. They've only ever helped—even when it puts them at risk."

Whatever Remy's face is doing, Idrian must interpret it as doubt.

"I'm not kidding. One of the Chancellor's dogs got too close a few years back and a sympathizer got a hold of his blood for us. I asked for Yves' help getting rid of him, and—"

Remy's on his feet and out the door before Idrian can finish, chest aching, but his palms are clean of ash and honey. When his hand goes to his sternum, there's nothing except the pendant to wrap his fingers around.

One of the Chancellor's dogs. It shouldn't come as any sort of shock that Cameron is not even a footnote in Idrian's story, merely an animal inconvenience.

Remy supports himself against the wall outside the door as something burns through him. It's anger, and it's grief, and it's a brand-new horror, and it has nowhere at all to go.

Some of the stray cats back home lash out with teeth and claws, the only way they know to protect themselves. At least Yves killed for the sake of a *planet*. Remy didn't even do it to preserve the living. He'll become a murderer in the memory of the dead. He's sick because he can't be angry and angry at how sick he feels, how small.

He passes people in the halls. Hollow people, tear-streaked.

He wants to scream, to grab anyone who will listen and drag them to his home, under the cool shade trees and the feathered ferns that grow thick beneath them, and show them the places where Cameron planted flowers that have thrived even though he no longer lives to tend them. He'll show them those ugly rainboots and the keys he always lost, the bouquets he drew on the walls. The trees that have grown to shelter the house. The houseplants that died with him.

He needs these people to know, with a desperation that expands like an explosion in his chest, that Cameron was generous with his affection, that his arms were warm and Remy never felt anything but safe inside them. He was so damn patient, too. He'd sit with Remy for hours and help him with schoolwork or tell him stories, even though he must have been exhausted after a full day at work. Sometimes they'd just work together, until Remy fell asleep against Cam's back, or Cam fell asleep on his paperwork and drooled on the table.

For their survival, these people took the life of an artist, a friend, a gardener. A *brother*. Someone who thought even a witherer's hands were for healing. Remy needs them to understand that he was barely fourteen the day he held his brother's body and begged him to wake.

How many of the children here will even survive to fourteen? Something bubbles up Remy's throat. When it comes out, it sounds like a laugh, but Remy's cheeks are wet.

Block D bears a fresh red X, still dripping, over its closed door.

It's like Lara with her rotten tether: Remy can't hate these people because he understands them. And it's so much worse, so much harder like this. His next breath chokes in his throat. The pain from his own frayed bond claws between his ribs, and he leans against a cold metal wall, pressing his hands to his eyes until color bursts behind the lids. He sucks in slow breaths, and when that doesn't work, he lets this place's flimsy gravity guide him to the ground where he shoves his head between his knees.

There, the sounds of Alta are dimmed, the darkness nearly complete. He takes in the honeycomb grate of the floor that Idrian's sister thought was so lovely and follows the neat corners of each hexagon until he can breathe again.

"Remy."

He opens his eyes to find Idrian, one hand self-consciously half extended.

"What."

"I meant to come tell you it was a bad idea to go running around but seems like you figured it out. Come on back. You die in the hallways, you'll just give Yves more work to do."

Remy doesn't say anything, but he stands.

They make it back to the infirmary, and Idrian directs him to a cot and then plops down on the one beside it after kicking it a few steps closer to Remy's.

"If it makes any difference, I'm sorry," Idrian says.

"For what?"

"I was an asshole when we picked you up. In there, today, the way you worked—I get why we're fatebound. I won't mind dying with you, if that's how this whole thing has to end."

"Maybe it isn't." Maybe the chain can break with him.

After a while, Idrian says, "Can I tell you a funny story?"

"I doubt we have the same sense of humor."

Idrian clearly doesn't care. He lifts an arm and spreads his hand in front of his face. "When I was a kid, I only ever really looked at my sister's and my own, so I used to think everyone's nailbeds were blue."

"That's messed up."

"Ha! Isn't it?" Idrian lets the arm fall over his face. "I've done everything I can to keep this place alive, to make sure everyone has one breath longer to live. I don't regret what I've done to make it happen."

Remy looks away, but his eyes only fall on ghost-lace and Yves' piles of books.

"I've bled for it. My *crew* has bled for it. I've killed for it. Jacques was a good kid, but the things he could have told them about our methods, our routes, our names and families . . . I didn't even think about it, I just acted." Idrian's bloody fist clenches in the cot's white sheets. "Like I did on Veida. I didn't mean for it to happen, but we needed the water, and I miscalculated, took more than the island could bear. It'd be nice if I could at least believe I were doing good, but the more I do, the more they die."

"That's not true."

"It is." Idrian turns to Remy, expression haunted. Without his sunglasses, he doesn't look anything like the childhood hero Remy so adored. He doesn't even look like a hardened criminal. How old can he possibly be? He has, what, a handful of years on Remy? Twenty-something, for sure. He can't be much older than Cam was, at the end. "You were a good student down there, I'll bet. How many years were the Isles occupied before everyone went back to Verdine?"

Jules Arbeaux

He wasn't *that* great a student. At one time, he learned precisely how long, to the day, the surviving Verdinians lived on the Isles. "A couple hundred, maybe?"

"Close. Two hundred and twenty-one. S'been a hundred more since they came down. How long you suppose these things were meant to last?"

A shiver runs through Remy.

"Not this long. I can't—I'm Roca's friend before I'm her captain, but she believes in me. They all do. These people think I can make something better than what I knew when I lived here. But the more I do, the more people I keep alive. The more who survive, the higher the population. The higher the population, the heavier the burden on every system. We've got engineers and scientists and skilled laborers for as long as they last, but there's only so many fixes they can concoct, and only so many supplies I can get my hands on to implement them. When I was little, one or two in every ten people would die between shipments. New arrivals kept things steady. I've cut that down to maybe 4%. Alta's got a higher population than ever. More than it can bear. That's the funny part. By keeping people alive and as happy as they can be on this rotten rock, *I'm making it faster*. Even if we survive this curse, there'll come a day when nothing I do will keep 'em alive."

"Why not bring them to the surface?"

"We tried, took as many as the ship could carry to an isolated fringe island. Should've worked. No idea how they tracked us, but those people were hunted. The *lucky* ones ended up back here. It hurt a lot of them, too, going back. The lower gravity here does things to you—to your muscles. Your bones." He gestures to his arms, to the hands he couldn't open to hold the hemostatic spray. "I've been away from the Isles for years and the ribbing in my coat is shock-absorbent, but they still break easy as anything. Some of the kids here wouldn't even be able to *walk* on the surface. The

Chancellor has the resources to help everyone adapt, but me? The stuff they'd need—I don't even know it, probably couldn't steal it if I did."

Remy squeezes his burning eyes closed. "Liar. That wasn't a funny story."

"Guess it wasn't." Idrian's arm goes back over his eyes, heavy like he can no longer lift it. "I don't know what to do anymore to keep them safe."

One life has weighed heavy enough on Remy. No one should have to shoulder the weight of three whole moons. Not even Idrian Delaciel. Loss made a knife of Remy, but it's made a tourniquet of Idrian—stemming the flow of blood only to kill the limb he seeks to save.

Remy bites his lip and buries his face in the pillow.

Bastard.

Remy can't let him die now. He can't let any of them die.

Slow, rhythmic breaths tell him Idrian has fallen asleep, and he creeps up from the cot and finds his way to Yves' desk again.

His eyes burn, jaw cracking with a yawn. It feels like weeks have passed since he left Auni this morning, but there's no time for rest, not with the withering already—impossibly—at his wrist. It shouldn't be advancing so quickly, not with so many people to share the burden with. Something's wrong. It should be going slower than Cam's, not faster.

In the back of the drawer, behind the supplies, there's a notebook. Remy pulls out the tin of ashes (terribly light—Yves' supply is nearly exhausted) and the supply containers and drops them on the desk. There's an emesis basin (blessedly clean) in front of the book. Remy supposes if you can't get your hands on a raw crystal bowl, any old thing will do.

He extracts the book, then examines the desk. First, he skims the titles of the books on either side of the plants. Half, at least, are aged copies of medical textbooks. But there are others. One book, out of place, bears the title: *On the Manipulation of Tethers*. A few others sit beside it, unmarked and hand-bound, with slips of paper or gauze marking pages. Remy adds them to the pile.

His knowledge of withering is functional, at best. His mother left behind one thin volume and a generations-old journal. She had only an academic interest in her ability. She was a Canta—she didn't need to sell severings to earn cash or perform witherings to take lives; perhaps she never even lost someone whose ash she could have used to perform them.

But here's someone who *clearly* has more than an academic interest.

Remy shoves the bottles and ash away to spread the textbook open. After a preface and basic introduction to tether theory, the chapter headings are fascinating: *On the long-term effectiveness of severing. On tri-tethers. On medically-assisted attenuation of rotbonds. On grief treatment by false-bonding.* In that last section, there's a diagram of a witherer tying two orphan tethers together. Remy shudders and tries to imagine tying himself to Lara's orphan tether. Even the thought feels obscene. There are days when he'd give almost anything to have someone living at the other end of Cam's tether, but it wouldn't be the same if it weren't *him*. Remy slaps the cover closed and grabs what looks like a personal notebook.

On the first page is a song. It's not one Remy's heard, but that hardly matters. The lyrics fill the first three pages of the book, and nearly every line has been crossed out. Cam's is not the only withering Yves has done for the sake of the Isles.

For all their organization in other aspects, Yves' personal notes on withering are a mess. On one page, Remy sees a circle with the word *Alterations?* At the center. Probably twenty or thirty lines branch off from the circle at different lengths, and at the end of each line are tiny, spidery lines of text. One reads, *fluids other than blood effective, yes or no? [undetermined]*. The next says, *failure to use fresh ghost-lace debilitates not kills [confirmed]*. Another, underlined, asserts, *use of witherer's bone marrow speeds and intensifies curse—pain for pain [Elyse, 226]?*

Remy's hands tremble over the paper.

There's so *much*. The following pages contain extensive notes on different additives and their effects on symptoms and progression, each with bracketed citations and notes on various levels of certainty. They are, without exception, ways to make a withering faster and more efficient (and, in one or two chilling notes that cite "Elyse" again and require self-mutilation on the witherer's part, unimaginably gruesome).

Remy doesn't see a single way to lessen or stop one.

But if one extreme exists, the other must, too. A quick skim of another journal—ancient and leather-bound, authored by Yves' oft-cited Elyse Matlacke—reveals "recipes," penned in a sweetly curling blue script, for hundreds of flavors of slow death.

At the bottom of one page, a note surrounded by delicate drawings of smiling mouths details a method by which a witherer can ensure the withered's teeth fall out one by one before death. It involves the witherer tearing one of their own out during the ritual and packing the hole with ghost-lace and ash—which can't be sanitary.

Pain for pain.

He's so engrossed in the books that he doesn't hear the infirmary's door whisper open. Doesn't hear someone entering, until Yves' cold voice falls on him from behind.

"What do you think you're doing?"

Chapter Eleven

Where all have homes and room to roam
and each man's ever free
to live and love and thrive uncaged—
Our planet rich: Verdine.

— Fragment from the Verdinian anthem

Remy jumps as Yves' hand lands on his shoulder.

"I didn't think I'd need to tell someone as cultured as you clearly are that it's rude to invade other people's privacy." They don't raise their voice, but that doesn't make it a drop less dangerous.

Yves snatches the tipped-sideways tin of ash from the table and pulls the drawer open, tucking it back in without breaking eye contact.

Shame burns up Remy's throat.

Whoever's ashes are in that tin, they're loved more than life. A witherer's work requires it. "Sorry."

Yves says nothing.

It's not like Remy can wriggle his way out of this one. "Um. Roca mentioned knowing a witherer. I got a bit overenthusiastic when I realized it was you. We can stop the withering, right? It hasn't advanced too far yet."

Yves picks up the little jar and gently rolls it. The baby tooth clinks against the glass. "That's not how witherings work."

He pulls at Elyse Matlacke's book of murder recipes. "But there are so many ways to make it worse. There has to be a way to reverse it!"

Idrian mutters something and shifts on the bed.

"*Quiet.*" Yves' hand closes on the back of Remy's chair. "Maybe there is, but I've read every text on withering I can get my hands on, legally or otherwise, and I've never heard of anything like that. Suppose you're right, though. We'd *still* need the witherer who started this. Everything hinges on intent; how willing do you suppose that witherer will be to undo their hard work?" Yves growls and shakes their head. "Believe me, it's been on my mind."

Yves spins Remy out of the way and grabs the emesis basin.

Remy can't help smiling. "Nice substitution, by the way."

Yves smirks. "I make it work." Then they pause, basin halfway to the drawer. "Substitution?"

"It's not exactly raw crystal."

Yves doesn't chuckle.

Silence grows like a living thing between them.

"I don't have any notes about crystal."

The speed with which the blood flees Remy's face leaves his lips numb.

Yves steps up, caging Remy against the back of the chair. "I *have* heard about it, though. It's an old clarification method. I knew someone who knew someone who let me examine some of the rare books in Astoria's library. I haven't tried it myself, obviously. Didn't have the luxury. You'll forgive me for wondering how you're so well-informed."

He swallows and resists the urge to lick his bone-dry lips. "My m-mother was a witherer," he blurts.

It's stupid. It's *true*, but he should've come up with someone else. A friend. A great-great-grandfather. A morbid fascination with tethers and how they're formed and broken. He could've even used Tirani as an excuse. Folks talk about her skills and Remy's in the same breath. It's not implausible to make the leap from learning about weavers to learning about witherers. His *mom*. How stupid.

Yves' expression is all polite curiosity, but Remy doesn't believe it for an instant. "How fascinating. Withering's often a family trait. My great-aunt was the last before me."

"Yeah, usually skips a generation." Clearly the way to get himself out of a hastily made excuse is to talk more. Oh, he's so fucked. "From what I've been told, Mom didn't like it much. I don't think she ever even tested it out. Apparently, the weaver she visited with my dad to ask about their relationship took one look at her tethers and recognized her for a witherer. I guess they're like . . . super-saturated? Or washed-out, or something?"

Shit. Great work, skirting Yves' suspicions by generously reminding them—just in case it wasn't already at the forefront of their mind—of the way to expose him. Tirani can't be used against Remy to identify him. Her connection to him makes all his tethers look colorless to her. But any other person with her unique vision could.

Thankfully, that's not the detail Yves chooses to fixate on.

"Ah, yes, I forgot. Everything's perfect on the surface. How nice, that a witherer would never even have to exercise her skills. Your mother is a lucky woman."

They throw the books one on top of the next, with thuds like punches.

"She was." Bile churns in Remy's stomach.

His mom *was* lucky, to never have to think of her inherited ability as anything other than a creepy fact she might pull out to liven up a conversation at a dinner party. To never even be *able* to use them—to never lose someone she loved and pay for her skills with their ashes. How strange, that Remy has more in common with Yves than with his own mother.

Yves shoves the books back where they were, a tight fit that bruises the ghost-lace leaves dangling over the edges of the pot.

"I'm not like your mother," they say, pale gaze seizing Remy's. Slowly, they lean back from where they've cast Remy in their shadow. "I've killed to protect the people in my care and I'd do it again."

Remy nods, speechless.

Yves looks away, and Remy tries not to breathe a sigh of relief.

With a quick huff, Yves banishes a ghost-lace bloom that broke off and straightens a stack of paper with sharp, efficient motions. They move to the glass cabinet stocked with gauze and bottles, pulling out an ampoule and several clean syringes. "I came for this. There are more than a few people in need of artificial calm." A sigh. "Myself included, but there's no rest for the weary."

"Uh . . . can I help?"

Yves blinks in his direction. Their casual reply is, "Who's Cam?"

Remy loses all his breath at once. "What?"

"You kept saying that name, back in Block D."

Remy forces his face to what he hopes is some semblance of calm, but it hardly feels like it's his mouth saying, "Did I? Must have been confused."

"You were a mess, I'll give you that." They grab a few more things from the cabinet and drop them into a handheld carrying case they pull from the wall. "Far be it from me to refuse an offer of help. Walk with me."

Mechanically, Remy finds his feet and follows.

Yves makes it out the door before frustration sweeps over their face. "Damn it! I forgot something." They hook an arm around the corner. "That way. Go on ahead. I'll catch up."

Remy walks in the direction Yves indicated until it breaks at a fork. There, he stops. He starts to scrub his hands over his face before he pulls back with a hiss. The spray stopped the bleeding, yes, but without the pain-dulling help of adrenaline, the pain hits him hard. The gauze he wrapped around them shows red at the corner where he probably just tore something open.

Footsteps in the hall slow as they approach, and Yves stops beside him.

"Let me see your hands."

Remy extends them.

"Terribly wrapped. Did you wash and disinfect?"

"A little?"

Yves sighs. "I'll have to go over it all again later. You got debris in the wounds. Your hands need to be thoroughly cleaned. Remind me when we get back." They hiss at the sight of Remy's withering, flicking at the line of it in the center of his wrist. "It wasn't there earlier."

Remy's stomach twists at the reminder. "No. It's going too fast. I don't know why—"

"Don't you? You've all been throwing yourselves face first into disaster. Every wound is a foothold for a withering, and you've given it hundreds. They take weeks on the *healthy*, and I wouldn't call any of you healthy." They release his hand. "It hardly matters. We do what we can with what we have. I grabbed topical analgesic for if your hands bother you too much."

"Why?"

Yves blinks. "Why analgesic? Well, you see, Greenie, when something hurts very *very* much—"

"No, I mean . . . why help?"

They gesture at their not-so-white coat. "Part of the job description."

Remy chooses not to remind them they're not a qualified doctor. Instead, dumbly, he offers, "You said you hated me."

"I did, didn't I?" A gentle push on his shoulder sets him moving down the path to the right. "It would be nice if I could. Anger and hate are simple—they create uncomplicated binaries. They feel *righteous*, give you something to do, put you above the object of your hate. Jealousy just makes you sick."

The dim hallway blurs past until Yves speaks again.

"I'm so damn tired of feeling sick, but you might've also noticed I'm not a fan of binaries. They tend to oversimplify things. Even you're more complex than I gave you credit for, Greenie."

"I have a name."

Yves looks at their feet. Something glints in their hair as they pass under a light, and Remy's stomach flips. They're still wearing the pink and lime-green clip Beni loaned them. Barely audible, Yves says, "Remy."

He nods.

"You did good in there today."

When he closes his eyes, though, he sees only the outlines of the bodies piled against the walls. The old couple silent in their beds, indicators screaming red. The unspeakable weight of the dead in his arms. "Not good enough."

"Depends who you ask. That baby's alive because of you. His mom made it, too, in case you were wondering."

Remy remembers the baby's soft skull against his hand, the way his mother begged for his life with what could have been her last breath. When he manages to speak, it comes out raw. "Good."

"*That's* why I'll treat your hands. Later. I'll make use of them now."

They end up in a massive, wide-open room. Long tables have been lifted away and stacked in the back, near what looks like a darkened kitchen. The room still smells just a little like food, and Remy recalls the promise of a "feast" when Idrian arrived with his supplies. It probably wouldn't have been anything like how Remy imagines a feast to be, but now, it seems, the feast is not to happen at all. Instead, the floor-space has been cleared to allow for rows of bodies. Only some are sheet-covered. Only some have their eyes closed. Only some are even body-sized. Too many are terribly small.

Yves slows as they walk between the rows, toward a door at the back. "It's a crime against sanitation, but we don't have another accessible room large enough for this."

Remy looks away when his eyes catch on a tiny, sheet-covered body with a dirty paper rose on it. "How many made it?"

"Right now? About thirty." Yves isn't looking now, either, eyes aimed at a door at the back of the cafeteria.

"Thirty." Remy doesn't ask how many were in Block D, doesn't need to. There were this many.

But as if Yves knows what he's thinking, they say, "There were 283 people in Block D. I haven't had time to do a count—it's possible that a few more were visiting friends or lovers and survived. Beni's brother was playing with some friends a block over and that's what saved him. Most of the survivors were close to the door and receiving some small amount of air. No one in the back rooms survived."

They push through another set of doors and arrive in what might be an extended dining room—smaller than the main cafeteria but likewise spacious. The tables haven't been moved from this one, and there's sound. The baby Remy pulled through the gaps suckles its tired mother's breast between whimpers. Two people hold each other in the back and talk, haunted and slow. Thirty, Yves said. Remy doesn't bother to count.

People in orange vests flit among them, administering or withdrawing oxygen.

Yves finds a boy first. Pale and freckled—Beni's brother.

He rocks back against the wall, face tear-streaked. Yves leans down and pats his knee, but he doesn't respond.

"Hey, shhh. I'm here. Can you look at me?"

It sounds awkward until Remy realizes what's missing.

If Remy were offering the same comfort, he'd punctuate it with a hundred *it's all rights*, and *it'll be okays*. Here, it'd be too obvious for a lie.

Yves pulls a small amount of fluid into the syringe they brought. "Patrice? I'm going to give you something that will help you rest."

Patrice doesn't answer, just hugs his knees like he's holding someone.

Yves gentles him with soft noises while pushing the meager contents of the syringe into his arm. He goes an awful sort of pliant, chin resting on his knees. Tears still chase each other down his cheeks.

Yves stands, supporting themself on the table behind them, and Remy follows behind as they start walking again.

"How can I help?"

"Just follow me."

They go to the mother and baby next.

Remy sits at the table while they treat the mother, who grabs Remy's hands and presses her face against them, breathing tired thanks into his bandaged skin. Remy waits, frozen, until she lets go, and Yves smiles.

When they move to the next person—one of the ones who recovered enough to assist with rescue—Remy helps put bandages on. Some knotted up thing inside him loosens at the sight of these people. The wounded skin he tends with Yves is warm and still has the ability to heal.

Between patients, Yves tells him, "The ones who survived are here because of you and Idrian. The time it took the hydraulics to arrive would've killed them."

Remy applies salve to tiny scrapes and talks to the survivors while Yves cleans and wraps more severe injuries and administers sedative to anyone else who needs it. It settles, as Remy uses his hands, for once, to heal, that Yves did not need an assistant. They did this for him.

Fingers locked around a roll of gauze, Remy whispers, "Thank you."

Yves nods without speaking.

Remy can't know if they would have said anything, because an earsplitting alarm kicks up, and all the sweet calmness swirling through Remy vanishes. "Is it—?"

Yves, face twisted in confusion, shakes their head. "That's the approach alert."

They race from the room and down the hall, Remy following behind. Finally, they burst into a small room filled with monitors.

A young woman with buzzed-short hair sits inside. "It's early," she mutters, confused.

The screens display, from every possible angle, an approaching ship. This one, unlike Idrian's, bears the Chancellor's seal and the mark of the OSS emblazoned on the side.

"Four days early," Yves mutters. "They're never early."

It seems like years ago that Yves told Remy about the dangerously-spaced deliveries. "Supplies?"

"We'll see."

The woman in front of the monitors, bulky headset in ear, is already picking up a small device to order someone on the other end to prepare for docking.

Yves and Remy step out into the hall, and the news must have reached everyone else already, because they flow through the halls with an energy Remy hasn't seen in anyone since they arrived. He's swept up in the crowd and pulled along, and Yves watches, expression conflicted, until they disappear around a corner.

∼

The crowd carries him, their flow as inexorable as the snatch of a strong undertow, their joy a living thing.

Someone Remy has never met smiles at him and pats his back. "Just wait. It's gonna be amazing," he says. "Boxes for *days*. You've never seen anything like it!"

Remy has, though: on the OSS, shelves running farther than his mind can fathom and ceilings higher than the stars. If they delivered even a fraction of the supplies rotting on the OSS, the Isles would be set for life.

Someone at the head of the group taps in a quick code, and the airlock between Alta and the docked ship performs a quick set of checks and then hisses open. The short hallway beyond the door glows silvery-clean and new, so bright it burns Remy's eyes.

The crowd walks forward blind, past row after row of sterile white lights embedded in the walls, and, finally, to the wide-open cargo bay.

Remy hears it before he sees it. The joyous motion of the crowd stops, a held breath released, like a stone dropped in water—and then, rippling through the crowd:

"What?" someone says, hollow with horror.

Another says, "No."

Remy blinks hard, squinting to see what everyone's upset about, but he finds nothing.

That's the problem.

In the center of the wide-open cargo bay, a few piles of boxes wait, stacked around an unmanned tower with a blinking console.

It's not an insignificant number of boxes, but in this huge, echoing space, it seems cruel and cold and very small. Remy walks to the glowing console while the others rush to the boxes, pulling them down to look inside.

A note sits on the keyboard, typed.

Dissidence has consequences.

Then, in blocky letters underneath, **accept the broadcast.**

A prompt line sits blinking on the screen, sky blue and innocuous on a black background. **PLAY RECORDING?**

The group gathers behind Remy.

"Play it," a man says, rough.

Remy selects **YES.**

Another prompt fills the screen. **UNIVERSAL BROADCAST PERMISSIONS REQUESTED. CONFIRM.**

"What is this?" someone yells from the back. "Where's the fucking food?"

Others join the chorus. The group fragments.

"We'll get it from 'em," someone growls. Before Remy can stop them, they stalk to the back of the room and beat against the door, pressing at the unresponsive keypad.

A calm voice flows through the speaker on the walls. "Play the broadcast. We attempted to auto-broadcast but were denied access. Please know, in the future, that this is unacceptable."

"This place is ours!" someone cries. "You have no right."

"The Protectorate governs all with peace. Accept the broadcast."

But someone has picked up one of the metal boxes and is using its brutally sharp edge against the door. When that yields only ugly dents, they bash it into the keypad. Now, the voice comes from a speaker somewhere overhead. "This vessel is property of the Chancellor and any attack upon it will be considered violent resistance. Cease your actions at once."

Lord of the Empty Isles

Who could cease, when over 200 bodies rest on the floor of the cafeteria that was supposed to prepare a feast?

The keypad is nothing more than a hole in the wall, destroyed circuitry spitting sparks. Someone picks up a can and throws it—with remarkable accuracy—at a light. The voice returns, just as calm. "Cease, or we will respond with force. Permit the broadcast."

Ignored. Something else shatters. A woman, face twisted with grief, uses a can to crack what looks like a camera.

The screen still blinks, gentle as the Chancellor has ever been to Remy. **CONFIRM**, it says.

It's not a request. There's no **NO** on this page.

Remy reaches out to confirm, but someone else pushes in. "If they're asking for universal broadcast privileges, only me or Shaia can do that. It'll be a non-optional announcement simultaneously played across all screens on the Isles and in any vessels nearby." The man chuckles. "And they wonder why we deny them."

The man, face set and grim, presses **CONFIRM** and then types in a dizzying string of numbers and letters and symbols too fast for Remy to discern.

RETYPE TO CONFIRM, the screen prompts.

Glass skitters over the metal floor as something else shatters.

The gentle voice doesn't issue from the ceiling again with either threat or promise.

Instead, the door with the sparking keypad opens once—a rapid, perfect whoosh, revealing an armored soldier. He looses a spate of bullets into the crowd and then steps back. The door closes. Quick as that.

The woman who broke the camera takes at least three of the bullets, driven back into the man behind her. Her expression as she falls is one of polite surprise. When she hits the ground, she doesn't rise.

I know this time of year is hard for you, the Chancellor said to Remy what feels like years ago.

The voice from the ceiling speaks again. This time it makes no threat. "Cease," it says. So much like CONFIRM.

The man retypes his code with trembling fingers that clench into a fist as soon as he's done.

As soon as he confirms, a massive screen flicks to life on the ceiling overhead, a magnified copy of what plays out on the smaller screen in front of them.

The screen overhead breathes with green. Remy had almost forgotten what it looked like. Trees rustle outside a window in a gentle wind, heavy with veiny, yellow-green apples and wrapped in ribbons for the Resurrection Festival. Remy can almost smell the orchard, the sweetness of apple blossoms and the sugary tartness of their fruit. Apples on every tree, and despite the best efforts of the Chancellor to gather and distribute them, hundreds rotting on the ground.

A gasp sweeps through the crowd, horrified and hungry.

In front of the window sits a long, polished wooden desk, marked at both ends with pots overflowing with a profusion of variegated, waxy leaves in purple and yellow-gold. It seems cruel. The Chancellor usually records his most casual broadcasts from this desk. His more serious ones, he saves for the armchair in the corner of his room, the one with the pre-ascension painting of a dying Verdine on the wall behind it—a skeletal wasteland against a flaming sunset.

Remy sat at that desk, once. He visited with Cameron and melted into the luxurious high-backed chair upholstered in rich lavender fabric and studded with gold buttons. He spun until he was dizzy.

The Chancellor sits in it now, wearing a gentle expression of paternal disappointment.

His hair is clean and brushed, peppered with gray. Instead of a suit, he wears a white shirt with a stiff, laced collar, sleeves unbuttoned and folded up, like this is a conversation between friends.

Remy aches with the urge to do what he's done since he was a boy. The slight bow. A closed fist behind his back for preservation. Open hand over the heart for progress.

Does the Chancellor think this is progress?

"Dissidence has consequences," the Chancellor begins, voice sonorous and warm. His lips quirk in a secret smile, like this is a shared joke. He pauses for a little stretch of time. Scripted perfection. Perhaps this is where they should laugh.

Instead, the silence reveals these sounds: someone holds the fallen woman's body and weeps, hoarse and graceless. Someone pleads for a bleeding teenager to *hold still, damn it, stop wriggling, I've got you.*

The Chancellor folds his hands before he continues speaking. Remy can't find the seams in his warm, open expression. "I suppose you probably know that. If you're listening, you've failed once to treat your environment with the respect it deserves, which has led to your current state of residence."

Curses greet this pronouncement.

"It has become clear to me that you've failed, yet again, to learn from your mistakes. The supplies I send to keep you all well, despite your unwillingness to do the same for the planet and people who nurtured you from birth, are a kindness which can be withdrawn—a drain on precious resources. I have overlooked many things in the past, out of a desire for peace."

Hands and torso smeared with the woman's blood, the person holding her cries, "You call this peace?"

But the Chancellor didn't script a pause for anyone's grief. "Andrew, if you would."

Someone steps into the frame, fitted suit ill-at-ease on his lanky form, though he hides it well enough to anyone who hasn't spent a lifetime in his company. Andrew Delacour looks handsome and put-together, hair combed back in a way it never is. Remy almost laughs, but his eyes, instead, find the one thing at odds with his professional image. Andrew wears his small, gunmetal-gray and red pendant over his suit, its form like a clenched fist or a beating heart. Remy's hand immediately goes to his own chest, where Cameron's identical pendant hangs over where the now-decaying tether once bound them, hidden by his tunic.

Andrew touches the pendant, quick and nervous, before he speaks. "It has come to our attention that the wanted criminal Idrian Delaciel infiltrated the Orbital Supply Station and, after stealing a portion of its supplies and severely damaging its backup fuel tank, murdered at least two of the dedicated young workers aboard it."

Remy's stomach is hollow, his mouth dry. He did this. *He's* the one that brought it to their attention. 8-8-4-1-2. He wishes he could take it back.

The screen flashes with the faces of the dead. Remy recognizes Jacques. He couldn't distinguish anything meaningful of the bloodied body at Roca's feet when he saw it, though, so the young, slightly soft face of a man with a lopsided smile and curly brown hair takes him aback.

"Furthermore, two beloved citizens of the capital have been reported missing, and witness reports put Idrian Delaciel in the place they were last recorded." Here, Andrew's voice breaks, and he clears his throat and lifts his chin. "We have reason to be concerned for their lives."

More photos. Remy, now—younger than he ever recalls being, smiling at someone. *Cameron* took that photo. Then Tirani, expression gentle.

"What the *fuck*," Remy says. "That's *bullshit!*"

Andrew *knows* why he had to leave. Except—

Remy goes cold.

Andrew doesn't. He knows Remy left and that's it. He doesn't know Remy found himself fatebound to Idrian and cursed alongside him. Doesn't know he had to join him to survive. All he knows is that Remy disappeared. Remy's stomach lurches. And that, just after, he used the number Andrew gave him to send out a call for help on the OSS. What did Remy expect him to assume?

Some buzz of noise swells behind him, and then what follows is a perfect and unnatural hush as the crowd parts. There's warmth at his side, and Remy looks up.

Idrian stands beside him, looking up at the screen. His arms hang at his sides, the blood tacky now as, on the screen, Andrew takes a deep breath and looks at the ground.

The Chancellor shares in his silence.

It's like theater.

"Take your time," The Chancellor says, expression benevolent as bodies bleed out beneath his gentle smile.

Andrew nods and clears his throat again, lifting a piece of cream-colored paper. Remy can't see the words, but he doesn't have to. Andrew begins to speak.

"For years, for the safety and wellbeing of everyone on the surface of our Verdine, I have remained silent on a matter of some importance. Many people know of Alister Delacour, who faithfully served as Minister of the Environment on the Preservation Committee until his untimely death. The story we told, so as not to cause unnecessary fear or public disturbance, was that his death was natural, though unexpected. I admit, now, to my lie. We have since sealed the gaps in our security that allowed it to happen, but to my shame as Vice-Enforcer, we failed to protect our own. Alister Delacour, my father—" Here he pauses. There is no calculated grace to the way his face flushes and his wet eyes blink too fast. Nothing at all beautiful or practiced in it, and Remy aches. "My father was murdered. I can't even comfort myself that his death was quick. By all indications, it was not. He loved his family, loved this *city*, loved the world we've all helped nourish together. Idrian Delaciel was the one who killed him."

He pauses to clear his throat. The paper in his hands falls, and he's looking directly at the screen. At Remy. "My father wasn't the only victim of Delaciel's violence, either. My close friend, the former Intermediary—youngest to ever inherit the position upon the retirement of his predecessor—was investigating a string of thefts when he got in Delaciel's way and was killed for it. *I* was the one who brought the investigation to his attention, the one who encouraged him to pursue it, and I watched as he died. He was only twenty-five." Andrew will turn twenty-five this year.

"Liar! Bastards!" Someone throws something that doesn't even get halfway to the ceiling before falling back down.

The crowd behind them erupts in disbelieving cries.

Andrew's voice fills the room. "I was helpless as a boy when my father died, and helpless as a young Enforcer when I delivered to my friend the investigation that took his life. I won't be helpless again."

Remy sees only Idrian: so still he barely seems to be breathing.

The expression on his bloodless face is a thing apart from rage. It's like just before Idrian pulled the trigger on Jacques, except it's infinitely colder, and it's directed wholly at Andrew. If he were here, Andrew would certainly be dead.

Instead, Andrew takes a deep breath and speaks again, raising the paper. "Now two more innocents are dead, and I cannot stand by and wait for more to die. Thus, with the authority vested in me by the Chancellor and the people of Verdine, I announce and will enforce the Chancellor's edict: Idrian and all who consort with him are now named enemies of Verdine. The full force of the city will be dispatched to apprehend them. All will be executed."

A pause, and Andrew lifts his eyes from the paper. "Alta, Fluora, and Toxys. Though your mistakes have separated you from us, you are our sisters and we would have you stand among us again. Renounce your connection to and protection of this criminal, or face the consequences of your dissidence. Your supplies have been reduced by 80%. We expect you will learn a hard lesson from this, but a valuable one. If you are found to be sheltering or associating with these criminals henceforth, your next warning will not be so kind."

The screen flicks black. Gentle, ocean-blue text reads, **END TRANSMISSION.**

Idrian stands still and pale in the aftermath, face lifted to the empty screen, hair partially loose from the blue ribbon that ties it and falling across his eyes. His hands are knotted into fists at his sides, stance unbalanced. Fresh blood drips to the ground with eerie, steady taps.

"Hey," Remy whispers, stomach twisting at how lost he looks. "Pretty sure you shouldn't be out of bed. You okay?"

Idrian doesn't answer.

Everyone else begins to file out. The person with the dead woman begins to pull her across the floor. The people with the dollies silently load stacks of boxes and, in so few trips a man even walks away with an empty cart, they clear out the boxes. Idrian remains.

"Hey," Remy taps at Idrian's shoulder. "Aren't you the one who told me we'd just be making more work for Yves if—"

As if Remy's touch was some sort of terrible signal, Idrian crumples.

"Shit. Idrian!"

Remy's clumsy attempt to stop him from falling fails, and Idrian hits the floor on his side. Remy hooks his wounded hands under Idrian's back and tries to lift him, but a piece of sharp debris grinds in his wounds and he pulls back, bandages reddening.

Someone strides into the room with a rumbling growl, dark curls swaying. "I wasn't even gone that long!" Roca cries, edging past the stragglers. Thom paces in behind her. Remy notices Emil last. He lifts one hand in a lazy wave. Remy's stomach sinks. Tirani isn't with them. "How did he get like this?"

Remy's lips part while Roca kneels to examine Idrian's wounds, but he can't bring words to his lips. Where can he possibly start?

Roca waves down the man with the empty dolly. "Bring that thing back! We need it."

The man obeys, but another voice stops everyone in their tracks, cold with authority.

"Do *not* pull him by his arms."

Yves.

Thom leans over to grab their hand, running a thumb over the partnership tattoo and between their knuckles. They share a look that says Thom has plenty of questions, but he lets go so he can get to work. Between the three of them, Roca and Thom and Emil make quick work of lifting Idrian at the torso and knees to get him onto the cart. He's already waking as they do it.

He slurs, "'M fine, lemme up."

"Oh, is this what you call fine?"

"Jus' needed a nap. 'M good now."

"I will *tie you to this cart*," Roca says primly.

"Couldn't sleep," Idrian tells her, bloody hand filthying her sleeve as he reaches for her. "Too quiet."

"I know." Roca gently pushes him down onto the cart. "I'm here. Get some rest, you crazy bastard."

"Bring him back to the infirmary," Yves says. "And *keep him there*. We'll catch up."

Remy means to ask where Tirani is, but Roca and the others file out before he can. Whoever had the woman's body is gone now, too, the only evidence of their passage a thick, uninterrupted line of red.

"You tore your hands open again," Yves says, flat. "I'd hoped the newest members of Idrian's crew might bring some common sense to the group, but it seems that a prerequisite of being fate-bound to Idrian Delaciel is having no fucking self-preservation instincts."

Idrian's crew.

It feels wrong, now, for an entirely different reason. Remy doesn't tell Yves that he has plenty decent self-preservation instincts. After all, he originally planned to free only himself from the withering, with no thought for what happened to the others. "I forgot," is what he manages to push past his dry lips. "Sorry."

"Don't apologize to me, you idiot," Yves snips.

Remy shuts his mouth, guilt stirring in him. That irritated tone, the brutal endearment—it's the same one they use with Thomlin and Idrian. *Sorry* sits again on his lips. He gestures to the place where Idrian collapsed. "What happened?"

"What *didn't*? If I know him—and I do know him—he hasn't slept well, if at all, in the days leading up to his little supply run. He probably has more hairline fractures in his hands and arms than I can count from his stunt today. He bled *all* over the damn place. Probably isn't hydrated. Plus there's that wretched withering doing its work. Your guess is as good as mine as to which one made rest non-optional—though I'd wager seeing his damn half-brother all over that screen didn't help."

Remy's every thought process grinds to a halt. There were only two people on screen just now. "*Half-brother?*"

Yves stops, too. "You didn't . . .?" They lift their glasses and scrub both eyes with their palms. "Of course you didn't. *Fuck.* I need a nap. That's not my story to tell. Half of it's not even a story I know."

Idrian has always been a caricature to Remy—flyaway hair tied back with a ribbon. Blue glasses shielding canny eyes. Trench coat and cruel smile. But now—

Andrew's hair is shorter, but it's barely a shade or two off. Their eyes aren't such different shades of blue-green, their noses identical.

Andrew Delacour. Idrian Delaciel.

Andrew's words return to Remy's mind and steal his breath. *He didn't go by any last name until he killed my dad.*

Did Idrian kill his own father?

Remy gathers everything he knows of Alister Delacour and Andrew's family and comes up with nothing except Regine in a kitchen filled with the sweet heat of baking cookies, entertaining Remy at the table while Andrew stress-baked his sixth batch. Her husband had been married once before meeting her, she'd mentioned. *A tragic affair*, was what she called it.

"So he's . . ."

"Pretend I didn't say anything. If I had my wits about me, I wouldn't have." The room is empty, now. "Come on, back to the infirmary with you."

The door into the Chancellor's ship snaps closed as soon as they're through it, and the empty hallway between the ship and Alta goes dark. A second door—this one the old, brushed metal of Alta, whirs closed to block off any sight of the Chancellor's ship, and the lights on the door flick from green to blood-red, lighting Remy and Yves' path.

"Sorry. I normally wouldn't make a mistake like that," Yves says. "But I had brothers on the brain."

Before he can reply, they've spun, brutally graceful, and slammed him against the docking hall's wall hard enough to crush the air from him.

"Remy." Yves' glasses glint with red light, their eyes translucent-blue and cold behind the lenses. Their next words land like a blow: "Remy fucking *Canta*, right?"

Chapter Twelve

*Know this: a knife, in use,
scars wielder and wounded both.*

— Verdinian idiom commonly attributed to Toxys,
Verdine's first recorded witherer

"I knew for sure when I saw the broadcast. As if I needed more confirmation. You're a wretched liar."

Whatever Yves is holding pinches against Remy's neck with the sticky-slick grip of something lethally sharp. Remy can't see the blade, but from the tapered handle in Yves' hand, it's a scalpel.

"I noticed how carefully they avoided naming you and your friend. How assiduously, too, they avoided naming or showing the *'former Intermediary'*. Cameron Canta, wasn't it? It was very smooth, but I was the one who killed him, so it wasn't hard to see the seams in their story. He had a little brother, didn't he?"

Remy swallows, and the shift of his skin drags the scalpel deeper. Warmth floods down his throat. He meets Yves' eyes without blinking.

"I'd guessed the shape of it before." They twitch the hand holding the scalpel. "I didn't *only* grab analgesic when I ran back to the infirmary. I hope you didn't think I believed your sad attempts to cover your ass when you knew *far too much* about the arcane specifics of withering. The broadcast just pulled everything together."

Yves knew, then.

When they told him about hatred and binaries, when they led him through the cafeteria past that row of bodies and into the room with the thirty people he helped save, Yves had already guessed Remy was the witherer they were seeking. They withdraw the blade a fraction of an inch—enough, Remy supposes, that it won't kill him to speak.

"Did you use his ashes to curse Idrian?"

There's little point in lying. "I did."

Yves laughs, sharp and humorless. "I thought so." They sigh, and the energy goes out of their stance. "Fucking poetic justice. I've wondered about it before, when I had time to wonder. What if someone I killed became an ingredient in the withering that'd take my life?" They pull the scalpel away from his neck, holding it so he sees the line of his blood that slicks it, and drop it into a small bag. "It's worse, of course, that it's not *my* life I endangered, but everyone else's."

Putting words to it makes it feel hollow, but Remy has to say it now that there's someone he's allowed to say it to. "He used to tell me my hands weren't meant for breaking."

"He was probably right, back then." Yves steps back. "You're bleeding all over your shirt. I've just given myself more work to do."

Remy blinks. "You aren't going to kill me?"

"Remember what I said about binaries? It's never that simple." Yves' fingers skim Beni's hairclip. "Anyway, Thom's my partner, not my blood relative, so I couldn't act as proxy and kill you to end the withering even if I wanted to. One of *them* would need to do it, and I wouldn't bet on Idrian in his current state."

Silence.

"Which leaves us with this." They gesture to the bloody scalpel in their coat. "I'm sure you know I could do horribly unpleasant things to you with that blood."

Visions of toothless gums and bone marrow and slow deaths dance in Remy's head. There's so little left of their ash and so few lines remaining in their song, but he could easily imagine Yves giving up the last of it or tearing out a tooth to make him suffer. "Will you tell everyone?"

He doesn't step away from the wall.

"That depends. Did you mean it when you talked about finding ways to unravel a withering, or were you just trying to cover your ass?"

"I meant it."

"I'm not asking if you'd do it to save your hide. I'm asking if it's what you *want* to do."

"It's what Cam would've wanted me to do."

"That's no answer."

"Yes, it is."

In the blood-red glow in the hallway, Yves stares at him as if seeing him for the first time. "You're a better person than I am, Remy Canta."

"I doubt it."

"I don't." Yves finally turns and begins walking. Remy steps in beside them. "It would be hypocritical for me to blame you. In your place, I'd've done the same—I *have* done the same, and I'll do it again. I won't let you take Thom from me. I'd do worse than murder to keep him safe. I can't promise you'll survive this, but I won't tell them what I've found out just yet." Yves traces Remy's brachial artery, almost to the ball of his shoulder, the thud of Remy's pulse a cold countdown. "If you can find a way to unravel the withering without killing yourself before it gets *here*—" they press against his shoulder "—I'll keep your secret. That should give you a couple days. After that, I'll tell them what I've learned. They'd kill to protect each other, too. I'm sorry it ended up like this."

They pass from the red hallway into the dim light and thin air of Alta's interior. Yves never did cut down the amount of air his canister fed him.

"Your brother's death bought *years* of life for us by keeping Idrian free. I won't ask for forgiveness, but it wasn't personal. He was an acceptable loss."

Remy clenches his teeth. "He wasn't."

"Agree to disagree." Yves slows on the way back in front of a nondescript gray door. At their bidding, it whirs open, and Remy reels at what's inside.

Light. His eyes blur with it, yellow-warm and blinding. His vision adjusts and reveals raised platforms—six or seven of them, wide and waist-height, running the length of a vast room. Greenery curls from the platforms. Some of it is small and pale, but plenty of it is vibrant—more so than the image Remy saw of the Chancellor's office, if only by contrast.

Against the cold, brushed silver and the ice-blue blinking status lights along the walls, the greenery here is both impossible and precious. Fruit and vegetables grow, fresh and fattening, from stalks and bushes and curling, thorny vines. An older woman, hair a halo of silver against darker skin, fills a basket with red berries, patiently picking them with pricked fingers. She hums a low song to the tune of her work. The door whirs closed behind Remy, cocooning him in the light and humid heat of this room. It's the warmest he's been since he got here.

This feels like a place he could breathe in, if he dared to.

Yves nudges him forward with a hand at his back, and the nearest platform blurs past, rich with frills of frosty green and purple lettuce and emerald vines winding up a trellis at the center. "We've given up so much just for this. We spend our water and power and light in hopes of making something for ourselves—something to sustain ourselves."

Some sort of tuber sends up hardy greenery in rows at the surface, growing to spite all the ugliness in this place. Cameron would have loved it here.

The path Remy walks is well-worn. He wonders how many people walk it every day to hold onto this hope. This, here, is a hope far closer than the blinding planet through the feet-thick glass that Yves showed Remy. It's something they made for themselves.

He and Tirani made something for themselves, too. And Remy, like an idiot, tried to break it. He longs to have her here beside him with an ache like a mortal wound. She'd love this place, too. She'd know all the best ways to describe these colors.

"It'll all die," Yves says.

Remy turns without meaning to.

"Gardens need water. More than I can easily imagine. Idrian brought a respectable amount, but his deliveries are meant to supplement the Chancellor's inadequate offerings, not replace them. His water allows this place to exist. What he brought *might* last two weeks on subsistence rations for everyone, but there will be little left for this. Never mind that with each late delivery, we lose more skilled workers. One of the victims the other day was the head of our sewage reclamation team. She had apprentices, but any knowledge she hadn't imparted is lost. You don't need to understand me, Remy, but I want you to understand *this*. We don't have much, but any one of us would do worse than murder to keep it safe."

Together, they pass the second platform, and Remy's feet slow. There, against the back wall of the room, a small crowd of people stands, hands dark with some sort of soil. The platform they stand in front of is empty. A cluster of red-eyed teens bows over it, rapt, next to an older couple. There must be twenty or thirty people in here.

Yves walks ahead of him and converses in whispers with the sniffling teens before accepting a small porcelain bowl from their hands.

Yves extends it to Remy. "Want one?"

Remy doesn't know what he expects to be in the bowl, but there are only seeds. Hundreds, probably, in every size and shape and color.

"There are 251 of them in here," Yves says, voice low.

That's when Remy notices the plaques on each raised bed. They're not alphabetized. The first bed, closest to the door, bears a plaque that says X. The next says S. Then come C, I, and V. The empty bed bears no plaque, but someone has repurposed a children's writing board to scrawl the letter D.

Remy's heartbeat throbs in his throat, his eyes stinging. "This..."

"Someone counted," Yves says. "The bodies. That's how many there were. We plant a seed for each." They sweep a gesture at the platform labeled 'S' the one with the thickest growth. "It didn't start like that, but after the second block went, it just sort of... happened. It helps, watching something thrive." They push the bowl toward him again. "You should take one."

"I shouldn't."

Yves sighs. "When all the seeds are planted, anyone who comes in to remember Block D will still have plenty of work to do." Yves plucks a small fruit from a bush on the end of Platform V and shows it to him. "The work never ends when you're trying to keep something alive. You're part of the reason we don't have 283 seeds here. Just fucking take one."

Remy thinks of Beni and her wild curls and her freckles. "Are there any that flower?"

"All fruit-bearing plants flower," Yves says, deadpan.

Remy chooses a small, ridged seed, almost fluffy, and Yves turns to converse with a young man who comes up behind them.

Remy presses along the back wall, looking for space at the platform. He finds some near the end.

As he passes the murmuring visitors, he hears hitching sobs and soft songs and a girl telling the gangly older gentleman beside her that her best friend Addie lived in a room with eight people she'd never met before coming here, but you'd never have guessed from looking at them. The older man tells her his Ulrich was good at mending socks and reciting poetry from memory, and they never ran out of things to talk about.

Remy stands in front of the platform. A barren expanse of dirt or some imitation of it stretches out to both sides. He clenches the seed in his palm and turns away. He can't do this. He can't take a seed from someone with stories like those. He turns to weave back through the crowd but nearly trips over the foot of a white-haired woman patting the head of a boy clinging to her side. Face buried in the woman's hip, the boy murmurs words Remy can't discern.

He recognizes the back of that head, though, fraught with wispy blond curls. "Patrice?"

The boy turns, freckles stark on flushed cheeks. He doesn't seem to recognize Remy—a blessing, considering.

"I have a seed. Would you like to plant it for your sister?"

Patrice clings to the woman's hips, whispering something.

"He says he can't reach," the old woman says. "He's too heavy for these old arms, I'm afraid."

"I can do it," Remy says.

The boy thinks about it before finally reaching out to Remy. He hooks both of his bandaged hands under Patrice's arms and lifts him, shocked at the boy's bird-boned lightness. Patrice's face crumples at the bare stretch of dirt. "It's empty," he says.

Remy swallows. "That's why we're going to plant something. You can come here to watch it grow, if you want. Would you like me to sing something for her?" The third verse of the lullaby Cam used to sing for him starts, *sleep, my dear, the stars your cradle,* and when Patrice agrees, Remy hums the words for Beni. When he finishes, he asks, "You ready?"

Patrice's nod is a tickle of hair against the underside of Remy's chin.

"Can you put your fingertip in the dirt? Not too deep, I think."

Patrice makes a dimple in the soil, and Remy passes him the seed. Patrice holds it between two gentle fingers, placing it inside. "How do I make it grow?"

"You need to bury it first." Remy gestures for him to press soil over the top of it—not too tightly. "But otherwise... plants need what people need." His chest aches as his lips form the words Cam used to chirp while flitting around the house with a watering can. "Food. Water." Something catches in his throat, and he manages to speak past it, his eyes caught on the yellow-green of the teardrop-shaped implant on Patrice's wrist. "Air. Love."

Patrice wiggles to be let down, then grips the edge of the platform, standing on tiptoes to stare at the place where he planted Beni's seed. "She said she'd play airball with me," he says at last, like it's a secret.

Remy doesn't know what to say to that, so he lets his hands drift over Patrice's back. "You can come and water it whenever you like."

Patrice nods. Even when Remy turns to go, his unblinking eyes don't wander from the little stamp of soil, like he expects the seedling to curl from the earth any moment.

Yves waits for him at the exit. Little baskets line the wall beside it, overflowing with vibrant produce. Without speaking, Yves swipes their wrist implant over the pad beside the door and it whirs open, this time to reveal the impenetrable dimness of the outside. The hollow dark outside raises goosebumps on his skin.

The air here, even with the suit Emil had him wear, feels colder than it did before.

Remy is silent as they move forward through the dimness.

The noise of running feet pulls Remy from his thoughts, and he looks up to see a familiar head of dense curls.

Tirani. She lasers in on Remy, racing toward him with wide eyes.

It's been less than a day, but it feels like weeks ago that he watched her leave the infirmary. Exhaustion crashes into Remy at the sight of her. Before he registers it, she's up next to him, running fingers through the still-wet blood on his neck and hovering over the thick bandages on his palms with a low noise of distress. Her hands cup his chin and he can't help pressing into her touch. He tried to take this away from both of them.

"I heard what happened here," she whispers. "I'm sorry."

"Me too."

"I was waiting for you in the infirmary. They said—they told me you'd be coming back, but I—" She presses her lips together. There's living green in her eyes, shot through with golden-brown and flecks of silvery blue, a whole planet in one place. In the quiet, Remy takes in the mole that makes a sideways exclamation point of her left eyebrow, the way she traces the shape of him with as much care as she ever traces the lines of tethers in the air. He *missed* this.

Remy wraps his arms around her and tucks his chin into her neck, holding so tight he squeezes a little *oof* of surprise from her. "I really am sorry," he says. "I was an idiot. I don't want to leave you. I promise I'll be better."

"Hey." Tirani's warm hand cups his skull, pressing him harder against her. She's shaking. Or he's shaking. Maybe they both are.

"I want to live," he confesses into her ear. She squeezes him tighter. "I want everyone to live."

He's not particularly good at living. He's spent the past five years chasing death. But there's so much more at risk than he knew. He doesn't want Alta's garden to die or to watch another brother hold the empty body of a sibling. He doesn't want to hurt Tirani again, or even Yves, who holds Thom like he's more precious than air.

"Okay," Tirani says, and her breath rustling the hair behind his ears is forgiveness he can only do his best to deserve. "Okay."

"Missed you, Tirani."

She laughs and flicks his forehead. "I wasn't gone that long."

"Tirani," Yves says, suddenly, voice flat.

"Hmm?"

"That's—sorry, this is very touching, but, fuck, did you say your name was *Tirani*?"

She pulls away, looking to Remy, then to Yves. "Yes?"

"That's not a common name, is it? Would you say it's pretty unique?"

"I've never met another. Why?"

Yves seizes Tirani's sleeve. "Follow me."

Chapter Thirteen

Grasping, or heart-connected, tethers are nurtured by nearness and signify an intimate and instinctive connection. Bearers of such bonds long to connect. These bonds are less likely than others to attenuate, but due to this resistance to gradual fade, they're more likely to rot when damaged by death or separation.

—From *On the Manipulation of Tethers*

Yves speed-walks through the hall, forcing Remy and Tirani to jog to keep up. "What are your parents' names? Or—your siblings, or . . . "

Tirani goes rigid, nearly missing a step. Remy throws out an arm to steady her. Ahead of them, the infirmary's door glows bright white. "I don't know. They left when I was a baby."

Yves paces into the infirmary, heedless of Roca crushed into the bloody cot with Idrian pressed against her and stops in front of the list tacked to the wall over their desk. They pull it toward them, running a long finger past the names while Remy holds his breath. He remembers, suddenly, how Yves greeted so many people by name in the blocks they visited earlier.

They skim down the names starting from the top, mumbling under their breath until they stop on a name and go still.

"I knew it. I've read this thing thousands of times by now. *Look*. There you are."

Tirani peers at the name beneath Yves' finger, one of hundreds on a thin, yellowed sheet less than halfway down the list. It reads, TIRANI (ARAVEL, OCHAR).

Quietly, Tirani says, "What does that mean?"

"Hey," Roca calls, extracting herself from Idrian's grabby arms. "Is everything all right?"

Yves doesn't answer, turning to Tirani. "Does the name Ochar sound familiar?"

"I—I don't—"

Roca frowns. "Yves, what is this?"

But Yves is looking at Tirani, eyes bright. "I always check in with new arrivals a few months after they get here. By that point, you can kind of tell whether they're going to—" Yves grimaces. "It's a good way to . . . determine their health needs going forward. After the check-up, I let them read this list and look for anyone they know. It's been carried on for decades, probably. The doctor before me inherited it from her predecessor. If they had to leave anyone behind on the surface, they can add the names of those people here, just in case they ever show up. Fluora and Toxys have lists, too."

"I don't get it." Tirani grips the paper where her name is printed.

"The name that comes first is the person they left behind. The one in parentheses is the person who added it here. If this is you—if *you're* the Tirani this Ochar was missing—then you have family here, or someone who loved and missed you."

Tirani hauls in a shaky breath, letting go of the paper to cover her mouth.

"*Yves*," Roca hisses, voice strained and low. "This isn't the time."

"It's exactly the time! This whole fucking *day* has been awful, and if this—if I can do *this*—" They kneel on the floor in the back corner, pulling a long, file-filled drawer open. "Fuck, just give me *one* win today."

Tirani staggers where she stands, and Remy pulls her close. She's tether-taut against him, trembling finely. "My family abandoned me."

"I wouldn't be so sure about that."

Roca levers herself upright in the cot. Idrian groans and tries to throw his arms around her again. "Yves, we need to *leave soon*."

"I know, I know, it's just—" They pull out a file with a huff, then discard it.

"Please," Tirani says, and her hands find Remy's and squeeze so tight it hurts. Remy isn't sure what she's pleading for, so he just squeezes back.

"He's gotta be in here. These files will have what block your Ochar's in, so I can—ah!" Yves pulls out a file. "Here we are!"

"Yves, don't!" Roca has somehow extricated herself from Idrian's grasp and is halfway across the floor toward Yves when they breathe a wrecked, "Oh."

The blood leaves their face. The file slips to the ground, pages scattering.

"Let me see." Tirani frees herself from Remy and kneels beside Yves, pulling pages from the floor. She stops, still as the dead, and stares down. After a moment, she traces the photo with her finger and makes a quiet noise Remy never wants to hear her make again. He moves to hold her. The grinning man in the image has Tirani's black curls and sandy brown skin, her button nose. The dimples on her cheeks when she smiles.

Aravel, Ochar, the file reads. Tirani touches the name, mouthing *Aravel*. "Where is he?"

Yves pulls off their glasses and rubs at their eyes. "I'm sorry."

"*Where is he?*"

"He was in Block S. It was before my time. I didn't realize—"

"What does that mean?" When Yves doesn't answer, Tirani turns, eyes skimming over Idrian, Thom, and Roca. "Someone, tell me what that means."

Remy recalls the faded X over the door, the red lights.

Before he can find words, Roca says—solemnly, from just behind them, "It collapsed. No survivors. I only lived because I was out playing airball with Idrian. Tirani . . . you seemed happy. I didn't want to ruin it."

Tirani idly traces the names below her father's, stopping on the second.

Spouse: Zana (Block S), the file says.

And beside it, *Child: Roca (Block S)*.

Tirani looks up, and Roca stares down, achingly kind, lips lifted in a half-smile and arms crossed tight over her chest. "Hey, Tiny. S'been a while."

Tirani shakes her head, hiding her face in Remy's neck. "I thought they abandoned me. I thought—I thought they were happy somewhere."

"We were," Roca says. "As happy as we could be without you. We didn't mean to leave you behind. Dad just wanted to meet and hand something over to a friend, part of a small group planning a protest against the overpopulation prevention statutes. It should've been quick, and we'd have been back to you before sunrise. It went bad fast, though. I'm glad you didn't have to grow up here."

Tirani just shakes her head again into Remy's shoulder, and Roca retreats. "I'll be here if you want to talk."

Yves' hand freezes halfway to Tirani's shoulder. Unsteadily, they find their feet. "I need to clean Remy's hand and bandage his neck," they whisper.

Remy shakes his head at Yves. "Tirani, wait, if—"

But Tirani just pushes back without looking at him. "Go on," she says. "I'm all right."

She's not, but Remy bites his tongue. When they're back in the *Astrid* with some privacy, he can try again.

Silent, Yves sits Remy in a chair and closes the tiny but prolifically-bleeding slice on his neck with a couple tape-like strips, then pours precious water into a basin and gets to work on his hands. Soon, flecks of dirt and two more pieces of glass filthy the red water.

Thom comes up behind them and plants his hands on their shoulders while they work. He doesn't speak, but the tension slips from their sharp, urgent gestures after a while.

"Shitty day," Thomlin murmurs, not a question but a statement.

Yves exhales a wet laugh. "The shitti*est*, I think. It's a day deserving of superlatives."

"So." Thom massages Yves' shoulders, lips ticking up in a weak grin. "Roca and the new girl. This secret sibling thing's getting to be a theme. Next thing we know, we'll figure out Remy's hiding one."

A high-pitched laugh bursts from Remy at Thom's words.

Yves digs a thumb into one of the wounds on his hands, and Remy yelps as they use a tiny pair of tweezers to lift a sliver of glass from the wound. "Oh, I'm sorry." A droll smile greets Remy when he looks over. Yves digs into a drawer and pulls out a small bag with long-ribbed cuffs inside, lifting it over their shoulder toward Thom. "Would you lace Idrian into these, love? I meant to do it earlier, but . . ."

"Got it." Thom takes the bag with a loose salute and paces over to Idrian's bedside.

As soon as he's gone, Yves leans in. "You need to practice the art of shutting the fuck up." They dab blood from his palms and then pause, sucking in a breath through their teeth. "I hoped I'd seen it wrong through all the blood."

Remy looks down to where Yves holds his palm up, and coldness unfurls in his stomach at the sight of the line of his withering already disappearing into his sleeve.

He darts a glance over at the group around Idrian's cot and whispers, "This is ridiculous. That—Cameron—" He bites his tongue. "It should take *weeks*."

Yves exhales a ragged sigh. "Perhaps for some."

Remy swallows. "When I first cast it, it went way faster than it should. I'd have been dead already if I hadn't found Idrian."

Yves nods and speaks so quietly Remy has to lean forward to hear. "Exactly. Finding them slowed down the advance for *you* because you got to split it with four other people, but it's making it faster than it otherwise might be for everyone else because they're carrying the burden of your sped-up curse between them. If your brother lasted weeks, it's because he was healthy and in an environment conducive to convalescence. Meanwhile . . ." They tug a twisted thread of metal from the weeping cut that bisects his palm and seem to consider that enough said.

Yves sprays his hands with a stinging disinfectant and pulls out a roll of bandages. When Yves finally releases Remy's hands, they're thick-wrapped and clumsy.

"All done over here!" Thom calls.

Yves pulls the books on withering from a shelf and drops them into a drawstring bag, pushing it toward Remy. They lean in to hiss, "Find your answers fast, Canta," and stand to join the group by Idrian's bed.

Remy follows, wincing at the sight of Idrian's bruised arms tied tightly with the cuffs.

"I can't trust Idrian to take care of himself, but these will help. Tighten them as the swelling recedes." They tap the ribbed material. "Shock absorbing. With any luck, the idiot at least won't make things worse."

"I mean, we're dying anyway," a voice says, and Remy jumps. *Emil.* He sits on the end of the cot, on top of Idrian's legs in a way that can't be comfortable for anyone involved. Remy didn't notice him there.

"You should come with a bell," Remy mutters.

Emil laughs. "I dunno, I think stealth is something we could do with more of right now."

Thom grimaces. "We're running lethally low on it. The OSS will have recalibrated their sensors so not even a shred of trash will go undetected. The Lamprey won't be able to make it in again. The supplies we brought won't hold you for long, will they?"

Yves steps away and tugs open the medical cabinet, uselessly rearranging the supplies inside. "No. I hate to ask more of you..."

"You don't have to ask," Roca says. "You know that. Whatever we can do, as long as we can still do it, we're yours."

"You shouldn't have to be." Yves crushes rolls of gauze into tight rows.

Idrian groans and shifts against Roca, eyes cracking open. Raw-voiced, he asks, "Roca?"

"I'm here. Go back to sleep."

"M'awake," he says. "Why're you here?"

"Because you were running around bleeding everywhere, remember?" Roca says cheerily.

"M'awake," Idrian tells her again.

"We know." Emil smiles over at Remy. "This is the *being obvious* part of Idrian waking up. Lasts a while." He turns to Yves, wrist with all the watches raised, tapping away. "What are your most urgent needs and at what volumes will you need them? Some things won't be easy—or even possible—to obtain, but we'll do what we can."

"I'll make a list," Yves says. "But fuel and water are the biggest ones. Something edible wouldn't go amiss, either, if you have a chance. Everything else—without it, we can survive at least a little while."

Emil hisses. "Fuel's gonna be tough."

Yves nods. "I know."

"We'll find a way."

Yves doesn't answer. "I'm on top of figuring out the witherer thing. I've sicced Remy on my books, so he'll be doing research on your end. Between the two of us, we'll handle it."

Yves is a much better liar than Remy, in that they're unshakably confident and haven't actually told a single lie.

Roca nudges Idrian. "*You* still need to make me that list of major fuck-ups and high-profile stuff people might want to kill you for."

A chill trickles down Remy's spine. Ah, yes. That. It won't take them long to find Cam, and with him, Remy. He really does need to find his answers fast.

"Yves, my arms hurt." Idrian struggles upright, and Roca, with a long-suffering sigh, braces him with a hand behind his back.

"You don't say." Yves turns a withering stare on him. "You brought it on yourself." But their hands are not unkind as they shake a few pills into one palm for him.

"Had to," Idrian says. And that, too, Remy supposes, is obvious.

"Maybe so, but this is where that has to end. If I hear even a whisper of self-destructive recklessness—"

"But I—"

"That's right. *You*." Yves pokes Idrian in the throat. "You are the nexus of this curse. That means taking care of yourself. That means not throwing your body into every bullet. It means getting sleep. Eating *food*. Letting yourself heal. A withering buries itself into every weak part, fills up every crack to get a foothold before it breaks you down. You've given it hundreds of cracks to live in, many of them literal." Yves' clenched fist in Idrian's coat drags him to his feet. It's oddly gentle, considering. Even upright, Idrian still looks half asleep, his hair pillow-fluffed.

"Remember this: your health is everyone's health. The withering is advancing far too quickly. Part of that is because it has so much to feed on. Roca's injury. Yours. Even Remy's. But unlike them, if *you* die, the withering is resolved. That means Roca, Emil, Remy, and *Thom* die the instant you do."

Idrian's mouth drops open. "No."

"Very yes. The way you buy them time is by treating yourself well, as foreign an idea as I'm sure that is to you." Their fingers graze the old stab wound on his side. "You don't have the luxury of recklessness anymore."

Idrian's eyes slide over to Roca, wide and almost childish. "You didn't tell me."

Roca smiles. "I did, darling. More than once. You weren't listening, is all."

"But you can't. There has to be a way to—cut you off, or something. It *has* to be just me."

"Not possible. We're bound to you because we love you and would stake our lives on your vision. I wouldn't cut myself off from you even if I could. Yves is right. The only thing we can do now is keep you from killing yourself and all of us prematurely."

Wouldn't cut myself off, Roca said.

Remy snatches the textbook from the bag, flipping through until he finds the section on false-bonds with orphan tethers. The diagram of a witherer tying two broken bonds together sits on the page—as unnatural and unsettling as it was at first glance.

It might be exactly the solution they need. If Remy could sever their fatebonds to Idrian and tie them to himself, wouldn't they be third-party connections, like Tirani's to Roca? He could free them from the curse, at least temporarily. He clenches his fists and closes the book. He'll run it by Yves before they go. It's not a complete solution, but it might buy them time.

Yves sighs and lets go of Idrian's coat once he's steady on his feet. "It's cruel of me to advise care when what I'm asking you to do will put you in danger, but my guess is we'll work through the supplies you brought within two weeks even if we're doing *barely* subsistence rations. Less if we try to keep other systems operational. The garden..."

Idrian tilts on his feet but rights himself. "We should get going, then."

"I wish you didn't have to," Yves says, one hand at his elbow.

Idrian ruffles their hair and regrets it by the instant, bloodless twist of pain on his face. "We'll be fine," he says. "We always are."

Yves sweeps away, eyes hooded. "You know better than to make promises, Delaciel."

Chapter Fourteen

*To ruin,
you must tend them, watch them flourish.
Grow them. Draw them
close enough to heal.*

— From "Gardener's Paradox," a surviving poem by one of the first criminals sentenced to the Isles, P.D. 36

Yves' list asks for water, so to Kuren they go.

The Chancellor's broadcast promised punishment if the Isles associated with Idrian, so the crew waits, white-knuckled, to be shot down or apprehended as the *Astrid* leaves Alta. No Protectorate ships emerge from the shadows behind Fluora or Toxys to give chase, however, and no ultimatums blare over the comms.

The silence they meet is almost eerie—far too strange to celebrate. They take advantage of it to re-enter Verdine's atmosphere and descend from airless, star-pricked darkness to the blazing light of day on the planet's surface; they have work to do.

Kuren is a tiny fishing island on the fringes of Remy's geographical knowledge—a crumb-sized, unlabeled blip on even the most detailed maps. Its lake will be their first of three stops for water. "To make sure we don't take too much from any one place," Emil explained.

An old woman lies in wait when they disembark, weathered and sun-bronzed hands clutching a spear. She squints as they approach.

"Ma Windsel!" Idrian calls, clapping a hand down on her corded shoulder. "Don't stab me. I promise I've been good."

The squint doesn't go. "Edie!" She laughs, delighted. "Back so soon? C'mere, let me look at you." She grabs him by the cheekbones and steers him down until his face is inches from hers.

Face so close their noses are nearly squished together, Idrian ventures, "Did you lose your glasses again?"

The more important question, perhaps: did she just call Idrian *Edie*?

"I never *lose* them. You know that."

Idrian smiles so wide his cheeks might split with it. "'Course not," he agrees.

"They'll turn up if I need them," the woman Idrian called Ma Windsel pronounces, pushing his grinning face away. "Don't need my eyes to know you look awful! Every time, I tell you to take care of yourself, and every time you come to me looking like a sick sapling! No one listens to Ma Windsel. Well, you'll listen today. You must be back for water again, but I caught more fish than an old woman can eat alone, and *you will be fed a meal* if it kills me. This way, all of you."

Light, warm laughter startles Remy, and he turns to find Idrian's face softened with joy. He didn't know Idrian could make an expression like that.

At the head of the group, Ma Windsel guides them uphill along a well-trodden path between the foliage.

"By the way, Edie, you're a terrible liar." She punctuates her pronouncement by thwacking his ankle with the non-business end of the spear. "'I've been good,' he tells me! *Nonsense!* 'Good' isn't the word I'd use for the things I've been hearing! Even out here, we get the Chancellor's broadcasts, dear."

Idrian winces.

"Newest one came through last night. They've been saying you *killed* that nice boy. Canta, I think he was." Remy's stomach twists, but Ma Windsel goes on, heedless. "He came here once, you know. All the way to Kuren! Years and years ago, of course. Got terribly seasick on the boat, but he was a charming lad. He said he needed to visit because he couldn't bear to speak for our people without knowing them. Isn't that the sweetest thing? I hadn't realized he'd died, but apparently it's been years. Shows you how well I keep up with things off-island."

Remy trips over his feet as they crest the hill into an open field dotted with fruit trees.

How could he have forgotten? It *has* been years. Five of them exactly, come tomorrow. He lands in the dirt, sharp rocks slashing his bandaged palms and heart stuttering with a dull gong of pain.

"Now, I don't believe that trash about you killing him, mind, but a lot of people do, and they're not happy." Ma Windsel pats Idrian's elbow. "You're both good boys. Ma Windsel knows these things."

Tirani helps Remy up. "You okay?"

He shakes his head, mute.

He *knows* which trip that was. He spent it with Andrew and Mrs. Delacour. Cam had gotten the Chancellor's permission to borrow a transmitter, and each night during the allotted time for non-urgent communication, he'd send a video. In one, Cam held up a wildflower bouquet and told Remy how the broad, furry red one in the center smelled—no lie—like a cross between smoked cheese and rotting meat.

They pass lima trees heavy with their dimpled citrus harvests. Baskets beside sturdy white ladders overflow with the small pink fruits.

Cam came home with a jar of lima preserves that time. Maybe he got it here. Maybe even from Ma Windsel.

Ma Windsel's shocked cry jolts him from his thoughts to find Idrian on his hands and knees in the grass, skin pale and clammy.

"Idrian?" Roca says, the word strung taut.

Idrian huffs, blowing a tuft of loose hair from his eyes. "I'm fine. Tripped, that's all."

But his splayed hands on the ground are shaking, even though Remy saw him eating pain meds and anti-inflammatories like candy before they disembarked.

"This planet's fucking *gravity* is nonsense on the bones," Idrian spits.

Roca offers her hand, but Idrian waves it away.

"Come on, this is nothing. Remy tripped and no one commented on that."

Remy, Remy doesn't say, *got up pretty quickly, too*. Idrian sits back on his feet, arms hanging at his sides and breath shallow and strained.

The only wounds Remy has to feed the withering are the ones on his hands, but exhaustion still throbs fever-heavy in his bones. It's breaking everyone down. Emil fell asleep at the control panel on the way here, Thomlin hasn't let the hemostatic spray out of his sight, and Roca's eye injury, despite Yves' best efforts, is a bare inch from infection.

Of all of them, though, Idrian must be feeling it the most.

Remy needs to find his answers soon, but when he presented his theory on false-bonds before leaving, Yves wasn't hopeful for its long-term success.

Intent—that's always the kicker. A severing without full consent from both parties will never be permanent. Even if Remy severs their fatebonds, the connection that created them won't vanish. Any knots he ties will soon unravel and return to Idrian, and the withering will pick up right where it left off.

Even if it worked, though, false-bonding won't save Remy or Idrian. Remy can't sever his own tethers, and it's not worth asking Yves to waste their dwindling ash on something that won't last. And Idrian's the nexus of the curse. There's no way at all to remove it from him, nothing Remy can sever to save him, even temporarily. He has maybe half a solution.

But Roca is Tirani's *sister*, and Remy has done to his closest friend exactly what was done to him. Half a solution isn't nearly enough. He needs to talk to her. After they eat, hopefully.

Idrian finds his feet while Ma Windsel tuts about getting some fish into him. They enter the village in brittle silence.

The marks of the Chancellor's work are obvious even on Kuren. The houses are taller than they are wide and closely-packed so that human dwellings grow up rather than out, and solar hivelights dot the slanted roofs. Inside Ma Windsel's door is the embedded screen that displays universal broadcasts from the Chancellor.

Ma Windsel waves them to mismatched woven chairs around the table and stuffs them with warm, buttered biscuits topped with lima jam. Evening finds the promised bounty of fish cooked to perfection, sprinkled with dried flecks of the island's fire peppers and topped with a glaze of lima syrup. The burst of eye-watering spice is softened by the flaky warmth of the fish and the sweet tartness of the citrus glaze.

Roca invites Tirani away from the table and out the front door before Remy can pull her aside to talk. Emil and Thom follow soon after, weighed down with baskets from Ma Windsel.

Idrian and Remy leave last. Bright light from the moons overhead paints the world in grayscale, every tree casting impenetrable black shadows behind them. Remy carefully doesn't mention how Idrian supports himself on the trees as they pass.

Lord of the Empty Isles

The *Astrid*'s shadowed cave of a cargo bay hangs open, as close to the lake as it can get. Accordion-like hoses trail from either side into the water, and Roca rests on her belly on the cargo ramp, binoculars in hand. She throws a small, rubbery device at Remy as he approaches. "In your ear," she says, in lieu of greetings.

When Remy obeys, Thom's voice echoes through the device. *"You ready?"*

"For what?"

"You'll be with me," Idrian says.

With a grunt and a loud clank, Roca shoves a full backpack across the floor toward him.

Idrian grabs it and swings one of its straps over his arm. "We'll keep an eye on the siphons."

"He means," Thom says, *"that he'll zip over the water like a child while we do all the work. Watch out, Idrian, or we'll replace you with Tirani."*

Tirani chirps, *"They let me press the button!"*

Roca's expression goes soft.

Emil chuckles. *"Suction's going. Hurry up, Idrian."*

"My pleasure. Remy?" Idrian's face-splitting grin doesn't inspire confidence.

"I . . . don't know anything about siphons."

"Too bad. Roca's out an eye and keeps running into walls, so you're up." Idrian shrugs. "Think of it as an adventure."

Roca tips her head in an apologetic shrug. "My depth perception's shit right now, so it's your turn to keep this idiot from jumping off cliffs. Good luck."

"There aren't even any cliffs here."

Thom says sweetly, *"That's never stopped you before."*

Roca's laughter is deafening.

Movement in the distance seizes Remy's attention. Through the sparse covering of trees around the lake and beyond an open field dotted with simple stone paths, the pale sand of Kuren's shore and the twinkling lights of shoreside shops stretch out. And beyond them—

"Binoculars." Remy kneels to grab them from Roca's slack hand. "Something's out there."

His breath freezes in his chest as the movement on shore comes into focus. Men in too-familiar uniforms pace from a boat marked with the Chancellor's crest.

"That boat," he gasps. "Roca—"

She snatches the binoculars back. "Don't worry about them. There's a Protectorate manufacturing facility an island over, and they visit Kuren on their off-time for the inns and the food. We'll be fine. They don't come out this far, and the trees do a pretty good job of making sure they can't see us."

Remy's pulse still races in his throat, vision sharp. "Are you sure?"

Roca's uncovered eye manages to convey a full expression's worth of scorn. "Who's the new kid here, me or you?"

Idrian grabs Remy's shoulder for a quick squeeze before walking out of the cargo bay and across the rocky shore toward one of the siphons. "She's right. Kuren's easy. In and out. We take some water off the top and go."

Remy swallows, eyes still fixed on the sand and the uniformed men striding across it. "Yeah?"

"Unless a fish gets stuck in the filter again," Idrian says. "That was early days. We had the filter to keep silt and debris out, but we hadn't yet rigged the sonic fish-keeper-awayer—"

"That's not what it's called," Thom drawls in Remy's ear.

"It's what it does. Anyway, the fish just sort of . . ." Idrian's fingers spread in a wiggly gesture that doesn't bode well for the fish's structural integrity. "I had to clean it."

Plopping down on the shore, Idrian slips the pack Roca shoved over to him from his shoulders. The first thing to come

Lord of the Empty Isles

from it is a short, thick-nosed rifle, which Idrian swings around his shoulders.

Remy gapes. "Do you . . . expect to have to kill someone?"

Idrian laughs. "No killing." He pats the rifle. "This one's kind of a good luck charm."

Next, he extracts a pair of chunky mechanical boots and slides his feet into them. They're not unlike the gravity boots Emil gave Remy on Alta, but they're bulkier along the sides and bottom. He pulls a second pair from his pack and passes them to Remy. "Put 'em on."

Remy stares dubiously at the boots. He tugs one over his foot and feels it shape itself to him, stiff and snug. "And these are . . .?"

"Water gliders." Idrian's eyes narrow. "You haven't used them?"

"Of course not!" Cam had to get permission just to send Remy videos. Of course he hasn't used illegal recreational tech.

Idrian jabs a button on the side of the one boot Remy has on. It whirs and loosens. Idrian tugs it off Remy's foot and shoves it back into his pack, then pulls the other boot from his slack fingers. "No glider for you, then."

"What? Why? How will I—"

Idrian's lips spread in a feral smile. "Tutorial first. Step up and hold on."

Roca's dry voice echoes into Remy's ear. "Idrian, don't drown the new kid."

"He'll be *fine*." Idrian steps into the water, and the instant his feet make contact, the boots lock in place and something expands from them—several inches from either side and several feet out in front and back.

"Climb on up." Idrian drifts into the water. "Clock's ticking."

When is it not?

Remy stalks into the cool water after him, soaking his socks and shoes, submerging himself to his knees. He grabs at the back of Idrian's coat and manages to get one soaked foot onto the glider. It changes immediately beneath him, expanding and thickening beneath his feet as the center of gravity changes. Remy lifts his second foot on.

"That's quite nice, actually," he offers.

"Wait'll you see how fast it goes."

That's all the warning Remy gets before the glider surges forward, nearly throwing him off. He crashes to his knees to avoid the sudden backward pull. Frothy water bursts against his face, and Remy chokes on it, hooking an arm around Idrian's boot to keep him secure as he swipes lake water from his eyes.

"I hate you," Remy rasps, but to his consternation, it comes out without a recognizable edge. A ripple split by their forward motion crashes over the glider and soaks him.

Roca's tired voice comes through. *"I told you not to drown him."*

Saintlike, Idrian says from above, "And I told him to hold on. Damn, this is great! Never could get anyone but Roca to come out with me on these."

"I wonder why." Remy hauls himself upright and throws a soaked arm around Idrian's neck, half-chokehold. "Yves'll kill you for getting the bandages wet."

"Ah," Idrian says. "Didn't think about that."

"I'm getting the impression you don't think about much of anything."

"Eh," Idrian says, which isn't a rebuttal. "There's stuff in the infirmary to rewrap you—pretty much everything you could want. Got some wake-you-up, some put-you-to-sleep. We've even got the hearty-starty stickers, if you'd like to *really* wake yourself up."

Remy coughs out a laugh. It comes easier than it should. "You're a bastard."

"Guilty as charged." Idrian tips an invisible hat.

Guilty.

The Chancellor's broadcast echoes in Remy's head. *Idrian and all who consort with him are now named enemies of Verdine. All will be executed.* Did Ma Windsel hear that on the broadcast she saw? Did she choose to give some of her island's water in spite of it?

Idrian must be thinking along the same lines, because his shoulders tense beneath Remy's hands.

After a moment, he shakes his head as if to clear it. "Anyway, we need to get you confident on these, or at least halfway competent. *So.* Pressure on your forward foot moves you forward. Start with light pressure until you get used to it." Idrian demonstrates. "Sitting back on your heels slows it, and leaning to either side starts a turn. Pressure of the lean affects the arc of the turn. Like this, though—lean too hard, and you might tip. It's *very* hard to right yourself when you do, but on the bright side, it'll be *hilarious.*" He demonstrates each move, then turns them in a lazy arc to bring them back to the cargo bay. When they arrive, he cheerfully shoves the spare pair of boots into Remy's arms. "Tutorial complete. Good luck. Don't drown."

"What? That wasn't—"

Roca, from her place on the floor, shakes her head and looks down too slowly to hide the soft smile on her lips. "It'll be all right. We'll fish you out if you fall in," she says.

"It's not that I don't trust you." Remy shoves his feet into clunky boots and walks to the edge of the water, staring at its lazy ripples. "But I really don't think I trust you. How am I supposed to do this?"

Idrian waits, arms crossed and straight-faced. "Just step on down." He gives it a moment. "Who wants to bet he eats lake before the night's out?"

Remy glares. "You are not *betting*."

Remy has one foot over the water when Thom's voice cracks through the earpiece. *"Idrian. Siphon one's blocked. Something must be clogging the filter."*

"And you said I don't do any work!" Idrian retracts his own gliders and joins Remy inside. "Better not be another fish. Good thing no one took me up on my bet. I get the dubious honor of being your first passenger." He removes his own mechanical boots, unstrapping the holster with his ever-present handgun and dropping it on the ramp with an echoing clang. Finally, he removes the thick-nosed rifle, looping it around Remy's neck instead. "Your good luck charm, now. Keep it safe for me while I'm down there."

Cold and heavy around Remy's neck, the rifle doesn't feel lucky at all.

"Just step into the water," Idrian says. "I'll climb on once you're in. Don't tip us, please."

Remy obeys, startling as the gliders expand. The foot he stepped forward with locks into place ahead of the other.

Idrian steps up and steadies himself with a hand on Remy's shoulder. "Pressure on your forward foot to move, remember?"

He remembers. *Gradual*, Idrian told him, so Remy exerts the lightest possible pressure with his little toe. His acceleration might be too gradual, but they arrive at the blocked siphon without tipping, so he considers it a win.

"You could be worse!" Idrian assesses when Remy finally pulls to a stop several feet past their destination. Moonlight catches the sheen of cold sweat on his face and makes something ghostly of him. The bulk under the coat on his left arm reminds Remy of the inadequately-wrapped bandages there, and the compression cuffs peek out from his sleeves. There's fresh blood on his shirt, still, from the wound that gave Remy blood for the withering.

"You're a mess," Remy says, stomach fluttering with a feeling he can't name.

Idrian stares, like he's waiting for a reason why that matters. He taps his earpiece. "Thom, tell him I've always been a mess."

Thom sighs. *"He really has."*

"I mean . . . I could do it."

Idrian grins. "You gonna tell me you've done this sort of thing before?"

"No, but—"

"No buts. My oxygen needs aren't as prissy as yours. I can hold my breath long enough to get the work done." Idrian tugs the earpiece from his ear and drops it into Remy's hands. "Be nice to my earpiece. We only have the one set."

Idrian dives into the lake before Remy can argue. The light on the water swallows the sight of him in seconds, leaving only sharply cut ripples.

Remy holds his own breath, counting time by the bubbles that break on the lake's surface. He has to haul in air before the third one rises.

"Will he be okay?"

Another bubble.

"He always has been before," Roca says, but when Remy turns to look, she's stock still, binoculars trained on the water where Idrian descended.

The ripples level out, and Remy grits his teeth. How long can a person hold their breath?

A flash of movement drags his attention to the trees, but he finds only the stark shadows of their trunks and hypnotic swaying of their branches, and, twinkling between them, the lights on Kuren's distant shore.

Something crashes into the underside of the glider, and Remy shrieks a curse. A mass of rotting leaves tangled up in a twisted branch screeches along the glider's underside before drifting away. The blockage, Remy assumes.

Idrian rises moments after, sucking in a breath and offering a quick wave before diving under again and swimming away.

"Hey, I'm right here!" Remy calls.

Roca speaks quietly. *"He wouldn't have been able to lift himself on. Probably would've tipped you into the water trying. Don't worry, he's a good swimmer."*

Remy watches the water until Idrian surfaces near the trees.

Something moves between the trunks again. They're eerie in the bright light of the moons—their shadows impenetrably dark and precise, and Remy's tempted to dismiss the movement as simple rustling of the leaves. The movement sharpens, this time, and gains its own familiar shadow as it slips out from behind a thick trunk.

A person. There's someone watching them. Adrenaline electrifies Remy's limbs.

He's such an idiot. He and Roca had their eyes on the water, like the only danger to Idrian was beneath it, but as Remy watches, a second figure follows the first, and a third.

The men slipping between the trees wear painfully familiar uniforms—dark trousers and a fitted vest over a high-necked dress shirt. Simple ribbon around the neck. A white shape decorates the vest's breast pocket, indistinct at this distance, but the placement and familiar cut of the uniform gives it away: it has to be the small form of the Protectorate's crest.

It's the uniform Cameron wore.

The men from the boat.

"You *said* they didn't come out this far," Remy hisses. He gets only a muffled curse and the noise of urgent scrambling on Roca's end.

"Idrian. *Idrian.*" Remy taps at his ear, but there's no response except the tinny noise of his own voice from the earpiece Idrian dropped into his hand. Remy shoves it into his pocket. That *idiot*.

If Remy yells, he's as likely to alert Idrian's pursuers as to warn Idrian.

"They won't carry anything lethal," Remy tells Roca. "But they'll have radios."

Idrian continues to glide toward shore with smooth strokes until it gets too shallow to swim, and then there's no grace to him. Remy knows only too well the first, cruel shock of gravity after rising from water. It must be even crueler to someone from the Isles. Idrian sags with it, knees giving out and dropping him in the muddy water.

The men slip from the trees as Idrian presses both hands to his knees to push himself upright.

If they capture Idrian or radio for support—

If they stop them from getting the water they need—

They won't have another chance. *Days without water*, Yves told Remy. *Minutes without air.*

Roca races to the rim of the cargo bay and pulls the glider boots on, seizing Idrian's handgun from where he dropped it, but she won't get here fast enough.

Remy thinks of Alta's airless atmosphere, of all the people who somehow found happiness there anyway, and his hands are shock-chilled as he grabs the rifle Idrian slung around his neck. A good luck charm, Idrian called it.

Lifting the rifle must take a fraction of a second. It feels like forever. Remy's never fired one before, so why does it fit snugly against the meat of his shoulder like it was meant to sit there? This must be what Idrian feels, this sick blankness, horror and resignation and determination a bile-sharp bite at the back of his throat.

Three men. Three, compared to thousands.

Remy steadies his stance on the glider. As one of the men pulls something from his belt—it could be a shock stick or a radio or a voice amplifier and it wouldn't matter—he swallows and takes aim. He can't hold back a horrified noise as he pulls the trigger, can't help the way he drops the rifle against his chest, turning away.

The noise that splits the air is not the lethal crack of a bullet but a muted *thunk* as something flies from the rifle's wide barrel and toward the group. It lands at their feet and white fog bursts out. They fall one by one.

Remy falls, too, landing on one knee with a crack and exerting enough pressure on his forward foot that he accelerates with a sickening lurch.

He didn't kill them. Whatever that was, it was probably non-lethal.

Relief, for once, is not at all a pleasant thing. It crawls through Remy, oily-hot, as the world blurs past. He would've killed them. He *meant* to kill them, put their lives in the balance and judged them a—what did Yves call Cameron?—an acceptable loss.

Remy forces himself upright and drags the glider to a halt not far from Idrian, gathering himself enough to extend a hand. "Climb on," he says.

Idrian doesn't reach for him right away, instead pulling the strap of the rifle from Remy's neck. Silently, Idrian swings it over his own head and situates it against his back. Remy winces at the sight of Idrian up close, barely upright in the water. Something dark drips in thick rivulets down his left hand. He must have reopened the wound on his arm.

He holds Remy's gaze for an electric moment before he says, "Thank you."

Without speaking, Remy passes over Idrian's earpiece.

The weather isn't terribly cold and the breeze isn't terribly stiff, so the water cooling on Remy shouldn't make him shiver, but he can't stop, teeth chattering something fierce as adrenaline withdraws its claws from him.

Just like it did for Remy, the glider expands to bear Idrian's weight when he finally steps up. Behind him, Idrian is lake-water soaked, but the place where he presses against Remy is warm, his heartbeat a wild, living thing against Remy's back.

Idrian tucks his chin over the top of Remy's head as Remy turns them and heads back toward the siphons. "You're not too bad on the glider. I suppose I owe you money."

Remy doesn't have the energy to remind Idrian that he didn't actually bet anything. He shivers harder. Idrian's arms go around him, and it's stupid that it helps.

"I owe you my life," Idrian says.

"*No.*" Remy shakes his head so hard they wobble in the water.

"Relax, kid." Roca soothes through the earpiece. "It was just knockout gas."

"That's not it. I thought I'd . . ."

He thought being fatebound to Idrian was a betrayal. But this—

His head tells him he made a hard choice to save lives, that those men are fine, that pulling a trigger today is not the most lethal thing he's ever done. His head tells him he's overreacting.

But he's never felt farther away from himself or from Cameron. His mind provides an image of Cameron in his old uniform with the spread wings of the Chancellor's crest over his heart and Remy, with a rifle loaded with real bullets. The weight of a trigger under his finger, heavy as a corpse. The crisp image of his brother in his mind's eye is clear in everything but its expression. The more Remy tries to recall his face, the faster it fades.

Maybe Cam wouldn't mind. He always said Remy should heal, not harm. But what about when it's not so easy? What about harming in order to heal, or because the only things you have in your pockets are knives? What if he *cares* about these people, who care about each other? What if Remy could see himself being friends with the man who engineered his brother's murder? That's not a thing that can be forgiven, not even by the extraordinarily forgiving.

Tomorrow it'll be five years since Cam died, and today Remy has chosen a side.

Something warm falls on Remy's shoulders, and he looks back, startled, to find Idrian pressing his long coat around him.

Maybe that's why he finds the breath to confess, "I would've killed them."

Idrian only squeezes Remy's shoulders, and then, quietly, as Remy sinks into the coat that smells like saltwater and leather, reaches to ruffle Remy's hair. "I wouldn't have made a murderer out of you."

Remy swallows hard, body aching with the curse he cast on all of them. He's done a good enough job making a murderer of himself.

Thom's voice comes through the earpiece. *"Idrian, you'll need to hurry back."*

Idrian tenses. "What's up?"

"They radioed out before Remy got them. They'll have reinforcements here soon. We've taken as much water as we safely can from Kuren."

A gust of air whistles through the trees. Almost too low for Remy to hear, Idrian says, "They'll be on high alert. We won't be able to hit Tulos and Matten Island for the rest. This won't be nearly enough." Idrian's voice goes lower still. "Thom."

"Yeah?"

"Take it. Take the rest."

"What?"

"From the lake."

"*I'll empty it if I do. We can't . . . Idrian, you can't want to make another Veida.*"

But his protests are hollow. Silence stretches between them.

"I don't *want* to," Idrian says, and his voice is level but his hands around Remy squeeze bone-breakingly tight. "But there're barely a hundred people on Kuren. Within the day, the Chancellor can evacuate them. He has the resources to refill the lake. Alta and Fluora and Toxys can't do any of that. Max suction on the siphons, Thom. Drain it."

Silence stretches out, broken only by the wind. Thom finally says, "*All right.*"

"I'm out. As soon as I'm inside and we have the water, we leave." Idrian presses on his earpiece and the static hum in Remy's ear cuts off as the noise from the siphons picks up. Idrian sags against Remy. "Can I borrow your shoulder?"

Blood from the reopened wound on his arm makes a watery puddle on the glider. A chill wind rides over the water, and Idrian shivers. Remy's wearing his coat, probably wearing his blood, too.

"Depends," Remy whispers, voice wrecked. "You dying?"

Idrian's laugh is quieter than a sigh. "Aren't we all?"

Remy shrugs, and Idrian smiles and drops his head onto Remy's shoulder.

"How . . ." Remy whispers. "How do you do it?"

"Mm?"

"Your 'judgment calls'. How do you *do* that?" The next words feel like they tear pieces from him on their way out. "How do you live with it?"

"Asking the hard questions today, huh?"

Remy can't tell if Idrian is shivering against him or laughing, but he takes forever to answer. Finally, he says, "'Cause none of us have the luxury of dying. Don't know anyone who'll pick up this thankless job if I quit."

The shore withdraws as the lake empties, and the gliders retract on their own, leaving Remy and Idrian to tread through sucking mud toward the *Astrid*'s cargo bay.

Roca waits on the edge until Idrian gets near enough for her to pull him in.

They all stop dead at the sound of a single, frayed word.

"Edie?"

Remy turns just as Idrian does.

Like she was there when they landed, Ma Windsel waits for them as they prepare to depart, hunched and alone on the shore of a mostly emptied lake.

"*Why?*" The moons cast the hollow of the lake in dense shadow behind her. The siphons withdraw into the *Astrid* with a whir.

Idrian's blood trails after him into the cargo bay. "I'm sorry."

Ma Windsel stands still as a statue. She must have found her glasses, because they're perched on her nose now. "Sorry don't work when you do it on purpose. You told me what happened on that other island was an accident, said you'd never let it happen again."

Idrian sags in Roca's hold like he'd be kneeling if he could. "I'm so sorry. I had to."

"You chose to," Ma Windsel says. "Like I chose to believe in you. It's in our nature to make mistakes, isn't it?" At that, Idrian recoils, but Ma Windsel keeps going. "I have half a mind to let them find you, dear, but I know I couldn't stop you. You go now. You live with what you brought to my home. What you took from it. You won't be welcome here again."

Her piercing stare follows them up into the stars, long after the cargo bay door has closed. Hollow horror throbs in Remy's gut, and something like anger, but there's no one to point it at.

"We need to get the water to Yves," Idrian says.

Softly, Roca says, "Emil got the first delivery loaded into the Lamprey from siphon two while you were dealing with the blockage. It'll auto-launch as soon as it's safe."

Idrian swallows and clears his throat, looking around the cargo bay like he's never seen it before. "Then . . . then I should—"

Remy *knows* sometimes the only thing that keeps a person upright in the wake of a loss is staying busy enough to banish it, but Idrian's hand is a map of red and the dirty lake water can't have done his injuries any favors. If he keeps going like this, he's going to kill himself and everyone else.

"You should *nothing*." Remy throws out an arm against Idrian's chest.

He expects Idrian to get angry, maybe. Push back. Maybe that's even what he needs. There's more than one way to banish pain, after all, and if Remy's learned anything from the throb of Cam's rotbond, it's that sometimes a newer, sharper hurt does the trick. But instead, Idrian staggers, slipping in a puddle of his own blood, and Remy has to throw his other arm out just to keep him from falling.

Roca gives Remy a silent nod. "I'm going to the infirmary. You drag this idiot to me as soon as you can, all right?"

Remy pulls Idrian's arm around him, bearing nearly all of his weight.

When they finally leave, the Lamprey launches itself unmanned, heading for the Isles to save at least ten times as many lives as they ruined today, but no one cheers for its departure.

In the dim glow of the hallway, Idrian looks at Remy like he's half his age. "We had to, didn't we?"

As if Remy, of all people, might have an answer.

"I need it to be just me," Idrian whispers, so soft the words fade into the hum of the halls. "The withering. All of this. Why does it have to hurt everyone else?"

Remy can't summon words to his lips, so he focuses on keeping Idrian on his feet.

In the infirmary, Roca and Thom tape Idrian's wounds.

"Get the first aid kit, would you, Remy?"

He finds a small box on the wall and brings it over, but Roca passes it back with a chuckle. "Little early for those," she says. "Those are our shock stickers. Kit's in the drawer in Thomlin's desk."

At Roca's urging, Remy dissolves two sleeping tablets from the kit (*at least two,* Roca told him, *or he'll wake in an hour and start deep-cleaning the whole damn ship*) into water for Idrian.

Roca sprawls out beside him on the bed, pulling a heavy blanket over him, and Emil settles into a folding chair and holds both their hands. Remy stands awkwardly next to the bed as Idrian's eyes get heavier and he relaxes back against Roca. He's clearly not welcome here.

Idrian seizes his hand as he turns to go. "Hey. Remy?"

It's strange to be called by his name—frightening because it doesn't feel bad at all.

Frozen in place, Remy doesn't dare to turn. "What?"

"S'really warm," Idrian says solemnly.

This time, Remy can't help turning. "*What?*"

"Blanket. You could sleep here, too."

Remy huffs, cheeks heating. "There's no room," he says, like that's the issue here.

"Mm." Idrian seems to consider this. "Your loss." He seems to consider his job done, because his grip on Remy's hand loosens and he tries to pat it. He misses on his third attempt, his hand falling to hang over the edge of the cot, eyes slipping closed.

"Kid," Roca says, quiet.

Remy scowls. "I'm not a kid."

"You're the same age as Tirani. I can't think of you as anything else. But for what it's worth . . ." She looks down at Idrian, lips lifting. "He likes you. That's . . . uncommon."

"Is it? He seems to get along with everyone." He gestures to how she's basically on top of him.

"Ha! Nah, this is—safety. Some of us who grew up on the Isles, we don't know how to rest unless we're crushed in with other people. Idrian's the worst about it. I don't think he remembers sleeping any other way. So we share. Emil doesn't mind." A soft smile blossoms on her face when Emil's lips graze her knuckles. "Idrian . . . he'll throw away his life for someone a bunch faster than he'll trust them, and he doesn't give trust in half-measures. You've either got all or none of it." Roca throws an arm over Idrian's chest, and he burrows into it. "Somehow, you've got all of it. He let you watch his back out there. He hasn't let anyone but me do that for him. I know you said this isn't your scene, but I hope you stick around if we survive this."

She wouldn't if she knew—and Remy shouldn't want to as much as he does. His next breath hurts, air whistling through a throat that feels like it's closing. "You barely know me."

It's a reminder as much as a response.

"Maybe. But I trust Idrian. And he trusts you."

Remy grits his teeth around the words *I'm the last person he should trust.*

Tirani arrives with two cups of algae-green meal-slurry, and Remy bolts the awful stuff down to keep from saying anything stupid and leaves without finding a response for Roca.

In the room he shares with Tirani, Yves' books lay spread out on the floor, pages open to arcane rules. *Pain for pain.* It's appropriate. Kuren's pain exchanged for Alta's. Pain is the core principle behind withering: witherers are useless, defanged without the ashes of the lost. They pay for suffering with suffering.

No one's ever written about what a person has to pay for salvation.

They make room for themselves between the nest of Yves' books on the floor and Tirani wraps Thomlin's ugly quilt around the two of them. She drops her head on his shoulder.

"Nothing makes it easier, does it?"

Remy tugs the quilt more tightly around her shoulders. "Hmm?"

"My parents. I always thought it'd be easier if they hadn't wanted to leave. But it just hurts a different way."

"Yeah," Remy whispers, and something stirs in him. He sits up straighter. There *is* a simple solution to all of this. "Tirani. She's your *sister*."

"Remy..." Tirani murmurs, barely audible. She tenses against him.

"No. She's your *blood sister*. She's—you get it, right? I would've done anything to save Cam." He swallows, dry throat clicking. He can't look at her. He's done this: Tirani is just the latest link in this awful chain. "It's okay if that's what you need to do, too."

Just like Remy could have ended Cam's withering if only he'd been able to find and kill Yves, Tirani—as Roca's blood relative—could end it, too. "You could save her. You have every right. Back then, I would've done it." If he'd had a blade and a guide when Cam first fell ill, he'd have hunted the witherer down himself.

Tirani pushes out from under the blanket with a desperate, frustrated noise. "You're asking me to kill you."

"I'm not asking. I'm just... I'm saying that you can."

Her eyes are wet as she stares at him. At last, she says, "Is that what you'd do now, if you could still save him?"

"I don't know." But the weight of that trigger lingers like a brand on his finger. In his mind, he hears Idrian's hopeless, helpless words: *I need it to be just me*. Remy gets it, now. It could be that easy. It *could* be just him.

Tirani just waits for him, silent and steady. She might not be arrogant enough to presume his answer, but she knows him well enough to understand he's lying. He does know.

"No," he finally whispers into the quiet. It's an ugly thing to be forced to admit, that he'd betray his own blood for these people. "I don't think I could, anymore."

Tirani smiles, but it's all sharp edges. She slides back under the blanket and tucks herself against him, turning her chin away. Remy pretends not to hear the hitching of her breath.

"Good," she says. "Me neither. I can't kill you, Remy."

He's not sure what he feels at the admission. Relief, maybe— at least a sliver of it. And something much heavier and darker, because it would've been so easy, if death were the answer.

"I haven't even really talked with her," Tirani says, voice a hum against his side.

"Hm?"

"Roca. She tried, I think, at Ma Windsel's, but then Emil came and told us to get back to the ship. It's all been so busy, I just haven't—and maybe I don't want to. Won't it be worse, if I get to know her more and then she just . . ." Tirani shakes her head. "She's going to leave me again. You both will."

Remy thinks he understands, all of a sudden, why Idrian and Emil and Roca cling so tightly to their optimistic lies about how everything will be fine, how they'll find a way. "I won't," he says, but he's no better a liar now than he's ever been, and the tired exclamation point of Tirani's eyebrow tells him she knows it. He swallows hard. "I'll do *everything* I can to keep her alive for you. I have—it's a mess, but I have an idea that could save her."

She sits up, eyes fixed on him.

"It's not the best."

"Tell me."

So he does. He tells her about his awful half-solution, how it'll turn the full force of the curse onto Remy and Idrian. He tells her it's ugly, and it's imperfect, but it's what he has. His withering throbs in the crook of his elbow.

Pain for pain. Maybe that's how it always has to go.

Midnight comes, probably, and with it comes the fifth anniversary of Cameron's death.

Remy clutches his fist over the aching bond in his chest and clenches his teeth against the numbing agony it brings, and it's worse because the pain doesn't have anyone to point at anymore. Because maybe it should always have pointed at him.

I need it to be just me, Idrian said. Remy can't earn the trust Idrian so freely gave him or stop this withering from breaking either of them down, but he can try, at least, to make sure he and Idrian are the only ones it hurts.

Chapter Fifteen

*To heal
you must cut down
to the beating heart of things.
You must prepare to ruin.*

— From "Gardener's Paradox"

Remy wakes with the world's most brutal sleep headache to the shameful crust of his drool on Tirani's shoulder.

He's not sure what woke him until several deafening crashes of a bell play over the interior speakers and Roca yells, as if this isn't the first time she's yelled it this morning, "Come one, come all! First bell for your last meal!"

He and Tirani never did move from the floor. Remy scrubs sleep from his eyes and pulls his legs beneath him. They have work to do.

In the common room, Roca arranges three heaping platters of food on the table.

In this light, her eye looks awful. The bandage over the wound is smaller, but the exposed skin around it is the livid red of a nascent infection. The withering won't allow her to heal. Remy doesn't even need to look at his hands. He knows from the hot, heartbeat throb of them that he's on his way to infection, too.

Thomlin steps in beside them, still looking half asleep—or like he hasn't slept at all, half-moons of exhaustion under his eyes bruise-blue. A tiny smear of blood under his nose has dried rusty brown. He lowers himself gingerly into his seat at the table.

If Remy's going to try out his half-assed plan to give them time free from the withering, he should do it soon. Tonight, preferably, before his withering gets past Yves' point of no return.

Not that he has any idea how to start, even after talking it through with Tirani. He can't ask for their cooperation. *Hey, I have this method I think could temporarily free you from the withering* sounds nice until they start asking how it works. It's all downhill from there, because the method is a severing, which makes Remy a *witherer* and he'll have to admit, *Oh, yeah, I'm the one who cast it in the first place.*

They'll eat him alive.

"Damn, that's grim." Thomlin frowns at the spread of food.

Remy chuckles. It's an appropriate observation for their current circumstances, even though Thomlin's talking about something else.

Roca shrugs. "It's what we had."

Springy slices of homemade bread sit beside a stick of soft butter and two jars of preserves on the table.

Remy recognizes them from Ma Windsel's home—the regular preserves and the spicy jar with its bright red flecks. Another platter holds steaming fish cakes sprinkled with delicate rings of wild onion, garnished with juicy pink lima slices.

It looks delicious. Remy has never wanted to eat anything less.

"Before," Roca says, quiet, as she arranges the plate of golden-brown fish cakes. "Before we left, she packed food for us. Seemed wrong to let it go to waste, even though . . ." She shrugs. "I'll get something for Idrian when he wakes up, but the pills should keep him out for a couple more hours, even with us gone. I piled like a million blankets on him, the heaviest we had, so hopefully he won't miss us. Anyway, dig in, for tomorrow we die, or whatever."

Remy drops into a chair so hard his jaw clacks. When he first sat here, being so close to Idrian made his skin crawl. Now, Idrian's empty seat leaves him just as unsettled. He manages a faint smile when Roca places the massive stuffed bear in the chair with a flourish.

"So what's the deal?" Remy says. "Last time, you did the food *before* a big thing, not after one."

Roca grins, sharp and predatory. "Oh, sweet child, you thought that was a big thing? We still need fuel."

Remy swallows. "Didn't we burn the OSS?"

"To a crisp. But we got a message from someone inside. A sympathizer. She says she and a few others can steal fuel for us and meet us outside the OSS's sensor range in a smaller vessel."

"That sounds easy."

"It does, and that's what should scare you. It's never easy. But we're in no position to refuse their offer. She seems confident she can sneak away without being noticed, says they won't be looking for interference from inside and are unlikely to notice the exchange. *I think we need to be ready for anything.*"

"Ready how?"

"This ship was originally a transport vessel, so it's not like we're armed if they're lying. Ready, in the best-case scenario, to get the fuel on the Lamprey and send it to the Isles before anyone tries to wipe us off the map." Roca falls into a chair. "I need a drink." She immediately stands from it. "We *have* a drink!"

She rifles through a pack thrown on the messy game table which is clearly never used for games until she withdraws a massive, corked bottle. "This stuff is wicked. Thom! Get the *fancy cups.*"

"I just sat down." Thom, unapologetic, butters a slice of bread with scientific attention, then heaps an embarrassing amount of spicy jam on top of it.

Remy sits up. This is perfect. "The cups, are they in the kitchen? I'll get them."

A plan crystallizes in his mind. The kitchen is just past the infirmary. And in the infirmary, in the first aid kit on Thom's desk, are the sleeping pills Roca had Remy grab for Idrian.

They're all about to drink. If Remy can knock everyone out, it'll give him time to tie the false-bonds without interference.

It's a horrible plan, of course. Good people though they might be, Remy has no reason to expect them to be anything but hostile when they wake from clearly drugged sleep. In their place, Remy wouldn't wait for an explanation. He'd boot himself out the airlock.

Which would be the last nail in their coffins, because if they boot him out the airlock *after* he frees them from the withering, they're denying Idrian the chance to kill him. He'd be floating, insensate, in the airless, lightless void of space, and with the last beat of his heart, his withering would be sealed. His clumsily-tied false-bonds would probably not survive his death. Which would mean their fatebonds would return to Idrian and then they'd all die.

A hopeless laugh scrapes its way from Remy's throat.

"What's wrong?" Roca asks.

"Nothing. I was just thinking a drink sounds fantastic."

"Get the cups, then. They're above the stove in that cushioned compartment at the back. You'll recognize 'em. They'll be the only things that match. Grab the corkscrew, too! Drawer in front of the door. It sticks—you'll have to tug to get it open."

"Nice!" Remy pushes himself upright and grabs the bottle beside Roca, tipping it in a dry salute. He gives Tirani a steady stare that he hopes comes across as *stay here, I've got this*. "I'll be back."

He forces a casual stride as he leaves the room, but no one seems to see a flashing sign over his head proclaiming his guilt, so he gets into the hall without interruptions. Even Tirani remains inside, awkwardly going to Roca's side when called to try some strange culinary combination.

Remy fast-walks through the halls until he arrives in the tiny kitchen, where he grabs everything he needs and drops it on the counter along with the massive bottle of alcohol. Then he sneaks into the infirmary and steals a handful of Idrian's sleeping pills from the kit. Idrian, deep asleep on the cot, doesn't stir while Remy does his work. Roca has thrown six or seven blankets over him so little more than his hair pokes out.

When Remy is finished, he and Idrian alone will bear the weight of the curse for as long as the false-bonding lasts. It won't be kind to either of them, but it'll at least give the others a *chance* of survival.

He just needs the right angle.

Intent. Pain and payment. Sacrifice. The principle holds in its own twisted way.

Ashes of the beloved dead to take the life of the living and loathed: paying for death with the dead. And the best-known solution, killing the witherer to free the withered: paying for a life with a life.

Balance.

The cost of Alta's survival will be Kuren's suffering. There must be something with equal weight to a life.

Remy's steps slow. Intent.

Everything hinges on *intent*.

Remy thought, last night, about how easy it would've been if death was the answer. Maybe it still is. He has one whole life to give. What if it doesn't have to be permanent? They have adrenaline. Remy saw it in the kit while looking for Idrian's sleeping pills. They have the resuscitation device.

After all, one wrenched-out tooth is not equivalent to a whole mouth of dead ones. It's a combination, some twisted up magic of suffering and sacrifice—meaningful but not always equal. It might work.

Resurrection on the eve of the Resurrection Festival sounds kind of appropriate.

It could be that simple. Perhaps it's never been written about because it's never been relevant.

There is, of course, one issue. He won't be able to ask Tirani to kill him. After Remy's done here, Idrian will be the only one still afflicted by the withering and thus the only person who can end it. Remy doesn't look forward to having that conversation.

So, I cursed you to death, which I'm mostly sorry for. I'm also responsible for the fact that the Isles are starving and the Chancellor is hot on your tail. Could you kill me, but like—nicely?

That'll go over well.

Even if Idrian agrees, the 'trust' Roca is so sure Remy earned will not survive this. He aches at the realization.

Fuck. For now, he'll free Thom, Emil, and Roca. When Idrian wakes, they'll figure out the rest. Maybe there are right words for this. Maybe, by the time Idrian wakes, he can find them. To fix this, he might not have to break this new thing he's found. Roca and Thom and Emil, the ease with which they move around each other—the generosity with which they invited Remy into their lives. Idrian, whose loss is the same shape as Remy's, who shed his coat to warm Remy and leaned against him without asking a single question, because he understood without Remy having to say a word. It's so easy and vital, fatebond-sure.

So fragile. All that understanding, but Remy would have to be the world's worst fool to think it could stretch far enough to cover the things he's done.

Remy returns to the kitchen with the pills clenched in his fist. Before he gets to work, he peeks out into the hall. It's empty and echoing, lit at odd intervals.

How many per glass? One? Half of one? More? Mixing them with alcohol will increase the effects and he doesn't want them to overdose, so he drops a pill in each cup except his and Tirani's and hopes. In the alcohol, the pills bubble furiously.

He can do this.

Heart hammering, Remy piles the faceted glasses on a battered metal tray and steps into the hall with the tray balanced on one hand.

"Remy?"

"Fuck!" One of the glasses is still bubbling, the last fragments of pill dissolving. Remy throws an arm around the glasses—half to hide them and half to keep them from tumbling off the tray.

The adrenaline-blaze of fear delays the realization that he's fine. It's just Tirani.

"Why are you here?"

"I wanted to help. Remy . . . what are you doing?"

Remy explains on the walk back and asks for her help. He can blindly grasp for their tethers if he wants, but Tirani's eyes will make things more efficient.

She has only one question when he finishes. "Have you figured out how we save *you*?"

"Still untangling that bit."

Tirani sucks in a breath, and Remy knows from the furrow between her brows that she wants to beg him to stop or tell him he's reckless, but she knows as well as he does that it's now or never. "Fine." She takes the tray from him. "Let's do this."

∼

They all drink, though Roca, by the time Remy returns, has sunken into an odd melancholy. Still, she takes a few healthy swigs and follows them with a fishcake or two.

In thirty minutes, everyone's out.

It looks like a slaughter. Roca and Emil and Thomlin lay in their seats or on the floor like ragdolls. When the drugs took effect, Thomlin slumped forward onto the table. Emil tipped sideways in slow motion. His body now hangs over the side of his chair in a way that can't possibly be comfortable. Roca, ever-graceful, managed to fall from her chair entirely. Her cup spilled when she fell. Only her left foot is still in contact with the chair, hooked uncomfortably over its arm.

Remy squeezes his eyes shut once he's retrieved his supplies from his pack, kneeling in the doorway of the now-dark room with ash and honey spread out beside him and his pack in front of him. He has a job to do, both like and unlike any other he's performed.

Tirani sits to his left, a line of warmth against him. Remy matches his breaths to hers and gets to work, smearing honey over his hands until they're obscenely sticky.

With a perfunctory swipe, he coats his bottom lip in the stuff.

Then the last step. His hands barely shake as he drops his fingertips into his brother's ashes. They soak into the honey, black as sin, and Remy taps his lips with them.

His fingertips tingle when the ritual is complete, and he traces down his sternum until he comes into contact with the frenzied heat of his rotten bond.

I'm sorry, he thinks to Cameron, as if this is only the first time he's betrayed his brother's memory and not the latest in a series. *It won't be for long. I'm not letting you go.*

"Tirani?" he whispers.

She squeezes his shoulder. "I'm here."

When he stands, she stands with him. Pins and needles stab his shins from kneeling for so long, but he walks toward the table.

Emil first. He's nearest.

Tirani guides Remy to the fatebond that connects him to Idrian. It's a ruminant tether, connected at the base of Emil's skull. Of course it would be. Vital and intellectual. Remy's ash-painted hands close around the dense weave of it. The rope is strong and warm with life. The knot beneath his skin thrums with something electric in the instant before Remy whispers the words to sever it and cinches his hands around it. The honey heats on his hands, hot enough to burn him, hotter than it's ever been.

This is where he'd normally let go. This time, he grits his teeth against the pain and uses his other hand to grasp Cam's dead tether. Remy grasps at its frayed end and brings Emil's tether to it, tying a quick knot halfway down so there's room to knot Roca and Thom's tethers in the excess and pulling it so tight he loses his breath.

It's perverse, what he's doing, and it won't be permanent, but it'll save Emil for now.

Next is Thomlin, whose tether extends from his foot—a reckless fatebond. The core of Thomlin's care for Idrian and dedication to his cause is a desire to be of service.

Dizziness washes over Remy when he finishes tying the second knot. The backlash will hit harder with each person he saves— the fewer people the withering can spread its effects over, the more he'll bear.

It's one thing to know in theory and another to feel in practice. His joints ache, eyes burning. He wonders what they'll think when they find out they owe their life to Cameron Canta, who died so they could live, and to Remy, who they treat like a friend—the one who cursed them in the first place.

Tirani catches him when he staggers and lowers him to the floor.

He's lucky Roca is already down here. Lucky that Tirani's sight is all he needs. Her eyes and his hands. He shuffles across the floor and lets Tirani lead him to the ropelike bond that connects Roca to Idrian. An anchored tether—it extends from her right hand.

"She'll be all right," he promises Tirani. One way or another, he'll make sure of it.

Remy hunches over her for a moment and hauls in shallow breaths, ribcage twinging with the pain of bones stretched to snapping. These bonds do not belong with him, and his body knows it. He's terribly aware of the slow, labored tread of his pulse, but he squares his shoulders and wraps his hand around Roca's tether.

Her hand wraps around *him*, tight enough to break bones.

"You," she slurs, unfocused eyes flicking open. "Why would you . . . ?" Her gaze moves to where Emil is sprawled, helpless. "What'd you . . . do to them? I should've known . . . we've never gotten caught on the OSS until you. Then the island, they never—they *never* come up that far."

"That wasn't my fault!"

But it was, on the OSS. He sent the message to Andrew. *I only betrayed you once* wouldn't earn anyone mercy.

Remy instinctively tries to sever her bond, but she's awake, and she actively does not want him near her. Her desperate intent is poison. Blistering heat bursts through her tether, searing his skin and sizzling in his veins. Remy doubles over and chokes on it.

Before he can get a hold of himself, Roca's hand tightens around his throat. "I swear, if you hurt them—"

She cuts herself off, like she can't concoct a punishment cruel enough or fathom a future where she could not protect them.

"Roca, please!" Tirani lets go of Remy and scrambles over to Emil, lifting his wrist to show it to Roca. Roca squints into the dimness, clearly not getting it. "Look! Look at his arm. The withering's gone. Remy isn't hurting them, he's saving them. You have to let him work."

"How?"

Remy licks his lips as Roca's grip on his throat loosens.

This is good. Unexpected, but good. It makes things easier, in a sense. Remy can work with it. "All I'll be doing is temporarily severing your tether and tying it to my—to a broken one for a short time. It'll go back to Idrian, but by the time it does, I'll have unraveled the withering for him, too. If you're willing, though, I have a job for you first."

Her eyes on him are steady and aware despite the laxity of her limbs. "*You* cast it."

"You killed my brother," he says.

Silence draws tether-taut between them.

"Why does it always have to be something like that?" Roca turns away. "Fuck. Figures. How will you save Idrian?"

He bares his teeth in an expression that probably looks nothing like a smile. "You'll like this. Everything I've found in Yves' books implies that a meaningful gesture with intent will worsen a withering. My theory is that it can be used to unravel one, too. Of course, there's also the part where the withered have to kill the witherer. Which is where you come in—and why I need to wait to free you from it."

"What do you mean?"

"I need you to help me die."

Chapter Sixteen

Ruminant, or head-connected, tethers signify a connection strengthened by shared interests or beliefs. Bearers of ruminant tethers long to discover, innovate, or effect change together. Their health and thickness may be affected by a change in priorities or interests. Ruminant bonds are among the most likely to fade healthily, without harmful decay—a simple drifting apart (and sometimes back together).

— From *On the Manipulation of Tethers*

Roca blurts, "You need *what*?"

"Remy!" Tirani grabs his wrist. "You didn't tell me—"

"I'll be fine. Just for a minute. If I die with the *intent* to unravel your witherings and at the hand of someone who still bears the curse, I think it should free us. Ideally, you'd bring me back as soon as it disappeared."

Roca's eyelids are heavy from the sleeping pill's effects, but her stare is unimpressed. "That leaves me a lot of room to let you stay dead."

Tirani steps in close. "You will *not*," she growls, and even though Roca has several inches on her, Tirani is knife-edged and angry, fit to kill. Remy wouldn't bet against her.

"'Course not."

Tirani's eyebrows go up, lips pressed together.

"Ahh, you've grown into such a little terror. No surprise there. You used to have me and Dad wrapped around your little finger."

"I don't remember that."

"I figured. I've been meaning to talk, but there hasn't been *time*, you know? Never is. We're always running, always an hour behind. It never bothered me as much as it did when I saw you. I recognized you the moment I learned you were a weaver, you know that? *Tirani*, never met another kid with that name in my life." With a smile, she reaches to touch the little mole by Tirani's eyebrow. "And this. I used to try to do your hair when you were a baby and you'd say *no* and give me *this exact look*, and it was the most brutal toddler takedown I've ever seen. I saw you, and I just knew. We lost a lot of years."

"Please," Tirani says. "Not now."

Roca twirls a finger in one of Tirani's curls before her hand drops, heavy. "It's rotten, isn't it? To have you back only when we're like this. Fucking unfair. You're a different person now, and I hate that I don't know her."

Tirani just shakes her head.

Remy pushes up beside her. "It'll be okay. I'll make it okay." He turns to Roca. "You've got shock stickers in the infirmary and adrenaline in the kit. Feed me CO_2 until my heart stops, then bring me back when the withering's gone."

"This is ridiculous, Remy," Tirani says. "There has to be another way."

"Maybe, but I haven't found it, and if I don't do *something*, we all die. Roca dies." He grabs Tirani's hands and holds tight. "You told me you wanted everyone to live. This is how."

Tirani bites her lip and looks away, which means he's won. There's no triumph in the realization, not when her eyes are wet with tears.

"I'll be fine," he says.

"Don't promise. Just don't leave me."

Roca lifts herself into a sitting position. "Look, if you need me to kill you, it'll have to be quick. I tried not to drink much because you were acting really suspicious—seriously, kid, don't go into crime—but I can't guarantee I'll be awake for long. There's a storage room next to the infirmary we can use. Tirani, help me up?"

Tirani and Remy and Roca support each other down the hall to the storage room. It's shadowed and grave-like, its corners brimming with boxes.

Remy perches on a cot under the single light in the middle of the room. Roca pulls up a stool while Tirani runs next door to get what they need. While she's gone, Remy says, "I can't free you from the withering yet because if you can't bring me back, it's important that you still bear it, so my death will save you. You, Tirani, and Idrian are the only ones left who can kill me."

"Ah," Roca says. "How morbid."

Tirani bustles back inside with the tools, ending the conversation.

"I'm no doctor." Roca raises the resuscitation toolkit. "But Thom's dead to the world and these things are supposed to be smart. They talk to you and shit." She stifles a yawn. "We'd better get started."

Roca places a half-circlet on her head, its bright display flicking to life over her right eye and showing Remy's vitals. A cheery voice from the headset guides her on the placement of the shock stickers, cold and sticky on his chest.

The display politely shows a beating heart. "Normal sinus rhythm detected. Do not shock."

Roca rifles around behind Remy for a minute, emerging triumphant. "All right. So! We don't have CO_2, but I was able to make this little guy." She holds up a mask, except it's not attached to anything and all the air holes have been closed with ugly matte-black tape. "Lucky you, I'm not entirely opposed to asphyxiating you."

Fear floods Remy's veins, acid-bright and urgent, his body remembering his airless gasps on Alta. He could run. Roca's clumsy with the drugs and Tirani wouldn't stop him. He could make it to the door—

"Ready to die?"

He grips the sides of the bed to keep himself in place, pulse jackrabbiting and vision narrow.

"As I'll ever be."

What if she decides not to bring him back? What if she tries and fails?

Worse, what if she succeeds? What'll happen when Idrian finds out what Remy did? Remy loses his breath trying to imagine it—Idrian's familiar grin shifting to cold disgust. Idrian looking at him like an enemy. How funny that a few days ago he'd have welcomed it.

"He'll hate me, won't he?"

When Roca only stares, he clarifies, "Idrian. When he finds out."

"He won't be happy, but I'll be with you when you tell him. I'll make him see sense. He'd have killed for his sister, too, if it could've saved her." She waves the mask. "In ten, okay? And nine, eight . . ."

Remy inhales, and it's not deep enough, not meaningful or satisfying enough to be his last. The air grows heavy, compressing his lungs and driving his spine into the knotted stuffing of the cot. The light overhead blinds him. He's not sure he could stand if he tried, but he shakes with the urge of resisting the flight adrenaline demands of him. He can do this. He will do it. He wants to.

Roca counts five.

Four.

Three.

Tirani grabs his hand in both of hers and holds it so tight it hurts.

One.

"Sorry." Roca's eyebrows draw together. She presses the modded mask over his mouth and nose until it creates a seal.

Remy tells himself he won't struggle. He'll go gently.

It's a lie. He dies with blood under his fingernails.

⁓

Sound returns first, garbled and desperate.

Breath is a revelation as his lungs expand. His heart plods, aching against his ribcage. Someone cries in the background. Something beeps.

A mechanical voice chirps, "Normal rhythm restored. Do not shock."

Someone says, "Thank fuck." And then, "Oh, *fuck.*"

Something peels from his chest with a mild sting.

Lifting his eyelids is nearly impossible, but he squints into cruel light, where blue and purple text from Roca's headset paints itself across her face. She's listing to the side, eyelids half-mast as the animated heart throbs cheerily in her display.

Something clatters to Remy's left and Tirani rushes into his line of sight, leaning down and pressing her forehead to his.

"How . . ." Remy hasn't done anything more strenuous than lay here and die, but his whole body aches with it, voice pathetically fractured. He swallows and licks dry lips. "How'd it go?"

"It worked!" Tirani says.

"About that." Roca turns her wrist to show him where the mark crawls back up her forearm. "It worked . . . while you were dead."

The truth sits in him with all the unassailable solemnity of an anchor. That's the end, then, isn't it? It's not like he has another life to give, or any other ideas.

His hand is an anvil, but he drags it up to cover his eyes. "Help me up?"

A smile pulls one corner of Roca's mouth up as she and Tirani help him sit, one hand behind his back. "Worth a shot, though. You look like death warmed over. And I feel like it. Not sure how much longer I'll be awake."

Remy sucks in a fortifying breath. "Let me do the severing for you, then. When Idrian's awake, we can talk about . . ."

Roca's lips press together. "What about Idrian? What happens to him?"

"Depends on which one of us dies first, and how long we last. If it's him, and he dies soon, the withering dies with him, I die with him, and the rest of you live."

"That's not ideal."

"Wait until you hear the next one. If it's him and he takes his sweet time to die—and he seems the type—your tethers will have plenty of time to travel back to him and we *all* die when he does. Same result if I die naturally: the second I'm gone, Idrian's withering is sealed, your tethers return to him because a false-bond won't survive the death of the bearer, and you all die after however much time the withering decides to make you suffer."

"Those are very shitty options, Remy."

"I know. But if it's me, and *he* kills me, you all live. I'm not a fan of being murdered—I can say that from experience, now—but that was my only idea. I don't want Tirani to have to live without you, so . . ." He shrugs. "So I guess that's it."

"Remy, no!" Tirani says. "You can't. Not like this."

Remy tries a smile. "I'm sorry. I put you in a really awful position. But I started this, and I can end it. Everyone else will live. That wouldn't be such a bad way to go."

"I won't let it happen." The words are low, but Remy wants to believe her.

Roca plants both her hands on the table, eyelids fluttering. "Well, I don't want to kill you, either. Not for good. I don't think Idrian will, either."

Remy's insides wrench, eyes sweeping away to skim the floor. "Won't he?"

Roca sucks in a breath through her teeth. "You might need to give him time."

"Thanks to me, we don't have time. Let me free you from the withering. That way, you and the others can recover so you'll have the energy to help us when we're being idiots."

"I like the sound of that." She grabs his wrist, her grip weak. "Damn, how many sleeping pills did you use?"

"Just one. But I doubt they were supposed to be combined with alcohol." Remy supports her shoulder when she lurches toward him. "I can get started. It won't take long."

"What's it going to be like?"

"Nothing you'll notice. He's still alive, after all, and tethers aren't architects of truth, they're echoes of it." The words Tirani has always told him slide off his tongue, and this time he believes them. Remy's hand drifts down his sternum, where Emil and Thomlin wait at the other end of Cam's rotten tether. "I doubt it'll feel any different to you. Think of it as spending a night with an acquaintance. Sleeping somewhere else doesn't change where you live. The place you go back to is still home."

Their tethers will return to Idrian. Remy's will return to stretching out into emptiness.

Roca laughs, but it comes out a sigh. Her elbows unlock and her hair tumbles over her shoulders when she falls onto the exam table where Remy died. "That's damn poetic. Fine. Go ahead."

She's half-asleep when Remy lifts the pillow from the table and puts it under her head. "You can rest."

The healthy rope of her fatebond beats like a heart against his hands. Severing a living bond is nothing like cutting a dead one. Remy ties her tether to his own and staggers when he loses her support.

Her withering recedes like threads unraveled and withdrawn, until she's free of it. Remy's climbs farther up his arm, hot like a brand.

Now it's just him and Idrian and a countdown that will either save the others or seal their fates.

Roca's breath is even and slow in sleep. Remy's is a riot in his throat. He's only half warmed over from his useless flirtation with death, but his work isn't finished. He stands.

"I'll check on the others. They'll be confused when they wake up."

He'll have to explain. But how can he tell them he learned this from a book, didn't even ask their permission, doesn't know how long it will last? They'll be calling for his execution before he speaks a word.

"You should sleep," Tirani says. "You're exhausted."

He is. His nap on the floor wasn't nearly enough to make up for his hazy half-consciousness on the boat to Auni the other day and his failure to get a decent night's rest since.

"I can't."

"You can. They'll make noise when they wake. I'll be with you. Here. You could use the bear as a pillow. I'll grab some blankets. And your tincture. You can sleep on the game table, or wherever. Just rest. Let your body heal as much as it can, okay?"

He nods, and she squeezes his shoulder.

"Good. I'll be back. You settle in." She vanishes down the hall.

Better to let her do this. Remy knows only too well that there's peace in staying busy. He heads for the common room where Thomlin and Emil sleep.

They both still rest on the table where they collapsed, wrists clean of the withering and pulses strong against his fingers when he checks.

Hopefully the false-bonds will last long enough to save them. Yves' book focused mostly on joining the broken tethers of the grieving. The single nod to doing the same with living tethers was that it was *unsustainable and short-lasted, disconnected in a matter of days.* At the rate things are going, Idrian and Remy also have a matter of days. Remy releases Thom's wrist when he hears light footsteps in the hall behind him.

Tirani's mention of sleep worked like a spell—days of exhaustion weigh Remy down. He'll gladly curl up in the world's most horrifying quilt and sleep for as long as they let him. "I have to be honest, the game table's actually looking pretty—"

But the person he finds when he turns isn't Tirani.

It's Idrian, sleep-mussed and furious, hand wrapped around the weapon at his side.

"What have you done?"

Chapter Seventeen

*Nothing
after all,
can be destroyed
which was not first loved.*

— From "Gardener's Paradox"

"Shit." Remy spreads his arms like it might hide the sight of Thom and Emil sprawled in the dark like the dead. "This isn't what it looks like."

For once, it actually isn't.

But Idrian is frozen, staring at something on the floor.

Remy's skin prickles with a flush of terror. His supplies lie right where he left them. Ashes, honey. Incontrovertible evidence of his nature. For one breathless second, he hopes Idrian won't understand. He hopes a lot of things. Yves and Roca both responded better than Remy could ever have hoped for. Maybe Idrian will, too.

But it's a stupid wish. Idrian's expression goes from anger to something far more frightening. It must help that Remy's bandaged palms are still dark with the mixture he used for the severing. His hands, raised in surrender, are all the evidence Idrian needs to convict him.

Idrian nudges the pot of honey with his shoe. "*What did you do to them?*"

Remy realizes what he's about to do a second too late. "Idrian, don't—!"

One flick of Idrian's foot and the honey overturns. Cam's ashes spill from their container and fan across the floor, staining the slow flow of honey black as rot.

Remy scrambles toward it without thinking, words stoppered in his throat. Idrian strikes with the merciless intent of a severing, one clammy hand closing around Remy's upper arm and preventing him from kneeling to gather the ashes.

"It was you, this whole time." Idrian's voice is no louder than it's ever been, but he might as well be yelling for the way it echoes in Remy's head.

On another face, in another situation, his expression might be curiously neutral, but this is the awful, placid blankness Idrian wore in the last few moments of Jacques' life.

I'll be with you when you tell him, Roca promised. *I'll make him see sense.*

Remy's hazy dreams of holding onto what he's found here scatter like so much ash. It shouldn't surprise him. He drew a deep dividing line between them, carving a curse into Idrian's skin and endangering everything he holds dear.

There's no give to Idrian's grip. Even with the compression cuffs and the painkillers and anti-inflammatories keeping Idrian on his feet, he can't be doing any kindnesses to his wounded arms. Remy will have to break bones—his or Idrian's, maybe both—to extricate himself, and he's *tired*. He was dead five minutes ago.

Cameron's ashes dust Idrian's boots, and nausea swells in Remy.

"We *took you in*." Idrian drags him into the narrow corridor.

Caged bulbs spill their glow onto the ground at odd intervals. The light paints Idrian impossibly bright and sharp-edged, vengeful. The shadows make a mournful ghost of him.

They don't stop until they arrive in the cargo bay. Idrian wrenches Remy's arm so he loses his balance, then lets go like he can't bear to be near him any longer. His hands clench into fists as Remy stares up from the ground, bandaged palms stinging on the floor and body heavy with the weight of his withering.

"We *protected* you."

Idrian's voice reverberates in the cargo bay, a thousand recriminations bouncing back.

It'd be easier if it was rage that echoed around the room, growing hollower with each repetition, but Idrian's ocean-clear eyes are narrowed with something like confused betrayal. He draws his gun and points it at Remy, as unwavering as he was when he killed Jacques. *I'll do you the same favor,* he promised back then, when Remy did not dare to call him anything more specific than *murderer*.

Remy rides a cresting surge of adrenaline and ignores the way it sets his teeth on edge. He doesn't have to shut his mouth anymore. Cam's name sits on his tongue and he can finally speak it.

Remy's lips twist up, and by the way Idrian shudders where he stands, whatever expression he's wearing must be horrible. "You protected me?" A laugh rattles free from his chest.

Idrian's lips press tight. "What did you do to Thom and Emil? Where's *Roca*? You—you're—" His face shines dully with sweat in the light of the cargo bay. The Lamprey with its murderous teeth rests on the floor, clearly having returned from its unmanned delivery while everyone slept.

Idrian could save a bullet, impale him on the teeth.

"I trusted you," Idrian says, so quiet it's hardly more than breath, rough like the words were cut from him. He turns halfway away.

Nausea twists in Remy—grief and guilt and anger blended, acid on his tongue. It should not hurt for this thing he's built to crumble. It's brand-new, barely formed. Surely it should be more fragile, hollowbond-thready. It shouldn't crush the breath from his chest. "I hated you," Remy confesses.

If only he could hate him now.

Idrian is human and monster at once—vulnerability and violence.

Yves talked about hatred so straightforwardly, but Remy sits across from the man he once wanted to kill, and hate is no easy thing between them. He'd give anything to make it easy, to swap this twisting sickness in his gut for something as pure and uncomplicated as rage.

But he couldn't, could he? He wouldn't, even if he could. Rage is a cutting, narrow-minded thing. It creates binaries—unkind simplicities. They're long past that.

The lightless eye of the gun stares at Remy, but Idrian won't even look his way.

He really is an idiot. If Remy had the energy, athleticism, or intention, he could wrest the gun from Idrian's hands and turn it on him. He ignores the twinge in his chest, the awful and unaccountable urge to reach out.

"You told me about your sister," Remy whispers instead. He might as well have charged Idrian, who staggers, wide eyes darting to Remy.

"You remember my brother, the Astoria grad? We talked about him, too. Remember how he was sick?" His voice grows louder, filling the space between them with phantom echoes. *My brother, my brother, my brother.*

If Idrian brought him here to do him the favor of a quick execution, he'll first hear what Remy has to say. "I watched that sickness eat him away until he couldn't even stand. I didn't know what was killing him until it was too late. And you know what? If I did, I could have *stopped it*. Back then, I would've hurt anyone to save him."

"Be quiet."

Remy holds Idrian's gaze. "Not him, though. I think he knew the whole time what you did. My brother, he was a thousand times kinder than I am. Our parents were dead and I don't know how he did it, but he was so fucking good, Idrian, so much better than I ever deserved. If he stood on Alta and understood what was happening, he would've taken every single person from that place and planted them somewhere they could grow. That *Chancellor's dog* who was on your tail, the one you had Yves *get rid of*, did you even know his name?"

The gun in Idrian's bruised hands shakes. His finger curls around the trigger. "Shut up."

But Remy's tired of shutting up when all he wants to do is scream. His eyes burn with lack of sleep and his heart clenches in his chest and aches with every beat and every breath. His bones are anchors dragging him down, tethers tying him. His bandaged palms throb. Fever sizzles in his blood. He wants to fall asleep with his brother at his back and wake tucked in. He wants to have had the chance to do the same for Cam.

He was given everything and he's given nothing back. He couldn't stop Cameron from dying. He can't even kill his brother's murderer. Can't even hate him, not when he understands him.

"You killed him. He was *all I had*." The words come out shredded as Remy's vision blurs, funneling the cool grays of the cargo bay into a colorless swirl. He blinks to clear it and wipes at his cheeks, smearing filth on them.

The dusky blend of honey and ash still paints his bandages wherever his own blood hasn't darkened them. Remy grasps for Cameron's bond, close enough to his chest that he can ignore the foreign knots in it. The tightness in his throat loosens enough to allow a ragged breath in.

He doesn't know how false-bonding was ever supposed to be therapeutic. It hurts so much. Five years today, and Remy hasn't atoned for failing Cam at all. Five years, and he'll die having tied his brother to the people who called for his death. The bond beneath his hands is ragged and rot-slick, and Remy is not sorry but he is ashamed.

"Kill me if that's what you brought me here for, but you remember his name. The man you killed was Cameron Canta, and he was my big brother, and I loved him."

"Stop talking!" Idrian pushes forward, and Remy braces himself.

He's died once today. He's a pro at it now, surely.

But there's no pain, no gunshot, no impact.

Remy opens his eyes at the noise of a mechanical hiss and a sudden pressure at the collar of his tunic. Idrian drags him back and then *up*. Up the ramp of the Lamprey and into its interior, where he presses the same button he pressed before and growls, "Yves, do whatever you want with this one." He shoves Remy against the wall as he enters the navigation code, using the gun like a pointer to direct Remy. "Don't move."

Fuck that. Remy pushes toward Idrian until the barrel of the gun kisses the skin of his neck. His mouth speaks almost without his permission. "That's a tad hypocritical, isn't it?"

Idrian jerks back, lips parting, but he doesn't say a word.

"Jacques got a bullet to the head. You told me I'd get the same, 'just like that'. Why are you getting cold feet now? What about your *judgment calls?* Shoot me, Idrian."

It'd be so easy. Remy recalls his own finger on the trigger—irrevocable pressure, then release. Remy's death at Idrian's hands would be the answer to all the ugliest questions they face. The withering will unravel, saving everyone. Tirani will have her sister, Idrian his crew. It should be easy for Idrian. Remy has watched him kill three times now—the brutal ease of it, that empty expression.

Idrian's expression is anything but empty now, but Remy couldn't put words to it even if he knew them. Idrian only says, "Don't move," again and backs out of the Lamprey.

But then: "Remy? Remy! Where are you?"

Tirani's voice, thready and distant.

She must've looked for him and found Cameron's ashes on the floor.

She sounds afraid.

"Tirani? Don't come in!"

Idrian's already out the door, and Remy takes a step forward, but the entrance to the Lamprey hisses closed and clicks with a lock. The console at the front lights up, and the Lamprey launches itself unmanned, knocking Remy to the ground.

Distance brings an instant ache. No more healing by proximity, then, for all the good it's done. Idrian probably has no idea how much worse he made things for them both by letting Remy live.

Stars stream past the front window, colder and farther away in the lonely vacuum of space than they ever looked from the planet's surface, and Remy tightens his hands around Cameron's bond and lets its sick beat lull him to rest.

Chapter Eighteen

*Those connected with blue **piecebonds** bring to a partnership complementary—and sometimes contrasting—personalities and skillsets. Such bonds can be business-related or personal. Bearers of piecebonds long to be challenged. Such connections may carry those who bear them to great heights and to feats immortalized in the annals of history but can just as easily implode. Given the opposing personalities linked by such connections, piecebonds are strongest when backed up by patient care or shared intellectual interest and are thus most likely to remain healthy when in ruminant or anchored positions; visceral piecebonds are more likely to rot than those linked at any other connection point.*

— From *On the Manipulation of Tethers*

A rough hand on his shoulder wrenches him from sleep.

"I take it things didn't go well?"

It could be minutes later when he processes the words. His lips are bone-dry, leathery tongue painted to the roof of his mouth.

The first thing he sees is the irritated line of his advancing withering. It's nearly to the ball of his shoulder, already reddening and beginning to branch. Idrian's probably isn't so urgent, since he's no longer sharing the burden of Remy's double-speed curse. But based on what Roca said when they first met on Auni, he's likely feeling the echo of what Remy's going through. If Remy dies like this, far away, his death will seal the curse. Everyone will die, and all his work will have been for nothing.

Idrian should've killed him. Why didn't he?

"This's ridiculous," Remy slurs. His blurred vision clears to reveal Yves crouching over him, dark circles beneath their eyes.

"I agree. You're all ridiculous. What're you *doing* here? I was sure Roca at least would've speared you through. Idrian, for sure."

"You'd think so, wouldn't you? But he flaked at the last second. The others, uh . . . weren't in any condition to provide input." Remy forces himself to his knees. Without the suit and its heavy boots, Alta's gravity is kinder to his bones. He finds his feet with Yves' help.

" . . . Idrian did this?" Yves sighs. "What a disaster. Does he *know?*"

"Some of it."

"I'm having trouble making sense of why you're still alive."

"You're not the only one."

"I don't know why I ever expect reasonable decision-making out of that man. What he expects *me* to do with you, I have no idea. Come along. Let me at least get some meds into you. Then . . . I hate to be blunt, but I need to send you back."

Remy closes his eyes, and his whole body feels dragged down. "It didn't work," he whispers. "I was sure I'd figured out a way to fix it, but it didn't work. I don't know what to do, Yves. I don't want to die, but . . ."

"It'd be nice if we could get what we wanted. Stand *still.*"

He's not sure how still he's standing (or how he's still standing), but it's enough for Yves to strap a mask over his face.

"Gotta keep you alive so I can send you to your execution, hmm?" They lift their glasses to massage the bridge of their nose, then offer a hand to help him out. "This is shit. I hate it. Come on."

Remy inhales oxygen through the mask as he exits with Yves, untethered and lightheaded. Yves' hand in his is cold, but their grip is reassuringly tight.

"So, what was it you tried?"

"Dying."

Yves' grip goes lax, and Remy staggers before they catch him. "*What?*"

"I figured if I was like . . . technically dead for a bit and was brought back, maybe it'd reset everything."

"Damn. That's dedication."

"It didn't stick. Came back as soon as I did. It should've worked."

"Yeah, well, withering's half logic and half poetry. Half nonsense, too, but that's one too many halves. Like the damn tooth thing. It's suffering, but it's not *equal*." Yves scowls. "And how you can only act as proxy if you're blood-related. My love for Thom is no less than a parent's or a sibling's, but there's nothing I can do. I can't say you're lucky, but I envy you."

"It just makes it worse," Remy whispers, "That the possibility was there."

Yves sinks into silence for a long while as they navigate the dim, claustrophobic halls. "It's all fucked up, isn't it? I'm sorry your thing didn't work. It should've. Witherings love morbid, awful little gestures like that, and dying is a damn sight better than a gesture. You sure you meant it?"

"I literally let Roca murder me."

"Ha! That is a point in favor of sincerity. Who knows, then. Walk slow. I'm not giving you as much oxygen as you're used to. We're rationing."

Remy can't help it—the absurdity of the whole situation crashes down on him, and he laughs, breathy and hysterical.

Yves bumps his shoulder. "Stop that. You're wasting air. This isn't funny."

"You're keeping me alive so someone else can kill me. It's a little funny."

It has to be funny, or it's something much worse.

~

Remy is floating on a seasick but pain-free haze, splayed out across one of the infirmary's cots, when the lights on the walls shift red and an alarm blares through the halls.

Remy has heard that tone before. It's the same one that announced the delivery from the Chancellor. The approach alarm.

Yves leans back in their seat. "Idrian's really going overboard with those deliveries." But then they glance at Remy and go rigor-mortis rigid. "He . . . didn't happen to get his hands on a second Lamprey, perchance?"

Remy shakes his head.

"Shit."

Yves runs. Remy pushes up from the cot and follows.

When he finally catches up, Yves and the young woman he met last time are bent over in front of the wall of screens. It's like the world's worst déjà vu. Just like last time, a vessel with the Chancellor's giant crest emblazoned on its side fills every screen. An alert pops up. BROADCAST PRIVILEGES REQUESTED.

Yves and the woman confer, and after a while, the woman types in a string of numbers, letters, and symbols, and speaks into a mic. "What do you want?"

"Allow us to dock."

"It's traditional to ask nicely."

"It was not a request. Allow us to dock. We have a new shipment of dissidents from the surface and are acting on the orders of the Chancellor. You are on thin ice, Alta; I would not suggest acting against us."

"How many in the shipment?"

"There are 212 prisoners to be distributed among Alta, Fluora, and Toxys."

The woman's hand falls from the button that allows her to speak. "That's more than we've ever—" She whispers a curse and turns to Yves. "We can't . . ."

Yves shakes their head. "We can't. They'll die. And if they don't, others will. Just feeding them would drastically shorten the longevity of our existing resources. We've already got more bodies than we can handle."

Yves presses the button. "No," they say, concisely.

There's a long pause on the other end. Then, "I'm sorry?"

"You should know the supplies you sent before aren't adequate to sustain our population until your next delivery. You have plenty of room on the surface for these people. Shit, there's more than enough room for *everyone* on the Isles aboard the OSS if you wanted us off the planet but actually cared for our wellbeing. Do what you will with your prisoners. We won't take them."

"*You don't want to do this.*"

Yves laughs into the mic. "About time you said something that makes sense. You're right. I don't want to be doing any of this, but you've made sure we have no other choice."

Another pause before the cold voice returns. "*You've made this bed yourself, Alta, with your disrespect for the life of the planet and your continued resistance to the Chancellor's peace-keeping laws.*"

"What's your name?"

"I'm—I . . . don't see how that has any relevance. What's yours?"

"I'm Yves Radenne, and I'm as much of a doctor as this place has. I'm fucking exhausted because I've been up all night dealing with the air-starved living and the corpses of the children you've killed by denying us the things we need to live. Who are *you*?"

"I'm . . . Communications Officer Brant, aboard the *Preservation*. And we didn't—if anyone is dead, we didn't kill them. You did."

"Communications Officer Brant, I hope you're as deluded as that makes you sound. If not, you're party to a calculated massacre. I'm tempted to allow you to board so you can see what you've created here, but as I said, I'm afraid I'll have to decline."

There's silence for a long while, and when the *Preservation* transmits next, it's a different voice, ragged and deep. "*Since we're introducing ourselves, doctor, I'm High General Hayeth. Understand that what happens next is on your head.*"

They don't leave. They don't fire on Alta. They drift gently around the moon for what feels like hours before finally departing.

"They're just . . ." Remy blinks. "Does that mean we're off the hook this time?"

The girl in front of the screen buries her head in her hands. "No. It means they've got something worse in mind."

Yves slumps against the wall when the *Preservation* is finally out of sight. "We're fucked." They extend a hand to Remy. "Get up. You can't die here or it's really over."

∼

Yves boards the Lamprey with Remy, sitting at the control panel while Remy sprawls out on the floor.

"Why are you coming with me?"

"I don't expect to be gone for long, if that's what you're worried about. There's nothing I can do back there, anyway. The way things are, people either die or they don't."

Remy blinks and his eyes long to stay closed.

A shrill beep pierces the silence, and Yves speaks, suddenly tense. "Alta?"

The voice of the woman from the broadcast room fills the vessel. *"Yves? It's Shaia. I'm glad you're still in range. There's something you need to see. I'm sending a broadcast request."*

"Should I come back?"

Silence stretches long between them. *"No. I don't think— there's nothing you can do. We skimmed the Chancellor's most recent broadcast off the satellite. It's . . . not good."*

Yves doesn't say anything, but they must accept the broadcast request, because the left-most window of the Lamprey flicks to milky translucence and begins to display a video.

Remy rolls onto his stomach to watch, forgetting the ache in his joints.

It begins like every other broadcast he's seen. First, the Chancellor's crest flashes silver-white on a background of star-swept blue, and then the Chancellor himself comes on-screen, sitting in the plush armchair with the dying-Verdine painting and lit by the cozy gold glow of a single lamp. A serious broadcast, then. "Good evening, people of Verdine. Per our last conversation . . ."

Why did he never notice, before, the artificial intimacy of these things? *Our last conversation.* As if the people listening have a voice in it.

Remy tunes back in as the Chancellor keeps talking. " . . . but our investigations have only uncovered further depravity. I'm appalled by the extent of the violence perpetrated on my beloved people and the world we sacrifice so much daily to preserve. Tomorrow, we will begin to celebrate the Resurrection Festival in thanks for the bounty Verdine provides in return for our thoughtful stewardship and in commemoration of the time when we failed to do so. I fear the only mask I am fit to wear during the festival is that of the Fool. I do not have the words to describe the things we have uncovered. I can only show you. Please be aware that these images are graphic. The footage you're about to see is not from Veida. This destruction is happening *now*. It's happening again, and it's a pattern I cannot bear to see repeated. Your children may wish to turn away, but I hope you will watch to the end if you can. Watch, and understand why we must unite to say *no*, once more, to the reckless cruelty that, if given room to grow, would wither our green world."

Remy loses his breath at the sight of Kuren—of lima trees heavy with pink fruits and no one around to pick them. Of boats crowding the shores, evacuating crying residents. A stuffed rabbit, hand-sewn and muddy with matte-dead buttons for eyes, lapped at by low tide. Of the crater the lake once filled, already mud-cracked at the rim. The tiny amount of water left at the bottom is more a mockery than anything, and barely visible with all the dead fish. There's a voice-over partway through from someone who saw the *Astrid* draining the lake's water.

She stands on the drying hollow of the lake, holding herself as she faces away, like she can't bear to see what they made of it. *It was all we had,* she says, over and over. The broadcast shows an echoing village square. Roadside stalls deserted. The once-lively stores near the docks, closed up and dark. An inn, lightless. Ma Windsel's home.

She said Idrian would not be welcome there again. It's worse, somehow, knowing she won't be there to curse them even if they return.

Jacques and the patrolling guard now fill the screen, along with images not of the bodies but of the stains left behind where they were found. In a few short words, the Chancellor describes their executions. What part of any of it isn't true?

An image of Andrew's father, again. Blond hair and blue eyes, just like Andrew. Like Idrian.

An image of Cam—taken upon his ascension to the position of Intermediary when Regine Delacour retired and recommended her young Vice-Intermediary for the position. Cam shakes her hand in the photo, and the set of his lips looks more or less professional, but Remy recognizes the twist that says he would be *beaming* if it weren't such a formal occasion. (There is another photo in which he is beaming—taken either before or after this one, most likely. It's one of Remy's favorites.) Regine should've held her position for decades longer. In the photo, Cam looks barely older than Remy.

Again, brutally efficient, the Chancellor describes their deaths.

Then, a picture of Remy—the same old picture where he looks maybe fourteen. "We have reason to believe that young Remy has also become a casualty of this man's brutal conquest—the last living members of the family wiped out. I knew both these boys, and I will mourn them."

"What the fuck?" Remy mutters. "Reason to believe I'm dead?"

Technically, he did die, but the Chancellor can't know that. The screen flicks away from Remy's picture and to cold footage of Alta. In horrifying detail, the slow pan of the camera reveals the frozen corpses that adorn Alta's surface. The Chancellor doesn't comment here. He doesn't need to. His audience, already primed with stories of Idrian's criminality, will draw their own conclusions, and they will be at least halfway wrong.

After about a minute of footage of the Isles, there's damning voiceover:

"*We have a new shipment of dissidents from the surface to distribute and are acting on the orders of the Chancellor.*"

And Yves' voice: "*Do what you will with your prisoners. We won't take them.*"

The image flicks back to the Chancellor, his expression hooded by lamplight. He leans forward, and Remy feels as if he's alone with the man as he delivers his final words.

"We have been kind to those who would harm our resuscitated world, sending them to consider their actions on the Isles which once preserved us while we sought our *own* atonement. We have wasted time and labor and supplies we could be using to enrich life for law-abiding citizens. But instead of ruminating on their misdeeds, these people have aided and abetted a man who has destroyed the lives of those who labor to help this planet thrive. They have blocked our transmissions, asserted their independence, and denied the Protectorate's rule. They have, in essence, armed themselves against everyone on Verdine. As your elected ruler, I take this threat to our abundance very seriously. The next time I speak with you all, I will have found a solution."

Remy gasps when the broadcast ends, his lungs hungry, eyes dry from staring without blinking.

Yves says, "Whatever he's planning, he's convinced everyone down there he's on the right side in this."

"That's ridiculous. Surely—"

"Tell me you didn't think we were barely human before all this. Where did you learn to think like that?"

His breath leaves him all at once, because he can't really say. There's no one moment, just a series of broadcasts over the last several years where the Chancellor's description of the Isles grew increasingly unkind. Subtly, he wove a tapestry of *us against them*, a tapestry that made Remy feel so righteous laying a withering.

He closes his eyes at the stab of pain in his chest.

How is he any different from the Chancellor? They've both justified murders with the gilded ideal of the dead. The Chancellor commits atrocities in the name of preserving the planet they once killed. Remy soaked up his fanatical zeal and used it as fuel for his own violence.

Idrian was wrong. The Chancellor hasn't made *dulled-down blades* of Verdine's citizens. He's sharpened every one of them and pointed them at his detractors.

"Even you had to see Alta at its most horrifying to understand what that bastard leaves out when he shows footage like that. Do you think there's a single person down there who has the context you do? If they do, they're on that ship of prisoners we denied. Even if they're down there, and they speak out, they'll be demeaned and dismissed."

Remy rolls onto his back and stares up blankly. "You think the Chancellor believes what he says?"

"Probably, but it doesn't matter. Even if he's lying through his teeth, he just turned the entire planet against us: no matter what he does to us now, it'll go down in history as a *victory* for Verdine against a corrupting force. You heard him. He thinks the paltry supplies he sends us are a waste. He *will* do something. We can't—shit, maybe he won't do anything. He doesn't have to. Without fuel, we'll be dead in a week. "

"What if we evacuate everyone?"

Yves laughs. "How? To where? That would give them the exact excuse they needed to blow us out of the sky. We'd be rebels. An advancing army, not desperate refugees. We don't have any vessel big enough to carry all of us anywhere, and if any significant number of us evacuated, it'd give them reason to kill anyone left behind and chase the escapees and execute them next."

"What about the Lamprey?"

"Look around. Sure, it's a stealth vessel and they're unlikely to notice or care about its comings and goings, but that means it's small enough not to matter. If we ignored safety protocols, perhaps we could fit twenty people inside. Sixty, if we packed them chest-to-chest. A hundred if they didn't have room to breathe anything except each other's breath. A *hundred* out of thousands, assuming they survived the journey. The *Astrid* isn't equipped to hold so many, either, and the surface won't be hospitable to people who have spent a lot of time here, never mind that we'd be sitting ducks. Even if we could get down there without being blown out of the sky, we'd be hunted."

"The OSS . . . ?"

"Large enough to hold those who would need time and accommodation before returning to the surface, but they'd kill us if we approached. Even trying would give them reason to attack."

"What if we got the people on our side? If he's spent such a long time courting public favor, he'd at least have to adjust his plans if the people turned against him, right?"

Yves laughs, raw and hopeless. "How do you propose we do that? Just accessing the broadcasts is the limit of our abilities. What could we say to change a single mind? That's the horrible part of what he's doing—very little of what he says is untrue. You heard what that man said earlier: we're lying in the bed we made."

"We could show them what I saw. The truth of what's happening to the people here. We could—"

"You're dying, Remy. *We* can't do anything. I'm taking you back to the *Astrid* so I can convince that idiot to kill you. Then I'm going to return with whatever supplies he has yet to send, and I'll share in whatever end the Chancellor has planned for us."

Remy's eyes sting, his chest on fire. "Aren't you angry? Don't you want—"

"I'm tired of wanting!" Yves spins to face him, eyes damp behind their glasses as they rocket to their feet. "I'm tired, okay? Of course I want. I want everyone to live. I want to be a doctor for scrapes and bruises, not a glorified undertaker. I want my hands to be clean. But Alta and Fluora and Toxys are falling to pieces and not one thing I want will happen. I want, at least, to rest."

Remy can barely breathe around the tightening of his throat. "I'll fix this."

The dim blue light from the END TRANSMISSION flickering on the screen makes a skull of Yves' face. "I'm sure you'll try."

They press a button to transmit. "Shaia? You're right. There's nothing any of us can do against that. If they come back, don't engage them. Adjust the comms rig to reject all contact except from the Lamprey. We'll call if anything comes up."

The woman's wry voice echoes into the cabin. *"Way ahead of you, Dr. Radenne."*

"I'll be back soon, assuming there's anything to return to," Yves says cheerily, then turns to Remy when the communication ends. "Sleep if you can, dear. It's the end of the world."

Chapter Nineteen

*Love
is not made by accident.
it is built. Carved. Cultivated.
To love is to crack open.*

— From "Gardener's Paradox"

The pain of distance lessens by shades as they draw closer to the *Astrid,* but even when they're in communications' range, Remy still feels wrung-out and half-dead. A harbinger of the end, perhaps.

"Idrian?" Yves transmits. "I'm here to return your wayward witherer. You shouldn't have thrown him away."

It's not Idrian's voice but Roca's that blasts into the Lamprey. "Thank goodness he's still alive!"

Remy croaks from the floor, "Didn't know you cared."

"Remy? That you?" Roca guffaws. "I don't. Not *much*, anyway. A little, maybe. The main thing is, you not being dead must mean Idrian's still kicking."

Remy forces himself up to his elbows. "What do you mean? Isn't he with you?"

A long stretch of silence, sharp enough to sever any tether. "We'll talk when you get here."

The rest of the journey is silent. When the Lamprey is settled in the *Astrid* 's cargo bay, Roca strides in, Tirani beside her.

Before Roca can say a word, Tirani grabs Remy and pulls him close. "I was so worried! I tried to tell him—"

"Are you okay? Idrian didn't . . ."

"I'm fine. Remy, I'm sorry it didn't work." She brushes her hands down his shoulders, then cups his chin. "You're burning up. You look awful."

"Only awful? I must look better than I feel."

She presses something cold into his hands: the container that held Cam's ashes.

Roca rubs the back of her head. "We swept up as much as we could. Wasn't much, but it's something. The floor was filthy, so there's probably all sorts of weird stuff in there."

Remy clutches the box to warm it between his hands.

"Idrian felt like an asshole when he realized what was going on. Tirani really laid into him, you should've seen it. *Damn* but the Aravel sharp tongue bred true in her. But it's not like he could've called the Lamprey *back*. Once it's deployed, it's an independent vessel, so we had to let it do its thing and hope—"

"You said he's not here?"

Roca winces. "Remember the folks I told you about who promised they could steal fuel from the OSS for us? He was a man on a mission as soon as he sent you away. He figured if he might die soon, he had work to do. Typical. He contacted the informer and arranged to meet. They refused to deliver straight to us and we didn't have the Lamprey, so they sent a small vessel for him. Just him. No guns, nothing else. We had him on the earpiece, but as soon as he got to the ship, radio silence. It's been . . . too long. We need to pick him up and get out of here, but they're on the fringes of the sensor range. We get too close, we risk being seen, and the OSS won't pull its punches. But they're not responding to our requests for contact and we can't leave without him. We have the Lamprey now, so we can approach. I can—"

"I'll go," Remy says.

"Oh you will, will you? What, you a pilot now?"

"No, but this withering will kill us both if I don't find him soon. I don't see how it makes much difference whether I die here or get killed looking for him. Can't you just send me to wherever he is, like he sent me to Yves?"

"The coordinates for the Isles are pre-programmed and they auto-approve its requests to dock when it arrives. I could *direct* it toward where Idrian went and teach you how to manually hail them, but I can't guarantee they'll respond."

"I'll make them let me in."

"Ha! You're not as good a liar as all that. Couldn't even keep your secret for a week."

"I won't have to lie," Remy says.

Yves raises a hand. "I'll pilot."

"No, you should stay here. It's better if you're safe, in case something happens."

"I'm hardly helpless, Canta."

"I know, but you've got people who need you."

"I *need* for you not to die and doom everyone."

"I'll be fine."

"Stop saying that. I brought you here so they could kill you, damn it."

"Then I'll take you," Roca says. "Or Emil."

"And leave the *Astrid* without its common sense or its only skilled pilot? Think about it. Sending me is the least wasteful option. If it's a trap, the people who were already doomed to die just die, and the rest of you are still alive to keep doing what you do. If it's not, I'll bring him back, and we'll figure out what to do from there."

The awkward silence lasts half a minute.

"Fine," Roca says. "It's not like we have a choice—none of *us* can kill you right now." She exposes her unmarked arm. "Bit of an asshole move, isn't it, making you save Idrian so he can do the honors?"

"A bit." What a strange position he's put them in. Will Idrian regret killing him? Will he hesitate at all?

"Take an earpiece. I want to hear everything."

He lets her put one in, and they return once more to the cramped interior of the Lamprey. Roca runs several checks and sighs before rapidly typing something into the computer. "I've programmed it to return if it isn't given permission to enter within five minutes once you're in range, so do your best. This screen will display your timer."

She sits him down in the chair. "Press this when you're close to open a dialogue and request entrance. This screen—" she points at a small, matte rectangle "—will light up if you tap it and display all the vessels in range. As long as you're closer to them than us, theirs *should* come up first, but if the vessel name starts with CRT and then a long list of numbers, that's us. It belonged to Emil's dad before Idrian adopted it, hence the Carteau. Anyway, select them, and press the button. If they refuse the request, keep pressing. Maybe you can annoy them into accepting. If they accept, the Lamprey will communicate with their vessel to enter or dock. You can record a note with your request. Maximum of ten seconds, by holding here. You got it?"

He slumps over the console. "Got it. We ready? Idrian's probably not feeling so great, either."

Roca sighs. "Yeah, he wasn't. Idiot still went when they asked, though." She leaves, and as the door closes, she says, "Bring him back."

As the Lamprey launches and draws closer to its target, his breath comes easier. He still feels unwell, but it's a bad flu sort of unwell, not a bones-on-fire sort. Roca's timer flicks on about halfway there, counting down.

"You doing all right, kiddo?"

Remy startles at her voice in his ear. He'd forgotten about the earpiece. "Still alive. The timer just started."

Remy sends his first contact request. The screen blinks yellow while it's awaiting a response, then flashes red after about thirty seconds.

Three minutes on Roca's timer.

Another attempt. By the time his second request is denied—with a message in a young woman's sweet voice: "Cease your approach, or we'll fire on you,"—Remy is too near to *cease* even if he knew how and too tired to care. The good thing about the death threat is that it jump-starts his hazy brain. Of course. He can send messages. Ten seconds, Roca said. He won't need that long.

He presses and holds to record with his request. "My name is Remy Canta. My brother was Cameron Canta. Idrian Delaciel murdered him."

He sends the request.

"The fuck? Remy, *what the fuck?*" Roca's voice bursts in his ear.

Remy recoils. He never learned how to turn down the volume on this thing. "Shh. Ow. What, do you think they're keeping him there for a fancy meal? You guys *killed* people on the OSS. You think they didn't have friends? Family? This is the way I get on board, if there's any way at all."

Roca is silent.

The screen blinks orange as the Lamprey draws close to the vessel. Twenty-one seconds remaining.

The screen flashes green.

Like Roca said, the vessel opens up and allows the Lamprey to drift inside. The Lamprey enters and settles like it knows exactly what to do.

The Lamprey's hatch hisses open after about a minute, and Remy emerges to find three people armed to the teeth. The first two are muscle-bound and expressionless, clad in the same uniform the murdered guard wore on the OSS and bearing scary-looking metal sticks. The third among them wears a different uniform—a soft jacket that sweeps across her chest and buttons on the right side. Curvy and pale with deep brown curls tied in a messy bun, she barely reaches the chests of the two men. The huge weapon she holds is half her size, and the dark bruises under her eyes make her look at least as tired as Remy is.

"Remy Canta." The woman holds out a hand. "Natalia Yrine. We have a lot in common."

Remy takes the hand, and her lips spread in a brutal smile that dimples both cheeks. There's a little space between her front teeth, and Remy's grip on her hand loosens. He knows that smile. He's seen it before.

A wave of nauseated realization sweeps over him. He saw it in a photograph, a close-up of a grin much like this one and freckle-spattered cheeks in a room where a lovesick boy swore on his tether and spat on his palm.

Natalia.

"Lia," he whispers. "You're Jacques' Lia."

"You met him?" The look in her eyes is a hunger Remy knows well. In the months after Cameron died, he subsisted on Andrew's stories about the two of them. Learning things he never knew about his brother made it seem like he still lived.

Remy doesn't have anything like that to share with Lia. "I was . . . on the OSS that day. I'm the one who sent out the alert from the supply room."

Roca's voice blares in Remy's ear. "You did *what?*"

Remy resists the urge to flinch. They plan to kill him anyway. It's not like he'll be any more dead when they're done with him.

Lia stares at him, stricken.

Remy wants, illogically, to kneel. "I couldn't stop Idrian from doing what he did. I'm sorry."

Lia's arms cross over her chest, chin going up and lips pressing together. "I saw your picture on the broadcast. What did he want with you?"

Various answers scroll through Remy's head and he discards them. "I cursed him to death," he admits, which is true, even though it isn't an answer.

"Nice." Lia's lips twist up. "I hope you don't mind that I helped him along a bit."

"Shit," Roca bleats into the earpiece.

A few days ago, news of Idrian's suffering would've brought Remy joy, or at least jealousy that he wasn't the one to inflict it. There is a thread of satisfaction to be had from the news, but the unnameable thing that crawls under his skin and speeds his pulse isn't as easy to pin down. "He's still alive, though," Remy says.

"For now." Lia flexes a hand at her side. "We could fix that, you and I."

There's only electric silence in Remy's earpiece—now, when he'd give anything to have some angry comment from Roca to distract himself with.

"Let's see what you've left me to work with," he finally says.

Lia sets off, and Remy follows close behind—close enough that, when she stops, he nearly runs into her back.

"Ah. I'll need you to remove any tech. We've got the vessel pretty well sealed and Karoyak excavated all the Protectorate tracking, but you can't be too careful."

One of the men with her holds out a thick black box.

Roca mutters, "Remy, don't—"

With an unspoken apology, Remy uses a fingernail to extract the earpiece and drops it inside. The second man, this one with a forbidding metal wand, leans in to whisper something into Lia's ear.

"You'll need to take off whatever's around your neck, too," Lia says.

Remy grabs at the strap around his neck and withdraws Cam's pendant. "This isn't tech. It was my brother's."

"I wouldn't be so sure those things are mutually exclusive. Those pendants are Protectorate-issued to high officials. Off with it. You keep it on, you don't leave the cargo area."

Remy's barely removed it for a moment since Cam pressed it into his hand the night before he died. Swallowing, he removes it, untethered without its weight and borrowed warmth.

He hesitates with his hand over the black box.

"It won't harm it. It'll just prevent it from transmitting. Drop it in."

It makes an ominous thud and rattle on the bottom. Like it broke something. The box snaps closed before Remy can check.

"This way."

They leave the cargo area—easily the bulk of the small vessel's size—and enter its cramped cockpit, where Idrian has been cuffed with his arms over his head to D-rings secured to the wall—meant, surely, for securing supplies, not people. He's barely upright, eyes closed and blood on his lips from a cut in the corner of his mouth. The way his cuffed arms support the majority of his weight makes Remy's body ache in sympathy.

"Delightful, isn't it?" Lia casts a sly smile in his direction, eyes crinkling.

"Delightful . . ." Remy tests the word on his tongue. It tastes wrong. His eyes slip away from Idrian, from the blood and bruises.

Lia traces Remy's loose fist with one hand until it opens. She presses something into it, a metal baton colder than a corpse and gummed on the end with blood. "Want to give it a go? I had my turn before you arrived."

Remy's fingers close around the baton, and he raises his arm. Idrian hangs from his bonds, unaware or uncaring. Vulnerable.

"He killed my brother," Remy manages, tonelessly. That should matter.

"You already said."

Remy draws the baton back.

He should *want* to hurt Idrian, at least.

But the thing that surges inside him and leaves a sharp aftertaste in his mouth is more like shame. The hand that holds the baton trembles.

"Oh, come *on*." Lia's hand closes over the baton's bloody end and pulls it from his hand. "Pathetic."

"I guess I am."

"Both of us." Lia smirks and drops the baton with a clang that shivers up through Remy's feet. Idrian's hazy eyes flick open at the noise.

"You know how many hits I got in?" she asks. "Two—maybe. They were good ones, though. Pretty sure I broke something."

"S'nothin' to brag about," Idrian slurs, bloody lips parting and feet slipping over the floor like he's trying to stand. "Got plenty of broke-somethings right now. You're not special."

"I didn't ask for your opinion." Lia kicks his ankle before his feet bear any of his weight. She scrubs her face with her hands when he sags against the cuffs again. "It doesn't feel like I wanted it to. Did it, for you?"

Idrian's eyes flick to Remy again.

"Not as long as I hoped it would," Remy admits.

Silence settles between them, until Lia speaks to Idrian. "Jacques trusted you, you know." Idrian flinches from this more than he has from any wound. "He did everything you asked him to, was so proud to have a part in what you were doing. Didn't even tell me about it, though he was a shit liar and I figured it out anyway. I let it happen because I *believed* in him, and in your cause. He'd have done anything for you, Delaciel."

"He'd have done anything for *you*," Idrian whispers. "I had two options—kill him or drag him along. But those pictures—he has family on the surface, people who could be used to sway his loyalty or coerce a confession. He had you. He wouldn't have left without you, and we were out of time."

"Two options? Is that what you tell yourself?" Lia's fists clench, trembling at her sides. "Does it make it easier?"

Idrian turns his face away, eyebrows knitted, and doesn't answer. He doesn't try to stand again.

"I wanted you to *hurt* for what you did." Lia grabs his jaw and turns his head to face her, smearing her palm with his blood. "I still do. But I'm better than you. You hear that, Delaciel? I'm better than you. I know this whole thing is bigger than I am." She turns away, grasping Remy's shoulder. "Give me your hand. I won't stop you from leaving with the fuel, or with him."

Remy blinks, at a loss, and extends his hand. "You won't?"

"I won't." Lia drops a key onto his palm. "For the cuffs. I can't look at him anymore. I'll be up front. My men are loading the fuel into your vessel now. Get this bastard out of here and leave whenever they're finished."

When Lia is settled into the pilot's seat with her knees pulled up against her chest, Idrian licks bloody lips and greets Remy coolly. "Traitor."

The edge to his accusation is duller than when he pointed the gun at Remy back on the *Astrid*.

"Murderer," Remy retorts, and savors the flash of guilt in Idrian's eyes. "I came to save your sorry ass. You could try being grateful."

"To the one who endangered it in the first place?"

"You did that that on your own. Consequences are a bitch." Pain and tightness he didn't even recognize in his chest dissipate as he speaks. He hasn't been allowed to speak honestly with Idrian since they met. There's something freeing in meeting him on level ground, all their secrets out in the open air.

The dark line of Remy's withering is stark against the pale skin of Idrian's hand, disappearing into his shirt.

Idrian gets his feet underneath him so he's supporting most of his own weight, and Remy steps in to unlock the cuffs. His hands, when Remy accidentally touches them, are the cold white of the blood-deprived. When the first cuff is unhooked, Idrian stumbles forward, and Remy props him against the wall with one hand while he works on the other.

As soon as he's free, Idrian's arms fall back to his sides, and he rolls his shoulders, hissing in pain.

"I'm not . . . entirely unhappy, seeing you like this," Remy admits. "Wanting you to suffer is a difficult habit to break."

Idrian takes a step and stumbles against the wall.

Remy sighs. "Can you walk?"

"I'll bet it'd amuse you to see me try."

Remy grabs one of Idrian's arms, pulling it around his shoulder. "Just to the Lamprey. We're on borrowed time."

The tank has already been pushed inside by the time they return. Remy drops Idrian on the floor of the vessel perhaps a little less gently than strictly necessary and backs away.

Idrian stares up at him, steady. "What we did to Canta, is that why you hate me touching you?"

"Half of it," Remy says. "The other half is, there was a time I wasn't sure if I could keep from stabbing you if you got close enough."

He startles at the ring of Idrian's surprised laughter. "I *am* very stabbable. Folks can't resist. I'm surprised you did."

Remy shrugs. "Things changed." He leaves the back of the Lamprey and finds Lia in the little vessel's pilot seat, knees pulled up to her chest. Verdine floats into view through the window, limning her and her men in light.

She pats the black box beside her as he draws up. "Back for your things?"

"And a few questions. How much time are we likely to have before they notice what you stole and come after us?"

"You don't need to worry about that. We didn't take from any of the monitored tanks. Once the Chancellor learned the OSS's backup tank had been damaged and its reserves drained by Idrian, he arranged to send more fuel. Luckily, we had a sympathizer among the delivery crew, and he siphoned some off into a portable tank for us. The OSS won't miss this fuel because they never officially received it. You've got plenty of other things to worry about, but this shouldn't be one of them."

"Thank you."

She nods. "You might notice the gauge on the tank says it's not quite full, but what we left you with should still keep the Isles safe for a while. We took enough to top ourselves off and resupply a couple times. Call it a transaction fee. I'm done with the OSS. It's been a while since I've seen solid ground."

She waves the two men off and extends a hand to him. "Travel safely."

He grasps it and holds tight. "You too. Lia, I'm sorry . . ."

He doesn't know how to finish. *For Jacques? About all of this? That we had to meet this way?*

She quirks a dry grin. "I am, too. I'll admit, I'd been told it would feel better than this to be a decent person. Shouldn't have believed a word of it." She lifts the black box and opens it, dropping two earpieces—Idrian's and his own—into his hand, then lifting his pendant out. "Good luck, Remy Canta."

Remy tucks the pendant back into his shirt, shivering at the dead-cold chill of it against his skin.

Back in the Lamprey, Idrian looks mostly liquid on the floor in front of the tank, leaning back against the bench set into the wall.

"How do I get this thing to head back?" Remy asks. "I'll admit, I'm not exactly a pilot."

Idrian waves a hand. "Green button on the keypad to your right. Press and hold. It'll communicate with this vessel to request preparation for departure, and once it's got permission, it'll auto-navigate home."

Remy obeys. In less than a minute, the cargo door whirs closed. Remy sits on the floor across from Idrian, crossing his arms, as the Lamprey leaves Lia's vessel and aims for home.

They've been en route for at least five oppressively silent minutes when Idrian breaks the silence, tipping his head farther back against the bench and not meeting Remy's eyes.

"I didn't know he had a brother."

Remy follows a sluggish drop of blood down the side of Idrian's face. "Would it have changed anything if you did?"

Idrian remains still for a long while. "Doubt it."

"Yeah, I thought you'd say that."

Idrian scrubs at his face, wincing at the motion. He and Remy now bear the whole weight of the withering. It must be thriving, with all the weaknesses they've given it to exploit.

Fever and exhaustion weigh Remy down. They're pathetic, the both of them. Remy pulls the neck of his shirt open. The withering has rounded the ball of his shoulder and sent fine, vein-like threads onto his chest. Funny—it's not so far from where it was when they first met. This will be their last conversation.

"Oh. I forgot to mention—they'll want you to kill me as soon as we get back," he says.

Idrian spins to Remy, eyes wide.

The expression on his face is so openly shocked that Remy can't help laughing. "You really know nothing about withering, do you?"

"Roca gave me an earful, but . . . It's been a weird few hours."

"The others are still false-bonded, so they're excused from execution duty for now. You'll have to do the honors. You fancy finishing what you started and taking out the last of the Canta family?"

Idrian grimaces. "Not really."

"Too bad."

Idrian turns away, forcing a weak smile that reveals bloody teeth. "I don't know what I'm supposed to say."

"Say you'll think twice before doing it again."

A hollow laugh pushes from Idrian's chest. It turns into a wheezing cough. "I'd think ten times if it'd make a difference. But if it's one life against the survival of everyone on Alta, I know what I'll choose every time."

Silence falls between them. After a while, Idrian says, quietly, "Tell me about your brother?"

Remy's hands go to his chest, but his clean fingers close around nothing. "Why?"

"Feels like I should know. I don't . . . I'm not angry. If it was Astrid and you'd done it, I'd've killed you, too."

"Is that supposed to make me feel better?"

"Not sure what it's supposed to do. I'm sorry he was your brother. But we were coming up on a supply run and he was half a step behind us everywhere we went. Couldn't risk him stopping us. It wasn't . . . personal."

"That doesn't make it better." Remy has hours' worth of things he could tell Idrian about Cam (he liked sweets to his own detriment; he sang really loudly while he worked, but only when it was raining; he was great at making connections but terrible at math and couldn't stand the tiniest bit of spice on his food) but none of them paint a perfect picture. Maybe that's how it's supposed to be. Remy's big brother was so much more than anything he said or did or loved. A person *shouldn't* be easy to sum up. That's what makes a life matter.

"Honestly, I can't say I regret what I did to you, either," Remy admits. "Cameron deserved more than I ever gave him. Seeking justice for his death is the least I could do. I don't know what kind of brother I'd be if I didn't at least try."

"I got my own justice once. Don't regret a moment of it, so you've got a heads up on me there."

The bitter anger in Idrian's voice and the distant expression in his eyes is so much like when Idrian watched Andrew on the big screen on Alta.

"Yves said Andrew's your brother," Remy blurts.

"Fuck Yves. Wasn't their story to tell." Idrian shrugs. "I guess he is. Never met him. After my time."

"How does that work?"

Idrian presses his lips together, tight and bloodless, and makes an expression like he's about to tell Remy to mind his own business, but he just shakes his head. "I was born Adrian Delacour. The bastard who contributed his seed was vice-head of the Preservation Committee at the time and met my mom at some fancy get-together. She was an environmental scientist in an advanced program at Astoria, though I doubt he cared. Apparently, she looked stunning in red. He 'liked her fire.' She liked their lively conversations. They went to a weaver who told them all the loveliest lies about how *complementary* their match was and how *meant for each other* they were, and they rushed the marriage."

Remy winces. "Is that why you don't like weavers?"

Idrian shrugs. "Doesn't help. I remember Mom, but I barely remember *him*. He worked a lot. Mom was working part time toward her doctorate when she figured out she was pregnant again. Timing would've been perfect. Astrid was due to be a summer baby. Mom wanted a girl. The Delacours are high officials, so it would've been okay. I think my father got careless, let something slip about the Isles. My mom didn't like the sound of it. They argued. He didn't like her fire so much when it was close enough to burn him, and she didn't like their conversations when lives were on the line. My guess? She threatened to make noise, because everything after that happened fast. He framed her for crimes against the city—as much as you can frame someone for something they'd have done anyway—and divorced her, which made her second pregnancy in violation of the Overpopulation Prevention Laws. We were sent to Alta. I was three."

"That's shit," Remy says.

Idrian rasps out a laugh. "There's more. When I got off Alta at fourteen, I looked into him, found out he'd remarried. You know how old Andrew is?"

Remy frowns. "Cam had six years on him, I think. That'd make him . . ."

"A little *less* than three years younger than me. He should turn twenty-five this year."

Remy stares blankly at the wall. If Idrian was three, then—

"That *bastard*."

"He had someone on the side. Maybe the whole time. Chances are, the whole thing had nothing to do with what Mom learned about the Isles. If the Chancellor figured out he'd gone and gotten the seated Intermediary pregnant in violation of the law, he'd've been in deep shit. But he made it all work. Got himself a nice replacement family, sent us far enough away that no one could contradict him, and the new wife clearly didn't ask any of the wrong questions. So I killed the bastard. Took me a couple years to plan it, but I waited until he was out of the capital on a trip and hunted him down. I was sixteen when I did it. He deserved worse than he got, but I didn't have three years to drag it out. Astrid suffered every minute from the time she was born to . . ." Idrian turns away. "Mom died in the Block S collapse, with Roca's parents."

"Andrew doesn't know, does he?"

"Don't see why he would. I bet he knows only what the Chancellor needs him to know to keep him pliable."

"He said he wants to kill you."

"He can damn well get in line."

"This feels like such a useless thing to die over. Not Cam; I'd die for him, easy, but *this*."

"It has to be me that kills you?" Idrian asks, something sharp and bright in his eyes.

"At the moment? Yeah."

"Ha! Good."

Remy scowls. "Don't sound so excited about it."

"No, it's just . . ." Idrian grins. "What happens if I refuse?"

"Wait. That's not—"

"Everyone'd just have to go along, wouldn't they?"

"If the withering resolves, *we both die*. If it resolves too late, everyone dies."

"You told me to think twice."

"Not about this!"

"Too late. You don't want to die, right?"

"I hardly think I have a choice. Consequences, remember?"

"Me believing I had no choice got us into this mess. Starting to think it's time to give that one a break."

"What if it's true this time, though?"

Idrian shrugs. "Might be. But we get in shit like this a lot. So far, we've managed to come out of it okay." He taps the withering they share. "You're one of us now, like it or not. Just wait. We'll find a way out for both of us."

Remy's beginning to understand why Yves was so hopeless in the face of Idrian's determination. His blazing confidence seems both laughable and unattainable—a fire Remy could warm or immolate himself with. "I already tried, Idrian. It didn't *work*, and I'm out of ideas."

"We have more heads for idea-making, and for once, we have time to think. I don't intend to waste it."

"You're an idiot. Roca's right. Reckless, self-sacrificing idiot."

"Mmm. She's usually right." Idrian breathes out an amused sigh. "Anyway, if it's true, what does that make you?"

"Huh?"

"Since we're fatebound. If I'm a reckless idiot, what does that say about you?" Idrian tips his head toward Remy, pinning him with his smiling eyes. "Fate saw fit to take everything from us and then put us in front of each other. You in the viper's nest, me out here—fatebound. I don't know much, but I know this: I won't kill you, Remy Canta. We haven't burned down nearly enough shit to justify the world binding us together. Not yet." Idrian's wild grin only expands when Remy has nothing to add.

"What you did for the others, it means only you and I are tied up in this. That's how it always should've been."

Chapter Twenty

*Bearers of **anchored**, or hand-connected, tethers find comfort in company; they thrive on both conversation and silent solidarity. Bearers of anchored tethers long to hold and to share. Of all tethers, anchored bonds are the most likely to be life-long, without traveling or fading.*

— From On The Manipulation of Tethers

"First things first." Idrian's lips twist into an apologetic grin as the Lamprey's rear cargo door hisses open to expose Roca and Yves waiting for them with wringing hands. "I won't be killing Remy."

Roca responds first, stalking up the ramp toward him. "*Idrian.*"

Slumped against the fuel tank on the floor, Idrian says with more authority than he can realistically command, "Hear me out."

"I will not. Your ideas are always bad. I don't want to kill him, either—"

"Thanks!" Remy calls as Roca pulls Idrian to his feet.

"Things are already bad," she says. "Don't make them worse."

"It's fine. We work best under pressure, right?"

Roca picks up the weight Idrian isn't bearing with a sigh. "Yeah, you bastard, 'cause it's the only kind of work we know."

Yves comes in next, grabbing his other arm to support him. "You *dare*, after I went to the trouble of returning him to you!

Even if you don't kill him, the both of you don't have much more than a day. This is not a matter of *does* anyone die, it's a matter of *how many* people die."

"I'm not ready to believe that."

"Then get ready! There's no progression of events where he survives. The only one that doesn't end with you or everyone else dead is if you kill him. I have—" Yves pulls a vial from their coat, but it rolls from their fingers and spins on the ground. They let go of Idrian and kneel to retrieve it, clutching it in one hand and not standing up again. "I have a sedative that'll make it . . . easier. I don't want to do it, but since when has that mattered?"

"Since now. We're unanimous. None of us want this, so we're not doing it."

"Idrian!"

"*Yves*. We have time."

"Not much."

"There's gotta be a way to undo it."

"Not everything can be undone."

"I know that." Idrian's eyes close. "I know."

Remy's head spins just from watching the conversation. The dizziness only worsens.

His vision speckles with static, stomach swooping. His knees hit the floor, cold sweat pricking up through his pores and making him shiver. The withering.

When his vision clears, he's staring at the floor and Idrian's feet are in front of him, a blurred hand extended to help Remy up. His pendant, freed from his shirt, swings gaily over the floor.

Remy accepts the hand and lets Idrian's solid grip pull him to his feet.

"You all right?" Idrian says. "You're looking a bit—"

He freezes like that, eyes on Remy's chest, where his hand idly cups the pendant.

"Why do you have one of those?" Quiet, words strung taut.

A hand flashes by in his peripheral vision and the pendant is gone from around his neck. Remy stumbles forward, reaching for it, but Idrian has already thrown it to the floor. He doesn't even have time to draw breath before Idrian raises his foot and stomps on it.

The glass filling the spaces between metal lies shattered and strewn over the floor, the cage of wire crushed toward the center on one side.

Idrian lifts his foot again, but Remy dives to the floor, covering the pendant with his hands and pulling it away.

"These things are *trackers*!" Idrian's hands twine in his hair. "High officials wear them. My dad wore one. This *whole time*—damn it, Remy, they've got an execution order out on us! They could hunt us down with this."

"It was Cameron's," he says, dumbly.

Idrian's expression does a complicated thing. "It's probably why they've been a step behind us this whole time. Who knows you have it?"

Andrew knows. He's always known. He was so supportive of Remy's choice to wear it after Cam passed. He never thought to tell Remy what its purpose was. All these years, Remy thought Andrew knew where to find him when he was chasing trouble because of his *keen investigator's insight*.

An incredulous laugh breaks free from his throat. He cups the ruined shape in his hands, and something slips out from inside. At first, Remy thinks it must be a final shard of glass, but it's fingertip-sized and black. It's one of the storage devices Cam would use to bring his work home. A tiny label along the side bears a note: *Remy*.

It's Cam's handwriting.

Cam pressed his pendant into Remy's hand the night before he died—the night he confessed the name of his killer. He'd said, *You have to understand.* Over and over, deliriously.

Remy's shaking hands close around the pendant for a moment before he drops it to the floor again. "Fine," he says. The storage chip, he keeps pressed against his palm.

Idrian frowns at Remy, pity and determination. He just says, "Sorry, but I'm gonna fry the fucker," and sweeps out of the room with the pendant. Roca follows.

That leaves only Yves. "You've been wearing that this whole time?"

Remy closes his hand tighter around the treasure in his palm. "Yeah."

"You should be dead."

"What?"

"You should be dead, all of you. If you've been wearing that thing since the start, They've had a traceable beacon informing them of your location at nearly all times. That means at any given moment, they could have captured or killed all of you."

"But they . . . it was only recently that they sent out that broadcast with the execution order."

Yves grabs Remy's wrist, and their skin against his is clammy-cold, voice flat. "You don't understand. Those things on the video, *what made them happen?*"

"What do you mean?"

"On the OSS. On Kuren. And me, on Alta. I refused the prisoners because we couldn't possibly handle them. Idrian took all that water because he had no time to get the rest in a way that was less harmful—and the drastically-reduced supplies the Chancellor sent to the Isles meant none of us would survive until the next opportunity. He chose to act in the best interests of the Isles every time, and every time it was a nail in his coffin."

Remy winces. *Pain for pain.*

Yves' clammy grip on his hand tightens until Remy's hand goes numb, the sharp edges of the storage chip clutched in his hand all he can feel.

"Remy, fuck, are you hearing me? They *manufactured* that urgency! They made sure we were cornered and we had *nothing* but tooth and claw to defend ourselves. They needed a monster so they made monsters of us. The Chancellor was making sure he had plenty of footage to turn everyone against us."

Remy shivers. They were on Kuren more than long enough for the Chancellor to arrange for his people to find them at the lake. It makes sense—and it makes everything else make sense. "I always asked why the Chancellor couldn't just capture him. They just kept telling me he *had a plan*."

"Exactly! He didn't take *thousands* of opportunities to bring in a criminal who's been a thorn in his side for years. They've made us the face of the opposition and given us plenty of rope to hang ourselves. We thought we were flying under the radar, that Idrian's few provable offenses weren't worth aggressive pursuit. We were naive. Not even ten years ago, public opinion of Idrian was surprisingly positive. Now, anyone who saw him would kill him themselves. If the Chancellor hasn't arrested Idrian, it's because Idrian hasn't hanged himself quite thoroughly enough yet . . . or he's still useful."

"The Isles," Remy breathes.

"My guess? He plans to get rid of every dissenting voice at once. We've grown too large, too loud for him. He's all about moving *forward*, and the Isles are ancient history—evidence of the people's failure to preserve their world."

"What are we supposed to do?"

"I don't know if there's anything we can do."

Remy swallows. "Let's tell the others. Maybe they'll have ideas."

"I doubt it. But they should know."

The path to the cockpit where Emil hunches over the controls seems dark and increasingly narrow. The events of the past few minutes and Remy's advancing withering conspire to steal the strength from his legs as soon as he arrives, and he drops down in the seat across from Emil that should probably belong to Thomlin or Idrian.

Something glitters on the flat stretch of space above all the screens and panels. A hairclip, gaudily-bejeweled. Beside it, there's a vibrantly-painted girl and her dog carved from wood on a cobblestone circle made from mirror shards. Remy pokes at it. For no reason he can discern, it's glued down. Everything is glued down. The entire space is filled with unusually adorable odds and ends. "Uh . . ." Remy says.

Emil looks up, flushing when he notices the direction of Remy's gaze. "That's, uh. That's mine." He pauses, lifting a hand now free of the curse. "I hear I should thank you for this? Or apologize to you. Or maybe be angry with you?"

Remy forces a brittle smile. "Idrian seemed pretty confused about it, too."

"Boy, was he! You made a real mess of him. Should've heard the talking-to he got." Emil laughs. "Everything all right? I'm guessing you didn't just come here for the great view."

Remy turns to Yves, who massages their temples. "Call everyone here, would you? I don't want to have to say this twice."

Emil depresses a button to his right. "Everyone to the cockpit. Yves has news." He turns to them. "Do I get a preview, or are you gonna keep me in suspense?"

"We're doomed," Yves says cheerfully.

"We're always doomed."

"Not like this."

Silence stretches between them, and as Remy unclenches his fists, something unsticks itself from his palm and falls against the loosening cage of his fingers.

Remy picks it out and his heart kicks up in his chest. The chip. Cameron's chip.

He should think about his next move more than he does. "Hey," he says loudly, just as Thomlin paces in. He finds one of the sparkly oddities—a hair ornament decorated with feathers and flecks of iridescent scales, on the other side of the cockpit, close to Emil—and points to it. "What's that thing?"

Thom and Emil's eyes both go to the hair ornament. Emil winces. Thomlin laughs, pulling Yves close to kiss their ear before he says, "Okay, so, remember I told you about how we tried to get Emil to steal something but he was nonsense-levels of awful at it and we all nearly died?"

"Yes." Remy's eyes skim the screens until he finds one with a slot the right size for Cam's storage leaf. He angles himself so he's in front of the screen.

"*So.* I wasn't lying. Only . . . one night, when Roca got him knockdown drunk, we realized he's an *extraordinary* thief, but only when he's plastered. Like he can literally steal food halfway to your lips and you wouldn't notice. But drunk Emil is also wildly belligerent and won't steal useful things. He only steals stuff he likes, right?"

Remy lifts the storage leaf while looking steadily at Thom and fumbles with it, trying to find the slot blind. "Right. So these things . . ." He gestures at the baubles.

"*Exactly.* He's like an allura bird! Drunk Emil loves sparkly things."

"I mean, no shade. I'd wear the hair ornament." The edge of the chip connects with the slot.

Thom grins. "And you'd *own* it. Anyway, this is our monument of appreciation to master-thief Emil, who likes to plunder the treasures of unsuspecting children. If you'd believe it—"

He's a fraying thread of an instant from pushing the thing in when a bright alert pops up on *that exact screen* and Remy has to palm the chip and swallow a shocked curse before either of them can see what he was about to do. The fear buzzing in his veins keeps him from reading the details of the alert right away.

Only when Thom and Emil go utterly silent does he absorb what the screen says: CONTACT REQUEST. PRIORITY: EMERGENCY.

There's a series of numbers and letters in parentheses beneath it.

Emil frowns. "Who would . . . ?"

Remy looks closer at the long string of nonsense. It's nothing he knows, but it plucks at something in his brain. He *should* know it. He's seen it recently.

"Should we reject it? Yves has something to say, right?" Thom ventures.

"Yeah, maybe? But—"

Emil's voice fades out as Remy recalls how he knows that parenthetical identifier.

He saw it when he was sending his own contact request to Lia's ship earlier.

He doesn't have time to say anything before another request comes through. CONTACT REQUEST. PRIORITY: EMERGENCY, it says. MESSAGE APPENDED.

The attached ten-second clip auto-plays.

It's incomprehensible, at first. Noise garbles through the speakers. There's panicked yelling in the background, indistinct. The grind of something mechanical. A hissing like a rush of breath.

Maybe five seconds in, Lia's small voice confesses, "*I don't know what's going on. Please, just answer—*"

"Lia?" he calls. But it's just a message. She can't hear him.

"We have to accept the request," he says. "That's Lia, the girl with the fuel."

He doesn't wait for Emil to do it. There's a box below the request and he taps the option to accept it several times before the screen indicates a channel is open.

"Lia, it's me."

Her voice blares into the cockpit, frayed at the edges. *"Remy, this is fucked up, this is so fucked up. What did you do?"*

"I didn't do anything."

A rattling whine nearly drowns her voice. "Our engines are overheating. These temps, we can't . . ."

Remy freezes, head filled with static. Yves' voice replays in his head, promising an end that would kill every person on the Isles, taking out every dissenting voice at once.

"Fuel," he whispers. Then, louder, "Lia, the fuel you took for yourself, did you put any of it in your tank?"

"*What? How could that—*"

"You did, didn't you?" Remy's fingers go numb as the realization settles. His hands fall against the dizzying array of controls without knowing what any of them do.

"*Remy, please—*"

The audio on the other end cuts off with a shriek. Something at the edge of the viewing window glows bright for a brief moment. Remy could swear a wave of pressure sweeps up against the *Astrid*, nearly toppling him, but no one else staggers.

A screen lights up in the corner of the right-most window, and its focus changes four or five times before settling on a single area and zooming in.

Charred wreckage, drifting.

Moments ago, Lia called Remy's name, like he could give her answers. Now, the monitor serves him the cold aftermath. Death can't be so sudden, surely. There's structure to it. A rise and fall.

Lia's pleas must have guided everyone else here, because they wait, silent, in the halls.

Remy turns to Yves, body moving a half-second slower than it should, like he's viewing the world through a distant window. "The fuel. That's how the Chancellor's going to do it."

Yves' eyes widen, understanding and horror dawning. They burst into motion. "Stop the Lamprey! Emil? Thom, call it back."

Emil blinks. "Was—was this what you wanted to talk about? What's going on?"

"I'll explain later. Call it *back*."

"We can't. It's a security measure to prevent remote hijacking. Once it launches, the Lamprey's radio silent. It'll communicate with its destination and no one else unless someone aboard manually initiates outside contact. Why? What's wrong?"

"It's—what I called you here for. The Chancellor's been toying with us."

"That's nothing new," Idrian drawls, leaning against the hallway wall.

"Shut *up*, Idrian. Emil, contact Alta. Or Fluora. Toxys. Anyone. Tell them not to take the fuel. We've been set up."

Lia seemed so pleased about the easy handover when she delivered it. A sympathizer in the group the Chancellor sent, she said. A tank of fuel set aside for their use.

How foolish, for any of them to believe in kindness.

It's so calculated, so utterly hands-off. The Chancellor manufactured yet another need and made sure they had only one way to fill it. First with the water, an opportunity to dig themselves deeper. Now, with the fuel, the dirt to bury themselves with.

"Emil?" Thom says. "Call up Alta."

"We're not in range."

"*Get* in range," Yves says. "Can you catch up with the Lamprey? Destroy it?"

"What? No! We only have the one, and it has too much of a head start on us. It's a stealth vessel besides—much faster than we are. I don't see us catching up."

"Contact Alta as soon as you can, then. If they use that fuel, it's over."

Less than half an hour until they're in range.

Emil sits up, hands hovering over the controls like there's anything he can do. Thom, Idrian, Roca, and Yves crowd the space behind the seats in the cockpit and the narrow hall behind it. Quiet settles. No one breaks it.

Seconds stretch out into endless minutes. The others shift awkwardly, staring out the window like something terrible will happen if they look away.

Cam's chip burns in Remy's palm. He presses the storage leaf safely between his fingers, mouth dry. There's time before they're in range.

He finds the slot from earlier, and the nerves that pull his shoulders high don't matter, this time, because everyone's feeling the same way. No one notices when Remy finds the slot and slides it in.

Probably, he should worry it's a trap, but that doesn't occur to him until the screen blinks. "PLAY RECORDING?" it asks, loudly, into the narrow space.

"Hm?" Emil tears his eyes from a busy screen at the sound.

Remy selects YES as Emil's eyes widen, his hand stretching out.

"Remy, stop. What are you—"

The screen fills with an image that knocks the breath from Remy's chest.

In front of him, almost life-sized, a shaky image shows Cam, tired and barely upright at his desk. "Heya, Rem."

He wants nothing more than to greet his brother back. His hand goes to his chest, but his clean fingers have nothing to grasp at, not even the pendant.

Back then, Cam was untouchably large in Remy's eyes. Five years on, Remy can only see how young his brother was when he died.

"If you're watching this," Cameron says, lips tipped into a sad smile, "I guess I'm dead."

Remy extends his hand until his fingers meet the cold, flat screen.

"Wow." Cam sinks farther into his chair. "Saying that was exactly as weird as I thought it'd be! So, uh, hello. I've been trying to sit you down and talk to you for days, but. Shit, Rem, you look at me like I'm your hero, and I can't—this is so much bigger than both of us."

Remy forgets to breathe.

Emil reaches across him, fingers scrabbling for the monitor. "Stop the playback. The thing could be corrupted. This could be part of their plan. You can't, after what we just saw—"

"Don't you *dare*."

Emil is twice as strong as Remy, but he stops when Remy closes his hand around his wrist and digs his fingernails in. Remy's voice is wrecked, and he can't take his eyes away from the screen where Cam sits, alive. "Don't you dare. I'll kill all of you."

"Already tried that," someone says, behind him. Remy ignores them.

On the screen, Cam rubs his nose and directs a flickering grin at Remy. "You probably know at least a bit about what happened to me by now, assuming I've gathered the gall to tell you, but I know myself well enough to know I won't be able to say even half the stuff I want to, and I'll bet less than half of that will actually make sense, so . . . here I am. Remember when I was gone a couple of months ago for that trip? Andrew brought me a report that sent me to one of the more isolated medtech facilities; Idrian had broken in and made off with a fortune's worth of materials." Cam smiles and shakes his head. "You were *fascinated* by him. I never could figure out why. I should've asked, shouldn't I? Should've listened. I'd heard the reports about him like everyone else—how his actions spat in the face of everything we were trying to build, how what just happened on Veida was a calculated act of destruction, and of course I believed them—but at that medtech facility, the things I was looking at were just itemized theft reports, and the cold data left plenty of room for the question I should have asked much earlier: why?"

There's silence in the cockpit as, on the screen, Cam rubs his eyes. "The public report said Idrian caused extensive damage when he was nearly intercepted on his way out and likely took the supplies to sell them to prisoners on Alta, Fluora, and Toxys. But the things he took, Remy, they were *basic*. Antibiotics, sedatives, local anesthetic. Gauze and disinfectant. We're not even talking steritape or nano-surgery machinery. No criminal with a strand of common sense would have any business with them. I started pulling at threads, and the only thing that made it all come together was the simplest answer: if Idrian Delaciel was risking capture to steal those things, it was because they were valuable on the Isles.

"But that brought up so many more questions." Cam drags a hand through his hair. "The other thefts weren't so different. Lots of water. The way our official reports spun it, it was a concerted effort at undoing the Chancellor's hard work. I saw pictures of the sinkholes and failing crops on Veida and got angry like everyone else. But *water*. When I stopped assuming it was purposefully destructive, I wondered. Why water?

"I started tracking down relocated Veida residents and visiting other islands where thefts had occurred. I spoke to everyone mentioned in the Chancellor's reports, and then I started looking for people who had refused to cooperate or who got shifty when I walked in. None of them wanted to talk, but I got the impression they respected Idrian—supported him. I started putting things together. We were so wrong. He was trying to *help* people, Remy. After what happened on Veida, he mixed it up pretty regularly, but I was able to predict, based on past reports, a time frame during which Idrian was likely to need more water. I wasn't usually in the right place, but I was close enough I could go in while everything was still fresh and gather information. I guess . . ." He gestures weakly and winces. "It got me noticed. By everyone. The Chancellor appreciated my zeal but delivered a major corruption case into my hands for me to shift my attention to, so I used my free time to investigate Idrian instead. Remember when I left my pendant behind on the kitchen table? I didn't want to raise any red flags with my movements, so . . ." He flashes a sheepish smile.

"I didn't think anything of it at the time, but I got jostled in the crowds by the Yenefria docks and somehow ended up with an impressive gash on my shoulder. A nice woman treated it for me. I suppose that's how they got my blood. I don't blame them. It must have looked bad from their end, me showing up everywhere they were. I was asking to get bitten.

"You're a smart kid. I'm sure you've guessed the rest. It took me a while to figure out what had happened. I'm sorry I didn't tell you. I kept looking for information as long as I could. I want you to understand I'm not dying with any regrets. Not on that front, at least. I chose to look into something I knew could get me hurt. I don't want to die, but this is bigger than us or what we want. I've got physical copies of the reports mixed in with Dad's recipes in the kitchen, and I have digital reproductions backed up on this storage leaf. I have . . . hours of interviews. I've broken down everything I learned in detail. Please use it. I hate to ask this of you, but please."

Lord of the Empty Isles

The video flicks to another day. Grayer light. Another Cameron, thinner. There's dried blood under his nose and bruises under his eyes, and the hands that set the recorder on top of his desk must be shaking from the way the video feed bobs. He exhales a breathy laugh as the image finally settles, like there's a single thing worth laughing about.

Remy swallows against a dizzying surge of fear and helplessness. He wants to look away.

Even when he was young, he couldn't bear to see evidence of his brother's mortality. He hasn't changed a bit, has he?

"I'm sorry, Remy." Cam tries a wan smile. "You have no idea how many days I've started recording and stopped because that's all I could think to say to you. I hope you know I'm not choosing them over you. I wish I could go on that field trip with you next week and just—live, the both of us."

Remy forgets to breathe. His eyes burn, but he barely dares to blink with his brother in front of him. Cam's arms wrap around himself, and Remy aches. It's so unfair that Cam had no one to hold him. Where was Remy, when Cam recorded this?

"Damn, this is hard. What do you say, right?" Cameron covers his face. "You're so little. I'm all you got, but I can't . . . You're *thirteen*." He laughs and scrubs tears from his cheeks, staring at the camera. "Shit, fourteen. You turned fourteen yesterday."

His hand covers the recorder, obscuring the screen in reddish-gray. When he pulls it away, he's gathered himself. "You've been asking for names, and I can't tell you, not yet. I can't let myself be someone who survives because you killed another person to save me. Call me selfish, but I'd much rather you lived for me. You don't need to be in such a big hurry to grow up. The way you see the world, it keeps me looking at everything the right way. Keep—keep drawing on the wallpaper, and anywhere else you want. Keep loving people with your whole heart and—collecting rocks and giving them names and making shitty porridge. It was *terrible,* Rem. It was so bad. I loved it. Thank you, and I'm sorry I won't see where you go after this."

He clears his throat, distracted by something off-screen that makes him smile. Remy, probably—outside playing instead of in there when Cam needs him. When he turns back to the screen, his expression is still soft. "If you can't, I won't love you any less, but if you can, see this through for me? If it makes you feel better, consider it a last wish. I respect the Chancellor's caution and agree that treating our world kindly is the way to help our people thrive, but *this* is not the way to preserve Verdine. A planet revived at the cost of so many lives isn't worth keeping. There's room here for every voice that wishes to speak. You've got a big heart, Remy. I know you'll understand."

By the time the video goes black, everyone's looking away. Emil, shoulders hunched, stares fixedly at the controls. Roca looks at her feet. Thomlin's found something fascinating about the hands he's clasped in front of him.

Idrian and Yves stare, unblinking, at the screen, long after Cam's image is gone from it.

Remy forces himself from his seat with a clatter. "That's him." The words are a dried-up thing in his throat. "That's the kind of person my brother was."

Yves whispers, "Remy . . ." and Tirani reaches for his shoulder.

"Not now." Even the air on his skin makes him feel scraped raw.

He pushes past Idrian and into the hall, taking in the grooves on the floor. He thinks of Astrid, who saw beauty in ugly places, and the mother on Alta with her infant son. Beni, face buried in a paper flower. Beni covered in a sheet twice as long as her.

All of this, this whole time. What would the world look like if Idrian hadn't made Yves perform the withering that killed Cam, if Remy hadn't done the same to avenge him? So much pain to lay this thing to rest, and for what?

"I need to . . ." He needs to go, but the hallway is too narrow, the space between Idrian and Remy electrically close even with Idrian pressed against the wall and staring at Remy's chin instead of into his eyes.

"He would have *saved* you," Remy manages to grit out.

His words land like a wound on Idrian. The rush of satisfaction lasts a fraction of a second before Idrian's nearness becomes suffocating. Remy shoves at him with both hands, but there's nowhere to push him. Idrian catches Remy's eyes at last, and the twisted-up expression on his face is pity and maybe regret, all the feelings with the cruelest double edges—but Idrian just waits, not even willing to cut with them.

Coward. Rage bubbles up in Remy. "Push me back! Hit me."

"Why?"

Too damn calm. Remy feels like a live wire. He flexes and clenches his hands to release the awful energy but it won't *leave*. "I want . . ." His next breath comes out a sob, and Remy catches it behind his teeth. "I want—"

Blood from his time with Lia has dried at the corner of Idrian's mouth, and Remy wants to draw more. He wants Idrian to fight him, blow for blow. Cam's rotting bond throbs with a perfect, brutal agony in his chest, so sharp it makes his vision pop with fireworks, and there was no point, really, to any of this. Cam sat alone in front of that camera, fading and afraid. Not one good thing grew out of his ashes.

"I'm sorry," Idrian says, and it's wrong, too raw and years too late.

"What good does your sorry do me? Let me past. I can't—" He can't breathe. Remy pushes again.

A cheery beep echoes into the cockpit, and Remy's not the only one who flinches.

Quiet, Emil identifies the alert. "We're in range."

It takes Remy longer than it should to make sense of the words, but he stumbles closer when they settle. Emil's right. The Isles' signal has appeared, faint, on one of the consoles.

Cam can't be saved anymore, and neither can anyone else who's gone, but maybe they can do this. Emil sets to hailing.

When Remy tried to contact Lia, the screen blinked gentle yellow while the request was under consideration. This time, there's nothing. A short message flashes on the screen. FAILED TO CONNECT.

Emil tries again. Again.

Failed to connect.

Remy's skin prickles with cold.

"That's not right," Yves pushes off from the wall. "That can't be right. Come on, Shaia! Surely they're not already . . ."

Shaia. Remy remembers Yves' last conversation with her.

"She won't answer." It's Remy's voice, but he feels worlds away from it, like he's watching his own life through a distant screen. "Remember?"

Adjust the comms rig to reject all contact except from the Lamprey, Yves said.

"You told her," Remy says. "Just the Lamprey."

Yves had surely assumed they'd be piloting it back in short order. If it hadn't launched unmanned, anyone aboard it could initiate contact.

Yves paces, a penned-in back-and-forth across the scant open space behind the cockpit seats. "We won't beat the Lamprey there."

"No," Idrian says. "We'd better hope they're slow at unloading."

"They aren't."

"This'll play right into the Chancellor's game, won't it?" Thom, this time. "We were warned against consorting with the Isles. Even if we arrive in time, he'll have someone watching the area. Our interference means more dirt on our grave—and theirs."

Yves laughs. "We're buried already. Do it."

Chapter Twenty-One

Sleep, my child, may earth protect you
Deep and wild the forest green
Sun will rise and paths direct you,
Stars will guide you home to me.

— From "Lullaby for the Left Behind,"
a popular Verdinian cradle song

Remy slips down the hall while Emil hunches over a screen. The farther he walks, the more the worried voices fade and the less tethered to the ground he feels.

Cam's video replays itself behind his eyelids. That weak smile, the way he held himself. The *uselessness* of it all. And Remy, off-screen.

With the lights off, the dingy room Remy shares with Tirani is crushingly small and dark. He's shaking by the time the door whispers open to admit him, and he backs up against the wall once he's inside and shoves the meat of his palms against his eyes.

"Hey." Tirani's voice, barely audible.

He shudders. He didn't notice her following him. Her hand settles, butterfly-light, on his shoulder, and he pulls her in, crushing his face into her neck as the words flood from him.

"I should've been there." Cam deserved better, so much better than Remy. "I let him down."

"You didn't." Tirani's arms tighten around him, painful. Remy holds on. "You were so young. It's okay if you were afraid."

"It's not! Not if—" They only had each other. When Remy skidded down three stairs and tore up his knee while running home from school, Cam was the one who recited weird plant facts to distract him from the sting of the disinfectant. When Cam fell asleep at the table in the sitting room, Remy was the one who wedged a pillow under his cheek for him to drool on. So when Cam had to deal with *that*, Remy was all he had then, too. He was so scared of losing Cam, but when he ran away so he didn't have to think about it, he took his brother's only support.

It's like he's back on Alta, gulping for air that doesn't satisfy him.

"I left him alone. He died—"

He *died*. All Remy can see is Cam holding himself and forcing a smile for the camera, unbearably young.

Tirani catches him when he staggers, guiding him down and pulling him close. She makes soothing noises, hums that vibrate through her. She says, "I'm here," and Remy can't bring himself to tell her that he wasn't, not when Cam needed him most.

"He only wanted to save them," Remy murmurs into her skin.

"I'm sorry."

"He wanted *me* to save them, and I can't. I don't know how. I've made a mess of everything."

"That's not news. I knew you were a mess the day I found you lying on your belly in the filth in the middle of an alleyway, trying to lure the ugliest cat I've ever seen with *an entire sandwich*."

"It wasn't that filthy."

The judgmental eyebrow goes up. "My point is, if you were a mess then, you were probably a mess before. I figure Cam kinda knew you might take the long way round." Her fingers trace the bandages on his palms. "The people who love us, they don't want us to hurt ourselves to earn their love or forgiveness or suffer because they're gone. It's like what Roca said on Alta. I wouldn't have blamed her for hating me, or at least hating that I got to grow up on Verdine. I've spent years thinking love is easy to lose, that you could do or say the wrong thing and people would leave." She shakes her head. "But did you hear her? She said she was *glad*."

Remy holds her tighter, and his ear against her pulse measures its joyful beats. "Yeah."

"The person I saw on that video would have been glad for you, too."

"Might be gladder if I wasn't dying," he says, but in the cage of her arms, nothing feels as urgent as it could. "I'm glad you'll have Roca, after."

Tirani pulls a hand from his face and leans back far enough to flick his forehead. "*No.* You don't get to talk like I can swap her out for you. We don't leave each other, remember?"

"I didn't mean . . ." Remy grimaces. "I'm sorry. I think I get what Cam was saying. I hate imagining the part of you that breaks when I'm gone. I want you to be happy and have people you love."

"I love *you*. Having Roca doesn't make that go away. I need you to swear you'll keep trying to save yourself until you can't anymore."

"Kinda meant to do that anyway."

"Promise me."

He presses his forehead into her collarbone. "I promise. Until I can't anymore."

Footsteps in the hall, followed by urgent knocking.

"Remy?" Idrian's voice.

Sickness winds through Remy. He drowns him out and doesn't answer.

Tirani's hand moves from the back of his head to cup over his ear. Into his other ear, she says, "You'll figure it out."

"Remy!" Idrian's voice is faint from the other side, but the knocking keeps up. "Shit, come on, my hands are killing me. Open up?"

The knocking picks up again, lower. Idrian's probably kicking the door.

"You want me to ask him to go away?"

"Please."

"I don't want to use the override code!" Idrian calls.

Tirani squeezes him tight, once, before letting go and standing. She stands so she fills the doorway as much as she can when the door hisses open, but Remy still sees Idrian staring, expression conflicted, over the top of her head. He forces himself onto his feet and wipes his face, daring Idrian to say something.

"He doesn't want to talk." Tirani spreads her feet wider and squares her shoulders.

"Sorry," Idrian says, quieter than Remy has ever heard him. "It's just—we're almost to Alta."

∼

For one peaceful moment, when Alta comes into view, as whole as Remy has ever seen it, they think they made it in time.

Shaia must have seen the *Astrid* coming thanks to the approach alert. She's the one who initiates contact with a cheery, *"Didn't expect to see you so soon. Don't tell me you brought another present. You keep this up and you'll really spoil—"*

Yves is leaning in to interrupt her when the radio crackles, just a bit. It's not even something that would worry them at any other time.

Shaia makes a startled noise, and then it happens: a flash of flame, doused instantly by the vacuum of space, somewhere near the center of Alta, and then a burst, soundless, a crumpling, and a flurry of debris.

"*What?*" Shaia's voice, over the radio, is faint. "*What's happening?*"

"No." Yves throws a hand against the screen that shows Alta. "Shaia? You there? What's happening?"

"*Shit. I think—just a—cond and I'll figure it—*"

The audio crackles.

Yves is whispering, *come on, Shaia, please,* and Idrian's saying *we have to dock,* and Emil blurts *like fuck we do. We need to get out before the whole thing blows!*

On Shaia's end, there's a long, awful silence.

Flecks of debris drift away from Alta. A few scrape against the *Astrid* as they pass.

"*Fuck, it was Tarsyn,*" Shaia says.

"Tarsyn?" Idrian echoes.

"The *fuel.*" Yves leans close to the mic like that'll make Shaia listen better. "Has it been introduced to Alta's supply?"

"*Yes and no.*"

"Shaia!"

"*You remember Tarsyn?*"

"No," Idrian says.

"We don't have *time* for stories. Did you use the fuel or didn't you? They did something to it. Is it—if you did—"

"*Yves, please.*" Shaia's voice is flat and tired. "*Just listen. Tarsyn.*"

Yves swallows and scrubs their face. "What'd he do?"

"*He—*" Shaia's voice fades out. "*He wanted to do something about the blackouts. He put together a rudimentary generator so next time we won't lose functionality in the rescue rooms when* the power blips, or food when refrigeration fails. Or light in the garden. He's been pestering me forever, and he made a nuisance of himself while I had the kids unloading the fuel, getting in their way and holding out this tiny little tank like a beggar—"

"Shaia."

"He wouldn't let them load it onto the dolly bot, and we had so much, I figured it wouldn't hurt to give him enough fill that little tank. The fool skipped on his way out."

Yves has gone pale. One hand reaches for the controls like they want to turn the audio off, but it curls into a fist before doing anything. "Sounds like him."

"Yeah. Yves . . . he was in the garden. He wanted to see if his prototype could power the grow lights."

Yves shakes their head, sharp, back and forth.

"It's gone."

Remy's stomach sinks. He doesn't treasure that place nearly as much as Alta's residents must, but the revelation still stings. All he can think about is the way Patrice patted Beni's seed into the soil and stared like he thought it could grow into something lovely while he watched. How that woman picked berries with thorn-pricked fingers and the baskets in the corner of the room were full of all the things Alta's people grew to sustain themselves.

"All of it?" Remy echoes, uselessly.

Yves paces away from the console and into a cramped corner of the cockpit, setting their forehead against the wall. They don't move, but their voice comes out perfectly calm when they say, "The rest of the fuel?"

There's a pause on Alta's end. "*Sent someone to stop them as soon as you made contact, but I think you need to come in. They're not happy. Some of them still want to use it.*"

"They *what?*"

"Dock. You'll see when you're inside."

They race through the halls when they're permitted entrance, Shaia pale and silent behind them. When they hunt down the Lamprey, the innocent-looking tank of fuel has only just been loaded onto an ancient dolly bot, and a knot of people argue around it.

"Why *shouldn't* we use it?" someone's saying, a slim boy with freckles and a shaved head. "The garden's gone. We either die now or next week, right, when the stuff we have runs out? Fuck dying slow, I'd rather go out with a bang. I hope the explosion tears the Isles to bits and sends them hurtling down on those bastards in their perfect houses."

The gathered group looks back and forth between each other.

The oldest of the group, a sturdy woman with coiled white curls, says, "I've always been a fan of big statements."

It's hypocritical, isn't it, to intervene?

Not so long ago, Remy was ready to let his own curse kill him as long as he'd take Idrian down with him. He wouldn't have been pleased to have his resolution questioned. This isn't a decision any of them are making lightly.

He steps forward anyway. "You don't have to," he says.

A couple heads turn his way, but the rest ignore him.

Tirani told him the same thing. He didn't listen to her, either.

Helplessly, Remy says, "You'd be letting him win."

"Letting?" The freckled boy grits out. "You think we wouldn't have chosen anything else if we could?"

Desperation is a stone in his throat. "But that's terrible. If everybody dies—"

"When," the freckled boy says. "When everyone dies."

Remy opens his mouth, but he can't find words.

The freckled boy pats the curly-haired woman's shoulder. "Mirta, you wanna go pitch it to everyone? We'll take a vote.

We'll share the truth with Toxys and Fluora when we send the rest of the fuel to them, and they can make their own choices."

It's too sad.

Back when Remy believed his death would kill Idrian—and thought that a worthwhile thing—at least he had a goal. At least he could've struck back, made some sort of difference.

The Chancellor has stirred up such hate that these people would never be safe on the surface. Alta and Fluora and Toxys cannot choose survival, only the lesser of two agonies.

They'll go down in history as monsters and rebels either way.

The group turns and starts walking. Remy follows, stomach twisting and words caught behind his teeth.

"Hey," Yves calls, and Freckles pauses at their familiar voice. "Dillon, you little bastard, listen up."

Remy stops and turns. Yves' arms are grasping for the top of the fuel tank, feet searching for a foothold. "Fuck," they growl. "Thom, a little help?"

Thom laces his hands and loops them beneath one of Yves' flailing feet to boost them. Yves crawls up, stands, and stomps their feet, a solemn thrum that echoes all through the tank. The apathetic group has paused their retreat—intrigued, if not engaged.

"All right," Yves says. "You all know I'm as happy to die as the rest of you."

Remy chokes on a flabbergasted noise, and Yves shifts toward him, tapping a foot. "Relax, Canta, it's true. You're all as happy to die as I am—which is *not at all*, but it doesn't fucking matter."

Remy opens his mouth to disagree, but he closes it again.

"Because no matter what we do, we're screwed. They've taken everything from us. Our children, our pride. What little we've managed to grow here. We either die in the dark, in agony, without air, or we go out in flames, and I'm with you in being more than happy to take the fast way."

Freckles—Dillon—nods.

"But it *galls* me—it fucking enrages me, if you will—that if we go out like that, we're doing just what their spoiled little Chancellor wants. My guess is, he already has some story prepared. You've heard it a billion times. We're all animals. It was all our fault. Our recklessness led to our own downfall. That's how we'll go down. That's the only story the schools will ever teach. Your children and grandchildren and great-great whoever the fuck you left behind down there, the ones you love so much we keep a list of them, that's the only story they'll know about you. And I'm all for a quick death by fire, but that's not something I'm ready to die with. They've taken everything else from us. I'll be damned if I let them take our story."

The older man behind Dillon crosses his arms, chewing his lower lip savagely between his teeth, eyes wet. "Then what?" he rasps.

"That's right. *Then what?* Canta, your turn."

All the hopeless, angry eyes turn toward him. Dillon's standing with his fists clenched at his sides, and he's younger than Remy would've guessed. He can't be more than sixteen.

"What?" Remy says.

Yves raises an eyebrow, piercings glinting as they stare down at him from the fuel tank.

"You had a lot to say just a minute ago. I'm assuming you have a plan."

"I..."

Remy's feet root him to the floor, his lungs too compressed even for breath. Everything Yves said is true. The world will see any attempt at survival as villainy, desperation as violence. The Chancellor has laid the framework for this narrative for ages. And either way, there won't be a single living soul to contradict him—not one the people would listen to.

Unless—

The soul doesn't *have* to be living.

"We use their own people against them," Remy starts, barely above a whisper.

"Can't hear you," the old man says, stepping up.

Remy clears his throat. "Your biggest obstacle isn't so much the Chancellor as it is public opinion. But now he's shown us his hand. I always wondered, I wondered for *years* why he didn't just arrest Idrian. But it makes sense, now. He had to ensure that Idrian was widely despised because he didn't want to turn his people against him if he captured and executed him. When I was little, it wasn't entirely uncommon for people to think Idrian wasn't terribly threatening. Some people even—even thought he was worthy of emulating." Heat rises on Remy's cheeks.

"Oh really," Idrian says. "Do tell."

Remy ignores him. "And that wasn't something the Chancellor could work with, so he changed the story the world was telling."

"Yeah, he's long since solved that problem," Yves says. "Where are you going with this?"

"All you have to do is take your story back. Turn public sentiment toward the Isles. We have to do what you all did for me." What Cameron did for himself. "We show them the truth. Every citizen, all at once."

"Like it's that easy!" Dillon spits.

"Maybe it's not," Remy says.

"The truth is cheap! No one's buying," the old man says. "I tried to tell my son. He turned me in."

Remy winces. He raises his hand, Cameron's storage leaf held delicately between two fingers. "That's why we use their own people against them. We have the start of it here. With his most recent broadcast, the Chancellor did all the work for us. He made a glorified martyr of Cameron Canta. He'll be the vehicle we use to send your story to the world. Even Ma Windsel remembered him," Remy whispers. Beside him, Idrian flinches. "I'll bet there's someone on every island who knew him like that. Who better than *him* to turn the tide of public opinion with his own words? And who better than all of you to show the truth?"

"The dead and the desperate." Yves chuckles. "I like the sound of it."

Emil speaks up. "I can record here. I'll do some editing to make for something broadcast-sized and make sure the file includes the packet with all the unedited footage so people can make their own judgments."

"This is all very nice, but how do you propose we *do* that?" Yves sits on top of the tank, kicking their feet against it with great, echoing thuds. "Picking up the Chancellor's broadcasts is the best we can manage here. The only way to send one of our own would be to do so from the Chancellor's personal estate."

"Exactly."

Yves leaps from the fuel tank and lands on the ground with an *oof* and bent knees. "Remy, please. One Idrian is already more than I can handle. Perhaps you've forgotten, but there's an execution order out for all of you."

A wild but familiar smile unfurls on Idrian's face—his jump-off-a-cliff smile. "You know I'm in, but people will be looking for us. You ready for that?"

"Tonight's the Resurrection Festival. We won't be the only ones wearing masks."

Idrian's smile expands, delighted. "It's like he's throwing it just for us."

Yves shakes their head. "We can't just mill around in the streets. It's too risky."

Remy's pulse pounds in his throat. "The last place he'd expect to find you is right under his nose. I know a place you can hide.

It's isolated. Abandoned. And it's *mine*." He wets his dry lips. He hoped never to go back there again. "The location is perfect. You have any idea how close the Canta Manor is to the Chancellor's estate?"

"You hear that?" Yves calls to the gathered group. "You *keep* that fuel. You light up the sky if you want to. But give us a day. We all have at least that much. We may be dead either way, but let's look lively on our way down."

Chapter Twenty-Two

The mourners hid their heads in fear.
The fools, they saw, but dared not hear.
The prophet—bruised and silenced—tried
to snuff the fires and soothe the dying.
Revelers, rich and rash, rejoiced.
The scribes, they gave the past a voice.
But not a one, nor one in all
Could stem the waves that drank the world.

"Recall, and through recollection forestall."

— Inscription carved at the base of the
Alta and the Lost statues

They return to the *Astrid* mostly so Idrian can change into less distinctive and less bloody clothing.

Without the sunglasses and the long coat and the holster, dressed in a simple white shirt and loose linen pants, Idrian doesn't look at all like himself. Or he looks too much like himself. He stops as he draws up to everyone, brows furrowed. Perhaps it's time for a rousing speech.

Instead, Idrian ventures, " . . . Did someone steal my bed?"

The solemn silence splinters.

"Emil! Damn you, you win!" Roca belts out between gales of laughter. "I took it days ago. Remy has it."

"You all bet on it?" Idrian rubs the bridge of his nose. "What am I saying? Of course you did."

They leave the *Astrid* on Alta and take the Lamprey down, going from the cold void of space to the cruel brightness of a cloudless summer in the Chancellor's city. The Lamprey lands, cloaked, in the thick woods at the rear of the city.

Remy and Idrian are the lucky ones—they'll head out to grab masks and festival-wear for everyone. It was Idrian's idea: if they're caught, the withering will likely kill them before they can reveal the location of the rest of the crew or be used to draw them out. If they don't return, Tirani can still guide everyone to the Canta Manor to rest and plan.

Idrian and Remy's journey is an uphill one, first out of the thick trees toward the city and then up the cliffside city's steep stairs. Remy has lived here all his life and takes the stairs two at once even with the narrow heels on the tall black boots he borrowed from Tirani and the hum of feverish exhaustion in his blood.

Not so for Idrian, who stops after only about five minutes of walking, supporting himself on the rail.

"*This* is how the Chancellor will kill everyone on the Isles," Idrian says. "Gravity. And walking up hills. Grab me by my foot if I pass out so I don't fall down this whole mountain. I'll die before I walk up these stairs again. Probably literally."

Up the hill, vendors set out their wares in the shade of cloth canopies. Bells tinkle and gauzy dancers' shawls sway with the breeze. The familiar spice of cooking meat for the festival's signature buns and the sweet crackle of ice candy float on the air toward them.

"You ever been?" Remy asks.

"The festival?" Idrian shakes his head. "If so, I was too young to remember."

They make it to the first booth selling masks and dance outfits, and Idrian stops in front of a delicate porcelain mask in blues that match his clothes. It's not nearly as bright as some of the others. The cradle-like crescents of its eyes and the shadows of the lids above are washed with paint in blue and violet, spattered with shining silver-white droplets like stars. Its sad slash of a smile is pocked with holes above and below at regular intervals, tied gently with a navy ribbon to create the implication of a mouth sewn closed.

The vendor sidles up. "That's a handsome match for you! The Prophet."

It's an eerily appropriate match for Idrian, is what it is. The mask of the prophet denotes those who saw disaster coming but were silenced or ignored. The bruise-like shadows in the eyes and temples and hollows of the cheeks symbolize the wounds the prophet sustained when they failed to hold back the coming tide. There's no way the iridescent pale-blue feather extending from the corner of each eye is genuine allura feather, but it's a strikingly close imitation.

Idrian's eyes travel to a smaller display with child-sized masks. His fingers skim a bright one with fake coins and fringed ribbons and brilliant paint in pink and turquoise and sunny yellow.

Remy taps on the hand that still holds the Prophet mask. "Get that one. It suits you." He picks up another—red and gold. "This one's for me."

The vendor's eyes twinkle. "Ah, we're all the Fool, aren't we? You'll carry it well."

The mask of the Fool is the most elaborate of all, fringed with airy crimson feathers and sharp-edged gold fragments meant to look like knives. The closed, smiling eyes signify the willful blindness of those who ignored the signs. The wide grin shows recklessness. If the knife-like fragments indicate the harm caused to the world, the delicate cracks filled with gold hint at the harm inflicted on the self. In previous years, Remy wore the mask of the Mourner. No wonder it never fit him.

Remy holds up a hand to the mask, comparing the lacquer on his fingernails. A perfect match. Before he left, Thom sat him down and painted his nails for him. Remy chose a lovebond-gold for his fate-finger, but Thom selected a vital, fatebond-red for the rest. "Fighting colors," Thom had asserted. "Go get the bastard."

Yves' contribution to the cause was a proud smile and the capped scalpel currently sitting in Remy's pocket. "Anyone tries to stop you," they told him, one long finger (patiently, they permitted Thom to paint their nails teal to match his) tracing their carotid artery. "One good slash should do it."

Remy gathers a handful of the remaining masks, sets of loose linen clothing, and matching dance wraps for everyone. Idrian quietly lays the child mask on top of the pile.

Remy pulls the money he got from Lara from his pocket, the coin purse pretty with its embroidered ghost-lace, to pay for the supplies. It feels right. The vendor thanks him for his purchase and waves him cheerily away with a traditional call of, "May we all celebrate still a thousand years hence!"

The Isles are faint whitish outlines in the cloudless sky, nearly blotted out by the sun.

From here, they look like they're in no great peril. There's no hint of the icy crack of Alta's surface. Remy wouldn't guess they're falling to pieces just by the shape of them. Late summer sun warms his shoulders and the air blows in salty and sweet.

"I know it doesn't matter," Remy says, "but I'm sorry."

"For what?"

Remy slants a glance at Idrian, unimpressed. He must be being purposely clueless. "Killing us both, I guess?"

"Eh, someone had to succeed eventually. Might as well be you."

Jules Arbeaux

They head downhill, away from the peak of the city where the Canta Manor drowses in the shade of its tall trees, an accusation without words. Remy doesn't realize how quickly he's begun to walk until Idrian's voice drifts to him on the wind.

"Hey, uh . . . could we pause a moment?"

Idrian's voice is always quiet, but now it's hollowbond-thready. That's what makes Remy turn. And Idrian is always pale—a sunless, Alta-raised sort of pale—but this is disturbingly close to the bloodless pallor of the dead. Several steps uphill from Remy, he's supporting his entire weight on the cliffside rail, knees bent like he wouldn't be upright without it. And the blood. His lips and chin are slick, the stair he's crouched over spattered with it, the faint layer of dust turned to red mud.

"Oh, don't look at me like that." Idrian pushes up the sleeve on his right arm so he can wipe his face with his forearm. "Shouldn't have dealt it if I couldn't take it, huh?"

Remy tries to make like he's sitting down on the stairs to give Idrian time to recover. He tucks his hands into his lap so Idrian won't see them shaking. The sun overhead sears him; the breeze draws out a cold sweat.

It's stupid. *He* did this. Seeing the consequences shouldn't leave him so shaken.

He hates that it has to turn out like this. Five years since he failed to save his brother. Five years of facing death head-on, unafraid. It figures he'd want to live only when it's not an option.

He reaches out toward Idrian but retracts his hands, not sure what he planned to do with them, anyway.

Idrian settles on a stair. "Gimme a second. Not exactly a chore to take a break. It's beautiful here."

It *is* beautiful here. Fruit trees spot open stretches of ground. The sun glints blue off the hivelights on the walls of cheery pastel buildings and paints the tip of every ripple on the Glass Sea below.

Lord of the Empty Isles

Little islands rise from the water in the distance, green-clad and bathed in light. Wildflowers push between cobblestones.

Five years he's been looking at his feet. Remy tips his head back to take in the sun, its rays bringing reflexive tears to his eyes. Its sizzle on his skin is almost tangible—both punishing and cleansing.

The world is full of sharp and unlovely things, but Idrian isn't one of them. Remy wishes he could show Idrian something truly beautiful. He deserves gravity that does not bind him and light that doesn't blind him and all the flowers blooming in the shade of the countless trees on this island that he never had on Alta. He deserves *time*, all the time that was taken from him and decades more.

Remy whispers, "You should kill me."

"Shut up," Idrian says genially. "I'm enjoying the view."

He finds his feet a few minutes later, and they don their masks and return to the Lamprey.

They spread the supplies out on the common room's table, and everyone chooses their own. Roca and Thom end up with Reveler masks—the ones with the colorful paint and ecstatic grin and fake coins that Idrian was so enthralled with in the child-sizes. Yves takes the black-and-white mask of the Mourner, with mirror shards glued to it. Emil and Tirani take the Scribe masks, with map pages glued into every hollow, outlined in silver and gold.

They each pull on their loose linen outfits and grab a wrap to match. The wrap for the Fool is gauzy red with gold stars. Blue and silver for the Prophet. Yellow-gold for the Revelers. Green and gold for the Scribe, black and silver for the Mourner.

Dressed like so many of the other people they pass, indistinguishable in the crowd, they slip onto and off roads, up the hills toward the top of the city where the Chancellor and the families of high officials live.

Remy knows he's close when he smells the flowers.

He knows he's arrived when he sees them.

Everyone behind him is tense, ready for a struggle, but even at this last, crucial step, no one leaps out to apprehend them. The irises behind the house, smoke-black and arterial blood-red at the tips with bruise-purple centers, look like a massacre, but Remy has only ever associated them with home.

Cam always said they didn't smell like corpses, but they kind of do. Some fool decided to call this variety Toxys Dawn—a prettier name than the flowers deserve.

It's no surprise. Against all odds, they were one of the first flowers that adapted to bloom in Verdine's damaged earth, before the planet became verdant again. At summer's end, with the city's rails festooned with ribbons and vendors chattering in the streets, the Canta Manor smells like a graveyard even in the shade.

By all rights, with no one here to care for them, the flowers should have died and been swallowed by the ghost-lace crawling over the ground, but they're in full bloom as Remy creeps up to the back door of the abandoned Canta Manor. By all rights, this house should have gone to the next Intermediary. The Chancellor must have thought he was being kind when he bequeathed it to Remy. He felt justified in neglecting it for so long. But how many residents from the Isles could it fit inside? The Chancellor knows how hesitant Remy has been to come back here; he won't expect him to return. Here, in the heart of the Chancellor's domain, at the home of the family that once served the man, seems as good a place as any to hide a motley crew of criminals.

Because his only other choice is heading inside, Remy gestures at the flowers. "My brother planted those."

Idrian's eyes slide over them. "They're, uh. They're nice."

"They're horrid," Remy responds. "Please, after you."

Lord of the Empty Isles

As they enter, they pass long-dead houseplants and furniture unused and draped in dust. Remy doesn't close his eyes this time.

Warmth swells in his chest at the sight of a small pot that once held an ill-fated cactus. Cam couldn't keep cacti and scrub and succulents alive for more than a month because he loved them too much. A week without water, and he'd get antsy. "They must be getting thirsty!" he'd declare, and he'd water the poor things to death.

It's like a bone cracked into place or air on a wound scoured clean. It hurts, but for the first time since Remy held Cam's body, it's not a wounding pain.

He could take the pots with the withered plants out back, maybe. Sometime soon, he could fill them with something new.

Tirani sticks close, hand open at her side should Remy choose to hold it.

He runs his hands along the wallpaper as they walk, tracing the pictures Cameron drew between the geometric print. No one mentions Remy's clumsy drawings of Idrian and the *Astrid*.

They arrive at their destination soon enough. The door to Remy's old bedroom is still open from when he performed the withering. He closes it, but he opens the doors and windows of the next three rooms. The faint corpse-smell of the Toxys Dawn irises floats inside. As Idrian and his crew wait in the halls, unusually quiet, Remy gestures to the open doors.

"Make yourself at home," he says, and he walks back toward the staff quarters where he can breathe. His feet lead him to the sitting room, though, and he falls instead onto the gold cushions in the window seat. If he weren't tired all the way down to his bones, he might get up and find a cloth to wash the glass. Instead, he sinks into the seat and loses himself in the way the light through the trees shifts in soft yellow bubbles on the ground outside.

"Nice house."

The voice pulls him back to himself, and Remy can't help flinching when Idrian walks in, dropping down onto the cushions beside Remy.

"I guess. I haven't lived here for years," Remy says.

Idrian coughs in a cloud of dust thrown up from the cushion. "I can tell."

Remy doesn't look away from the ground outside where he used to play.

Idrian leans back against the wooden sill. "You know what I hate?"

"I'm sure you'll tell me."

"I hate—how little I know about myself. About what I want. Who I want, if anyone. Never had time to figure it out. More than fucking... brittle bones and shit, that's what I hate. That's what your Chancellor took from us. I'm not a kid like you, but a kid like you probably still knows what he wants, right?"

Remy turns a dry look on Idrian. "I was..." He shrugs. "I was barely fourteen when Cam died. I haven't wanted anything but to kill you ever since."

Idrian's pale eyes flick up, clearer than the Glass Sea. "Remy, I'm..."

"No apologies. If we start with those, I don't know if it'll ever end."

"Then what?"

Remy traces circles into the dust on the window. "I'm not sure. Hey, I can tell you what I *used* to want. You ready to hear something hilarious?"

Idrian chuckles. "I think we've established we don't think the same things are funny."

Remy says it anyway. "Would you believe that I wanted to be you when I was young?"

Idrian swears loudly. "*No you didn't.*"

"Yeah. When we played Lord of the Empty Isles, I was always you."

"That fucking *game*," Idrian says to the ceiling. "That's not funny, it's just sad."

Remy stretches his legs across the window seat. It wasn't made for two. He grumbles when his feet run into Idrian. Well. Idrian sat here without asking. Remy kicks his feet into Idrian's lap and raises an eyebrow. Idrian just sighs.

"Hey," Idrian says after a minute. "I got a game."

"Hmm?"

"We take turns. One thing we want. Figure if we practice enough, maybe we'll hit on a real answer or two."

"We're dying." Because of Remy's withering, it hardly matters what they want. "That's a bit morbid, don't you think?"

Idrian doesn't answer. Instead, he says, "I want the Isles to be safe. Not for now, but always. I don't want any more kids to watch their siblings die."

Remy stares outside to where the leaves cast flickering puddles of light on the ground. "Doesn't count. That's what you've always wanted."

"Fine." Idrian kicks one of his legs against the wall. "I want . . . to live in a place with flowers. All sorts. Bright ones that don't smell like dead things. Your turn."

"I guess I want . . ."

Cam. His laughter. The way he'd come inside with the knees of his trousers muddy.

Remy hates this game. "I want . . . damn it, Idrian, I don't know! I want to punch you in the mouth."

"Doesn't count," Idrian says, lips curling up. "That's what you've always wanted."

Not always. "I can't do this."

"I'd let you, you know."

"What?"

"Hit me. If it'd make you feel better."

Remy scrubs his eyes, forcing out a breath. "You can't keep doing this."

"Doing what?"

"You can't keep—like this. Throwing your life at whoever will take it away from you. It's rude, okay? After—after Cam . . ."

Idrian's voice is softer than a confession. "I don't know how not to."

"Well, I don't know how not to want to kill you, but I think I've been doing okay at it."

Idrian chuckles. "Except for the part where we're still dying."

"Except for that."

"Let's keep playing, all right? It's fine. Start small. You hungry?"

Remy glances in the direction of the kitchens. "I want porridge. But like, the savory kind. With onions, and thin slices of meat. Rare, with that sauce, so it melts in your mouth."

"Rich kid."

"It's not your want, it's mine. Your turn."

"Fine. I want that candy from earlier. Got a fucking sweet tooth a mile wide, and you know how little sugar there is on Alta? And I want . . . fresh fruit in slices, on that spongy cake, you know the kind? With the cream and sprinkles of spice. I think I'd literally kill a man for it."

That startles an unamused laugh from Remy. "Don't joke about that."

"Sorry."

"What did I say about apologies? Is it my turn now?" Outside, the wind blows the trees and sways the feathery, gold-tipped ferns they shelter, casting patches of light over Idrian's solemn face. "I want . . . to be someone my brother would've been proud to know."

Idrian opens his mouth to say something but closes it again. After a while, he tries again.

"You know, I never thought I'd say this, but . . . I really, really want to live to see tomorrow. I could let Thom paint my nails, couldn't I? Blue, I think. With stars. I'd like to see Roca and Tirani be absolute terrors together. And I think I'd like to get to know you better."

Remy might want that, too. The words catch like a stone in his throat, his eyes burning. He throws up an arm over his face. "Damn it, Idrian, you ruined it," he rasps. "We should—we should stop. We'll need to get ready soon."

They can't have any of these things they want, but if nothing else, they can give the people on the Isles a chance—a choice. If they manage this, Tirani and Roca will have plenty of tomorrows and the space to decide what to do with them.

A warming, inquisitive meow punctuates the silence. Incredulous, Remy turns to find a small, dirty gray cat in the doorway, slow-blinking her yellow eye at him. Remy tilts his head at her, taking longer than he should to reconcile the sight of Grisly with his childhood home. At last, it settles. He never did close his window, did he? She could've come in through any of the ones he just opened, too.

He shouldn't be surprised after she nearly foiled his escape attempt through the washroom window the other day. She's good at being in places she shouldn't be.

Idrian blinks at the cat, nonplussed.

Rolling off the window seat, Remy stoops to pick Grisly up. She's all bones under the pillowy poof of her fur, and she rattles fit to shake apart with purrs as he tucks her against his chest. She shoves her skull up under his chin with a greeting so fierce it rocks his head backward, and he chuckles, returning to the window seat with her securely in his arms.

After a moment of pause, he deposits her in Idrian's lap.

Both man and cat stare at each other, unsettled, before Grisly resumes her purrs, turning around twice on Idrian's legs before claiming the dip between them. Idrian sits still as Alta's statue, like he's afraid he'll break her if he moves. Quietly, he says, "*What?*"

Remy grins. "Her name's Grisly. She likes you. You can try petting her, you know."

Idrian's expression softens as he stares down at her, and he extends two tentative fingers to stroke her head. Grisly, assertive as ever, angles her face so he'll rub at her chin and cheeks, then grabs his fingers with her sharp claws, licks them aggressively, and then rubs her own face against them—forcing him to groom her. It startles a laugh from Idrian, and the feeling that grows in Remy is an aching sort of joy.

This, he realizes. He wants this.

For himself and Idrian. For Tirani and Roca and all the others. Soft things in a safe place—the unhurried way the dappling of tree-filtered sunlight sways between the tall grasses outside, like the day will never darken.

Outside, the sun inches across the sky like it's loath to set. When it sinks, the festival will begin in earnest, and they'll have their opportunity. Remy pulls the neck of his floral tunic aside to press at the tender, inflamed skin where the withering has unraveled into a mass of mad, vein-like threads reaching once more for his heart.

Tonight. One way or another, everything will end tonight. All the wealth in this house, and the one thing it's never been able to buy the Canta family is time.

Chapter Twenty-Three

*Hand over heart for progress, they say
closed fist at the back for our past.
But what, my dear,
can a closed fist hold
that it doesn't already have?*

— Unknown poet, P.D. 66–89. Sentenced to Fluora

When night falls, the tinkle of bells fills the air. Torches flicker along the paths to the Chancellor's estate, the seat of Verdine's government, a flawless moonlight white embraced by trees. Fever and exhaustion make something otherworldly of the festivities, every sputtering flame a condemnation or epiphany.

Tirani, Thom, and Emil stayed behind to relocate the Lamprey into the woods behind the manor and ensure a quick escape if they need it.

That leaves Idrian, Yves, and Roca with Remy. He takes up the lead, slipping into the crowd swaying up the road in the setting dark, the ghostly white of the ribbons twined into the safety rails guiding them upward. The moons cast long shadows behind them.

Dancers swoop like the ocean waves that swallowed most of the world. The bells and tassels on the fringes of their scarves make something beautiful of the destruction they're committing to physical memory with their dance. Remy finds himself mirroring their motions.

Jules Arbeaux

The group arrives, at last, in front of the Chancellor's home. The trees in the orchard have been festooned with ribbons, the rotting apples picked from the ground. Solar-powered beams light the Alta and the Lost statues solemn blue. People gather in the orchard on blankets to watch the fireworks that will fill the sky at full dark.

A simple stage has been set out in front of the massive building that serves as both the Chancellor's personal residence and central offices for the Protectorate of Verdine. No one takes note of the stage until a man strides toward it. On his face, he wears a mask cracked down the middle—painted on one side with the colors of the Prophet and adorned on the other with feathers for the Fool.

Idrian and Remy watch, breathlessly still, as he ascends the steps.

"Good evening, citizens of Verdine." The man lifts his mask so part of his face is visible, revealing the Chancellor's paternal smile. Idrian tenses beside Remy.

The Chancellor paces and gesticulates on the stage, and the crowd sways toward him, enthralled. Remy hears *Alta* at least once, but he tunes it out. Soon, whatever clever half-truths the man is telling about the Isles won't matter.

The Chancellor blared Cameron's image everywhere and claimed Cam's tragedy for Verdine. Just like he planned for the Isles, he'll become the architect of his own ruin.

With all eyes turned toward the Chancellor's speech and the Chancellor's own attention on the crowd, it's an easy thing to slip to the side of the building.

Andrew gave Remy his personal code—for emergencies, he said. Surely, he didn't expect Remy to use it this way. Andrew has worked through the festival every year since Remy's known him. If he's lucky, it'll be the same this year. Remy paces up to a closed and dimly-lit side door and punches the code into the keypad beside it.

8-8-4-1-2.

Those numbers set all of this in motion. If he's lucky, they'll help him end it, too.

He presses the send key and waits, positioning himself at the fringe of the flickering illumination of a torch. Idrian and the others wait just outside the door.

After a while, the side door whirs and clicks, and Andrew emerges. Light spills around him onto the grass, and he squints into the darkness. "Remy?" he whispers. "*Remy?*"

Remy steps out from behind the fruit tree he sheltered himself behind, blinded by the light from the door, but his movement attracts Andrew's attention just like he hoped it would. The way his knees knock and dizziness nearly sends him to the ground is owed entirely to his advancing withering, but it only underlines the effect.

He waves at Andrew. "You said I could use it in an emergency, so..."

Andrew's eyes widen, expression slackening, and he takes a step forward. "I thought you were *dead*."

"Not quite."

Andrew sighs, shoulders dropping. "I kept an eye on your vitals through the pendant when I could. Your heart *stopped*. We thought someone had killed you and kept the thing for themselves."

"Ah, no. That was..." Frankly, more complicated than he has time to explain right now. "I'm fine. Alive, in any case. Andrew, there's something I need to talk with you about. It's the pendant. It broke—"

"We noticed that."

"—and I found something inside. Cam recorded a message for me."

Andrew's expression softens. "That's good. I'm happy for you, Remy."

"You need to see it. Can I come in?"

"Of course, of course. Nothing exciting to see here, but . . ." Andrew reaches to pat Remy down as he approaches, bending to peer into the dimness. "You look awful. I've been so worried. I've made like six hundred pastries since you vanished; I hope you're hungry. What I said back then, I didn't mean for you to *leave the entire city*. What happened to your hands? Is that blood?"

"I'll tell you everything soon."

It's when he's halfway inside, catching Andrew between his own body and the door, that Idrian and the rest flood in after him.

That nearness is why he feels the sudden tension in Andrew's body. As Idrian enters, mask half-lifted, Andrew's expression shutters. Maybe it's only because Remy has never seen that look on his face that he didn't connect the dots on his own. That chilly blankness is so much like Idrian's, it's scary. They've never looked more like siblings.

Remy presses his hands to Andrew's chest and gently pushes him back against the door. "Cam's message was about *them*."

Andrew barely moves, but the door slips closed and Andrew's arm is suddenly a protective bar around his chest, and the hand once holding the door now holds the gun previously holstered at his side. "Did they make you do this? You're being coerced?"

"No."

It turns out betrayal makes every face look younger. Andrew's expression, for an awful moment, is wide-open with shock.

Idrian has his handgun out, bruised arms holding it steady. "Remy said you have a card that'll allow you to initiate an emergency broadcast."

Andrew's arm around Remy tightens, but his eyes never leave Idrian. "You *told* him?"

"I'm bound to him." Remy lifts his arm and lets his sleeve slip back, baring his forearm. "What I did to him, it's going to kill me, too."

Andrew shakes his head with all the determined authority of his position. "That's ridiculous. Did I—" Horror dawns on his face. "Should I not have washed your things? Did I cause this?"

Remy laughs. "No. I mean, you probably shouldn't have washed them, but more because of the whole *becoming an accessory to my crimes* thing than anything else. This is . . . I think you'll understand when you see what Cameron had to say."

Idrian takes a step forward. Without his coat, there's very little bulk to him, but he widens his stance to put Roca and Yves behind him. "You don't have any power here. Remy said you might help and forbade us from hurting you. We'd be glad if you followed willingly, but we're not without choices if you refuse."

"My father . . ."

The smile on Idrian's face is knife-edged. "*Our* father," he corrects, voice steady even though his expression goes taut and brittle. "Not that he deserves to be called one."

Andrew's expression blanks.

Idrian steps in close. "Don't tell me you haven't noticed the resemblance. Neither of us took after our mothers. You with all your secrets and lies and pretty stories. Your Chancellor told you so much, but he never mentioned this?"

"No."

"Oh, yes. I took great pleasure in changing my name after he was gone. I don't suppose anyone ever mentioned you had a half-sister, either. Astrid. She'd be almost as old as you are now. While you were getting spoiled with gardens and good food and fresh air, she barely lived to see her third birthday. Your *father* sent us there to die so he could play at happiness with you and your mother. It's too bad you lost a parent, but I'm not one bit sorry I killed him. Arrest me, shoot me, kill me later if you have to. I won't stop you."

Roca steps out from behind Idrian. "I will."

Idrian leans closer to her, his arm pressing against hers, but his eyes stay steady on Andrew. "We'll do what we came here to do, whether you're a willing participant or a hostage."

Andrew whispers, "That's not possible..."

Remy pries himself free from Andrew's hold. "Look, not to interrupt your reunion, but can I just remind you all that we're dying here? Watch the video." He presses his fingers to where he was once connected to Cam. "On my bond, I'll accept whatever judgment you pass on me afterward."

Andrew stands tether-taut and pale, eyes flicking between Remy and Idrian.

"Please, Andrew. You told me Cam asked you to look out for me, and you have—more than you ever should've had to. I'll be out of your hair soon thanks to the withering."

"How long...?"

Remy pulls the neck of his shirt down to show the threads of the curse snaking over his ribcage. "Not long. This will be the last ridiculous thing I'll ever drag you into."

Andrew's teeth clench, gaze flitting away. "I don't like this. *Any* of this."

"I know, it's messed up."

Andrew sets one hand on Remy's shoulder and offers up a pale smile. "I've gotten used to messed up, keeping an eye on you. I hope you didn't think your clumsy attempts to *illegally purchase a criminal's blood* went unnoticed all these years."

Remy actually had assumed that to be the case. "Uh..."

Andrew sighs. "We can talk about that later. I'll—" He waves toward Idrian with a cutting gesture, not even looking his way. "There's more we need to..." he trails off, shakes his head, and points himself down the hall, ahead of them. He stalks away before anyone can follow, shoulders tight. "This way."

The hall is filled with paintings, both modern and pre-ascension. The pre-ascension paintings depict the world as it was—skeletal and starving, burnt-out. The post-descent ones capture Verdine as she is, green and thriving under the Chancellor's rule. No one could walk these halls without understanding the Protectorate's goals.

Andrew leads them to the room where he and the Chancellor recorded the ultimatum they sent to Alta—soft maroon carpet, gleaming wooden desk with hardy plants spilling their leaves from pots positioned at the corners—and sits in the Chancellor's high-backed chair to wake the darkened screen set into the surface of the desk.

"The message you want me to see?"

Roca passes him the storage leaf Emil prepared. "We edited the clips to put together something pithy and consumable, but I've been told to tell you that the packet attached to the file has the evidence in its entirety. You're welcome to peruse it at your leisure *after* we've got the recording out."

"I'll decide when it's ready to send, if at all."

"How sweet," Roca says, knife-sharp. "He thinks he's in control here."

Andrew inserts the storage leaf as if Roca didn't speak, and a request to autoplay comes up in an instant.

"Cam recorded this?"

"Yeah, just a couple weeks before..."

Andrew squares his shoulders and plays the file.

Cameron's face fills the screen, exhausted but put-together. "Aria, Hanne, Auni, Kuren—beloved citizens on any of the Protectorate's two hundred islands and beyond, I've come to you before to see the places where you live. I've been the grateful recipient of your hospitality. I've heard your stories and your requests. I come today with a request of my own—the only one I'll ever make. I don't know what any of you will have heard by the time this reaches you. I'm here to make a case not against but *for* the people responsible for taking my life. I hope to present it without bias, so I beg you to receive it with open hearts and minds."

What follows is a visual flood of information, carefully arranged to concisely build Cam's case. Theft reports with the odd items circled. Water. Medical supplies. Short snippets of Cam's voice. Fragments from interviews he conducted on some of the islands he tracked Idrian to. Between, Emil has inserted footage of the Isles from the outside to the inside. The dying people in the halls one moment. A crowd of smiling children waving madly and yelling their hellos.

Emil didn't have much time to gather footage, but he made the most of it. Dark hallways. The dripping X over Block D's door. Yves, exhausted, explaining the situation in fifteen seconds. A peek into a dimly lit room with one bed and eight occupants. The garden in the aftermath of the explosion, lightless and decimated. Emil included clips from short interviews with Alta's inhabitants. He asked no leading questions. He posed only two questions to the people, the same no matter who he spoke to.

"What's one thing you love about Alta?" he asks an elderly woman. A young pair of siblings. A married couple, expecting. And then, "What's one thing you'd want to see if you could go to Verdine?"

The answers are crushing. A little girl describes the ocean in abstract, like any other child might talk about tethers—a concept they believe in but accept on faith, unable to see. Trees. Air. Sunlight on skin.

"I want to show my baby a place that will nurture her," the expecting mother says.

Patrice, with curls and eyes like Beni's but no one beside him in the frame, says he wants his family.

A shaky recording of Remy and Idrian follows. Remy takes the lead, introducing himself as Cameron's brother and outlining what he knows of ways to offer the people on the Isles a safe place to recover until they're able to return to Verdine's surface—whether they do so to have their crimes re-examined or pardoned. Remy is awkward on-screen, without any of his brother's peace or presence, but the information he shares is what's important, so he tries not to cringe at seeing himself on the screen.

The recording ends with Cameron just as it began. When the image fades, Andrew sits, silent. At last, he shakes himself. "They're exaggerating, Remy. It's what they do."

"They're not. I was there. It's falling apart up there."

Andrew scoffs. "That's the point."

Remy's whole body goes numb, and it hits him that perhaps he's been foolish. All this time, he thought Andrew must not have known. That if only Remy could show him the truth, he'd make the right choice. "What?"

"Those people showed an egregious lack of care for the world we're trying to preserve. We *know* the Isles have grown old. Sending them to a place where their wellbeing depends on their ability to competently repair and care for the world they live in is a calculated move. If they cannot care for Verdine when the consequences of neglect are not immediate, we will put them in an environment where the need is more urgent. The punishment fits the crime."

"No, it doesn't!"

Andrew startles. "Remy, I thought you'd agree. It's—"

"This isn't just shit they can *repair*, Andrew. They don't have enough air up there. I couldn't even breathe."

Andrew pushes from his chair and paces in fast, even strides across the floor. "That doesn't make sense."

Remy extends a hand to stop Andrew in his tracks. "Have you even gone there? Have you seen it for yourself?"

"The Chancellor said—" Andrew cuts himself off before he runs into Remy's extended hand. He sucks in a pained breath as he cups a palm under the blood-stained bandages.

"When I was visiting, one of the blocks collapsed." Remy's lips are dry, but he has to say this. "There were so many bodies, Andrew, hundreds of them. *Children*. There was a little girl. I couldn't save her."

Andrew's face twists with shocked grief. "Remy," is all he manages to say. He closes his hands, feather-light, around Remy's bandaged one. "*Shit*. I didn't—that's not okay."

"Yeah."

"The Chancellor must not know. There's—if that's what's happening, then there must be corruption or—or miscommunication somewhere along the line."

"I don't think so," Remy says.

Andrew shakes his head. "We can figure it out. I'll look into it. But for now, people who deserve to be judged for their crimes—" at this, he glares at Idrian "—will surely be judged, but if Cam wanted the world to see this, I can let it be seen. I can't guarantee it'll change anything."

He taps in a code and pulls the recording from one screen to another, dropping it into a solemn-looking window and filling the window that pops up with text. After a moment, he leans back. "I sent it through as high-priority."

A dialogue box comes up asking him to confirm the transmission of a priority universal broadcast.

"You're a lot like him, you know," Andrew says.

Remy shakes his head.

"No, you are. In all the ways that matter. And a little like me, for better or worse." His expression brightens. "Oh. Let me try something . . ."

He spins in his chair to peer out the window after a moment, and sure enough, flickering light sifts through the blinds on the windows. Remy flinches at the deafening sound of Cam's voice coming through the walls. Cam's broadcast is playing outside.

Andrew grins. "We set up that screen for a rather different purpose tonight, but I think the folks who've gathered for the festival will enjoy this, as well."

Remy grins. The Chancellor will be livid. This won't be an easy thing to charisma his way out of.

But there are people out there right now, learning the truth, because of Cameron. Cam and Astrid and Beni and the thousands who've died on the Isles won't come back, but perhaps they can prevent more deaths like theirs. This planet has seen far too much murder in the name of preservation.

This is where they break the chain.

"Thank you," Remy says, stepping up to Andrew. The lights in the room spin in his vision, and he's no longer sure if his chest aches and his heart squeezes out painful, skittering beats in tribute to Cam or because of his withering. "That's all we needed."

Andrew stands, lips tipped up in a wry smile. "We wouldn't be a Protectorate if we didn't protect, right? This'll complicate things, but I've been watching over you for years." He ruffles Remy's hair. "I'm used to things getting complicated. And you'd better believe we'll be looking into ways we can keep you alive. We have the considerable resources of the city at our disposal. I'll bet—"

Something awful and hot twists in Remy's chest, and then his world tips. He stumbles against the desk, his first thought that this might be the end—wretchedly ill-timed end that it is. He'd have preferred to not make Andrew watch.

But once the off-kilter feeling vanishes, Remy feels not worse but better. There's only one thing that could mean.

He gasps, turning to Roca, who grimaces with one hand held out in front of her.

"Oh, well," she says. "That was nice while it lasted."

"No," Remy whispers. He didn't expect the false-bonds to last very long, but if they'd only made it a few more hours, Emil, Thom, and Roca would have survived.

Idrian stares, stricken.

"I don't know if I can do it again," Remy says. "I'm sorry. My supplies—not that I've got much left—are back at the house, and if nothing else, you all sharing the curse again gives us more time. If we can make it back—"

A loud noise draws everyone upright. Footsteps crack double-time down the hallway, shattering the stillness.

Andrew winces. "I'm sure that's the Chancellor. He's . . . unlikely to be pleased, but I think he'll understand. He wants what's best for Verdine, too, though I imagine I'll be out of a job for what I did. More time for research, I guess?"

"I'll tell him we forced you," Remy blurts. "That we took you hostage."

"True though that may be," Andrew says with a pained smile, "this room is monitored. He'll be able to tell by the footage that I was acting of my own accord—if from nothing else, then from me putting it on the screen outside. That's not something any of you could've had the inside knowledge to ask of me."

Idrian hurries to the doorway, gun drawn, as the footsteps draw closer.

"I wouldn't if I were you," Andrew says, dryly, without looking at Idrian. His head stays down, fingers skimming over the keyboard. He hums consideringly and drags a few things to a window. At last, he looks up. "I'm not kidding. Put it down. With the broadcast I'm sending, with the truth you've told, the world's eyes are on you. Resistance will only put you in a worse position. I suggest you all go peacefully, if that's how the night must end. You'll be treated fairly."

Idrian rasps a laugh. "It's cute that you actually believe that."

"It's embarrassing that you don't." Andrew scowls. "I might be convinced to visit you in prison, if you survive long enough. I have questions."

"As long as your Chancellor's in the cell next to mine, I might be convinced to answer them."

The door swings open before their conversation can go any farther. The Chancellor stands there, flanked by two guards.

Remy can't remember their names, but he knows their faces. One of them gave him a tour and spun him in the Chancellor's seat when Cam had to come here for a meeting. Remy laughed until he nearly puked and rolled off onto the plush carpet until the room stopped revolving. The guard shared a half-sandwich with him while they waited for Cam to pick him up. It had always been a good memory.

The guards wear no indulgent smiles today. Both carry weapons as they enter the room in a concerted push. They're dressed for the festival in uniform whites with gold-fringed gloves. One wears a ring of woven flowers around his neck.

Idrian says, "Put your guns down."

After that, it all happens almost too quickly for Remy to process. The first man turns and points his weapon at Idrian. The second—the nearest, the one who played and shared his food with Remy—ducks and elbows Idrian in the stomach, using his own bulk to drive him back against the wall.

"Delaciel, stop!" Andrew calls. "Lower your weapon. Go peacefully. They won't—"

The guard drops his own weapon and twists the gun from Idrian's hand while he gasps for air.

Remy stumbles forward a step, running up against Andrew's shoulder, and thinks, *I should pick up the dropped gun.* But fear roots his feet to the floor.

The guard settles Idrian's weapon into his own hand and executes a smooth quarter-turn. That's what Remy notices. The grace and precision in the movement. The intent.

Not for the first time, his ears ring at a too-close gunshot. Two. Three of them.

A gasp—surprise and pain, just beside him.

Andrew coughs out a short noise and staggers, chest blooming red.

The Chancellor strides into the room, smile-lines crinkling at the corner of his eyes, and he finds Idrian, who's clutching at no-doubt bruised ribs, halfway upright against the wall.

Andrew falls.

"Adrian Delacour," the Chancellor says, voice warm like floral tea in winter. "Look what you've done."

Chapter Twenty-Four

*Those connected by gold **lovebonds** share a mutual and abiding care—whether platonic, fraternal, familial, or romantic in nature. These gilded bonds, uncomplicated and unconditional, indicate a loyal and lasting connection. They are likely to linger even after the separation or death of one party, and are among the slowest to fade.*

— From *On the Manipulation of Tethers*

"Andrew!" Remy says.

Or he thinks he says it. His own voice comes to him through a haze. He throws his arms around Andrew's chest to keep him on his feet, but Andrew's weight bears him down, his blood impossibly warm between them.

Remy's knees hit the carpet, soundless. Yves hurries to examine the wounds, hooking an arm behind Andrew's back and guiding him down.

Andrew's expression twists as he glances between Remy, Idrian, and the Chancellor. Of all things, he looks confused. Blood bubbles between his teeth, red hand reaching for Remy.

"Don't move." Yves whips the dance wrap from their shoulders and folds the gauzy black cloth over the wounds in front. "You'd better hold on, you bastard. I'm *done* watching people die, you hear me?"

Andrew's lips only part, blood sliding down to slick his chin and jaw.

The Chancellor strides in like nothing is wrong and takes a seat at his desk. "It's a shame. He was a hard worker. Alas, youth is the great destabilizer. Inconstancy nearly broke us once. I won't let it happen again."

"You killed him," Remy breathes.

"I think you'll find Idrian Delaciel's gun killed him," the Chancellor says, eyes warm and fatherly, fingers steepled.

Bloodied up to their elbows, Yves growls between clenched teeth, "He's not dead yet, you asshole. Remy! Pressure here."

Yves stands when Remy presses his palms over the folded cloth, the guards' weapons following them as they stride across the room to the sunny yellow emergency treatment box. Andrew's blood has soaked the wrap, and it throbs up to fill the spaces between Remy's fingers.

Yves drops once more to their knees, blood spattering onto their loose trousers from where it's made a swamp of the maroon carpet. They drop the box beside Andrew and open it.

"You know," they mutter, pulling a pair of scissors out and splitting Andrew's shirt to bare his chest, too bloodied to distinguish anything. Yves drops the scissors and withdraws a vial from the ordered compartment in the box's top. "Andrew fucking Delacour, do you have any idea—" with a nail, they flip the vial's top open and pour its powdered contents over the wounds "—how many *lives* I could've saved with a fraction of these supplies?"

One of the wounds is bubbling oddly, and Andrew only wheezes in response. Yves pulls out a roll of biotape and seals it over the bubbling wound while the Chancellor watches with his mild smile and clean hands, then withdraws a needle.

"It's good to see you, by the way," the Chancellor offers with an open-handed gesture. "Adrian. Remy."

"That's not my name anymore."

"Nonsense. I held both of you when you were this tall. I think I know your names."

Idrian pushes himself up against the wall, seething, but the guard with his gun turns the weapon on him before he can lunge.

"I'd advise against haste," the Chancellor says.

"I'll *kill you*."

"Oh, will you? Don't get ahead of yourself. I made you. It's much easier for people to be good when they have someone whose atrocities they can test their own choices against. You kindly offered yourself up for the role—a leech of our planet's resources, a potential destroyer we could unite ourselves to oppose. I simply accepted your application. You shouldn't have any complaints. You were free, more or less, to do as you wanted."

"To do as *you* wanted."

The Chancellor shrugs. "The Isles were a good symbol, for a while. A reminder of our missteps. But today marks a hundred years since our return. People have grown tired of symbols and less fearful of the damage we all once wrought. There's a very thin line between a reminder and a safety net. *We used them once to escape the consequences of our actions* can too easily become *we can use them again if we poison our world once more*. We must continue to preserve our world. The Isles need to disappear, and so, too, must the recklessness that made them necessary. You'll see. In a world without the Isles, things will be better, cleaner. Instead of wasting resources to feed criminals, we'll sentence them to *true* rehabilitation, laboring to help our planet thrive. I've already chosen an island for it. I'm no longer in need of your services, Delacour."

"Delaciel."

Yves sits Andrew up and leans him against Remy. He's translucent-pale with blood loss, eyelids flickering at half-mast, ready at any moment to slip closed and stay that way. All Remy can think is *not again*.

"Everything I do," the Chancellor says, "I do to protect Verdine, to ensure its people will live to see the planet thrive."

Yves darts a glare over the top of the desk, smearing Andrew's blood over their forehead when they try to wipe sweat from it. "*Which* people?"

"The ones who obey the law," the Chancellor says mildly, "may partake in the planet's bounty."

Andrew's body is terribly heavy on Remy's shoulder, his forehead tipped against Remy's chest as if seeking comfort. His breath is fainter than a butterfly's wings.

And his gun. His gun is holstered against his hip, in the shadows between his body and Remy's.

"The law!" Idrian scoffs.

The guards with their weapons focus almost entirely on him, watching the way he stands, trembling probably in anger more than pain. No one looks at Remy and the body slumped against him. He slips his fingers along the outline of the gun. The frigid metal tugs a shiver from him.

"Your arbitrary *laws*," Idrian says. "Even your Intermediary was horrified by your actions. If you have to keep what you're doing a secret and lie to your people to justify it, maybe we're not the fuck-ups?"

"Cameron." The Chancellor reaches across his desk to swipe a drop of Andrew's blood from the wood. He glances at the vibrant red liquid and smears it to invisibility between his fingers. "I wasn't opposed to his appointment when Regine had to retire. I was looking forward to seeing what he'd make of his role. He was a smart young man, very dedicated. Andrew was just the same when he came here—single-minded in his dedication. It's truly unfortunate what happened to him."

"He's still alive, you bastard," Yves snarls, standing. The guns take aim at their chest, but Yves doesn't flinch, turning away from the weapons to face the Chancellor. "He's as stable as I can make him, but he needs surgery. You need to call for someone."

Andrew's breath against Remy is faster and fainter, his skin clammy.

"I don't think I will." The Chancellor raises an eyebrow. "Not unlike you, he's outlived his use. Too hot-headed, it turned out. That's the problem with the young. They're so eager to tear out the foundations their peace was built on. The justice of youth is a fickle thing. He, like you and so many others before him, failed to see the larger picture."

"Larger picture!" Remy closes his hand around the grip of Andrew's pistol. "The larger picture is that people are dying because they disagree with you."

The Chancellor sighs. "Remy. A *minute* percentage of the population is sacrificed for the health not only of the majority but of every single life that will populate this world for generations—millennia to come."

"I'm not your sacrifice," Yves hisses. "*We* are not your sacrifice."

"Hypocrisy. I think you'll all agree that sometimes a small number of people must die for the good of all. You understood that when you killed my Intermediary, didn't you, Adrian?"

Idrian flinches.

The Chancellor looks directly at Idrian. "For all that we stand on different sides of this divide, you and I are quite alike. It's a difficult choice, but sometimes the death of one is necessary for the lives of many. It's why I knew I could use you. See, I was banking on your reaction when I had my man inform you of his location."

Heat floods Remy, and his mind serves up memories of the Chancellor's hand on Cam's shoulder, his paternal grin wide and warm as Cameron presented cases or proposals.

The Chancellor smiles at Remy. "Remember when you were little? You'd make us play that game with you. You'd hide for hours in cubbies and cupboards and hideaways none of us were small enough to crawl through. Sometimes, when your opponent is difficult to pin down, you have to try more creative methods. You got *hungry* from all that sneaking. Your brother and I simply settled in the kitchen while he made a snack, and when he called you down—"

When he ran downstairs at Cam's call, forgetting he was playing a game, the Chancellor swept him into his arms, laughing and tickling him until Remy couldn't breathe. It was fun, and perfect. It felt like *family*. It took Remy days to realize he'd lost.

"Sometimes," the Chancellor says, "the best move is to find the right man for the job and create an opportunity."

I had my man inform you of his location, he said.

"*You?*" Remy traces the cold ridges on the trigger guard.

"It wasn't personal." At this, Yves shudders and looks away. "It was a matter of pragmatism."

"You killed my brother," Remy says, voice hollow even to his own ears. Andrew's gun slips from the holster and into Remy's hand, as heavy and cold as any corpse.

Remy started this thing with blood. He could end it that way.

"I presented an opponent with an opportunity. Because he's like me, he accepted it."

"I'm *nothing* like you," Idrian snarls. He lurches forward, but the guard with the gun fires off a warning shot that grazes Idrian's shoulder and sends him back against the far wall.

"I don't need you to believe it when you've proved me right so many times. And *you*—dear Remy. You and I aren't altogether different, either. I gave you an opportunity, too."

The gun gets heavier in Remy's hand. Heavier than a life. A hazy truth begins to take shape, growing distressingly clearer. "No."

"It was even the same *island*. Yenefria. Surely you don't think I'm incapable of stopping the illegal trading happening there? I created a flytrap and people like Idrian are drawn there again and again. All my men had to do was wait with a knife until one of his regular visits so they could harvest a bit of the blood I knew you'd need. They didn't even have to wait long. 'Idrian Delaciel' had served a purpose, and it was about time for that tale to come to a close. And you were the right man for the job."

The same urge that nearly knocked Remy down on Alta comes back to him now. The urge to explain himself. To push the blame onto the Chancellor, to anyone but himself. But he can't. He had Tirani beside him advocating for healing and memories of Cameron urging him to use his hands to shape, not break. Presented with a choice, he *chose* death over life.

Idrian chose death. Yves chose death. They both chose what looked, to them, like the least dire option. What good has it done any of them?

Remy's pants soak up Andrew's blood where he kneels. He lets the gun slip to the plush carpet between them, breathing an apology into Andrew's hair. The weapon's landing reverberates up through Remy's knees, but it doesn't make a sound.

He doesn't have to choose death today.

"To be fair, you also surprised me. I *didn't* expect the two of you to end up traveling together. I'd love to hear how that happened sometime. I'm even more shocked that you ended up working together. It's an unusual pairing. Idrian, you look like you've been through a lot, and I think I know why. I'm sure you've guessed who the cause of your recent troubles is."

He points to where the rust-red threads of the curse peek from the neck of Idrian's shirt.

The Chancellor looks to Remy, and it settles: the man thinks Idrian doesn't know who cast it.

Remy grins. "Ah, yes," he says. "About that."

"If you're talking about the withering, that's old news," Idrian says. "We talked that out already."

"But it's... you're—" The expression on the Chancellor's face is delightfully baffled. It's not a look Remy has ever seen the man wear, in public or private.

Despite everything—despite the blood cooling on his arms and torso, it's almost funny.

It *is* funny, in the way nightmares are funny when you wake up and realize how little sense they make. A breathy, nearly hysterical laugh tumbles past Remy's lips, shaking him until tears roll down his cheeks. The man at the desk just continues to look embarrassingly befuddled, no doubt attempting to piece together how that conversation might have gone.

Perhaps he was expecting Remy and Idrian to go after each other—a clean resolution to his problems. The trash taking itself out. He glances between them, but by the looks of it, his examination doesn't yield any answers.

No surprise. The Chancellor could not predict a choice he couldn't imagine making.

The realization cuts Remy's laughter to a tired trickle, and he slumps, exhaustion thrumming through his bones. Andrew begins to slip, and Remy's arms go up around him. He's *tired*. It's more sad than it is funny, that the one thing this planet's leader couldn't predict was reconciliation and unity.

Remy's hand fists instinctively over his sternum, where the ache from Cam's tether has weakened to a faint thrum.

He'd be proud. After five years, Remy made another choice today. To live and let live. To let go.

Andrew deserves to live, too, to find his own peace with Idrian and with his loss.

To let go. Remy's eyes swing to Idrian, fingers twisting in his shirt, realization like air after minutes underwater.

The withering was never about Remy or Remy's life. No wonder his attempt to sacrifice himself failed to unravel it. His life, though comparable, was never *equal*. It was a throwaway thing. A tooth and a drop of blood can substitute for a mouth full of them and a whole life if that's how little the witherer thinks of their victim. A life for a life is a lousy trade when Remy's life meant so little to him for so long. It was *always* about Cam.

Remy cast the curse in his name, sustained it in his honor. Used the pain of his rotten bond as reminder and punishment for himself. Blood for blood makes a cycle, makes a withering work—makes it worse. Choosing death was easy.

Choosing to heal, though . . . He forces the words through dry lips as he turns to Idrian, fist over his heart loosening until it's fully open. "I think I know how to end this."

The possibility wrenches the breath from his chest. It dries his mouth and shakes him to his bones. That's how he knows he's found the right answer—because this, too, is a thing he longs to run from.

Idrian's face twists in confusion, lips parting, but he doesn't have time to ask for clarification.

"Sir . . .!" The guard's voice is urgent, and Remy spins to find a crowd of festival-goers filling the hall outside the open door, shocked silent.

Remy examines the faces and settles on the familiar ones.

Lara, standing with her little boy's face pressed into her shoulder, whispering, "Baby, don't look."

Old, gaudy Fluora beside Ma Windsel. The ship that took her away from Kuren must have brought her here, and perhaps

Fluora did for her what she did for Tirani when she was without a home.

Someone in the crowd speaks up. "We heard everything. From outside."

The Chancellor goes stock-still, then bursts into a flurry of motion, tapping and swiping on the screen set into the surface of his desk.

Remy remembers Andrew's frantic work just before the Chancellor arrived, remembers him warning Idrian to put down the gun.

The world's eyes are on you, he said. He must've meant it literally.

A weeping woman pushes through the crowd, graying hair tied back into a bun. She pushes past the guards with their guns until she's in front of Remy.

In front of Andrew.

Regine Delacour. Intermediary for decades before she ceded the role to Cameron. She kneels in the mess of blood without comment and takes her son from Remy, tucking him against her. A few people in medical uniforms carry a portable cot through the crowd and settle down next to her, ready to save a life if there's life left to be saved.

"That Canta boy," Ma Windsel says, clear and loud. "He was a good one. Mr. Chancellor, I don't think you should be sitting in that seat."

With Andrew's head pressed into her shoulder, Regine speaks next, voice rough but steady. "According to the Rites of Leadership, Section III, subsection c.i, you will cede your position while the claims made against you are investigated. In the absence of an acting Chancellor, your verdict will be rendered by majority vote from the heads of the existing ministries. The detainees on the Isles will be recovered and moved to a place which will serve their needs until such time as we're able to review their cases and render judgment. I will accept your willing secession from your position."

And so the world makes its judgment.

~

Remy bargains with Regine for house arrest until the other high officials can figure out what to do with them. It's not a difficult bargain to strike, with a monitor reporting Andrew's heart rate in steady-enough blips and Yves, exhausted, in the corner, having fought for his life. Yves is freed first, permitted to return to the Canta Manor to change clothes. Roca goes next, hurrying back to the *Astrid* to tell Emil to call up Alta and inform them they won't need to blow themselves up just yet. Remy leaves last.

Idrian meets him at the manor's back door, holding out Remy's most gaudy shirt—he and Tirani decided on it while wretchedly drunk. It bears glittering gold tassels on the shoulders and pink, yellow, and powder-blue floral detailing on the sleeves and neckline.

"Looked like a good 'we're not dead yet' shirt," Idrian confesses, giving it a celebratory shake so the tassels wiggle. "Good shirt to die in, yeah?"

"No."

Idrian seems to think Remy is offended by his shirt choice, so he pulls it back. Remy snaps it from his hand and pulls the tunic soaked with Andrew's blood over his head and uses it to scrub at his skin before pulling the new one on.

"No, what I mean is, I know how to fix it." He says the next words more quietly. "Idrian, I think we can live."

He paces down the hall to his room, Idrian following close behind.

Andrew was true to his word: the bowl and the blood are gone from Remy's old desk. Pre-dawn light drifts into the room in dusty rays that billow when Remy pulls the quilt from his childhood bed and sits on the end. The bed is too small for him, now, the room too quiet.

Yves spins in Remy's desk chair while he shares his plan. When he finishes, they offer, "It sounds about as reasonable as anything else. I hope it works."

"It has to." If it doesn't, nothing will.

Tirani slips in silently from where she's been standing by the door with Idrian and drops onto the edge of his bed. "It'll work," she says, quiet. She presses Cam's ashes and what little remains of the honey into his hands. "I figured you might want this."

He nods and prepares his own hands. He can't cut Cam's tether, but he'll hold it until it's gone.

Yves sets out their supplies on the same desk Remy used to lay the withering, and Remy grips the sheets on his bed. Above him, an old map he and Cam glued to the ceiling curls at the edges. Remy's eyes find Kuren, nameless at the fringes. On the opposite side of the room, his bookshelves overflow with stories. In the past few days, Remy has been on adventures broader than the world map and the bookshelf can cover. The whole room—the whole house feels too small for him, now.

This, though, right here—it's the scariest thing he's done so far.

"Ready?" Yves asks.

He isn't. Not at all.

Still in the doorway, Idrian steps awkwardly half-inside. "Didn't know if you'd want me here for this."

Remy laughs. "Sure, why not?"

"We'll be better able to confirm that the withering is fully gone, if it works," Yves adds.

Idrian slips in, feet silent on the floors, and stands by the bookcase.

"Don't you dare," Remy rasps. "Get over here."

Silently, chastened, Idrian perches on the opposite side of the bed from Tirani, his weight negligible, like he's balancing on his heels, ready at any moment to flee. Remy throws out an ash-stained hand and grabs Idrian's, holding it tight enough to crack bones. Remy won't let him run from this.

Even though it's untrue, it'd feel so damn good right now to say *I hate you*. With all its hairline fractures, Idrian's hand in his must be aching, but he holds Remy back just as tight. It's not true yet and may not ever be, but he thinks he could almost say *I forgive you* if he tried hard enough. He could certainly say *I understand you* and mean every word of it—understanding is a treasure worth keeping.

"I'm glad you're here," he says instead.

"Canta," Yves murmurs.

He only turns when Yves lifts their hands, ash-dark, expression solemn.

"I know you've heard the spiel—you probably have your own—but it feels weird to do a severing without it. So . . ." Yves draws in a breath. "I can't guarantee this will be permanent, though with an orphan tether, the likelihood of it coming back is much smaller. The ritual will not be painful. It won't take anything from you that you aren't willing to give. It's not a one-step solution—it won't erase your feelings of loss, but it may ease pain caused by rot-sickness. It'll only give you a chance to heal, but you still have to choose to heal every day. It'll be over quickly. Are you ready?"

"I don't want him to be gone," Remy whispers, and Idrian's hand tightens in his. On his other side, Tirani grasps his shoulder.

"I won't move forward without your consent. Do you want this?"

It's cruel, that he has to choose it.

But he already has, hasn't he? He chose to align himself with Idrian, whose desperate desire to heal harms as much as it helps, who is just as broken as Remy. He chooses this strange new family he's formed on the *Astrid*.

After five years, he chooses to heal.

"I do," Remy rasps. "I'm ready."

Yves doesn't question his resolve, just silently sets to the work of breaking.

Their long fingers close around the lovebond that once tied him to Cam, and it feels *wrong* to have the hands of his brother's murderer on the only thing Remy has left of him, but Yves' fingers are gentle, the expression on their face both kind and grim when they trace the rot-slick rope from its frayed end to its anchor and hum a sweet and unfamiliar tune, gentle as any lullaby Cam ever sang for him. Remy's eyes sting, breath stuttering when he presses his hands against his own anchor, hard, to feel the fading, heart-like beat of it.

"Now," Yves says, soft, and cuts.

It was awful when Remy did it to Lara.

It's infinitely worse now.

His tight-clenched hands close around themselves as the tether collapses. There's no warmth, no pulse except his own—drumbeat-fast and faint against his shaking fists.

The fact that he has nothing to hold isn't even the worst part, especially when Tirani and Idrian's free hands both fall on top of his—a welcome pressure.

The worst part is, it doesn't hurt anymore. Tirani said it was like cleaning an infected wound. Lara cried after her bond collapsed, and Remy didn't know why. He gets it now.

This is what it feels like:

For the first time in years, Remy can breathe. It's like he's had a band around his chest, rib-crushingly tight, and his lungs are finally free to expand. The scalpel-stabs of pain that have always accompanied thoughts of Cam—reminders, reliable as sunrise—are duller and fainter and vanishing, and he *can't*.

He doesn't know what to do without it.

His breath comes in shivering bursts, eyes pricking hot. Healing feels like betrayal, like releasing a fragile, precious thing kept from crumbling only by the pressure of his hands.

And because he can breathe, he suddenly can't.

Cam's been gone for years but it feels like only yesterday that he died while Remy slept in another fucking room. Remy should have *been there*, should've slept beside the bed so his brother wouldn't have to die alone. He shouldn't have been afraid when Cam grew so thin he was barely recognizable, an alien in his own body. He shouldn't have gotten distracted and fidgety and impatient to play while scooping up spoonfuls of soup when Cam got too weak to hold a utensil.

He looked out the window when he could've looked at Cam. When he looked at his brother, he saw the end of something he couldn't stand to let go of, so he ran out into the yard, away from the promise of loss. He should've talked more, should've asked more questions—should've learned every story his brother was willing to tell him. He should've read stories to Cam, too, should've told him everything, told him he loved him every time he saw him. Once for every day he wouldn't be able to say it again. He should've let Cameron cry on his shoulder instead of crying onto Cam's. A good brother would have found a way to treasure even the ugly parts. A good brother would not have slept through his last chance at goodbye.

It should hurt. Letting go shouldn't heal him.

He huffs bitten-off sobs through his teeth and turns his face into his shoulder.

"Hey," Idrian says, too gentle.

Yves murmurs something and stands to go. Everyone's voices are funereal-faint, making the wretched noises Remy can't hold back the loudest sounds in the room.

Small hands close around Remy's. Tirani. "Remy, it worked."

Of course it did, Remy thinks. And then, *it shouldn't have*. It should be something that ends him.

Remy shudders away and off the bed, feet tangling.

He gulps in breaths until his head feels balloon-light, vision fizzing grayish. The pain—a companion for years—is barely even a twinge now. There's nothing left of his brother but the sweet mess of ash on Remy's hands.

He makes it out of the room, down the echoing halls as his tunneled vision closes. Sand between the floorboards, eyes burning and vision blurred.

Out the front door, onto the porch where the first rays of sun glow on the horizon.

His eyes blur and his chest contracts. A wracking barrage of grief steals the strength from his legs and he sinks to his knees there, the racket of his own breath all-consuming.

Soft, small hands—Tirani's hands—follow him down. She pulls him between her knees and against her chest, her palm like a cup against the back of his head, so there's no part of them that's not in contact. Remy sobs into her neck, and he must be making a mess of her shirt. A long arm wraps around Remy's shoulders, and Idrian leans in to mercifully blot out the sun.

Idrian makes soothing noises, hums that vibrate through him. He doesn't tell Remy anything will be okay, and maybe that's why Remy can almost believe it might be. "I'm here," is all he says. He is, and that matters—the being here.

"I wasn't," he confesses. The words are poison on his tongue, the sort he shouldn't be allowed to speak but can't survive swallowing again. "I wasn't there. He must have been so afraid."

He's never let himself speak those words aloud. The one person back then who loved him ruinously, without condition, and Remy didn't love him nearly well enough in return. He trembles in the silence that follows his admission, and the comforting warmth and weight of Idrian's arm leaves him. Maybe this is it. Remy has done so much to try to tear their bond apart from the moment he knew it existed, and maybe now that he wants it to last, he'll break it with this. He can't look up.

But Idrian stays right where he is, and from where he's staring at the grains in the wood of the porch, Remy can only see shifts in the level of light as Idrian moves.

"Here," Idrian breathes at last into the space between them.

Something small and faint and rope-like falls into his empty hands and Remy's fingers close around it, desperate.

"How's that?" Idrian says, close to his ear. "Kinda like a tether, right?"

Remy traces the string in his hands, satin-slick and smooth, so much thinner than Cam's. His vision returns—light, then outlines, then colors in all their crispness—and Remy's riotous breath calms as he identifies the thing laying across his palms. It's a ribbon, maybe eight inches long, sea-blue and worn smooth, frayed at the ends. The ribbon Idrian uses to tie his hair. He looks a bit ridiculous without it, silver-blond curls dusting into his eyes.

"I'm getting it dirty," Remy rasps. He should give it back, but he pulls it closer, instead.

"I'll wash it."

"He's gone."

"No more than he was before," Idrian says. "He would have been proud of who you've become. The beauty of living things is that they grow."

Something swells in Remy's chest, but before he can find words to put to the feeling, Idrian keeps talking.

"That was Astrid's." He points to the ribbon, and now Remy can't take his eyes off it. "Only thing I have of hers. I don't have her ashes, don't even know what they did with her body. I can't touch her tether, nothing."

Nothing but the ribbon Remy's staining with his dirty hands. Quietly, he hands it back to Idrian. "It worked," he says, barely above a whisper.

"Yeah."

It worked, and they have tomorrow, and the day after, and the many tomorrows after that just waiting for them. The reality of *after* hits Remy like a boulder to the chest. He can't recall the last time he thought in terms of tomorrow. He has a *future*.

A ragged laugh catches in his throat and comes out more like a hiccup. Remy has a future, and he has no fucking idea what to do with it. He turns to Tirani and then to Idrian, desperate.

"What now?" He squeezes his eyes closed, the landscape in front of him an imperfect, writhing darkness. "What are we supposed to do next?"

Tirani doesn't answer in words, but she settles in on his other side and twines her fingers in his, dropping her head against him.

Idrian's hand falls on his shoulder, an anchor and a tether at once, to keep him from drifting. "We live, I suppose."

Remy's eyes fly open to the sight of Tirani's hair in its thick curls under his nose and Idrian's sad smile.

"How?"

Idrian traces the back of his own hand, up the compression cuffs still on his arms. "Mm, I'm not actually sure. But we have time to figure it out."

Remy's left hand is clean of the curse, now, the line of his withering gone almost without a trace. His fingers, ash-smeared, reach for the tether that binds him to Idrian. He misses it at first, and panic lurches through him. It's not where it used to be.

He finds it a little farther up and to the right, as silky-strong and healthy as it's ever been. It's traveling, like only living tethers can. It could end up anywhere. Remy's fingers close around the sturdy rope, and he doesn't bother to wonder where it'll end up. He'll find out when it gets there.

Chapter Twenty-Five

*Wake, my child, and face the morning
Shake the daze off from your eyes
Can't you see your future dawning?
I will follow close behind.*

— From "Lullaby for the Left Behind"

Remy enters the Canta Manor through the front door.

Tirani left with a quick squeeze not long ago and promises of a feast. Remy's already resigned himself to some savory-sweet fruit-filled thing. Idrian, meanwhile, sits without speaking beside him until Remy finally moves to stand.

He freezes at the closed front door, hand half-extended.

"We can go around back," Idrian whispers.

No. Remy's done enough floating through this old house like a ghost. He pulls the door open.

The early morning sun peers through the doorway and into the dusty interior, lighting the keys on the door-hook and the shiny metal handle of Cam's floral umbrella. They're exactly where Remy thought they'd be: just where Cameron left them. The sight of them there even though Cam will not lift them again brings not agony but pain of a lesser sort—the dull stretch of a scab pulling at the edges of a raw wound.

He is not healed. This, Remy is finding, is not the sort of thing a person heals from. It's something, though, that he thinks he'll learn to carry.

Remy stands on the threshold and shivers.

Idrian steps up behind him, one hand on his shoulder gently urging him to step up out of the entranceway where Cam's shoes still wait.

Remy should go inside and supervise the meal-making so Tirani doesn't overwhelm the thing with chunks of rainfruit, but instead Idrian pauses. He bends toward a bucket in the doorway and extracts something from it. A trowel, five years dirt-crusted. He puts it in Remy's hands.

"Follow me," he says.

Remy follows.

Out the door. Through the high grasses bowing in the field, to the place beside the road, under the trees that shade the lush ferns. There, Idrian stops. Two soft fingers on Remy's shoulder urge him to kneel.

He does.

"It's a good view, isn't it?" Idrian stares across the road, to the steep drop-off and its breathtaking view of the pale-blue sea, clear all the way down. The sun is just rising, weeping crimson light into the waves and emerging golden. It gilds the islands napping, green-blanketed, in the distance. After the noise and late night of the Resurrection Festival, dawn arrives like a secret, most of the world asleep in their beds. "This is a good place. A beautiful place."

"I suppose it is."

"Good. Dig."

"I'm sorry?"

"Here." Idrian points. "A hole. Dig."

"Why me?"

"'Cause my arms still hurt."

Remy laughs and digs, until he has a nice-sized hole and the ash-stained bandages on his hands run red and his cheeks are damp with sweat or something else. "What now?"

The most important question. What, indeed, after all this?

Idrian puts in the ceramic child-mask first, then pulls the ash-stained ribbon from his hair and lets it drop. "I wanted to leave her someplace beautiful. You have anything you want to put in?"

Remy has so many things he could put in, far more than will fit in a hole of this size.

There's a pressure on his palm, and he looks down to see the broken, bent cage of Cam's pendant. Like this, warped and empty of its red glass and the message it hid inside, it no longer resembles a clenched fist or a heart, but it's warm from where it must have sat in Idrian's pocket.

"Meant to give that back to you earlier, but it never felt like the right time."

Remy tips his open hand and lets the pendant fall.

It rolls into the hole until it finally stills on top of the ribbon.

It's a bit pathetic. Awfully small things made so much smaller by the dimensions of the hole Remy dug. "It's too big," he says. His eyes sting and he's not even sure why. "We need—"

More. There's so much more they should put inside.

Idrian's hand closes around his and that's all that's really needed to keep Remy from rising. "It's okay," Idrian says. "It's a good start."

Remy wants to sleep.

The officials can come take their testimony tomorrow.

The world can pass its judgment on them tomorrow.

Idrian tips fresh earth into the hole with cupped hands and Remy joins him, handful after handful until the earth is rich black under his nails, their beds flush pink with the sea air.

The red sun lifts at a frantic pace, like it was waiting all this time for permission to rise, and Remy pats fresh dirt into the hole in the cool shadow of a man he once called an enemy.

Tomorrow, Remy will wake and they will be criminals or saints. It won't matter which. He sighs and licks his lips and tastes brine.

"Yeah. It's a good start."

Acknowledgements

To anyone whose pain is kin to the pain portrayed in these pages—I wrote this for us.

This book wouldn't be a book without the support of many incredible people. My life-changingly wonderful agent, Maddy Belton, saw something worth fighting for in this story, and my editor Molly Powell is possibly the most brilliant editor in existence. Thank you both for believing in me!

A lifetime of gratitude wouldn't be enough to thank Caroline Ambrose and the readers at the Bath Novel Award, whose kind words about an earlier draft of the story meant everything during a tough year. Many thanks to the sadly now-defunct Pitch Wars mentorship program and especially Sunya, my talented mentor, who deserves every good thing.

I can't forget my most excellent and beloved critique partners, friends, and DM scream-team! Eternal gratitude to Sadhana, the first person to ever read this book in its entirety, back when I wanted nothing more than to hide it in a dark place. Libby, Leanne, Anna Rae, Jessie, Morgan, Suzy, Emily, Sophia, Ayida, Arianna, and Alice—you're all extraordinary. Language fails when I try to thank you, as it does in so many situations, and I'm desperate to hold every one of your books. And Chy, J.B., Nina, London, and Tobias, the crit group that gave me the faith to put my feet on this path: I hoard you like a dragon hoards treasure.

I'm hugely thankful for the rest of the excellent Hodder team! This book has been in the very best hands from day one. Thanks so much to phenomenal editorial assistant Sophie Judge and to my

Acknowledgements

amazing copyeditor, Alyssa Ollivier-Tabukashvili. I'm so grateful to Laura Bartholomew in marketing, Kate Keehan in publicity, Inayah Sheikh Thomas in production, Will Speed in design, and Andy Ryan who handled proofreading! Many, many thanks are also due to Tom Cole for bringing this stunning cover to life, and to audio editor Dominic Gribben and narrator Georgina Sadler for giving my characters a voice. Even if we haven't yet had a chance to speak as of the writing of these acknowledgements, I so appreciate all the work you've done to make this book real and put it into the hands (or ears, as the case may be) of readers.

To my family, who believes in me more than I've earned and who all listen when I wax wordy about the mysteries and miseries and majesty of publishing without rolling their eyes (too much)—I love you, always.

And, finally, to Rexann, the girl who dug into my belongings at summer camp, unearthed my writing notebook, and made fun of it in front of everyone: my spelling was impeccable, thank you very much. It's my handwriting that was atrocious.

About the Author

Jules Arbeaux was born in Sacramento but raised reckless and barefoot deep in the Midwestern woods. When not writing, Jules paints, folds increasingly tiny paper animals, and artfully neglects a throng of thriving succulents.

WANT MORE?

If you enjoyed this and would like to find out about similar books we publish, we'd love you to join our online Sci-Fi, Fantasy and Horror community, Hodderscape.

Visit hodderscape.co.uk for exclusive content from our authors, news, competitions and general musings, and feel free to comment, contribute or just keep an eye on what we are up to.

See you there!

HODDERSCAPE
NEVER AFRAID TO BE OUT OF THIS WORLD

@HODDERSCAPE   HODDERSCAPE.CO.UK